Measures of Grace

HEART
QUEST®

More to Love

HeartQuest brings you romantic fiction
with a foundation of biblical truth.
Adventure, mystery, intrigue, and suspense
mingle in these heartwarming stories of
men and women of faith striving to build
a love that will last a lifetime.

May HeartQuest books sweep you
into the arms of God, who longs for you
and pursues you always.

Measures of Grace
LAWANA
BLACKWELL

HEART
QUEST®

Romance fiction from
Tyndale House Publishers, Inc., Wheaton, Illinois

www.heartquest.com

Visit Tyndale's exciting Web site at www.tyndale.com

Check out the latest about HeartQuest books at www.heartquest.com

Copyright © 1996 by Lawana Blackwell. All rights reserved.
HeartQuest edition published in 2004 under ISBN 0-8423-7227-X.

Cover illlustration copyright © 2004 by Robert Papp. All rights reserved.

HeartQuest is a registered trademark of Tyndale House Publishers, Inc.

Scripture quotations are taken from the *Holy Bible*, King James Version.

Library of Congress Cataloging-in-Publication Data

Blackwell, Lawana, date
   Measures of grace / Lawana Blackwell.
      p.   cm. — (Victorian serenade ; 2)
   ISBN 0-8423-7956-8 (softcover : alk. paper)
   1. Women—Crimes against—Fiction.   2. Revenge—Fiction.
I. Title.   II. Series: Blackwell, Lawana, date. Victorian serenade ; 2.
PS3552.L3429M43   1996
813′.54—dc20   95–36082

Printed in the United States of America

10   09   08   07   06   05   04
9   8   7   6   5   4   3   2   1

To Joseph,

You have been a blessing ever since that day your father and
I brought you home from the army hospital in Germany.
May God continue to fill your life with joy.

With special appreciation to Gilbert Morris,
my writing mentor and friend.

He will feed me with the treasure
Of His grace in richest measure;
When athirst to Him I cry,
Living water He'll supply.

Henriette von Hayn, 1778

Prologue

LIGHT inside the half-timbered cottage was fading fast, but Mary Satters waited until her eyes began to ache before finally taking a match to one of the tallow candles. As if that were her signal, the child who had been sitting under the table put down her straw doll and padded over to a bench under the window.

"Be careful, Jenny," Mary gave her usual warning as she resumed the preparations for supper at the fireplace.

The child paused long enough to send a somber look back at her, then hitched a dimpled knee up on the bench and pulled herself up to the window. Tightening her lips, Mary stirred the contents of the caldron with a long wooden spoon. She knew that little Jenny would wait there with her forehead pressed against the dark glass for as long as it took, like a sentry tied by duty to his post. How could a child watch so anxiously for a mother who was so cold and indifferent?

Ten minutes later, the sound of a horse's hooves, distant and muffled against the dirt road, drifted through the cracks in the wooden door. "Do you see her yet, Jenny?" Mary asked.

The child obviously had seen something, for she climbed back down from the bench. But to Mary's surprise, she didn't go on to her second post at the door. Instead, she scuttled back under the table, sat down, and picked up her doll again.

It must be Roy, Mary thought. But her husband's thatching job was in Harton, ten miles away. Surely he wouldn't make it home this early in the evening. The hoofbeats grew louder, then ceased. Seconds later the door was pushed open. Thomas Hammond, her brother-in-law, stood framed in the doorway.

"Your sister's gone," he said, not even looking over at his daughter.

Mary's spoon clattered to the hearth, and she bent to snatch it up. "What do you mean?"

"She ran off with some man."

"What man?"

"Don't know." His hands curled into fists at his sides. "Someone who was staying in town." Finally he sighed and glanced at the child under the table. "I can't keep her and work, you know."

Mary closed her eyes for a second and rubbed her forehead. "I just don't know. Roy won't like it none."

"I got no kin. It's you or a charity home."

"You can't do that to your own daughter!"

"She don't eat if I don't work. What choice do I have?"

Mary looked over at Jenny. The child, still clutching her doll, watched them both with a solemn expression, as if she understood the gravity of the situation.

"I'll ask Roy," she said at last.

"Thank you," Thomas said with a broken voice, then turned on his heel and left.

There was nothing Mary could do now but turn her attention back to the stew in the caldron. Two lives were being shattered and a family torn apart, but if she burned the supper, they would have nothing to eat until tomorrow.

After the sound of the galloping horse faded into the distance, Mary caught a movement from the corner of her eye. Jenny was crawling out from under the table again. Mary watched in despair as the child climbed back on the bench and resumed her watch at the window.

1

1863

JOSEPH Price pulled his collar up around his neck and squinted into the drizzle. The churchyard had been cast in a dismal gray pall since dawn, but this chilly rain made the mid-June morning feel more like late autumn. Standing under the gabled roof of a lych-gate, Joseph listened to the drops pelting the wood above him and wondered again what was keeping Squire Nowells.

Joseph frowned, absently brushing at a stray drop of water that had landed on his cheek and trickled down into his beard. He had been waiting for almost an hour, and he was beginning to have doubts about making it to York in time. If he missed the train to London, there wouldn't be another one until Saturday. He didn't relish the thought of a two-day wait.

He peered ahead through the headstones and crypts. Squire Malcolm Nowells III was finally limping his portly bulk past a stand of yew trees, most of his head concealed by an open umbrella. Joseph would soon be on his way.

"We can talk over there." Squire Nowells's voice reached him above the patter of the rain. He motioned toward the church. Joseph held the wooden gate open for him, and the two men shared the umbrella, stepping carefully over the slippery wet stones of the walkway.

At the front of the church, a Norman doorway arched over a plain door of oak planks. Joseph removed his hat as the squire reached out for the iron door handle. There was a squeaking sound, then a click, and the door swung on its hinges away from them. Once inside, both men paused for a moment to allow their eyes to adjust to the feeble light coming in from high, slitlike windows. When he was finally able to see, Joseph brushed the raindrops from his gray frock coat, while the squire propped his closed umbrella in a stand against a wall.

"What time does your train leave?" Squire Nowells took a seat on the back pew of the small sanctuary and motioned for Joseph to sit beside him.

Joseph took his watch from his watch pocket and squinted at it. "One o'clock. Four hours from now."

"You've got plenty of time, despite the rain. York is only a two-hour ride from here, and the roads are quite good."

"I appreciate the use of your coach and driver."

The squire nodded and drew an envelope from his waistcoat pocket. "Here is your bonus for delivering Gerald Moore's body to me."

Solemnly, Joseph tucked the envelope containing fifty pounds into his waistband. He tilted his head in the direction of the churchyard. "Did you have him buried out there?"

"Certainly not!" Squire Nowells snorted. "Not in the same ground where my father lies." A bitter smile curled the corners of his fleshy lips. "Mr. Moore's body is under six feet of ground in my east pasture, where he can listen to the sound of my father's horses trampling over his grave. I fear that he is lonely, however." His voice twisted with sarcasm. "I'm anxious for you to bring back his woman as soon as possible."

"I've told you once before that I'll have no part in the killing of a woman. Moore's death was an accident, however well-deserved."

Squire Nowells raised an eyebrow. "And I still can't talk you into arranging another *accident* for Corrine Hammond?"

"Not a chance."

"Well, no matter. Once I've arranged to have Mrs. Hammond incarcerated, it'll be only a matter of time before she joins her former lover. Only I don't think the two of them will look so pretty after a while, do you?"

The glint in the squire's eyes, obvious even in the dim light of the church, made Joseph uneasy. Again he wondered if he should have declined to take this case. He had tracked down many an estranged son, and even a few criminals, for gentry with more money than patience. But this was the first time he had been told by an employer that the authorities were *not* to be involved.

And yet the law *was* involved, in a covert sort of way, for Squire Malcolm Nowells was the justice of the peace of Treybrook, this little farming village in Humberside.

"My mother has suffered enough. I don't want her to go through the humiliation of a public trial," Squire Nowells had told him just a month ago.

And the family had certainly endured more than their share of suffering. Gerald Moore and Corrine Hammond were apparently quite expert at their little extortion game. Moore would find just the right prey—a wealthy, usually married, man with an ego to match his assets. A man like the elder Squire Nowells, in fact. Mrs. Hammond would seduce him out of several thousand pounds sterling, and she and Mr. Moore would then disappear for greener pastures.

Usually it worked like a charm—the victims would rather

sacrifice the money than press charges and lose face. In the case of Squire Nowells II, however, the scam went far beyond the loss of a few thousand pounds. Humiliated, the squire hanged himself in the cellar of his house. And a powerful enemy was created in his son.

Now Gerald Moore was dead, but Corrine Hammond was still at large, and Squire Nowells III was demanding that she be brought to justice. But Joseph wondered as he watched the vindictive fire in the squire's eyes just how much justice the woman would get.

Joseph turned back to the squire. "Just how do you plan to have Mrs. Hammond incarcerated without a trial?"

"Easily, Mr. Price," the squire replied. "It's done more often than you think. You see, one of my duties as justice of the peace is to enforce local law and order. Under British law, the sentences of petty criminals within this jurisdiction are totally within my discretion."

"What about the assize courts?"

"The assize judges only come around twice a year. Surely you're aware that their business is to try the more serious criminal and civil cases."

"Yes, but I wouldn't exactly call Corrine Hammond a petty thief."

The smile returned to the man's face. "But that's where we differ, my good man. I intend to have her arrested for stealing half a crown from my father and have her duly incarcerated."

"Half a crown?" Joseph couldn't believe his ears. "Surely she managed to take much more than that."

"Ah now, I can't be certain of the *exact* amount Mrs. Hammond extorted—she and her partner. But gentleman that I am, I'll give the lady the benefit of the doubt and assume that it was only half a crown. Petty thievery. Jail without a trial, and for as long as I declare."

"But the constable—"

"Is a wise man," Squire Nowells cut in with a wave of his hand. "And in complete agreement with me about the matter. My father was influential in having Constable Martin assigned to his position, you see."

Frowning, Joseph said, "I can't say that I approve of your methods."

"Don't you agree that Mrs. Hammond should be called to account for the deeds she's committed?"

"Of course."

"If I bring charges against her and turn her over to the superior courts, she'll undoubtedly be sentenced to hang. I'm allowing her the opportunity to live a while longer . . . that is, until the croup overtakes her. I'm afraid our lockup is quite drafty—but then, it's been around since the Saxons, so what can one expect?" The squire's expression turned to worry. "You're not thinking of backing out of our agreement, are you?"

After a thoughtful pause, Joseph shrugged his shoulders. "I don't suppose it matters to me how Mrs. Hammond pays her debt to society. Once I've brought her to you, she's no concern of mine."

~

Squire Nowells had been right about the length of time it would take to get to York. Stepping out of the stuffy coach, Joseph was pleased to find the air cool and clear. Apparently the rain that had drenched Treybrook was showing mercy to the ancient city and its centuries-old limestone walls.

After purchasing his ticket and a newspaper at the booking

office of the City of York Railway Station, he left his gripsack and traveling bag with a porter, then walked two blocks to an inn on the river Ouse. A carved wooden sign above the building said Noel Arms. Most of the tables on the back verandah over the water were filled, but Joseph settled himself at the one remaining table. After ordering a lunch of trout, fresh from the river, he divided his attention between his newspaper and the people at the surrounding tables.

His natural curiosity concerning those around him had served Joseph well in the fifteen years he'd spent as a detective. He often amused himself by playing a private mind game, trying to figure out the backgrounds and occupations of complete strangers. The dark-haired man at a table to his right reminded Joseph a bit of his brother Benton, and Joseph's mind drifted to his family.

Joseph had known from his earliest years that he was different from his three brothers. Collins, George, and Benton were content to stay in Bristol, their lives and the lives of their families revolving around their father's bakery business. If his brothers had ever been seduced by the possible adventures that waited down the road, over the next hill, or across great bodies of water, they had never shown such inclination. Yet they were good men, and at times Joseph found himself envying the stable domesticity of their lives.

When he had finished his newspaper and his lunch, he took out his watch again. Almost an hour until his train would board for London. He got up and pushed the chair under his table, then decided to cross the bridge and walk the short distance to the Cathedral of Saint Peter, which dwarfed the city and everything around it.

It was apparently market day, and Deangate Street was thick

with people. He walked as briskly as the crowds would permit, regretting that he didn't have more time to fully explore the city. In certain quarters, York had the appearance of being scooped up out of medieval times and set down gently into the year 1863. Timbered houses nodded forward to one another across narrow streets, and alleys meandered to the river with an ancient air of leisure. Echoes played in little squares and open spaces, through sheltered gardens where Stuart kings surely must have jested with their courtiers.

Corrine Hammond lived here for a while, he reminded himself as he reached the shadow of the thirteenth-century cathedral. That was how she had managed to make the acquaintance of the elder Squire Nowells, for he often came to York to spend time at his club.

Staring up, awestruck, at the medley of colors in the stained-glass windows, Joseph wondered how anyone could live in such aesthetic surroundings and still plot to rob his fellowman. Had Corrine Hammond and Gerald Moore even noticed the beauty around them? Or had their predatory eyes been too busy scanning the area for more opportunities to advance their own selfish desires at the expense of others?

Perhaps I'll ask Mrs. Hammond to enlighten me while I'm bringing her in, Joseph thought wryly. *We'll have more than enough time for some scholarly discourse on the subject of greed versus morals.*

2

As Corrine Hammond pushed the bench back under the dressing-room table, a knock sounded at the door. "Come in." Before she could get to the door, it was eased open, and Bernice walked in with a tray in her arms. The cook's face was even ruddier than usual from the exertion of climbing the stairs.

"Oh, Bernice . . . I was just about to go downstairs for lunch," Corrine fretted, reaching out to take the tray from her arms.

"Well, accordin' to Doctor Gilford, you shouldn't be goin' up and down the stairs so much," Bernice answered with a firm set to her jaw. She might be Adam Burke's servant, but she had a good deal of control over what went on when her employer was away. "Here, set that tray down on the foot of the bed."

Corrine did as Bernice commanded, then turned around to protest. "You don't need to be climbing the stairs so much, either. Not when I'm feeling so much better."

She looked better, too, than she had two weeks ago when she was brought bruised and bleeding into Adam Burke's London home. The purple streaks under her eyes had faded completely, and the swelling had gone down quite a bit from the bridge of her nose, leaving her face with a slightly Mediterranean cast.

"Besides," she added to Bernice, "you've got enough to do without having to wait on me."

"I don't mind waiting on you, and you need to be doin' what the doctor says. Patience is always good medicine."

"Patience," Corrine sighed. "That's another virtue I've got to learn, isn't it? I never realized there were so many of them."

The red-haired servant laughed, bringing back two ruddy spots to her cheeks. "It seems that way, don't it missus? But it all boils down to doin' what's pleasing to our Father. Besides, you've got the Holy Spirit inside you now. He'll help you figure out what's right to do."

"Oh, Bernice . . . you always know just what to say. Do you think I'll ever have as much faith as you do?"

Bernice motioned toward the armchair beside the bed. "Here, sit down, and let's get this tray across your lap first." Corrine sat, and the cook went on. "As much faith as me, you ask? Well, that's where patience comes in again, Mrs. Hammond. Right now you're like a newborn babe."

She picked up a small china pitcher of milk from the tray and poured some into Corrine's steaming cup of tea. "You can only understand the simple things about God . . . like a baby can only have this milk here until it grows."

"But how will I grow? Am I going to have to wait until I've been a believer for as long as you have?"

"It ain't accordin' to how *long* you've been a Christian, but how much of that time you spend drawing closer to the Lord, talking with him." Bernice pointed to a Bible on the nightstand, the one Adam Burke had bought for Corrine just three days ago, before he'd gone off on his honeymoon. "The Word of God is important, too. Stay in the Word, missus, and it'll help your faith grow."

Corrine wanted so desperately to believe that. Whenever Bernice was around, everything about her newfound faith seemed so simple. But the cook had a family and her other duties, and certainly couldn't spend all of her time reassuring a repentant fallen woman. When the room was quiet, especially in the still hours of the night, the doubts came creeping up to torment her.

A lump gathered at the base of her throat, and she looked up at the woman hovering over her. "All those terrible things I've done," she managed to whisper. "You don't even know the half. . . ."

Putting her hands on her ample hips, Bernice straightened. "That's right, missus, I don't know. And the Lord don't know, either."

"How can God not . . ."

"How can he not know? Because the Good Book says that he'll put our sins down in the deepest part of the sea and remember them no more if we'll come to him. If God is willing to forget about them, we've got no business pullin' them up and grieving over them!" An understanding smile came to her face and softened her voice. "Nothin' worse than soggy, wet sins dripping all over the place, missus."

With the edge of her linen napkin, Corrine wiped her eyes. "You know, I think that Gerald Moore did me the biggest favor of my life when he almost beat me to death."

Bernice gasped, clapping a hand to her cheek. "The things you say!"

"It's true. If he hadn't tried to kill me, I wouldn't have had to stay here these two weeks. You wouldn't have gotten me to sit still long enough to hear about Jesus."

"But to say that a beatin' is . . ."

Corrine smiled up at her. "Isn't my soul more important than my body?"

"You've got me there, ma'am," Bernice chuckled. "Perhaps you won't stay a babe for very long after all." She leaned down to remove the silver cover from Corrine's dish. "Now, this mutton stew is gettin' cold while we're talkin' about the Lord. I don't reckon God minds if you take time to get some nourishment."

"Does that mean you can visit with me a while?" Corrine said, brightening.

The cook had already turned to pull the bench back out from the dressing table. "Only if you'll eat your lunch first, ma'am."

Corrine smiled at the kindly servant and lifted her fork. Not too long ago, she would have despised anyone as selfless as Bernice. Concern for others was a weakness, a flaw that kept one from reaching one's goals. Even as a child growing up in Leawick, Corrine's every action had centered on making herself happy.

So single-minded had she been in the pursuit of that goal that, eight years ago, she had left her husband and her two-year-old daughter to take up with Gerald Moore. Gerald had been disinherited by his titled family because of a past scandal, which made him seem worldly and exciting. He was even more ruthless than Corrine and immediately undertook the task of apprenticing her in his new vocation—extortion. Corrine was the perfect accomplice.

Until just weeks ago, that is, when contact with a pitiful

foundling in an orphanage caused her to start thinking about the child she had deserted—and about her countless other misdeeds.

Her confidence had already been shaken, for her latest prey, Adam Burke, had instead fallen in love with Corrine's housemaid, Rachel Jones. Corrine and Gerald had been certain that the wealthy Mr. Burke would be an easy target—a lonely, isolated man, his face scarred from a battle injury. But Adam Burke had proved to be a match for Corrine's wiles.

Gerald's impatience with Corrine's ever-increasing remorse, and with her failure to attract Adam Burke, finally culminated in violence. Corrine shuddered. She remembered all too well the beating she had received from Gerald—the terror and the pain. She had given up everything for him, and he had left her to die on the floor in the house they had shared.

As Corrine later learned, Gerald's fury turned then on the maid, Rachel, for whom he had lusted for months. He was in the process of dragging the girl upstairs when a man, a stranger, broke in through the back door. As Gerald wheeled around in surprise at the intruder's appearance, he lost his balance, stumbled down the stairs, and broke his neck.

Battered and bloody, Corrine had managed to drag herself outside while Rachel struggled with Gerald. An acquaintance of Corrine's found her in the street and took her to Adam Burke's house. Adam had rushed off to save Rachel, only to discover her alone at the house. The stranger, apparently, had disappeared with Gerald's body.

Had it only been two weeks? It seemed like a lifetime.

Now Rachel and Adam were in Italy on their honeymoon. The couple had forgiven Corrine for her misdeeds, assuring her that she was welcome to stay as long as she needed.

But Corrine didn't plan to stay for a day longer than necessary. She was anxious to go back to Leawick and try to make amends for the hurt she had caused by leaving. She owed that much to her family—and to her God.

~

"Oh, Bernice, Jenny will be ten years old," Corrine said when the cook had taken the tray from her lap and set it back on the foot of the bed. "Do you think she'll even recognize me?"

Bernice's smile did not quite mask the concern in her eyes. "You never can tell, ma'am. I believe little ones are smarter than we give them credit."

"But eight years is such a long time. And Thomas . . . my husband. I wonder if he still hates me."

"You can't know that either. You're doing the proper thing, though, goin' back home."

Corrine nodded sadly. "I just wish I could make things right for everyone that I've hurt."

"Maybe someday you'll be able to," Bernice replied. "And maybe not. But you can ask our dear Lord to heal the wounds of those people."

"I already have, Bernice. Most likely, I'll be doing so every day until I die."

3

AT half past noon, Joseph turned back to retrace his steps to the railway station. He bought some oranges from a greengrocer's cart and a couple of meat pies from a woman with a basket, to save for his supper. Meal stops at train depots along the way were often no more than twenty minutes, and the tasteless fare that was offered usually wasn't worth the hurry—or the indigestion afterwards.

The North Midland Railway's locomotive hissed jets of steam as Joseph stepped onto the boarding platform. The first shrill blast of the whistle pierced the air, and the crowd of waiting people scurried toward the compartment doors.

Joseph hung back for a while, watching other people choose the compartments where most of them would spend the next sixteen hours. A weary-looking father and mother herded six noisy children toward a compartment in the fourth coach from the engine, and Joseph made a mental note not to go near that one. While he enjoyed his nieces and nephews, bringing them gifts every time he visited Bristol, he generally did not seek out the company of small children—particularly while trying to sleep sitting upright on a rattling train.

When almost everyone had boarded and a second shriek of the whistle sounded, he decided upon the sixth coach from the engine, middle compartment. Only four people, three men and a lady, were visible from the window, and none looked to be under the age of twenty-five. *Old enough to behave on a train,* he mused. He stepped inside and greeted the other passengers with a nod.

Since it appeared that no one else would be boarding this particular compartment, he stored his hat and gripsack behind a rail on the shelf to his right, over a leather upholstered seat, and wondered why all the seats on a train were not designed the same way, facing the front.

There was something unnatural about traveling backwards, whether in a coach or train, and a bit unsettling to the stomach. The few times he had been forced to ride in one of the rear-facing seats had not been pleasant. He had crossed the English Channel several times in choppy seas and had experienced not even a hint of seasickness, yet he couldn't ride backwards in a coach without feeling nauseous.

Old man, you're getting more set in your ways every year, he told himself. *One day you'll be too fussy about the travel arrangements to go anywhere. That's what living alone does to a person.*

Propping a foot up on his other knee, he couldn't help but smile at the finely dressed man and woman holding hands in the seat across from him. It was obvious to Joseph that they had been married for some years. They were far too comfortable in each other's presence to be newlyweds. And they appeared to communicate with each other with their eyes, needing very few words.

A brief image flitted across his mind, a vision he had entertained before, of himself with a wife at his side, her gloved hand resting in his. The thought was enjoyable for a second, but then the usual empty feeling followed in its wake. *It's too late for me to change.* A man with a wife and family couldn't expect to do only the things that made himself comfortable. *I should have gotten married a long time ago. Now it's too late.* Never had he stayed in one place long enough to cultivate any deep friendships, much less a romance. Travel and adventure had been his first loves, and they demanded a solitary lifestyle.

One last scream of the whistle and a groan from the iron couplings, and the train started rolling. From the window Joseph watched the steep heather-covered hills and moors of Yorkshire for almost an hour, so lost in thought that the first stop, Doncaster, caught him by surprise. The married couple and one of the men gathered up their traveling bags and left Joseph's compartment, and just as the second whistle was sounding, another man boarded. He appeared to be a few years older than Joseph and took the seat facing him, where the couple had been sitting.

"The name's Quinton Locke," he announced after he had stashed his satchel and hat on the shelf overhead. He was a short man with bushy muttonchop sideburns. In contrast, his thinning hair was slicked straight back over his scalp and coated so thickly with Macassar oil that Joseph could smell it over the cigar the man was holding.

Joseph watched with interest as the man reconsidered and brought a ledger out from the satchel. *Must be a salesman,* he thought. Yorkshire was famous for its wool and coal, but the man didn't seem the type to be associated with those businesses. *Perhaps stationery supplies?*

Remembering his manners, he reached out to shake the man's hand. "Joseph Price. I'm pleased to make your acquaintance."

"Are you headed for London?" When Joseph replied in the

affirmative, Mr. Locke said, "My home is there, in Chertsey. I come up north twice yearly on business. The land's lovely up here, but I'm always eager to get back home." He inhaled appreciatively from his cigar, then glanced at the only other passenger, a young man absorbed in his newspaper at the opposite window. "Why, I do believe this is my lucky day. It looks like we're to have a nice peaceful trip. No children about, eh?"

"None so far."

"Let's just hope it stays that way," said Mr. Locke. Taking a pencil from his waistcoat pocket, he flipped open his ledger.

Not stationery. Let's see . . . he must be in pharmaceuticals, Joseph amended his earlier guess. "What business are you in, if you'll pardon my prying?"

"I sell supplies to several chemists in London," Mr. Locke answered. "A little company here in Doncaster manufactures certain elixirs from herbs on the moors, compounds that can't be bought elsewhere. Every so often I have to pay a visit."

Joseph smiled to himself. *Right on the nose.*

"And yourself?" asked Mr. Locke. "What is your occupation?"

"I'm a detective."

The man looked impressed. "Scotland Yard?"

"Private, actually."

"Interesting." Mr. Locke took another puff on his cigar, then turned his attention back to his ledger. The train started moving again, and Joseph felt his eyelids growing heavy. He leaned his head back against the leather seat, closed his eyes, and absently counted the clicks of the wheels upon the rails. Before too long, he had drifted into a comfortable half doze.

~

Telsa Knapp could feel her heartbeat quickening at the first sound of the approaching train. Standing outside the Little Danworth depot, she turned to her husband for one final plea.

"Can't we stay in the house by ourselves until it's over, John? After all, it's only Mrs. Gatter's what's got it, and we ain't been near her for days."

John looked down at the children standing pressed against them, their heads turned toward the advancing column of black smoke. "Nay, Telsa. If it were just you and me, I'd risk it. But not the little ones."

"Then come with us."

Her husband gave a sad shake of the head. "You know I've got to tend the sheep. I'll send for you when it's safe to come back home."

Swallowing, Telsa nodded and drew closer to her husband's side. "As soon as it's safe. Not a day longer."

~

Joseph blinked and sat up straight, suddenly aware that the train was no longer moving. From the window he could see a tiny hamlet consisting of one winding lane and a couple dozen flint cottages. The hand-lettered sign above the depot, a rubble-stone building suspiciously resembling a converted farrier's shed, read Little Danworth.

Seven people stood waiting in front of the depot—a man wearing a farmer's smock, a woman with a baby in her arms, and four children. The children's faces were anxious, as if they couldn't quite believe that this great smoke-belching, screeching monster had stopped for them. A trunk and large wicker basket were nearby, and a burly Negro porter from the train ran out to shoulder the trunk and take it to the baggage car.

As the porter disappeared with his trunk, the farmer's expression revealed his uncertainty about what he was supposed to do next. "Get on board!" Joseph heard another porter call out, and then he watched as the farmer took the basket on one arm and lifted one of the younger children with his other. Speaking to his family, he then led them toward the nearest coach . . . Joseph's coach. And Joseph's compartment.

"Oh, bother!" Mr. Locke groaned in horror as he watched the brass latch on the door move. Papers from his satchel were spread in three different stacks on his knees and on the seat beside him. "I suppose I won't get any more work done on this trip. Why did they have to choose *this* car?"

Joseph cringed with embarrassment, even though the farmer was just stepping inside and hadn't heard the man. Having his very thoughts spoken aloud by someone else now made them seem petty, mean-spirited. He studied the sour expression of the man across from him and wondered if his own face would look the same way in a few years.

"Here, let me change cars so your family will have some room," offered the young man from the opposite window. Grabbing his satchel, he passed the farmer and stepped down out of the compartment. Mr. Locke watched the man leave with obvious envy, then looked down helplessly at his papers, as if contemplating the bother of having to organize them again.

The farmer gave a timid nod of greeting to the two men still on board, then settled his family into the seats at the opposite window. With a quick squeeze of his wife's hand and a pat to the top of the baby's head, he left the coach, and the wheels began turning again. The stop took all of five minutes.

Ignoring the martyred looks of the man across from him, Joseph watched the family from the corner of his eye for a little while. While their clothes were the simple garments of a farmer's family, they were clean and well made. The children, from the oldest to the youngest, wore shoes—clogs with wooden soles—and the girls had on clean cotton gloves.

It was obvious from their wide-eyed expressions that the children had never been on a train before, which was perhaps why they were so well behaved. Even the baby hadn't made a sound at the last screech of the whistle, which relieved Joseph greatly. Perhaps this trip wouldn't turn out bad after all.

One of the children, next to his mother on the facing seat, was a rosy-cheeked lad with blond curls, about three years of age. He studied Joseph through curious, yet solemn eyes. When Joseph sent a wink in his direction, however, the boy turned shy, snuggling closer to his mother and looking elsewhere.

The child's probably heard what a crab I am, Joseph told himself. *Perhaps every tot in England who misbehaves is threatened with a visit from "The Grouchy Mr. Price."* He could just picture flustered mothers, nannies, and governesses all across the country tucking in their charges with the warning, "Mind you, stay in bed and keep quiet—Mr. Price could be peeking through the window at you."

Mr. Locke glanced up from his ledger and evidently misunderstood the expression on Joseph's face. "I've always believed that the poor stay poor because they don't know how to handle their finances properly," he commented. "Wouldn't you agree?"

Joseph wasn't quite sure what the man meant. Surely he

wasn't referring to the mother and children who had just boarded. No one would be *that* rude, he told himself. "I'm not sure I understand your meaning," he finally said.

The man sent a pointed look in the family's direction, then lowered his voice. "You'd think that such people as *those* would want to save a few pennies by riding third class, wouldn't you?"

Wincing inwardly again, Joseph glanced at the woman and children. The woman had her face turned toward the window beside her, but it was obvious from the rigidity of her posture that she had heard.

He felt like striking the pompous Mr. Locke across the face. Though he himself would just as soon not have children around him when he traveled, Joseph was offended by the arrogance in the man's words. The only difference between the third-class cars and the ones used to haul livestock were the rows of wooden benches in the open third-class accommodations. In his most irritable mood, he would never condemn a family to travel in that fashion. He leaned closer to the man across from him, lowered his voice and said, "I believe this is a free country, sir. Is it not?"

The man looked stunned to receive such a reply from one he had earlier taken for granted as being a kindred spirit. "Here, here now," he scolded, his face clouding. "There's no call for rudeness!"

"My feelings exactly," Joseph answered in an even tone. "So I would appreciate it if you'd keep your opinions to yourself." He darted a covert glance in the direction of the family next to him, hoping he hadn't embarrassed the woman any further. She met his eyes with a shy smile of gratitude, then turned her attention to the sleeping baby in her arms.

The train pulled into Newark upon Trent at a quarter of

seven, and a porter stuck his head into the coach to announce a thirty-minute stop to take on and let off travelers. "There's a decent restaurant here, too," he added with just a hint of a smirk. A handful of passengers left the train, some of them taking their bags and parcels, and some carrying nothing, going to the station only for supper. Mr. Locke was one of the latter, taking his leave without a word to Joseph.

This was the longest stop they'd had since Doncaster, and dining in a rattling compartment was sometimes hazardous to clothing. Joseph could imagine that people up and down the length of the train were now taking advantage of the lack of motion to dive into baskets that they had packed. His neighbors did the same, the woman reaching into her large basket for sandwiches wrapped in brown paper.

Think I'll wait till the next stop, Joseph thought, still sated from his huge lunch. He reached past his lunch into his gripsack for a well-worn copy of *A Tale of Two Cities*. He had read only two pages of chapter twelve, when a soft voice to the right said, "Mister?"

Joseph looked over at the farmer's wife. She was holding out a sandwich made with thick slices of brown bread. "Would you like something to eat?"

He smiled at her, realizing that she thought he had brought no food. "I've got some packed," he answered. "But thank you for your kind offer."

The woman went back to tending to her children's supper. The earlier shyness of the young ones had eased a bit, and they chattered softly to each other. Strangely, Joseph didn't mind now. In fact, it was rather pleasant, listening to their young voices.

The pleasantness lasted only a moment longer, for the lad

who had been watching Joseph earlier was refusing his mother's attempts to get him to take a sandwich. When his mother insisted, the boy turned his face away from her and began to sob. The more his mother tried to calm him down, the louder he cried, until Joseph wondered if the child would burst a blood vessel.

"Oh, sir, I'm so sorry," the woman apologized as she handed the baby to her oldest daughter and lifted the boy up into her lap. Her attempts to quiet him were in vain, and after a while it looked as if she were ready to cry herself.

"Here," Joseph finally said, standing and holding out his arms for the lad. "Let me try."

The child wailed louder and tried to cling to his mother, but Joseph was stronger and pried him from her lap. "We'll just get some fresh air and have a chat," he said over the boy's wails, stepping toward the open compartment door.

"Now you see, there's nothing to cry about," he soothed when they were outside. "Look over there, can you see that clock tower? It's going to play us a fine tune in just a minute."

By the time the clock began chiming the seventh hour, the little boy had stopped weeping, although tears still clung to his rosy cheeks. He lifted a finger to point at the clock, still wearing the solemn expression he'd had since his family boarded the train.

"You're not much for making small talk, are you lad?" Joseph asked him as they stepped back into the coach. To the mother he said, "He may not have an appetite for sandwiches today. Would you like me to try to feed him?"

The mother gave him a grateful smile, and Joseph sat down with the boy on his knee and took his parcel of food out of his satchel. *I can always get something at the next depot if I'm hungry,* he told himself.

"Now, how about a bit of orange?" he asked the child, all the while peeling one with his pocket knife. To his surprise, the boy accepted a section of the fruit without protest, even holding out a hand for more when he had chewed and swallowed the first slice.

By the time the whistle sounded, Joseph was peeling the second orange for the child. Mr. Locke came back to the compartment, looking disgusted to find one of the farmer's children right across from him. Without a word, he snatched up his satchel and moved to another coach.

The lad finished both oranges, never cracking a smile as he ate. Joseph wiped the boy's face and hands with a clean handkerchief, then offered him half of a meat pie. "Too full of oranges, are you?" he asked when the boy shook his head. "Well, it's back to your mother, then."

"Thank you so much, sir," the farmer's wife said as Joseph set the child back next to her.

"I'm glad to help out." Joseph's natural curiosity about people took over, and he wondered why a mother and children would leave home without the father. "Are you going to visit relatives?" he asked.

A shadow crossed the woman's face, then she nodded. "My sister lives in Wittering. We're going to stay with her for a while."

There was something so sad, so touching in her expression that Joseph's heart went out to the whole family sitting beside him. He didn't want to make the woman uncomfortable by prying further, but it just didn't make sense, a family being split apart like that. He remembered the look of love and sadness

that had been on the farmer's face when he had said farewell
to his wife and children. Surely this was a painful separation.
Could it be for economic reasons? Have they lost their home?

Joseph wasn't what could be called an extremely wealthy
man, but most of the time he enjoyed a comfortable income.
Even with all the traveling that was required of him, he had
only himself to look after, so his expenses were minimal.
While he wasn't exactly frugal, he didn't like to waste money,
so he traveled second-class coach most of the time.

What he didn't spend, he saved, and his account at the Bank
of England had grown into a considerable nest egg over the
years. He thought about the leather money pouch tucked
away in his waistband. Even now, there were probably enough
banknotes inside to help the family find another place to live,
where they wouldn't have to separate. *What good is having
money if you can't help someone now and then?* he thought.

"Excuse me, madam," he said to the woman, keeping his
voice low so that he wouldn't embarrass her. "Forgive me for
prying, but is your family having problems of some sort?"

"No, sir," she replied quickly, yet her face grew sad as before.

"I'd like to help if there's something that I can do."

~

Telsa Knapp shook her head. The gentleman was nice enough,
but he couldn't help. No one could. *There's naught that anyone
can do but get away.* "We just have to leave Tidestone, to stay
with my sister for a little while."

"Tidestone?"

"The town where we live, some fifteen miles from Little
Danworth." Glancing at the baby, who was now back in her
arms, she wondered if they were taking action too late. Why

had she fought her husband's decision for almost a week, giving the scarlet fever that had stricken a village dairymaid time to get a firmer grip on the community? Were the children now going to have to suffer the consequences of her delay?

The man was staring at her with such kindness in his eyes that Telsa wondered if he had guessed the reason they'd had to flee their home. John had told her not to tell *anyone* but her sister, for where could she and the children go if they were run out of town by panicked villagers?

It seemed not to be the case though, for at length he asked, "Have you enough money to pay for your return fare?"

Telsa's shoulders relaxed. "Oh yes, sir. My husband does smithin' work on the side, and he's even been able to hire a couple of men to help him tend the sheep."

He nodded. "You must be wishing he could have come with you."

Blinking away the tears that stung her eyes, she answered quietly, "I'm wishin' he could."

~

The woman and her children got off the train at Stamford in Leicestershire. Joseph carried the little boy and his sister to the platform, then tipped a station porter to take care of the family.

I didn't even ask their names, he realized on his way back to his compartment. From a window in the next coach, Mr. Locke glared down at him as he passed. Joseph looked up at the heat in the man's expression and thought, *Maybe I'm not the grouchiest man in England after all.*

4

EVAN, don't put that in your mouth!" ten-year-old
Jenny Hammond cried. She dropped her pail and
sprinted toward the tot, who had taken off most of his
clothes and was seated in the grass in front of the sheep pen.

Wearing only a linsey-woolsey shirt, Aunt Mary's youngest
child was inspecting a beetle he had picked off the fence post.
After hearing his older cousin's warning, he brought his hand
up to his mouth and put the unfortunate creature inside.

"Nasty!" Jenny cried, kneeling down beside him. With her
fingers she pried his mouth open, but the bug was nowhere in
sight.

The boy gave her an angelic grin. "Nasty!" he echoed.

She had to laugh. For all the trouble he caused, Evan was the
most pleasant of Aunt Mary's four children. Not that Trudy,
Rebecca, and Diana—ages six, five, and three—were bad, but
the girls had inherited their father's more serious nature.

Jenny had lived with Aunt Mary and Uncle Roy ever since
she could remember, so her father's death from consumption
six months ago hadn't made much of an impact on her life.
Still, he was her closest kin. Even though she'd rarely seen the
man—and he was drunk every time she did see him—she still
grieved over his death.

Her mother she couldn't remember, although once in a while at night she would dream about a dark-haired lady. She would usually wake up with an unexplainable feeling of sadness after such a dream.

Aunt Mary, her mother's sister, had once said that her mother had beautiful dark hair, like the lady in her dreams. Jenny didn't know if she really remembered such a person or if her own imagination had created her.

Rebecca came running around from the back of the cottage, Evan's damp, grass-stained napkin dangling from two of her fingers. "He took this off," she said, wrinkling her nose and handing it over to her older cousin.

"You silly boy!" Jenny scolded lightly as she reached out to brush a spider from one of the baby's dirt-caked feet. "I can't take my eyes off you for a minute, else you're stripping your clothes and eatin' bugs!"

Evan laughed, then pointed to his open mouth. "Bugs!"

"Watch him, Becca, and I'll get another napkin from the wash line," Jenny said. Shaking grass from the front of her skirt, Jenny walked to the twine stretched between two oak tree trunks and took down one of the wool napkins thrown over the line. A movement from the cottage a few feet away caught her eye. She could see her aunt through the window, kneading bread at the kitchen table.

Aunt Mary had always been good to her, treating her like one of her own children. But life in the tiny dwelling was hard, and her aunt always seemed tired, especially when Uncle Roy was unable to find any work thatching roofs in and around Leawick, their little farming village in the county of Shropshire. Though Jenny was only four years older than firstborn Trudy, she had become the children's nanny of sorts, keeping them clean and fed and out of their parents' way.

She bore no resemblance to her four cousins, save for her wheat-colored, baby-fine hair. While the others had their Uncle Roy's brown eyes, Jenny's were gray. Huge and luminous, they drew attention away from her delicate chin line. "You ain't exactly pretty," Aunt Mary had once told her, "but when your face grows up you'll be beautiful, like . . ."

She had closed her mouth then and gone back to shelling peas.

~

Later that morning, Jenny dropped another handful of blackberries into her tin pail, then turned to make sure that Diana and little Evan hadn't strayed from the clearing where she had ordered them to sit. To her relief, the two were still caught up in pulling apart honeysuckles from a vine weaving through the meadow grass.

She brushed a strand of hair from her eyes and smiled, recalling the mixture of surprise and delight that had come to Evan's face when she had first dabbed a bit of the clear, sweet nectar onto his tongue. Diana, a year older than the lad and the worst of Aunt Mary's children to wander off, had been impressed by this discovery enough to stay at her little brother's side.

Satisfied with the whereabouts of her two youngest charges, Jenny set her pail on the ground and gathered up her skirt to see how Trudy and Becca were faring on the borders of a briar patch several feet away.

"We've been here all morning," Trudy complained at the sight of her older cousin. "Haven't we got enough for a pie?"

Jenny came closer to peer into Trudy's pail. The bottom was barely covered with berries, while the girl's lips and chin were stained purple. She didn't even bother to look into Rebecca's pail, for there were almost identical smears on her face.

"Almost enough," Jenny answered. She wasn't about to scold the children. Sweets were a rare thing lately.

She went back to her own pail, warned the two littlest ones to stay put, and worked a little faster. An hour later, when Diana and Evan had grown weary of the honeysuckles and were beginning to get cranky, Jenny decided that enough berries had been picked. She called to the older girls. Together, they had enough for a couple of pies, or perhaps even a cobbler.

Handing her pail to Trudy and charging Becca to hold little Diana's hand, she scooped Evan up to her bony hip and herded the children down the hillside path through the tall grasses toward home. A sudden breeze, laden with the scent of wild roses and honeysuckle, bathed their faces as they walked, as if rewarding them for a job well done. The children soon forgot how tired they were and skipped along, chattering all the while.

Uncle Roy and Aunt Mary's cottage was just in sight in the glen below them. Jenny shifted little Evan to her other side and quickened her steps. Aunt Mary would be pleased with the berries they had picked. Perhaps having pie for dessert would lighten Uncle Roy's mood.

As the children neared the front door of the cottage, Jenny was dismayed to see Uncle Roy's wagon under the eaves of the barn. His leggets, knife, and shears hung from nails on a post—ominous signs that there were again no roofs begging to be thatched.

Aunt Mary met them at the door, wiping her hands on her apron. The worried look on her face made her look older than she was. "Come fetch your dinner, children," she said, nodding briefly at the pails of berries Trudy held up for her inspection. She went back to a kettle hanging from a hook in the fireplace and began dishing out bowls of stew made from a hare Uncle Roy had trapped yesterday in the woods.

Without waiting to be told, Jenny took the half loaf of bread that Aunt Mary had set on the table and began slicing it into six portions—Uncle Roy's she sliced thicker than the rest. From a crock Trudy brought over from the cupboard, Jenny spread each piece of the brown bread sparingly with butter. She then helped little Evan and Diana up on the bench in front of the handmade plank table.

By the time all the children were seated, Uncle Roy, a stoop-shouldered man with a pinched expression, came inside from the back of the cottage. All conversation at the table died down immediately. Even baby Evan sobered up and stopped fidgeting.

Without even nodding at his wife and children, the man sat down on a rush-bottomed chair at the head of the table and began sopping his stew with a piece of bread. Aunt Mary served up her own dish and came to sit with the family, and the meal was eaten quietly, with only the occasional clatter of tin spoons against stoneware bowls.

Uncle Roy's stew was finished within minutes. Catching his wife's eye, he frowned down at his empty bowl, then stared out the window as she jumped up and served him seconds.

Jenny, at her usual place between Evan and Becca, forced herself to take another spoonful of the stew. She had come to the table hungry, but for some reason her appetite was now gone. An air of anxiety filled the tiny kitchen, adding to the usual tension that came with Uncle Roy's presence. *Did I do something wrong?* she wondered, forcing another bite down her throat.

~

Roy Satters resented the burden that had been put on his shoulders of having to provide for his family. He likened his situation to that of a convict in prison, being forced to walk a ceaseless treadmill or to pick apart mile after mile of hemp rope.

And there was no end to it as far as he could see. Why, Mary had just told him four days ago that she was with child again!

Whether he could find work or not, the one constant in his life was the need to provide food for the people under his roof. While he entertained no thoughts of abandoning his wife and children—like the grandfather who raised him, he would do his duty—he saw no need to go beyond that obligation and nurture their souls.

And he felt that he had more than done his duty with Jenny, his wife's niece. Any man who would support a child that was not his own for eight years deserved a medal! A lesser man would have packed the child off to an orphanage a long time ago.

He glanced at Jenny, now helping the baby manage his spoon. *She's been a good help with the little ones,* he mused. *She does give Mary more time to cook, mend, and tend the cow and garden. But Trudy's old enough to watch the others now. And we may as well get something back for taking the girl in.*

His meal finished, Roy tipped his mug to drain the last of his ale, then pushed away from the table. "Trudy, take the others outside now," he ordered. To Jenny's timid, questioning glance he simply added, "You stay here."

~

Jenny's stomach lurched. What could she possibly have done to make her uncle look even more stern than usual? She got up and lifted Evan to the stone floor. When she had finished helping Trudy shepherd the younger children to the front door, she turned around to find Aunt Mary still at the table, crying.

"I've found you a position in Sir Feldon's fields," Uncle Roy began, not even waiting for Jenny to sit back down on the bench. "You're to start work in the mornin'."

"Please, Roy, don't make that child go to the fields," Aunt Mary pleaded through her tears. "She's still just a little thing . . . it'll kill her!"

"She's big enough to help put food on the table," he answered matter-of-factly. "I started workin' when I was barely six."

"But you didn't have a fa—" Aunt Mary's voice died, silenced by her husband's venomous look.

"She don't have a father either, Mary. And she can't expect to live on charity all her life." With that, he got up from the table and walked out of the room. He did not look at the trembling girl as he passed her by.

~

The morning sun was just beginning to send its first tenuous rays above the treetops when Roy brought the wagon around to the front of the cottage. He whistled a rare tune as he loaded his thatching tools in the back. He had found some work in Fletcher's Down, just over the hills to the east.

First he would take Jenny over to his landlord's fields. The baronet's fields were within walking distance, only a couple of miles away, but he wanted to see the farm manager this first morning, to make sure that the salary arrangements were what he had understood them to be. With his mood lightened considerably at the prospect of two incomes, he paid no attention to the fear etched into the face of the young girl seated next to the driver's box, her hands clenched in her lap. Nor did he look up when his wife came out into the yard carrying something in her hands.

~

"Now, see that you eat every bit of your lunch, even if you ain't hungry," Aunt Mary said, coming around to the front of the wagon to hand Jenny a parcel of food tied up in a bandanna. "There's a slab of berry pie in there, too."

"Thank you, ma'am," Jenny said meekly. She wondered what she had done to displease her aunt, for the woman had avoided looking directly into her eyes all morning. A shiver of dread went through her, and she longed for a reassuring word from someone—anyone—about the day that stretched out before her.

A lump came to her throat when she thought of her little cousins waking later without her to help them get dressed, lace their shoes, and put the right amount of honey in their bowls of porridge. Would they miss her terribly today? She wished that she could go back into the loft, where they all slept together on a flock mattress, and kiss their little sleeping faces again.

"Keep your bonnet on, lass, so your face don't burn," Aunt Mary was saying. Her eyes started to glisten, and she wiped them with the back of her hand. "And don't go round with your head in the clouds and forget to drink enough water. You'll get the sun fever if your insides dry out."

"Leave her be, Mary," Uncle Roy ordered from under his cap, as he checked Dan's harness. Dan, Uncle Roy's gray speckled dray horse, had given Jenny a mournful sidelong glance when she came out to the wagon as if he, too, knew what lay in store for the lass.

Uncle Roy climbed up on the wagon box and took the reins in his weathered hands. Clicking his tongue, he gave a flick to the reins, and the wagon started forward with a squeak of the wheels. Jenny braced herself and sat as straight as possible beside him, not daring to look back at the little cottage where she had spent most of her ten years.

She would return this evening, but nothing would ever be the same. This was not her home, Uncle Roy had reminded her yesterday. She was not part of the family. She was just a charity case, a burden to her relatives.

A tear seeped from the corner of her eye and trailed down her cheek. Jenny didn't want the man beside her to see it, so she turned her face to the side. They were passing the hill where she and her little cousins had picked blackberries just yesterday morning. The tall meadow grass, laden with honeysuckles and bluebells, nodded and waved, as if calling her for one last frolic before leaving her childhood completely.

~

A dozen or so people were already gathered in front of one of Sir Feldon's barns. They all turned curious faces toward Roy Satters's approaching wagon.

"Mr. Blake around?" Roy asked, reining Dan to a halt.

"Over here!" came a voice from the shadows of the barn

37

doorway. A man wearing a brown linen shirt stepped into the emerging daylight. Of medium height, he had massive shoulders and a face that was tanned and leathery. Mr. Blake walked over to the wagon, ran an appraising eye over Jenny, and then scowled. "Ye didn't tell me she were so little," he said to Roy in an accusing tone.

"Aye, she's little," Roy answered. He pointed toward the group of workers that stood there staring. "You've got two over there that's smaller than her."

"They been working here for a couple of years. They're used to it."

"Jenny's used to hard work, too. She's helped my missus with her garden ever since she could walk. Give her a chance and you'll see."

The man looked up at Jenny again, then shrugged his shoulders. "One week. But if she don't work out, don't come round asking again. Sir Feldon pays me to run his farm, not be a nursemaid."

"She'll work," Roy assured him.

5

JOSEPH'S train pulled into London's King's Cross Station at six o'clock the next morning. Stepping down from the coach into a city blanketed by fog, he took his gripsack in one hand, got his traveling bag from a porter, and hailed a hansom from the line of cabs waiting just outside the station.

He was weary to the bone, and his neck ached from trying to sleep with his head leaning against the rattling window of the train. But he was anxious to get started, too. He would go right away to the rooming house on Charing Cross Road, the one he had used the last time he was in the city. After stashing his bags he would have breakfast, then get back on the trail of Corrine Hammond.

She was still in London . . . he could sense it. And he intended to find her—whatever it took.

After a hurried breakfast of sausage and eggs, Joseph left his rooming house and boarded an omnibus that came within a block of Charles Street. If luck was with him, Corrine Hammond would still be living in the house where Gerald Moore had met his end.

He was not ready to bring her in. For that, he would need to hire a coach and horses for the trip back up to Treybrook.

He certainly could not expect her to stay by his side on a long train journey.

But it wasn't time to hire the coach. For all he knew, Corrine Hammond could have died from the injuries Moore had inflicted upon her. He remembered the blood on the sitting-room floor, leading out to the street in front of her house. Someone had taken the injured woman away—but where? She could be back at home, in a hospital, at someone else's home, or even in a cemetery somewhere. He had to find out before proceeding with any other plans.

But he couldn't just walk up to Mrs. Hammond's door and ask. If the woman was still living there, she would likely get suspicious if she thought that someone was looking for her. And what if her maid answered the door? Mrs. Hammond's maid had seen him, had even spoken with him on the day that Gerald Moore fell to his death. She had been in too much shock to ask why a complete stranger had happened on the scene and saved her from his clutches, but by now, surely she had wondered about him.

Joseph spotted a group of ragged boys on a street corner, playing chuck-a-luck for matchsticks with homemade dice. One boy, smaller than the rest, hovered just at the perimeter of the group, obviously wishing for a chance to play.

"Would you like to earn a penny?" Joseph leaned down and asked the lad when he got close enough to speak.

The boy's head shot up. "What I got ter do?"

"Just knock on a door and ask for a job doing yard work."

Disappointment shadowed his young face. "Don't know how ter do yard work, mister."

"Don't worry. You don't have to take the job if one happens to be offered," Joseph reassured him. He didn't have the heart to tell the lad that such a possibility was very remote anyway. "I just want to see if someone still lives in a certain house not too far from here."

"Like a surprise, you mean?"

"That's it. In fact, if you're convincing enough, I'll raise your salary to twopence. What do you say?"

"Twopence? Where's the house, mister?"

They walked the last block together, turning the corner onto Charles Street. It was a pleasant, tree-lined road, with neat terraces alternating with ancient houses standing in high-walled gardens with carriage drives. The house Mrs. Hammond and Gerald Moore had leased, a Georgian-style red brick, was just ahead to their left. "Now, you go on ahead and knock on the front door," Joseph instructed the lad. "I'm going to stay here and wait for you under this tree."

The boy glanced down at his patched and worn shirt, then turned fearful eyes to the house. "The front door? Ain't they gonter get mad?"

"I don't think so." Joseph found himself moved by the lad's embarrassment with his clothes. Reaching into his pocket, he brought out a larger coin and held it between his finger and thumb. "Anyway, even if someone does, you'll still have a half crown in your pocket. You can buy a dozen new shirts with this." *I must be crazy,* he told himself. *He'll probably waste it all away before the day's over.*

"For me?" Looking down at Joseph's hand with eyes as big as saucers, the boy reached out a tentative finger to touch the coin.

"Just don't look back at me if someone answers, whatever you do," Joseph cautioned as he put the coin in the child's palm. "You understand?"

The lad gaped down at the coin in his hand, then closed his fingers around it. "I'll do it right now, mister!"

While the boy ran down the street to Mrs. Hammond's house, Joseph stepped close to the trunk of a nearby beech tree and watched. Not looking back, the boy boldly climbed the steps to the front porch and rapped with the brass knocker. When there was no answer, he knocked louder a second time, then a third.

That doesn't mean she's gone, he told himself, motioning to the boy that he could stop knocking. But he had a sinking feeling that was exactly what it meant.

"Want me ter try the back door?" the boy asked, made bolder by his sudden wealth, as he came back over to where Joseph was standing.

"No, thank you." Joseph smiled at the lad. "You did a good job."

~

His next stop was at the Park Lane home of Eugene Graham, the man who had rented Gerald Moore the house on Charles Street. To his relief, the elderly man was at home and in a talkative mood.

"The house is empty," he said over a cup of tea. They sat in opposite chairs in the front parlor, a room infested with bric-a-brac. "Your Mr. Moore seems to have vanished into thin air."

Stirring his tea, Joseph didn't think it odd that Mr. Graham wasn't aware that his tenant had died. After all, he himself had spirited off the body in a wagon just minutes after it happened.

"So you've heard nothing from his . . . companion," he asked. "I believe her name was Mrs. Hammond?"

Mr. Graham's eyebrows lifted. "A Mrs. Hammond, did you say?"

"Yes," Joseph answered, his heartbeat quickening.

"I received a post from a Mrs. Hammond less than a fortnight ago, but that was the first time I'd heard of such a person. The letter said that the house was vacant and that she was terminating the lease. There was an extra month's rent in the envelope, along with her apologies for such short notice."

"And this was the first time you'd heard from her?"

"It was."

Leaning forward to put his teacup on the table in front of him, Joseph asked the man if he still had the letter from Mrs. Hammond.

"I had no reason to keep it," Mr. Graham answered.

"Do you remember the return address?"

He shook his head thoughtfully. "Somewhere in north London. I can't recall the name of the street."

"Well, I appreciate your allowing me to take up so much of your time." Joseph reached for a slip of paper from his waistcoat pocket, then stood. "This is the address of the inn where I'm staying. Would you please send for me if you remember anything else?"

"I'll be happy to," said Mr. Graham, rising to his feet as well. "There is just one thing that isn't clear to me, and that's the whereabouts of Mr. Moore. Do you have any idea where he is now?"

Joseph smiled faintly. "Humberside, I believe. Something to do with horses."

~

Joseph left Mr. Graham's at noon, too anxious to get back on the right trail to think about lunch. It was time to do some serious investigating, and for that he would need more mobility than the omnibuses could provide.

He hired a hansom cab just outside Hyde Park, instructing the driver to take him back to Charles Street. As he rode through the streets of the busy city, he wondered if Mrs. Hammond had possibly found another lover and partner in crime to replace Gerald Moore. Was that why Moore had beaten her, because she decided she preferred someone else—possibly the man they had come to London to extort?

That was a possibility he hadn't considered. If only he knew what prey, what magnet, had drawn the couple to London, he felt he would be close to an answer. There had to be a way to find that out.

Right now he had to figure out how Corrine Hammond managed to disappear on that fateful day two weeks ago when he had come so close to capturing her. Surely some neighbor, perhaps a servant, had seen something. After all, a battered woman stumbling out to the street had to attract someone's attention.

He would ask every person who lived or worked in the vicinity. Now that he knew the house where Corrine had lived was empty, he instructed the driver of the hansom to pull up in the carriage drive. He then stepped down and walked past the lawn to the neighboring house to the west and pulled the cord of the brass bell on the doorpost.

Presently the door cracked open and a long, thin section of a frowning face appeared, presumably the housekeeper. "We've seen nor heard nothing out of the ordinary," came the pickled answer to Joseph's inquiry; then the door was closed again.

Undaunted, Joseph retraced his steps to the house on the opposite side of Mrs. Hammond's former home. Another housekeeper answered, with more cordiality than the first. "We never even seen the lady what lived next door up close," she explained. "Just her maid now and then, on her way to market. But there's rumors goin' around that she—Mrs. Hammond, that is—ran outside with blood all over her face one day and waved down a carriage. Don't know how we could have missed seeing something like that, but we did."

"And where did you hear this, madam?" asked Joseph. As was his usual custom, he was careful to keep any eagerness from his tone of voice. So far, no one had thought to ask about his connection with Mrs. Hammond or why her whereabouts were any of his business. He would just as soon keep it that way.

The housekeeper eased the door open wider and pointed a freckled arm to the house directly across the street. "Mr. Warrick's cook, Mrs. Turnley. She said she saw the lady next door bein' helped into a carriage a couple o' weeks ago."

Thanking the housekeeper, Joseph crossed the street and went around back of the house to the kitchen door. *Might as well go right to the source,* he told himself. A comely young woman wearing a ruffled cap and spotless apron answered his knock. She appeared startled, pleasantly so, to find a well-dressed gentleman on the stoop. Usually only deliverymen and other servants used back doors.

"My name is Joseph Price," he said, giving her a smile as he took off his hat. "May I speak with Mrs. Turnley?"

"That might be possible," the young woman said. Fluttering her lashes at him, she tucked stray wisps of brown hair under her cap. "And what business would you have with her?"

"Are you Mrs. Turnley?"

She folded her arms and leaned against the door frame, a little smile playing about her full lips. "Well, I am and I ain't," came the answer with a little laugh. First taking a quick glance over her shoulder, she continued. "You see, Mr. Warrick is gettin' up there in years. He's . . . forgetful, you might say. Half the time he thinks he's about to fight that Napoléon bloke. The cook who was here a long time before me, her name was Mrs. Turnley, and that's who the old gent thinks I am most of the time. The name just stuck. Wages are good here, so he can call me Mary Queen of Scots if he wants to.

"By the way," she added before Joseph could speak, "the 'Mrs.' part is all in the master's fancy, too. I ain't married. Never have been." Her eyebrows lifted meaningfully. "What about yourself, love? Got a wife at home?"

"No, I haven't," he replied easily, resisting the urge to take a step back away from the hungry look in her eyes. "Would you mind if I asked you some questions?"

"Only if you'll come inside and sit like a proper gentleman," she teased.

Joseph waited until she had stepped out of the doorway before following her into the kitchen. The stone-walled room was pleasantly cool, rare for a kitchen. As the young woman motioned toward the chairs at the kitchen table, she explained that she had to heat the oven to bake bread only once or twice a week.

"Most of the time Mr. Warrick just wants broth and cheese or porridge for his dinner," she said. "We ain't even got a scullery maid round here, but the work's so easy I've still got time to spare." She gave him a pointed look. "Time to have tea and scones with my gentleman caller. Or would you be wantin' some brandy instead?"

"Nothing for me, thank you," Joseph answered as he pulled out a chair on the opposite side of the table and sat down. It

46

was past three o'clock and he was beginning to feel rumbles in his empty stomach, but he didn't want to obligate himself to "Mrs. Turnley" any more than strictly necessary.

Standing across the table from him, she looked disappointed. "Are you sure?"

He smiled. "Well, perhaps some tea would be nice. If it's not too much trouble."

"No trouble at all!" She was at the cast-iron stove in an instant, fishing a match from a tin box to light the gas jet. "My real name's Mildred, by the way," she said as she filled a kettle of water from a spigot over a large metal basin. "Named after one of my aunts. She was always a mean old thing, though. I was glad to get this job and get away from the likes of her, even if Mr. Warrick's a bit half baked most of the time." She chattered on about the other eccentricities of her employer while she made the tea, asked again if he wanted some scones, and finally brought the kettle and a couple of empty cups on a tray over to the table.

Joseph kept an attentive face toward her, all the while his thoughts racing through any clues he might have overlooked this morning as to the whereabouts of Corrine Hammond. When Mildred was finally seated across from him and had stopped talking long enough to take a sip of tea, he took advantage of the silence. "I wonder if you'd mind telling me," he began, "about what you saw the day Mrs. Hammond was injured."

Her expression turned immediately wary. "Mrs. Hammond?"

"The woman from the house across the street. I was told you were outside on the day she disappeared."

"Why do you want to know? Are you in love with her?"

Joseph blinked. "Excuse me?"

47

"Is that why you're lookin' for her?" she asked through lips that were forming a pout.

Stunned, he shook his head. "In love with Mrs. Hammond? Absolutely not—I've never even met her."

She seemed mildly satisfied with his answer. "Well, she had a gent livin' there, too, you know. I seen him slippin' out the house plenty of nights and comin' back before dawn. I figure he's the one what beat the stuffin' out of her on the day she left. I don't know what happened to him."

Setting his half-filled cup of tea on the table, Joseph said, slowly, "So you did see her that day?"

To his utter frustration, her expression became wary again. "Are you with the law, mister?" she asked, narrowing her eyes as she studied his face.

"Please call me Joseph. And, no, I'm not with the law." He swallowed his impatience and gave her another rendition of the smile he had first greeted her with, wondering briefly if he should have opted for a career on the stage instead of detective work. It seemed at times that he was just an actor, playing any part necessary to accomplish his task. Lowering his voice, he added, "I would be in your debt for any information you could give me."

It seemed to do the trick, for she returned his smile with an affectation of coyness. "Joseph. It suits you, that name." But then she came out with, "I just want to know why you're lookin' for that Hammond woman."

"I've been hired to find her," he replied carefully, through clenched teeth. "There is no personal interest involved, I assure you. Now, would you please tell me what you saw that day?"

"But how do I know that you're tellin' the truth?" Mildred was aware that her visitor was her captive until she gave him the information he had come for—and obviously intended to make this visit last as long as possible. "Mrs. Hammond was a fancy-looking lady. You could be—"

Unable to take any more, Joseph doubled his fist and slammed it against the tabletop, causing both teacups to rattle against their saucers. "That's enough!" he barked. Wide-eyed, the girl jumped back in her seat.

He stared down at his fist, even more surprised than the girl, for he had always thought himself capable of keeping his emotions under control. Was the fact that he had slept very little on the train last night, combined with the hunger rumblings in his stomach, affecting his temper? Or was he simply getting too old for all of this?

"Look, I do apologize," he told her gently. "I don't know what came over me."

"You didn't have to hit the table." She sniffed, wiping the corner of her eye with her apron.

"No, of course I didn't. And you have every right to be angry with me."

After a pause, where she appeared to be wondering whether to sulk and draw out his apology a little longer, she finally gave her shoulders a shrug. "She got into a hired carriage."

"I beg your pardon?"

"Your Mrs. Hammond. I seen her with blood all over her face bein' picked up out of the street by a driver. There was this other woman in the carriage, tellin' him to put her inside."

Joseph leaned forward, his mind conjuring up a mental picture of the scene. "You said the carriage was hired. Was it a hansom?"

She nodded. "And I recognized the driver."

Barely daring to draw a breath, Joseph urged her with his eyes to continue.

"See, that's why I scooted back into the house, quick as I could," she went on. "He—the driver, I mean—he's a cousin o' mine, and I don't want my kin knowing where I'm workin'. They'd all be over here with their hands out quick as you could say 'Bob's your uncle!'"

Joseph's smile was genuine this time. This was more information than he'd dared hope for on his first day in the city. His thoughts briefly flitted to Corrine Hammond. What was she doing at that very moment? Did she have any inkling that she was about to account for her past misdeeds?

"What is your cousin's name?" he asked, his casual tone of voice belying the eagerness he felt.

"Gregory Hammers," she replied, wrinkling her nose in distaste. "Worse gossip than any woman I ever saw." She rolled her eyes and grinned. "Even worse than me. I'm glad I spotted him before he caught sight of me."

"Do you know his address?"

The girl nodded.

"May I have it?"

"Maybe so." An impish look crossed her face. "That is, if you'll stay and have another cup of tea."

"I'd love some more tea." He smiled, holding out his cup.

"And a scone." She shrugged again and returned his smile with a sheepish one of her own. "It gets lonesome in this kitchen."

Joseph nodded. Loneliness he could understand. "A scone would be nice, too."

6

EELING the eyestrain from reading for over two hours, Corrine finally shut the book and set it down on the cast-iron bench beside her in the conservatory. She closed her eyes and drank in the aroma of the moist earth, flower blooms, and green plants.

With the fingertips of her right hand, she reached down and lovingly traced the two words imprinted against the fine leather of her Bible and wondered if any other book between its covers could match the beauty and comfort of the Gospel of John. *I'll find out,* she determined. *I'll read all of it, if it takes me the rest of my life.*

Pity that her eyes, used to reading nothing heavier than *Godey's Lady's Book* and the most shallow penny-dreadful novels, moved so slowly across the words that told about her new Lord.

Yet I wonder if that's what Bernice calls a "blessing in disguise." There was so much to absorb; one shouldn't hurry through the pages. She had read the part about the woman at the well three times. *She was just like me before she met Jesus, and now she's in heaven with him. When I go to heaven . . .*

She drew in a deep, shuddering breath, still in awe of such a thing happening to her. *When I get there, I'm going to look for*

51

that Samaritan woman. Perhaps they could even sit down for a while and tell each other how good it felt to be clean after feeling dirty for so many years.

Corrine wondered sometimes how she could possibly contain the love she felt for her Savior. She wanted to run through the streets of London and shout what a miracle had happened, just as the woman at the well had done in Samaria.

Would she always have this fire burning in her heart? The thought of her feelings growing cold was a frightening one, so much so that she raised her eyes and whispered, "Lord, please help me never to take for granted the grace you've shown me."

~

Later, Corrine sat down to a lunch of boiled beef and potatoes in the servants' hall with Bernice and the others. It was a relief to finally have meals at a table, and it didn't matter where the table happened to be located. After all the fuss they'd made over her by bringing trays to her bed and sometimes even helping her handle the fork and spoon, she refused to allow the maids to set the dining-room table just for her.

Having looked down upon servants for so long, Corrine was pleased to discover that she greatly enjoyed their company. Jack and Lucy, Bernice's husband and daughter, were there, as well as Hershall, the only other manservant, and maids Dora, Marie, and Irene. *It wasn't too long ago,* she thought, *that I would have scoffed at anyone who treated people like this as equals.*

She determined that she would save the memories of these moments for later, like pressing a flower into the pages of a book. Then she could take them out and dwell upon them whenever the more shameful memories cropped up and threatened to take away her peace of mind.

After lunch, Hershall brought her trunk up to the guest room and set it on the carpet with a muffled thud. "Would you like me to unbuckle the latches for you, ma'am?" he asked.

"No, thank you," Corrine answered. "I'm not quite finished sorting out what I plan to take."

She was in the process of doing just that, with dresses lying in stacks across her bed, when a knock sounded at the door. "Come in."

Bernice walked in with a parcel wrapped in brown paper in her hand. "This was just delivered. Perhaps you'd like to pack it with your things."

"Delivered for me? What is it?"

The cook gave a casual shrug of the shoulders, but her eyes suggested that she knew good and well what it was. "Why don't you open it and see?"

Corrine took the package from her, pulled off the twine, and tore open the brown paper. Folds of indigo blue muslin fabric fell out of the package. "A dress?"

"Well it's a dress all right, but it's not for you."

Corrine glanced up at the cook with a puzzled expression, then held the new garment up to her shoulders. Although she was petite, this gown had obviously been fashioned for a child. Suddenly she realized who the gown was for. "Jenny?"

"I wanted you to have something pretty to bring her." Bernice averted her eyes as if her own emotion embarrassed her.

With tears blurring her vision, Corrine gathered the soft fabric up into her arms. "It's so beautiful. What a thoughtful thing to do."

"Oh, well, likely it won't even fit the lass," the cook muttered, bending down to pick up some twine that had fallen to the carpet. "Do you need some help with the packing?"

"No, thank you," Corrine answered, still moist eyed. "I've got almost a week to get it done, so I can take my time." She motioned to the stack of gowns lying on top of the bedspread. "I won't be able to use several of those dresses."

"Why not?"

She looked embarrassed. "They're a bit . . . revealing. I just wouldn't feel right wearing them."

Walking over to the stack, Bernice lifted the hem of one of the gowns, a fashionable shade of plum. "Be a shame to waste such pretty material. Can't we see about havin' them altered for you?"

Corrine shook her head. "Most people in Leawick aren't able to keep up with the latest fashions. I'm sure they already resent me for leaving my family—I don't want to show up in town looking like I'm putting on airs." She walked over to where Bernice stood and looked down at the garments. "There's quite a bit of fabric in the skirts—do you think they could be cut down for children's clothes?"

"Perhaps the women's missionary society can cut them down for the orphans in Spitalfields. Just set aside those you don't want to keep, and I'll talk with Mrs. Morgan about it next time I see her." The cook smiled. "You've got enough on your mind as it is."

"Thank you, Bernice." Impulsively, Corrine leaned forward to give her a hug. "You've been a great help already. And I do thank you for this dress." She held it up again. "Jenny will love it."

Her cheeks glowing, Bernice folded her arms and nodded. "You can't wait to see her, can you?"

Corrine laid the new dress down lovingly atop the others on the bed. "I can't wait. But I'm still afraid she'll hate me."

"Maybe there'll be some resentment at first, but you're her mother. There's a bond there that can't be denied."

"I hope so."

"What about your husband?"

"Thomas?" A cloud passed over Corrine's face. "I was a terrible wife the short time we were together. We hardly knew each other. No doubt he hates me more than anybody."

"What will you do if he won't take you back?" Bernice asked gently.

"I don't know. I just have to try and convince him that I've changed."

"Do you have any feelings for him?"

Corrine shook her head sadly, then answered in a flat, expressionless voice. "Never have, if you want to know the truth. But I'm married to him. And I've got to do what's right, haven't I?"

~

The address that Mildred, the cook, had given Joseph had been correct at one time. But it turned out that the sometime carriage driver, sometime loafer had moved several times since, each time to a seedier tenement.

An inquiry to the manager of the Hansom Cab Company had not been fruitful, for Joseph was told that the man had been fired a week earlier. It seemed that he had shown up for work in his cups and had taken a hapless couple on a wild ride along the railroad tracks leading from Paddington Station.

Fortunately, no train had come along, and the man and wife, though bruised and battered, had been so relieved to finally get out of the carriage that they had not threatened legal action.

It took Joseph three frustrating days to find cousin Gregory, now living with some drinking companions. The man had just gotten up from his bed the afternoon that Joseph knocked on his tenement door. Broke and sober, Gregory was desperate to find the means to end his sobriety. He was as eager to talk as the cook had described him to be, and a gold half sovereign from Joseph loosened his lips even more so.

"It weren't every day that I picked up a woman what's been beat like that," he said. "And the house I brought her to was a fine one I don't see the likes of very often. Most people livin' on Clifton Hill have got their own carriages and drivers."

Not only did he remember the house, but he was willing to give Joseph directions—for an extra half sovereign, of course.

By six o'clock that evening, Joseph was seated on the box of a coach he had rented, directly across from the house that Gregory had described. From his lofty perch, he could easily see the front door of the greystone Georgian—where, he hoped, Corrine Hammond was still a guest.

It was the perfect surveillance place, out there in plain sight. It was common to see carriages and drivers waiting in front of the finer homes of the city, as the members of the peerage and the gentry spent great amounts of time making calls. Since the occupants of each estate would assume that the carriage was waiting for someone calling upon a neighbor, no one would be so impolite as to ask what Joseph's business was in being there. *We Brits are nothing if not mannerly,* he mused.

He was reasonably certain that Mrs. Hammond was still here. After all, she would need to stay put for a while to recuperate from her injuries. Now it was time to plan his next course of action.

He would have to discard his earlier notion, which was simply to kidnap her whenever she came outside. Even the smallest estate on Bow Road would have servants, and plenty of them. Mrs. Hammond would not likely go anywhere in the city without at least a footman to escort her. *That is, if she's able to go anywhere.* Resting his elbows on his knees, Joseph squinted at movement outside the house—it turned out to be a gardener with pruning clippers in hand. *For all I know, she could be in there with a leg in a splint.*

Before he could plan any further, he had to know what was going on inside that house. He watched the gray-haired gardener at work and thought about the countless times he had used servants to garner information. But there was too much risk this time, for he didn't want Mrs. Hammond to have an inkling that someone was interested in her.

He thought about Corrine Hammond's maid, who had seen him on the day he took away Gerald Moore's body. He had asked the girl the whereabouts of her mistress, but she had been too dazed from her struggle with Gerald Moore to answer coherently. Joseph had to assume that this maid— Rachel Jones had been her name—was with Mrs. Hammond now.

Absently scratching his beard, he wondered if the girl could give him the excuse he needed to get into the house. *After all, I practically saved her life.* A smile curved his lips, and he wondered why he hadn't seen the answer sooner. *I'd wager she doesn't even remember my asking her about her mistress that day. She could be my ticket inside.* Not covertly, slipping into the kitchen and bribing members of the household staff, but right through the front door.

The temptation to walk right up to the door was almost overpowering, but a quick glance down at the wrinkled suit he was wearing forced him to reconsider. *I look like a mudlark,* he thought. *And probably smell worse. No one would allow me past the foyer.*

Ever since he had arrived in London four days ago, he had been so eager to pick up Mrs. Hammond's trail that he had subsisted on minimal sleep. He hadn't even taken the time for anything longer than sponge baths at the washstand in his room. He stroked his beard again—it was ragged and needed a trim, and his hair felt oily.

Tomorrow then, he decided.

~

At ten o'clock the next morning, a cleaner, much more presentable Joseph Price knocked on the front door of the house on Clifton Hill. A maid opened the door seconds later, an older woman with striking blue eyes. "Yes, sir?" she said.

"Good morning, madam," Joseph said, smiling and holding his hat. "My name is Joseph Price. I'm looking for a Miss Rachel Jones. Would she happen to be here?"

"Miss Rachel?" The maid returned a shy smile. "She's in Paris, sir—on her honeymoon."

"Her honeymoon? You don't say?"

She nodded. "Got married last week, to Mr. Adam, the man who owns this house. Would you care to leave her a message?"

"I don't suppose it's necessary." Joseph shrugged. The look of discouragement he gave the maid came easy, for he was beginning to doubt the wisdom of this rash course of action.

"Is there something wrong, sir?" asked the woman at the door.

"Of course not," he answered right away, then let out a sigh. "She probably doesn't even remember me anyway."

"Are you a relative, Mr. Price?"

"A relative? No, not at all. I just wanted to make certain that the lady is suffering no ill effects from . . ." He stopped and smiled. "But of *course* she's fine now, isn't she? After all, she was well enough to get married."

"Ill effects, sir?" The maid tilted her head. "Are you talkin' about that bad man who . . ." Her voice trailed off, and she watched him with a questioning expression.

There we are! Joseph thought. Of course she had heard about the girl's struggle with Mr. Moore. As in other households, it was impossible to keep the goings-on from the servants. Wearing a frown, he offered, "The fellow was a scoundrel, ma'am, not deserving to be called a man."

Her face brightened. "You're the gentleman that helped her get away, aren't you?"

Joseph hung his head modestly. "Any gentleman would have done so, madam. I just happened to be nearby when the lady was in distress." Taking a reluctant step backward, he replaced the hat on his head. "But since she's away, I suppose . . ."

"Wait," she said, opening the door wider. "Mrs. Hammond will be wantin' to meet you, I'm sure."

He stopped short, his heart quickening in his chest. "Mrs. Hammond?"

"Mrs. Burke . . . Rachel, I mean, was her maid. Mrs. Hammond is stayin' here for a while. She's been wondering about the man who helped Miss Rachel get away." Her eyes took on a pleading expression. "Wouldn't you have time to let me tell Mrs. Hammond that you're here?"

Removing his hat again, Joseph clutched it to his chest and smiled. "If you think it's important to your Mrs. Hammond, I've got all the time in the world."

The woman led him down a central hall to a large drawing

room, its walls pale green above rich cherry wainscoting. She motioned to a comfortable-looking wing-back chair, then asked him to have a seat. "Mrs. Hammond was in the conservatory a little while ago," she said as she started back for the door. "I'll see if she's still there. May I fetch you some tea?"

Joseph was settled into the chair. "Why don't we wait and see if Mrs. Hammond cares to have some?"

With a nod the maid was gone. Joseph listened to the sound of her shoes against the quarry tiles, counting the steps mentally until they faded away. Presently, two sets of footsteps approached.

A stunning woman, petite and shapely with raven black hair, came through the doorway, followed by the maid. Rising from his chair, Joseph opened his mouth to speak but found himself at a loss for words.

"Mr. Price," the woman said, walking toward him with her hand outstretched. Her voice was low, almost husky, but still very feminine. "How good of you to call."

"Thank you," he managed, irritated at himself as he gave a little bow over her hand. He had expected the woman to be beautiful, of course, but he hadn't expected that she would make him feel awkward, like a schoolboy. Her simply cut ecru gown he would have considered plain on any other woman. But the lack of decoration on her garment drew attention to her huge, smoky gray eyes, delicately cleft chin, and flawless complexion.

The only thing that rescued her face from being classically beautiful was a slightly Roman nose. Far from hindering her looks, it gave her face character, something he was not expecting to see.

Remember all the poor fools she's destroyed, he reminded himself as he watched her lower herself into the chair facing his. She was waving away the maid's attempts to assist her. "I'm all right, Dora." She smiled up at the woman. "Would you mind bringing some tea?"

"Right away, Mrs. Hammond," said the maid and left the room.

Corrine Hammond was looking his way now. "Dora tells me that you're the one who rescued my former maid, Rachel."

He was disconcerted to feel warmth in his cheeks. "Actually, the scoundrel fell down the stairs. I just surprised him, and it caused him to stumble."

"How fortunate that you came when you did." She studied his face, her gaze direct without seeming bold. "I've thanked God for your intervention, sir, ever since Rachel told me what happened."

Thanked God? He was taken aback until he reminded himself that the Corrine Hammond he had heard so much about was an expert at presenting herself as a proper lady. "I'm just glad the girl wasn't hurt," he finally replied. Leaning forward, he looked at her with concern. "But what about you, Mrs. Hammond? I seem to remember the girl worrying that her mistress had been injured."

"I'm fine now." A look of sadness passed over her features, and she murmured, "That was a terrible day."

Joseph could *almost* feel sorry for her. "At least it's in the past now," he said gently.

"Yes, the past." Her gaze grew direct again. "One thing I don't understand. How did you happen to be at my house that day?"

"It was your house?"

"You mean, you didn't know whose it was?"

"No," he lied. "I was just passing in the street when I heard the struggle inside."

"Really? You must have extraordinary hearing."

"Sometimes, although my mother would argue that point." He feigned a look of boyish mischievousness. "I had a habit of pretending not to hear her calling me in for nap time."

She was smiling now. "Did it work?"

"Well, I tried it last week, but she ended up finding me anyway," he answered, returning her smile. *I can be just as charming as you can, Corrine Hammond.*

She laughed—a rich, low sound. In spite of the intense dislike he felt for the woman, he found himself joining in.

"Tell me more about your family," she said after the laughter had died down.

"Well, my father and brothers bake the best bread in England."

"Oh? Are you a baker, too?"

He grimaced and shook his head. "I never liked the feel of raw dough on my hands."

The maid named Dora showed up with the tray at that moment. "Would you like some tea, sir?" she asked Joseph.

"I'd love some," he replied, "but I'll wait until Mrs. Hammond has hers."

When Dora had set a cup and saucer on the tea table in front of him, she asked if he would prefer milk or lemon.

"Lemon, please." He normally took milk and sugar with his tea, but his throat was becoming a little dry and scratchy—probably the result of not getting enough sleep lately. Maybe the tartness of the lemon would help.

"I'm positive that Rachel and Mr. Burke will want to thank you in person when they return from their honeymoon next month," Corrine said after taking a sip of tea. "If you would please leave your address, I'll ask Dora or one of the others to give it to them."

"And why wouldn't you be able to give it to them yourself, if I may be so bold as to ask?"

"Because I'm leaving town this Thursday."

Joseph inhaled a mouthful of tea and had to cough several times into his napkin. "Are you all right?" Mrs. Hammond asked with concern on her face.

"Yes, thank you," he finally was able to answer, blinking watery eyes. "Just need to be more careful when I drink tea, don't I?"

She smiled. "It happens to everyone now and then."

"And almost always in public, at least in my case." He smiled back, slightly irritated at her sympathy. He cleared his throat and pressed on. "Are you going on holiday, Mrs. Hammond?"

She took another sip of her tea. "No, not a holiday."

He knew better than to prod for an answer that wasn't so vague. Besides, he had a fair idea of why the woman was leaving. *This Mr. Burke who owns the house—he must have been her last intended victim. Only he ended up marrying her maid instead. Perhaps that's why Gerald Moore beat her, because she failed to seduce Mr. Burke.* What a crushing blow it must have been to a woman so beautiful, to have a man prefer a servant to her.

If his theory was correct, he couldn't imagine why Mrs. Hammond was now a welcome guest in the Burkes' home. Perhaps, for all her past misdeeds, she had treated the maid well. *Even Judas Iscariot likely had one or two good qualities,* he told himself.

Since Mrs. Hammond was going to be tight-lipped about the purpose of her departure and destination, he was going to

have to at least find out any crumbs of information that she would let slip by.

"Well, if you happen to be traveling by train," he ventured casually while brushing an imaginary piece of lint from his sleeve, "I strongly recommend that you bring your own food." He gave a mock shudder of distaste. "But no doubt you've already experienced depot meals."

"I have," she answered with a nod. "Awful, aren't they? But the cook here—Bernice is her name—has already said that she'll be packing a basket for me. There will most likely be enough food to last a week."

"Oh? Then you must be going somewhere far away?"

"No, it's just that Bernice is quite generous."

"That's a definite asset in a cook," he said. "Generosity, I mean. So it's to be a short trip, then?"

"Not *too* short. Would you care for another cup of tea, Mr. Price?"

He sighed inwardly and thought, *What I'd care for is a little less tea and a little more information.* "Thank you, Mrs. Hammond, but I really must be going. Perhaps we'll meet again one day."

"I'm sorry you weren't able to speak with Mr. and Mrs. Burke," Corrine said. "Please don't forget to leave your address."

Joseph set his empty cup back on the tray, then stood. "My business takes me in and out of town on short notice. I'd hate to miss their visit. Perhaps it would be best if I called upon them some other time."

"Do, please. They should be back by the end of July."

"I'll make it a point to call." He told her that he could find his own way to the front door, then after a little bow, left the room. The meeting had not been a total loss. He had been able to meet face-to-face the woman he'd been pursuing and had found out that she was leaving town in two more days.

A wry smile came to his mouth at the thought that he had finally taken the time yesterday evening to unpack the rest of his clothes and have them pressed. He would just have to repack his bags.

~

That night Corrine, dressed in her dimity nightgown, pushed aside a pillow on the window seat in her bedroom and sat down, turning toward the glass. She blew out the candle and pressed her forehead against the windowpane. The sky was brilliant tonight, and she squinted her eyes in the direction of a cluster of stars and wondered if she were looking at a constellation. Little Bear, perhaps?

Gerald Moore had taught her many things about the world, but everything she had learned had been for the purpose of getting ahead by using people. There were so many little things that she didn't know, so much knowledge that other people took for granted.

The sense of loneliness she had felt all evening had settled in her chest, causing an actual ache. She wished she could talk with Bernice now, but she had taken enough of the good woman's time away from her family. Lucy needed her mother, and Jack needed his wife.

Besides, she wouldn't want to see the disappointment that would be on the cook's face if she knew. Bernice and the others had been so proud of her when she decided to become a Christian. How could she reveal to any of them that she had failed so soon?

I was sure that part of my life was gone forever, she thought, frowning bitterly. How easy it had been to fall back into her old ways, if only for a moment.

As grateful as she had been to that Mr. Price for saving Rachel, she now wished that he had waited just a few more days to visit. Why did such a handsome, charming man have to call when her faith was still so obviously weak?

This morning, as she sat across from him, she had found herself wondering if he had a wife, if he thought her broken nose made her look unattractive—even, for just a moment, how his strong arms would feel around her! A shudder of humiliation racked her. *I'm a married woman!*

She chewed on her knuckle. *What if it happens again? Am I going to have those thoughts every time I talk with a man?*

Bernice had warned her that temptations would come, but Corrine had been too wrapped up in the joy of her salvation, too certain that she would never want to go back to her old ways again, to pay the warning much heed. She had glibly imagined that when temptation came, it would be to commit an act that she wouldn't want to commit anyway, like using bad manners at the table or even killing someone.

I didn't know it would be something so hard to resist. What had Bernice told her about that? A picture of the cook's face came into her mind. *"Resist the devil, and he'll flee,"* she had said.

That was what she was going to have to do. If men were still her weakness, she would have to make sure that she didn't get into another situation like the one she was in this morning. And she would pray to God that if the temptation came again, he would give her strength to resist it.

7

LENORA Dunley lay sideways on her bed and watched streams of sunlight slant through the chintz curtains of her bedroom window. Bringing a hand out from under the goose-down counterpane, she held it up and squinted so that the sunlight seemed to seep through the spaces between each finger. *Get up, get dressed . . . up and dress,* the voice in her head ordered in its usual singsong manner. *Up to dress, down to sleep. Water so cold and dark . . . can't breathe . . .*

A groan escaped her lips and frightened her with its volume. She pulled her hand back under the covers and drew her knees up to her chest. *Down to sleep.* She shivered.

The door opened, and Alice, her lady's maid, stuck her head in the room. "Did you call, m'lady?" she inquired softly.

"What?" Lenora raised herself up on one elbow so that she could glare at the girl. "Were you listening at my door, Alice?"

"Course not, ma'am." Seventeen-year-old Alice had worked in the baronet's household for almost four years now, and still she trembled in Lady Dunley's presence. "I was just about to peek in and see if you were awake yet, that's all. Then I thought I heard you call out."

"I didn't call out." *Wasn't my fault. Water so cold.* "Bring my wrapper."

The servant obeyed immediately, taking a silk robe from where it lay across the Grecian couch at the foot of the bed. She held it out for her mistress. "Would you like me to bring you some hot chocolate?"

"What? No, never mind," Lenora replied, slipping out from under the covers in her shift. "I should have my bath first."

"I've got the water heating now." Alice helped her mistress into the robe.

"Has Sir Feldon had breakfast yet?"

The maid nodded. "I believe he had an early breakfast, ma'am."

"He must be inspecting the fields."

"Yes, ma'am, I believe so."

Lenora sighed, "Then there's really no sense in my getting up after all, is there?"

"Of course there is, ma'am."

"Why?"

"Why?" The maid looked uncomfortable again. She was a dull creature, though a pretty one, and obviously would much rather be outside flirting with the gardeners. "Because it's time to get up."

"Why shouldn't I go back to bed and stay there all day? What is there for me to do?"

Shifting on one foot, Alice suggested, "Perhaps a walk in the garden would be nice?"

Lenora ambled over to her dressing-table mirror. Leaning over, she studied the fine lines that were beginning to creep up around her hazel eyes. She was only thirty-five years old and had been a handsome woman at one time, but now her skin was turning sallow from never seeing the sun. Streaks of gray were beginning to leech the color from her waist-length brown hair, too. "How old are you, Alice?"

"Almost eighteen, m'lady."

"Do you have a beau?"

The girl looked pleased. "Yes, ma'am. Two of 'em."

Her eyes sad, Lenora turned around to face the girl. "You'll get married someday then, won't you?"

"I expect . . ."

Lenora let out a faint groan. Squeezing her eyes shut, she began rubbing her temples.

"Do you have another headache, ma'am?"

"No," she sighed. She looked up again. "You're right, I need to stay up. Can't stay in bed all day." *Can't stay in bed all day,* the voice in her head echoed.

~

She always felt better after her bath. Mrs. Styles, the head housekeeper, had warned that excessive bathing caused a number of illnesses, but Lenora liked to be clean. Sometimes she bathed at night as well. And her long hair was washed every morning, no matter how much trouble it entailed. Alice would bring a pitcher of cold water straight from the pump for her rinse. The brisk water pouring over her head shocked her senses and seemed to temper her feverish thoughts, if only for a little while.

After she had bathed and Alice had towel-dried and combed her hair, Lenora opened her armoire and ran her hand listlessly along the assortment of gowns hanging there. She chose a lavender calico, not because she cared what she wore, but because Feldon had gotten so angry at her several months ago.

"It's been two years!" he had raged, his voice thick with

emotion. *"Every time I see you dressed in those black clothes, it makes me think about what happened!"*

"Why do you want to forget her so much?" Lenora had screamed back. *"She's your daughter, too!"*

"But she's gone now! We can't bring her back by living this way!"

"We can't bring her back by living this way," Lenora murmured as she handed the dress over to Alice to shake the wrinkles from the folds of the skirt. She allowed Alice to dress her in silence.

With hair hanging in damp ringlets down her back, Lenora then went down to breakfast. She would have Alice coil her hair up at the nape of her neck when it was fully dry. There was a time when she would not have dreamed of coming to the table dressed so casually, when they used to entertain houseguests from the city. But that was back when she cared about things like that.

Neil, her younger brother, was already seated at the table behind a platter of fried eggs and ham. He was thirty years old, with trimmed muttonchops framing his cheeks and eyes, which were the same color hazel as his sister's, and the once-handsome lines of Neil's face were beginning to go soft from too many hours spent in the local pub. "Good morning, sister," he said with his mouth full.

"Good morning, Neil." She slipped into the chair a manservant held out for her. "You're up rather early, aren't you?"

He looked wounded. "It's after nine o'clock. I've been up for hours."

"Doing what?"

"Well, business matters." When she laughed, he shrugged helplessly. "All right, maybe not *hours*. But I'm not the layabout you think I am."

"Of course not." Another servant brought tea and plain porridge, and she picked up a spoon and took a small bite.

Neil frowned across at her bowl. "You're wasting away, sister."

"I haven't got much of an appetite in the mornings."

"Nor in the evenings."

She shrugged her thin shoulders. "What does it matter?"

"It matters to your husband. How long are you going to punish him?"

The spoon clattered to the table from Lenora's fingers, and she stared down at her distorted reflection in the silver. *He doesn't understand, either.* That wasn't surprising, of course. How could a man, who had never felt the soul-wrenching agony of stillbirth after stillbirth, understand the feelings of emptiness and failure that they brought on. And then to finally have a child!

Not just any child, but an angel child, one so perfect in every way that she was given the name Angelica. Worth the physical agony that had brought Lenora so close to the icy arms of death. Even worth having the physician warn her that she would not live through another attempt at giving birth. What did it matter that she couldn't have another child when Angelica filled her life so completely?

She had been a beautiful child, too—delicate and feminine, with gray eyes that seemed almost too big for her face. They would walk out to the garden together every day, and she would tell Angelica all about her own childhood and some-times repeat the fairy tales that her mother had taught her. Often they would sing nursery rhymes—Angelica's warbling little voice would trill out songs in perfect pitch. As the girl grew a little older, Lenora would bring her into the sitting room to sing for company after dinner. The guests would clap and shout, "Bravo," and Lenora would beam at the child and wonder how she had ever lived without her.

Feldon had been a fool over the girl, too. When Angelica was four years old, he taught her to play croquet on the lawn, and when she was six, chess. He would put her on the seat beside him when he took the gig to inspect the fields. All of this had pleased Lenora greatly, for when their daughter was born, Lenora had been afraid that Feldon would be secretly disappointed that he didn't have a son.

Angelica had brightened both of their lives for seven years, and then the light was abruptly snuffed out the day the child drowned.

It had happened at the lake on their property, Lake Chestnut, right in the presence of four adults who could swim. Lenora became so distraught after it happened that she had to be given laudanum and put to bed for days. She had no recollection of the funeral, which she had reportedly attended in a drugged stupor on the arm of her husband. That was the last time she had been outside the house.

She never really forgave Feldon for not being able to rescue the girl, even though the accident wasn't his fault, and even when she realized what a great loss he felt inside, too. The very fact that he could still tend to business matters concerning his beloved farm proved to Lenora that his sorrow did not come close to matching her own.

Just one day, she thought, staring down at the pat of melted butter in the center of her porridge. She would gladly trade the rest of her life if she could have just one more day with Angelica. *Clouds for baby's pillow . . . sing me a nursery rhyme, one more time.*

Lenora suddenly became aware that her brother had been speaking. She raised her eyes to find him looking expectantly at her.

"What did you say?" she asked.

Neil shook his head. "Never mind. We've gone through this before, and it's not going to do any good."

"Just tell me."

He put down his fork and leaned back from the table. "That dress looks pretty on you. Why don't you have Alice fix up your hair, too?"

"She's going to do it after breakfast."

"I don't mean in that awful knot behind your neck. You used to wear it in curls, with ribbons and things like that."

Lenora reached up to touch a damp ringlet at her shoulder. "Why should I?"

"Because you used to care what you looked like. I'll wager it would make you feel better."

"I don't think—"

"Then we could take the gig out and visit Feldon in the fields," he cut in. "The weather's glorious out there this morning. How long has it been since you've been out?"

Sing me a rhyme, round and round. She blinked and tried to recall what she and her brother had just been talking about. "Been out?"

His jaw tensed under his mustache. "In the sun, Lenora."

"Maybe tomorrow."

"He won't be inspecting the fields again for another week. Why not surprise him today? You could even tell Cook that you'll deliver his lunch."

She had to smile at the thought. Feldon's mouth would likely drop open at the sight of her outdoors. But then an awareness of the effort involved in undertaking such an activity made her feel suddenly drained.

"I don't have the strength today."

Neil wiped some egg from his mustache with his napkin. "I knew you'd say that. But you're never going to have any strength if you spend all of your days up in that room. You used to love to get outside and—"

"Oh, all right!" she cut in, waving her hand.

"What?" Her brother's napkin was poised in midair.

"Maybe for just a little while." She didn't care a whit about getting back her strength, but lately it had been more and more difficult to sleep at night. Doctor Clayton had refused ages ago to give her any more laudanum. Perhaps if she didn't spend so much time in bed during the day, she would be so tired at night that the voice in her head wouldn't keep her awake.

She sighed and touched the lace on her collar. "Do you really think it would be good for me?"

Neil gave her a smile. "I do."

~

"Ye got to move faster, girl!" Mrs. Farrel, a spry, hunch-shouldered old woman, followed Jenny down the row. She expertly used a hoe to push up dirt to cover the trench that Allen, the boy walking several feet ahead, dug by dragging his hoe at an angle.

Jenny's job was to take a fistful of turnip seeds from the leather pouch slung across her shoulder, then sow the tiny seeds by allowing three to fall into the trench at eight-inch intervals.

The chore had seemed easy when it was explained to her,

but six hours later, she grew more and more flustered with her attempts to catch up to the boy hoeing the trench. Sometimes the seeds would cling to the sweat of her hand, and she would have to rake out just the right amount with her fingers. Then other times, too many seeds would fall at once. With no time to go back and correct her mistake, she thought ahead to the time weeks later, when they would all come up through the dirt in tangled clumps, irrefutable evidence of her carelessness.

However great her fears, Jenny had learned by midmorning that there was no reason to be afraid of Mrs. Farrel. Though the woman had been constantly at her shoulder, hurrying her along, there had been no anger in her voice. And Allen, who appeared to be only a couple of years older than Jenny, was silent, never turning back to see how the two behind him were faring. Even when he turned to come down the next row and passed Jenny and Mrs. Farrel, he did not raise his eyes, under his straw hat, to look at them.

It was Mr. Blake, the farm manager, who had caused dread in the girl's thoughts all morning. Every hour or so he would show up on a horse at the end of a row and survey the work with cold eyes. "Move faster or don't bother comin' back in the morning!" he barked at Jenny once.

The threat was effective, for Jenny feared Uncle Roy's wrath more than she feared anything that Mr. Blake could do to her. She moved faster, though her limbs ached with the effort.

"Yer doin' fine now, lass!" Mrs. Farrel was able to say when the sun was high overhead. It was almost time for lunch, the only break in the day that the workers got.

Minutes later, the farm manager blew a whistle, and the workers immediately put down their tools and headed for the shade of the hedgerows. Mrs. Farrel walked alongside Jenny, her weathered face creased into a grin. "Come a week, and I'll be huffin' to catch up with you."

The thought of doing such wearisome labor for a whole week caused Jenny to shudder. Then it dawned upon her that she would likely grow old and stoop-shouldered in these fields, just like Mrs. Farrel.

~

Lenora adjusted her straw bonnet as her brother drove the gig down the dirt road leading to the fields. She had forgotten how pleasantly the sun could bathe one's face with its gentle rays. For just a few minutes, she breathed in the heady scent of red dog roses from the hedgerows and barely thought about Angelica.

"Now, isn't this nice?" Neil commented from beside her.

"Yes," she said and turned to smile at him. "It's a lovely day."

"Do you remember how you used to conjure up plots on how to give our tutor the slip so we could play outside on days like this? And most of your plans would result in my getting punished."

Lenora's smile grew broader. "You were so easily led, little brother."

"You're right," he chuckled. "Do you remember our first tutor's name?"

"How could I forget Mr. Teagle?"

"Teagle the Beagle."

Lenora laughed. Her eyes full of merriment, she turned to look at the road for a fraction of a second, then froze. Leading off to the right was a well-worn path, etched by carriage wheels. How could she have forgotten? Her lips began to tremble as she wondered how she could have been so disloyal.

"I wonder whatever happened to . . ."

She turned glaring eyes on her brother. The timing of his sudden attempt at conversation was obvious—he had wanted to keep her from seeing the path to the lake!

"Take me back home now," Lenora ordered.

Neil turned to her, his expression filled with disbelief. "What?"

"I want to go home." *Water so cold . . . can't move my legs. Sit down, Angelica!*

"But look." Neil's finger was pointing down the road. "The fields are just ahead."

Clutching her brother's arm, Lenora said, "I don't care. Take me home."

"All right. But at least let's give Feldon his lunch."

"Then you'll take me back?"

"Yes," he sighed and gave the reins a flick.

Feldon was standing by the gate with his farm manager, Mr. Blake, when they drove up. "Lenora?" His eyebrows raised in surprise as he approached the gig.

"We brought your lunch," Lenora told him. She leaned down to pick up the basket from the floor of the cart.

"Well, let me help you down and we'll have it together." Feldon gave Mr. Blake a nod of dismissal, then held out his arms to her. "We could have a picnic by the apple trees."

Lenora had forgotten how handsome a man her husband was with his ramrod-straight posture and enough gray creeping into his sideburns to give his face a scholarly appearance.

The boat, all that water. Her little yellow dress had little carved ivory buttons down the back. "I'm too tired," she answered, handing him the basket instead.

The hurt washed over his face as he stood there. "Can't you

77

stay for a little while?" Reaching out to touch her arm, he said, "Please?"

She drew back from him. "Not today. Maybe tomorrow." A lightning-quick look passed between her husband and brother, and it made her angry. "You don't understand!" she said sharply to both of them.

A shrill sound pierced the air, causing Lenora to jump in her seat. Pressing her shoulder to Neil's side, she turned to look where Mr. Blake was standing, now on the other side of the gate, several yards away with his whistle.

"He's just signaling to the workers that it's time to go back to work," her brother told her with just a trace of impatience in his voice. "They've been having their lunch in the shade."

"All right, I guess you'd better take her back," Lenora heard Feldon say to her brother in a weary voice. But her attention was caught by a group of workers heading back for the fields.

"Who is that?" she demanded, straightening in her seat so that she could see over the juniper bushes.

Feldon looked over his shoulder. "Just the field-workers. Why?"

"The girl over there. Who is she?"

He looked again. "There are several girls out there, Lenora. Which one?"

"The one walking with that old woman." Lenora pointed at the girl. "See, now she's staring at me!"

Lenora's heart started beating out a rapid cadence in her chest. She stood and squinted in the direction of the fields. "Angelica," she whispered, her hand at the base of her throat.

Her husband turned to look in the same direction. "Take her home," he told Neil in a grim voice. "Now."

78

~

During her hurried lunch, Jenny wondered why the hours in the turnip field seemed so much longer than the hours in the blackberry patch. She had been walking the rows for ages, it seemed, and yet the better part of the day still stretched out before her.

The other workers must have the same feeling, she thought, for there was no joy in any expression—only the weary knowledge that at the end of the day, meager meals awaited the workers in meager huts, and after a few precious hours of sleep, the whole cycle would start all over again.

She wondered about her cousins. Did they miss her? Would Trudy remember to caution the younger children to keep away from the hornet's nest under the eaves of the barn? Could she keep little Evan from sticking his hand in the meat drippings bucket? A tear traced a dark path in the grime on her face, and she smeared at it with the back of her hand.

She couldn't think about sad things, else her work would slow down and she would be let go, and Uncle Roy would be furious at her for ruining her chance to help out the family.

She would save the tears for tonight, when everyone else was asleep. Right now she would force herself to think about other things, like when Mrs. Farrel told her that she was getting faster.

Then she saw her—a lady in a lavender dress, talking with Mr. Blake and another man. Even from a distance, Jenny could tell she was pretty, and her dress looked so crisp and clean.

The whistle signaled the workers back to the fields, and Jenny started walking back with Mrs. Farrel and the silent Allen. Something compelled her to look back in the direction of the lady, and when she did, she was startled to find the lady looking straight at her.

Jenny's steps froze, and she found herself unable to look away. The lady raised a hand and pointed straight in her direction!

Was the lady telling those men that she wasn't keeping up with the other workers? Her uncle would never forgive her if she lost this job! With her heart pounding fit to burst, Jenny turned and ran to catch up with Mrs. Farrel.

~

The gig bounced along at a much faster rate on the way back to the house. Lenora glanced at her brother from time to time and wondered what she had done to cause the frown on his face. It seemed that nobody was willing even to make an attempt to understand her anymore.

"Don't be angry with me," she pleaded, putting a hand on his arm. "You're the only friend I've got."

After a little while he sighed and looked over at her. "I can't stay angry with you, Lenora. It's just that you won't even try to get better."

There's nothing wrong with me, she thought, but she knew better than to say that. "I came riding with you, like you asked."

"Yes, I guess that's something."

She took a deep breath and prepared herself for the argument to come. "Please turn around. I want to go to the lake."

"You *what?*"

"The lake. I need to see it."

"Why?"

"I just need to." How could she explain when she couldn't understand it herself? Just a few moments ago when they had passed the turnoff, she had felt an inexplicable compulsion to go down the path. Had seeing the girl in the field been some sort of sign? Was there an answer to all of her torment in the place she feared most?

Now that the house was looming ahead, the need to go back was overwhelming.

"Feldon would kill me," Neil declared with a shake of his head.

"He doesn't have to know."

"I'm sorry, I just can't allow it."

"All right." Lenora feigned a casual shrug, amazed that Neil had no idea just how easily led he still was. "I'll just take the dogcart when we get back."

Her brother shot her a panicked look. "You can't go out there alone!"

"And you can't stop me! It's my house, too, remember."

He said nothing, but seconds later pulled the reins to turn the horse around. "I can't let you go there by yourself," he sighed, a look of resignation on his face.

8

LAKE Chestnut, kidney shaped and shaded along the shoreline with tall fir trees, covered five acres of the Dunley property. A boathouse big enough to hold eight rowboats sat over a small inlet, and a long covered pier stretched out toward the middle, its boards bearing numerous scars from hooks and knife blades. The lake was a magnet for houseguests from more urban places, and generations of Dunleys had enjoyed its waters.

When Neil brought the gig to a stop several feet from the boathouse, he turned to his sister with an uneasy expression. "Let's just sit here for a minute," he suggested. "You don't want to overdo . . ."

But Lenora was already gathering her skirts to climb down to the ground. As her brother hastened to tie the horse, she walked out to the beginning of the pier and stopped. She looked from right to left at the expanse of water, took a deep breath, and stepped out onto the first boards. They gave an ominous creaking sound when she put her weight upon them.

"Lenora?" Neil caught up with her and was pulling at her arm. "Don't you think we should go back now?"

"No," she murmured, jerking away from him. "Have to think."

When she got to the end of the pier, Lenora eased down to sit with her feet hanging over the side. Her brother sat down next to her, his movements stiff and tense. "I don't know why you'd want to come here."

"I don't know either."

A long silence stretched between them, broken only by frogs calling from the tall grasses along the shore. Finally Neil gave a sigh and said, "Maybe it's good that we came, after all. It's time you accepted what happened."

Lenora did not answer. Mesmerized by the sunlight dappling the surface of the water, she thought she heard the laughter of children, the way she had heard it on that terrible day two years ago. . . .

~

"Mama, why do I have to wear so many petticoats on the boat?" Angelica asked again, her hands brushing against the flounced sides of her yellow calico skirt. "I won't be able to sit down."

"Yes, you will." Lenora frowned and wondered if the girl needed still another petticoat. How could Feldon allow another extended visit from his uppity cousin Kendall and his insufferable wife, Simone? Every summer they could expect at least a fortnight of the couple and their three children.

She had met Kendall before his marriage to the French-woman and found him to be quite pleasant. But now, all he seemed to be capable of was boasting about the success of his business and, even more, the successes of his children. He seemed jealous of Feldon's title and thus compelled to prove to everyone that he was just as good.

Simone was far worse. In her breathy, accented voice she

would go on about the beauty and talents of their daughters, Henriette and Dominique, and their son, René—three of the most spoiled children Lenora had ever seen. Why, the girls arrived with trunks of the latest designs from Paris and seemed to spend all their time changing clothes. If they had been older and trying to attract beaus, Lenora would have understood. But these girls were only nine and twelve years old!

Eight-year-old René was as bad as his sisters. He spent most of his time grooming himself rather than doing the fun things that boys usually did in the country. Next to that, whining about the food on his plate at mealtimes was his favorite activity. He was built small and slight, like his mother, but with his father's enormous ears. Just yesterday he had shown up for breakfast wearing a red velvet jacket, and Lenora had had to cough to cover up her laugh, for she imagined him dancing at the end of a leash for an organ grinder.

It was for René that the whole outing at the lake was being arranged.

"I can't believe that stupid woman," Lenora muttered to Angelica after ordering Helena to fetch another petticoat. "Promises the brat a boat ride in exchange for eating his breakfast. What're they going to give him when he gets older and won't eat? A racehorse?"

"But why do I have to wear all of this on the boat?" Angelica asked, her voice a shade too close to a whine.

Lenora picked up a brush from the dresser and began pulling it through her daughter's hair. "Because Simone will have her little popinjays dressed as if they're going on an outing in Hyde Park. I'll not have you looking like some ragpicker's child."

They had to take the barouche and the gig to the lake,

a picnic basket secured in back of the larger vehicle. Feldon and Kendall put two rowboats in the water and rowed out to the edge of the pier, where they helped the women and children into the boats. "One of you will have to ride with Uncle Feldon," Kendall told his children. After five minutes of arguing and bribing, Henriette was finally persuaded to volunteer.

"Now, isn't this fun?" Feldon asked, the muscles of his neck straining as he rowed the boat away from the pier. He sat at one end of the boat and Lenora at the other, while Henriette and Angelica sat stiffly on the middle seat, both surrounded by yards of skirts and petticoats.

"Yes, it is," Lenora finally answered, irritated by the effervescent laughter of Simone in the other boat. She forced a smile, determined not to let the Frenchwoman make her look like a shrew. "Isn't this fun, Angelica . . . and Henriette?"

"Yes, Mama," Angelica answered.

Henriette's attention was drawn to something in the water. "Is that a fish?" she asked, leaning to peer over the side of the boat.

Angelica was on her feet in an instant. "Where?"

"Sit down!" Feldon ordered, holding the oars poised above the water.

"Oh, I see it!" cried Angelica. In her excitement the girl moved an inch closer to look, pitching the boat sharply to the right.

"Angelica!" Lenora cried as she grabbed for the sides of the boat. A look of panic passed between her daughter and herself, and the next thing Lenora knew, darkness, colder than death, was closing in around her.

Help me! her mind screamed as she flailed her arms in the

water and tried to swim. The heavy fabric of her skirt was wrapped around her legs, hampering their movement. She had gulped water into her windpipe when the boat first went over, and now more water was burning its way up her nostrils. Her mind, numb with terror, refused to tell her where the surface of the water was.

Suddenly, Lenora felt a hand latch onto her arm. Her shoulder felt as if it were being pulled out of its socket, but in a second her face was above the surface.

"Help me, Feldon!" she sputtered, lunging for her husband's neck.

"Grab the boat, Lenora!" he yelled back. The overturned boat lay just in front of her in the water, but it seemed like miles away to her.

She felt her husband's hands on her arms—he was trying to loosen her grip on his neck. "Don't let me go!" she screamed, the water lapping at her face.

"Grab hold of the boat! I've got to find Angelica!"

"Angelica!" Clinging even tighter to her husband, Lenora tried to will her legs to move. "Angelica!"

"Lenora, let go!"

She could hear screams in the background and splashing to the side of her. Kendall, gasping for breath, had an arm wrapped around Henriette's shoulder. He was swimming toward the second boat, which the sobbing Simone was making a frantic attempt to paddle closer.

Again Feldon tried to get away from her, this time using both hands to push at her shoulders. In her terror, she locked her arms around his neck again.

"Let go and grab the boat!" he screamed between gasps for air. "You're pulling me under!"

"Angelica—where is she?" Kendall's voice came suddenly from her side, but Lenora could not make her arms loosen their grip on her husband.

"Help me get her to the boat!" Feldon sputtered.

With Kendall holding his cousin's shoulders out of the water, the two men pulled Lenora the short distance to the overturned boat. "No!" she shrieked as Kendall pried her arms away from her husband's neck.

"Just hold on to the boat!" Feldon ordered, then shot away from her.

Lenora threw both arms over the hull of the boat, as far as she could reach. By kicking her burdened legs in the water, she was at least able to stay afloat. "My baby!" she screamed over and over, leaning her forehead against the wet wood.

~

"My baby," Lenora whispered.

"Lenora?"

She turned to look at her brother with tear-filled eyes. "My baby's gone."

Neil's face was sad. "Yes, she's gone."

Wiping her eyes with the back of her hand, Lenora said, "I never want to see this place again."

9

R EALLY, missus, you could easily wait another week to go home," Bernice said Thursday morning, as she watched Dora put the finishing touches to Corrine's hair.

"I don't think I could wait another day," Corrine answered. "In fact, I could hardly sleep last night for wishing morning would come."

"But what's rattling about in one of them train compartments going to do to your side?"

"My side hasn't hurt in days." She turned to smile at the cook. "I do appreciate everything you've done for me."

"You will write and let us know how you're doing, won't you?" asked Dora while Bernice wiped her eyes.

"Just as soon as I'm settled."

Jack and Hershall showed up to get her trunk. "Careful now," Bernice told the men as they heaved it up to their shoulders.

It turned out that all of Adam Burke's servants wanted to see Corrine to Eusten Station, the point of departure for the London & Birmingham Railroad. The men loaded the trunk, Corrine's carpetbag, and the hamper of food that Bernice had prepared into the back of the wagon.

"Just a minute," Corrine said. "I think I may have forgotten something." She ran into the house, and when she returned, they were all sitting in the wagon and carriage, waiting for her.

Hershall picked up the reins. "Ready?"

Corrine settled herself into the carriage seat. "I'm as ready as I'll ever be," she sighed.

She took one last look at the house where she had been a guest for three weeks, where she had ultimately found Christ and a whole new life. She had so longed for the day that she could leave, but now a heaviness was centered in her chest. *I hope I can come back and visit one day,* she thought. Hershall snapped the reins, and they began moving up Clifton Hill.

~

So, she's going to Birmingham, Joseph thought, peering out of the window as the carriage and wagon up ahead passed under the great arch of the Doric Prophlaeum. The more humble Eusten Square station, origin of the London & Birmingham Railway, lay beyond that grand entrance.

Now that he was fairly certain of the train Mrs. Hammond would be taking, Joseph called out for the driver to halt. He shouldered his gripsack and stepped out of the coach. After paying the driver, he took the last block on foot.

He had packed lightly for this trip, not wanting the bother of keeping up with a traveling bag. An extra change of clothes was folded inside—he could always buy another suit in York if necessary, after he had delivered Mrs. Hammond to Squire Nowells.

He waited until he was certain that Mrs. Hammond had purchased her ticket before approaching the booking office. Sure enough, he could see her on the platform from the corner of his eye—she was giving farewell embraces and hand-shakes to the group of people that had accompanied her. *No wonder she's been such a good con artist,* he thought. To look at Corrine Hammond right now, one would think that she really cared about those people.

Inside the booking office, he had to stand in a short line to purchase his ticket. When he reached the window, he asked the agent if he had just sold a ticket to a beautiful woman with dark hair.

"Aye," the man replied with a grin. "From Birmingham she's goin' to Shrewsbury, in Shropshire. Made me wish I was going there, too."

The boarding whistle sounded soon afterward. Joseph watched from the very edge of the brick-fronted platform while Mrs. Hammond, holding a valise and hamper, walked toward the open door of a coach. She turned several times to wave at the group of people that had accompanied her.

Watching her closely, he realized again why so many men had become enamored of her. The dove gray traveling dress and matching hat gave her a businesslike and sophisticated air, while the tiny waist and glossy ringlets cascading down her back left no doubts about her femininity. *Pity her character doesn't match her looks,* he reminded himself.

He had decided last night that he would have to let her know that he was on the train, but not at the very beginning of the journey. Since she had already told him that she would be leaving on Thursday, it would look too suspicious for him to show up right away. There would be plenty of stops and ample opportunity to "accidentally" make her acquaintance again.

He had a plan, one that he hoped would work. Without Gerald Moore to guide Mrs. Hammond's dubious career,

Joseph was certain that she must be worried about the future. Perhaps that was why she was taking the train to Shrewsbury, to find another source of money. It was likely that, before Moore's death, he had already planned out their strategy for the next victim. Evidently a man in Shrewsbury.

Joseph had told Corrine very little about his personal life when they had had tea Tuesday. And he didn't know if he was just being a vain fool, but even though she hadn't actually *flirted* with him that day, he thought he had seen some interest in her eyes. What if he pretended to be a wealthy man with questionable morals? Perhaps a bored patrician with too much time and money on his hands.

Why, bringing Mrs. Hammond up to Treybrook would be so much easier if she could be convinced that he was suitable prey. Surely she wouldn't pass up an opportunity right in front of her for one that wasn't certain.

He would pretend to have a wife and family, too, since most of her previous victims had been married men. After all, they had more to lose from scandal and would be more likely to pay when blackmailed.

Perhaps he could even persuade her to forget Shrewsbury and accompany him to some town close enough to York— to save him some trouble when it came time to bring her to Squire Nowells—but far enough away to keep her from suspecting anything. *Leeds would do nicely,* he thought.

And if that didn't work, he could always follow her until she left the train and then fall back on his original, more troublesome plan. He would hire a horse and coach, kidnap the woman, and take her to Squire Nowells against her will.

A clammy coldness snaked down his spine, causing him to lean back against the brick wall for a moment. He hoped that

Mrs. Hammond would make things easy for him. *After this job, I'm going to have to get some rest,* he told himself. He felt drained, worn out. And the scratchiness in the back of his throat had gotten worse, despite the spoonfuls of peppermint oil he'd been taking.

~

From her seat by the window, Corrine put her hand up to the glass and watched her new friends walk away. When they were almost swallowed up by the crowd of people on the platform, she pulled a handkerchief from her purse and wiped her eyes. The irony didn't escape her that servants—the class of people she'd looked down upon for years—had helped her the most when she had felt the lowest. After eight years with Gerald Moore, she had forgotten that people could treat each other decently, expecting nothing in return.

She saw Bernice turn around and smile in her direction one last time, and she lifted a hand again in farewell. *God bless you and your family, my friend,* she thought.

There were four other passengers in her coach. At the opposite window was a middle-aged man dressed in the tweeds of a country squire. Between the man in tweeds and Corrine sat an elderly woman, her white hair coiled under her bonnet. It turned out she was traveling with the married couple on the facing seat.

"My name is Mrs. Watkins," the elderly woman told her with a smile, introducing the married couple as her son and daughter-in-law. The man in tweeds wasn't a squire after all, but a yeoman farmer by the name of Mr. Elmoor.

Corrine introduced herself to the people who would be her companions for the next several hours, careful to keep the smile that she directed toward the men nothing more than cordial.

Then she rested her head on the back of her seat, folded her hands in her lap, and listened to the last blast of the steam whistle from the locomotive. The train moved forward, starting her on the journey toward her husband and daughter.

~

There were stops to take on passengers at Watford and Wendover, but Joseph sat in his compartment, three coaches down from Corrine Hammond's, and bided his time. The stop at Milton Keynes would be longer, with at least twenty minutes for any reckless passengers to buy their lunches at the depot.

When the train finally pulled into Milton Keynes Station, Joseph took down his gripsack and hat, made his way to the door, and stepped down onto the platform. Nausea swelled through him, and he stopped to let it pass. *Must have gotten up too quickly,* he thought.

When he reached the door of the compartment he had seen Mrs. Hammond enter, he stepped inside. She was there, her lunch basket open on her lap. He looked at her and blinked, feigning astonishment. "Mrs. Hammond?"

"Mr. Price?" At the surprise in her voice, the other passengers looked up from their lunches.

"Would you mind if I shared your coach?" he asked, though it really wasn't necessary to do so, for there was an empty space directly across from Mrs. Hammond. Unfortunately, it was a rear-facing seat, which wouldn't help the nausea that still lingered, but he had to take what he could get.

She didn't answer, just looked at him with gray eyes still

wide with confusion. One of the men, the one seated with
a woman on the rear-facing seat to his left said, "Of course
you may, sir."

"Thank you." Stashing his gripsack and hat overhead, he sat
down, marveling at the luck that would put him so close to
Mrs. Hammond. He exchanged introductions with the others
in the compartment, then smiled at Corrine and said, "Well,
you told me you were going out of town today, didn't you?
What a coincidence that we would be on the same train."

"Yes," she replied after a short hesitation. Though she'd
given him a quick smile, she seemed uncomfortable with his
sudden presence, which puzzled him. She had been so amiable
the day before yesterday when he had called upon her at
Mr. Burke's house. Did she suspect that he had arranged this
"coincidence"?

"When we spoke, I had no idea that *I* would be leaving
London on the same day," he told her, putting a hand up to
his chest. "But I got word last night of a fine Arabian for sale
in Birmingham, so here I am!"

Corrine's brows lifted. "An Arabian?"

"Stallion," he said, smiling. "As black as midnight, so I'm
told."

She nodded, seeming just a little more at ease. "Of course."

"Anyway, I wanted to get a chance to look at the animal
before any other buyers found out about him. We're very
competitive—people who deal with horses."

"I didn't think to ask about your occupation," she said.
"Do you breed horses for a living?"

"Racehorses. But as a hobby, not an occupation." He
lowered his voice. "I was originally three coaches down, but
there's a gentleman in there who has hit the bottle one time

95

too many. Ever since Watford he's been entertaining us with songs." He gave a chuckle. "It was quite amusing for a while, but the ears can only take so many off-key renditions of 'Rule, Britannia.'"

There was laughter from the two other men in the compartment and smiles from the ladies, even from Mrs. Hammond.

"I suppose if you're going to be a drunk, you should be a happy one," Mr. Elmoor chuckled.

"I suppose," Joseph agreed, "but I don't think the poor man's going to be so cheerful come tomorrow morning."

Mr. Elmoor chuckled again, then the passengers turned their attention back to their meals—except for Mrs. Hammond. Though her basket was still open on her lap, she was absently staring at the contents and made no move to take out any of them.

"Please don't let me keep you from your lunch," Joseph told her.

She looked up at him, obviously noticing that he hadn't a basket. "Didn't you bring anything to eat?"

"I packed a couple of sandwiches in my gripsack, but I haven't got an appetite just yet." This time he was telling the truth, for the idea of food was not appealing at all, even though he was still feeling a little weak and really thought he should eat something. He hadn't been hungry at breakfast, either.

Whether his lack of appetite was from the excitement of being so close to the end of his chase or from the scratchiness of his throat, he didn't know. He watched the woman across from him close her hamper again.

"I don't seem to have an appetite either," she said.

"Oh, I'm sorry. Perhaps I should have chosen another compartment."

LAWANA BLACKWELL

Corrine gave him a questioning look. "I beg your pardon?"

"My story about the inebriated man was hardly fit for decent company. If it caused you to lose your appetite . . ."

"No, not at all." The corners of her lips twitched downward slightly, and he thought he detected a moistness in her gray eyes. "It's just that I'm on my way to meet someone, and I'm rather nervous."

No doubt you are, he thought wryly, listening to the sound of the boarding whistle. After all, she was on her own now and didn't have Gerald Moore to make arrangements ahead of time. Realizing that his opinion of her surely must be showing on his face, he stopped frowning and tried to look sympathetic. "I would imagine that it's hard for a woman to travel alone," he said with gentleness in his voice.

She bit her lip and turned her face to look out of the window. Still Joseph pressed on, leaning forward in his seat. "Please, Mrs. Hammond, if there's anything that *I* can do . . ."

Corrine gave him a quick grateful nod, then turned back to the window again. She looked strangely vulnerable sitting there, and for a second he felt all sorts of protective feelings surging through him. If only she were some other beautiful woman that circumstance had put in his path and not the Corrine Hammond he knew her to be . . . *What would you do then?* he asked himself. *Fall in love? You've let other chances to settle down slip through your fingers . . . and you're too old to change.*

The movement of the train brought Joseph out of his reverie. He had only about three hours to convince her that he was easier prey than whatever unsuspecting bloke waited in Shrewsbury.

Glancing around at the others who shared the compartment, Joseph wished fervently that they weren't there, for they all

97

seemed like decent people. Especially the elderly woman seated next to Mrs. Hammond—she reminded him a bit of his mother, which increased his discomfort. *They're all going to think I'm an obnoxious fool by the time we reach Birmingham,* he thought, wincing inside.

That was the worst drawback about being a detective—occasionally having to take on a distasteful personality. In this case, he absolutely despised the role he had to play, and there was no way that he could let his fellow passengers know that it was just an act.

Still, what Mrs. Hammond thought about him didn't matter, he told himself, as long as it worked.

Reaching into his frock coat, he drew his leather pouch from his waistband. Then with his brow furrowed with concentration, he pretended to count the bundle of pound-sterling notes inside.

The movement caught her attention, as he had hoped it would, and he smiled at her with just a hint of suggestiveness as he replaced the pouch. "You know, the wisest thing I ever did was to marry a wealthy woman," he chuckled, loathing the oily tone in his voice.

Her returning smile was polite, nothing else, so he shifted to another tactic. "I'm rather disappointed that I won't be meeting your friends the Burkes any time soon."

That time it worked. "Rachel—Mrs. Burke—will be disappointed, too," she said, her gray eyes serious. "But won't you be going back to London after you buy the horse?"

"I'm afraid not, Mrs. Hammond." He shrugged. "You see, my horses are kept at my wife's ancestral home in Leeds. I spend as little time in London as possible."

Before she could say anything, he crossed a boot-clad ankle

up on his knee and continued. "You see, my wife loves the city, and—" he waved a hand in the air—"and all of the social life that comes with it. You'd think that there would be nothing to do right now, with so many of her friends spending the summers in the country, but she finds enough to keep her busy." Giving her a meaningful look, he added, *"Too* busy."

"Oh," she gasped softly, then stared down at her hands. Was he imagining the color that came into her cheeks? He would have thought Corrine Hammond was incapable of blushing. *It has to be an act. After all, she can't let herself appear too easy when most men enjoy the chase.*

"In fact," he continued, "she very likely won't even know I'm gone until she needs an escort for some dreary soiree." Reluctantly, Joseph glanced at the other passengers. He definitely was not imagining the disapproval set into the jaw of the elderly Mrs. Watkins as she stared straight ahead. *I'm not the cad you think I am!* he wanted to say, but with the way he was acting, no doubt she'd want to hit him with the crocheted handbag in her lap.

"I'm . . . sorry," Mrs. Hammond finally stammered.

"Oh, well, that's life." He stretched his lips into a conspiratorial smile and wished again that Mrs. Watkins were not present. "As long as she's generous with the money, I shouldn't complain. At least I don't have to work for a living."

When she didn't reply, he leaned closer and lowered his voice. "Just gets lonesome once in a while, do you know what I mean?"

Color suffused her cheeks. Again she mumbled, "I'm sorry." Then to his utter astonishment, she stood to get her valise from the shelf, opened it, and took out a Bible. She sat back down, and as Joseph watched her flip through the pages and then begin to read silently, he felt himself grow smaller and smaller in the seat.

Worse than that was thirty minutes later, when the train came to a halt at Northampton. She put her Bible back into her valise, took it and her lunch hamper by the handles, and stood. "Good day, Mr. Price," she said in a chilly tone before stepping through the door.

His cheeks burned as he watched her through the window, entering another compartment in the next coach. He had never spoken to a woman in such a manner before. Any woman. In spite of knowing what type of person she really was, he even thought about following her and apologizing. But he had humiliated himself enough.

As the train started moving again, he didn't dare look at Mrs. Watkins. Blackness swallowed up the compartment ten miles later as the train entered Kilsby Tunnel, one and one-quarter miles of track through Northamptonshire iron-stone. Leaning his head back against the seat, he wished that the darkness would last the whole journey so that his shame could be more private. His temples were beginning to pound, and he wondered what had ever possessed him to agree to track down a woman.

All of this was Corrine Hammond's fault, and his dislike for her intensified. Who did she think she was, rejecting his flirtations in such a pious manner? He had never thought much about his looks, but surely they weren't so repulsive that even a woman like her would turn away from his advances.

Perhaps she was pretending to be hard to get, Joseph thought, trying to repair the damage she had inflicted upon his pride. Well, if that was the case, she was carrying things too far.

He would just have to go ahead with his second plan and follow her to Shrewsbury. He just wished that his stomach would stop rolling.

10

THOUGH it was past noon, Lenora Dunley still lay in bed with her head under the covers, drawing air through a tunnel she had made under the comforter. *"That wasn't Angelica you saw!"* her husband's voice reverberated again through her consciousness, as it had for the past two days.

She could hear herself answering back, *"I know she's not Angelica! I just want to see the girl up close!"*

She had pleaded and pleaded, but to no avail. Feldon had not budged but instead gave her his usual maddening lecture on carrying on with her life and not thinking about their daughter every minute of the day, until she had wanted to pull out her hair and scream!

As if she could forget! What kind of mother would she be if she forgot her child so easily?

Her breathing came faster, racing against her heartbeat. She could picture the little girl in the fields so clearly, just as she had seen her the day Neil had talked her into going for a ride. The child was walking with a group of workers, and for some reason she had stopped and turned to look in Lenora's direction with huge eyes.

Lenora hadn't been able to tell the color of her eyes from that distance, and before she could ask Feldon to have the girl brought over, he had ordered Neil to turn the gig around.

But she knew in her heart that the eyes were gray. *Angelica's were gray, so gray. Serious sometimes, laughing sometimes. Looked like a princess, my daughter, my little girl. So beautiful.* She could feel a tear rolling across the bridge of her nose, dampening the sheet below her face. *Angelica, let mama sing you a lullaby.*

"White clouds for baby's pillow, and the dew for her drink," her voice warbled past the lump in her dry throat.

At the sound of her door opening, she closed her mouth abruptly and lay there waiting, her senses sharpened. It would be Alice, she knew, again pleading with her to eat something. Or Neil, or maybe even Feldon, though he had stormed out last time and said he wouldn't be back. When had that been? Last night? This morning?

What did it matter? She was glad for the rumblings from her stomach, the dryness of her throat. She would lie under the covers like this and shrivel away to nothing. Then the voice in her head would stop reminding her what a bad mother she was to let Angelica get in the boat.

"Lenora." Her husband's voice.

Slipping her arms up over her head, Lenora gathered handfuls of the soft counterpane that covered her and held on tightly.

"Please let me talk with you." The voice seemed to break a little. "I'm sorry I shouted at you."

White clouds for . . . pillow, dew for drink . . . Lenora squeezed her eyes shut, though it was already dark under the covers. *The breeze will comb baby's hair, and the frost make her blink.* She could feel a hesitant tug on the comforter. She tightened her grip until her fingers ached.

"Please, Lenora," came the muffled voice. "Don't do this to me . . . to us."

"Leave me alone," she finally rasped.

"I brought you some soup. You've got to eat something."

"Go away!" *White clouds, white clouds, not my fault, round and round.*

~

A pebble had worked its way between Jenny's stocking and her clog shoe, pressing against the side of her foot. Every other step, Jenny would give her foot a shake, trying to shift the pebble to the toe, where at least it would not be so uncomfortable.

She couldn't think of stopping to unlace her shoe and take care of the problem. As it was, the pebble had slowed her down; she was now seven or eight feet behind Allen, and Mrs. Farrel was at her shoulder, urging her to hurry.

They had come from lunch only an hour ago, so there would be no chance to do anything about it for a while. She worked faster in spite of the pain in her foot, narrowing the gap between herself and Allen by a good three feet. It was not enough to satisfy Mrs. Farrel, for she began poking Jenny lightly in the back with the rounded end of her hoe.

"Mr. Blake's comin'!" came the old woman's voice behind her. "You got to hurry, child!"

She dared not look around to see the farm manager and had no idea where he happened to be, yet Jenny could feel his eyes burning into her back. In despair, she moved as fast as humanly possible. She had kept up with Allen all morning, and now, with Mr. Blake somewhere glaring at her, she'd fallen behind!

"Jenny! He's callin' you over!" Mrs. Farrel sounded startled. "Run over there and see what he wants before he gets mad!"

Her knees turned to water. She stopped and turned to look toward the beginning of the row they had half finished. Sure enough, Mr. Blake was seated there on his horse, the perpetual frown on his face.

"Hurry, girl!" urged the old woman, pushing at her elbow.

Jenny nodded to the man on the horse that she understood, then pulled the seed pouch over her head and handed it to Mrs. Farrel. "Thank you for . . . being nice to me," she stammered, then turned and started limping as fast as she could toward the beginning of the row. She was dead certain that she was about to be let go, but she would do her best to show Mr. Blake that she was an obedient worker.

"What's the matter with your foot?" Mr. Blake called down when Jenny was close enough to speak with him.

"I've got something in my shoe," she answered meekly. "A pebble, I think."

The man frowned again. "Well, why didn't you get it out?" He didn't give her time to answer but turned to point to the horse and wagon on the grass several feet away. "Sir Feldon wants to see you."

Jenny gaped in the direction he was pointing. On the seat of the wagon was a man Jenny had never seen before, clad in a gardener's smock. She trembled, then turned back to Mr. Blake. "Why does Sir Feldon—"

"I don't know, girl, but you'd best get the rock out of your shoe and get going!"

The gardener was brown and stocky, with a pipe clenched between his teeth under a bushy dark mustache. He was as silent as young Allen when Jenny climbed up on the box seat beside him, except to cluck at the horse when he lifted the reins. Nonetheless, he smiled at her and slowed the horse when he saw that she was having trouble staying in the seat, for the wagon bounced her unmercifully. Finally they passed the barns and came upon a dirt road leading to the Dunley manor.

In spite of her apprehension, Jenny felt a slight shiver of anticipation when she realized they weren't headed to the barns. She had heard of the great manor house that had sheltered Dunleys for generations, but even Aunt Mary had never had the opportunity to actually see it.

After a few minutes the dirt road linked up with a wider, tree-lined carriage drive off the main road which led to a pair of open, wrought-iron crested gates. A stone lodge sat just to the right, so large in comparison to Uncle Roy's tiny cottage that for a moment Jenny thought it to be the manor house itself.

The wagon continued on, over a stone bridge spanning a running brook and past a wide lawn graced with a fountain and colorful flower beds. When Jenny could finally tear her eyes from the flowers, the house was almost upon her. She let out a gasp at the imposing mansion and thought it the most beautiful thing she'd ever seen. The roof was steep and covered with slate shingles, not the thatch reeds that Jenny was used to. A dozen evenly spaced white-sash windows and a white portico made a pleasing contrast to the mellow red brick.

Then a panic seized her, and she looked down at the dirt encrusting her bare arms. Quickly she rolled down her sleeves, but the effect was almost as bad because she only owned the one faded blue dress, and there had been no time to wash and let it dry when she had come from the fields yesterday, or the day before. She had gotten up before the sun, too weary and too disheartened to comb yesterday's tangles from her hair, and the black under her fingernails from today's work looked permanently imbedded. Hugging her arms to her thin body, she realized that she had no right to be near such a beautiful place. Surely someone had made a mistake!

The gardener was guiding the horse to a smaller path leading around to the back of the house. He noticed Jenny's discomfort and finally spoke. "Only lazy folk never get dirty, lass," he muttered around his pipe. "Nothing wrong with good, honest dirt."

Honest or not, Jenny wished with all her heart that she could go back to the brook and wash herself. Wherever she was going, it would be better to go dripping wet than filthy dirty. And just where was she going? If she were to be let go and sent home, as was her earlier fear, why hadn't Mr. Blake simply told her so back there in the field?

She closed her eyes tightly and imagined with all her might that the past three days had been a dream, that she was still on the hillside picking berries with her cousins. Why, she could almost smell the honeysuckles in the air and hear Evan's laughing voice!

But before she even opened her eyes again, she knew that such imaginings were futile. Something was about to happen to her, perhaps another change in her life as drastic as going to the fields had been.

The wagon came to a stop at the back of the house, and the gardener nodded toward a stone staircase leading below-ground. "Housekeeper's expecting you," he said. "Go on inside." He puffed on his pipe while she climbed down from the wagon seat, then clucked to the horse again and left.

Jenny watched the horse and wagon disappear in a cloud of dust. Then there was nothing left to do but approach the house.

A thin young woman with several pockmarks on her face

opened the door to Jenny's knock. Waves of heat and the scent of fresh bread wafted out from behind her. The young woman was wearing an apron that looked damp and stained, and she told Jenny that she was one of the two scullery maids. "Cook said you'd be comin' in here," she said. "She'll be back shortly."

She let Jenny into the kitchen, a steamy room with a lofty ceiling, dominated by a long pine worktable. Two other women, one stirring a cauldron at the range and another putting more wood into a brick oven beside a huge fireplace, stopped talking long enough to look her over. "You can wait right there," the scullery maid said, motioning toward a bench at the table. Then she went back to what she had apparently been doing before, hanging an assortment of polished copper pots, pans, and molds onto a cast-iron rack.

While Jenny watched the women get back to their gossip and work, she raked her fingers through her tangled hair, trying to look at least a little more presentable. A short thick woman came in through the double doors to the left of the fireplace. Jenny knew right away, by the increased pace of activity of the workers in the kitchen, that she was the cook.

The cook looked her way while the scullery maid explained that she had just arrived, then walked over to where Jenny was seated. She had small, round eyes over a pug nose, and there was surprise in her expression, mingled with distaste.

"Come with me, child," she said. Her voice was business-like, with no animosity but no warmth. "Mrs. Styles wants to see you."

"M-Mrs. Styles, ma'am?"

"She's the housekeeper."

Too intimidated to resist, Jenny nodded and followed the cook across the room, back through the double doors to a short hall. An open pantry door was to the left, and a woman sat on a stool inside. She appeared to be counting jars and sacks of food on the shelves in front of her, then writing something down on a pad of paper in her lap. She seemed much older than Aunt Mary, with lines in her face and thick, graying hair braided into a knot at the crown of her head. When the cook cleared her throat after she and Jenny had been standing in the doorway for several seconds, the woman finally stopped moving her pencil and looked up.

"Mrs. Styles, the girl is here," said the cook. She nudged Jenny into the small room. "She needs a bath—and she's much too scrawny for scullery work."

"She's not here for kitchen work," the woman answered. "Sir Feldon wants to see her."

Sir Feldon? Jenny thought again, her pulse quickening. *Why does Sir Feldon want to see me?* She had only seen the man once in her life, from a distance, the day that the lady had stared at her. What had she done that would warrant the attention of the most important man in Leawick?

"I'll take her on upstairs," the housekeeper said with a tone of dismissal in her voice.

After the cook left with obvious reluctance, Mrs. Styles stood, set her paper and pencil on the stool, then stared down at the girl with curious eyes. "I just don't see the resemlance," she murmured, more to herself than to Jenny. Her face eased into a warm smile. "What is your name, child?"

It was too much. The smile broke down the self-control Jenny had tried to maintain ever since she had walked into this house. Unable to answer, she just looked up at the woman through the tears welling up in her eyes.

"There, there now," soothed Mrs. Styles, reaching out to

take her hand. That act of kindness brought even more tears, until Jenny was helpless against the wave of low, tortured sobs that came from somewhere within her thin body.

The woman suddenly dropped Jenny's hand and stepped out of the pantry, leaving her alone and even more terrified. But seconds later she returned with a damp dish towel in her hands. "There's nothing to be afraid of, child," she soothed, kneeling down to wipe the girl's face.

The towel felt cool against Jenny's burning skin, and after a little while, she was able to stop crying. Her throat was raw, though, and she could not stop her teeth from chattering.

"You don't have to be afraid," Mrs. Styles said, a reassuring smile on her face. "No one here is going to hurt you."

When Jenny could finally speak, she rasped out, "I don't know why I'm here."

"Why, Sir Feldon wants to speak with you for a few minutes. That's all."

"Is it because I couldn't keep up with Allen?" Fresh tears came to her eyes. "My shoe had—"

"You're not in trouble, child," the woman interrupted kindly. "Is that what you thought?"

When Jenny nodded, Mrs. Styles patted her shoulder. "No wonder, then. This big house and the lot of us can be frightening to a little thing like you." The kindness in the housekeeper's eyes calmed her, and her breathing began returning to normal.

"Now, would you like to tell me your name?"

"It's Jenny."

Mrs. Styles's eyes were shining. "What a fine name to have." She straightened and held out a hand. "Now, Jenny, it's time to go see Sir Feldon."

"Will you stay with me?" Jenny's meek voice asked.

"I imagine that I will. But you don't have to be afraid, no matter what. The baronet is a kind man."

Jenny took Mrs. Styles's hand and walked with her out of the pantry to a set of iron-railed back stairs. They led up to the ground floor and a carpeted inner hallway with three doorways set on each side. At the end of the hall Jenny could see an open door, with part of a polished dining-room table showing and a chandelier overhead. She thought they were headed toward this room when the housekeeper stopped at the second door on the right and knocked.

"Come in," came a man's voice from the other side. Mrs. Styles gave Jenny's hand a quick squeeze, then opened the door.

A gentleman wearing a white shirt, cravat, and black waist-coat sat behind a desk. His clean-shaven face was long and narrow and bland, and his thinning auburn hair was gray at the temples. At the tug of her hand, Jenny approached the man's desk with Mrs. Styles, hanging back as much as she dared.

"This is Jenny," the housekeeper said. "The girl you sent for."

The man nodded. "You may sit down." Jenny thought he wore the same worried expression that Aunt Mary usually had on her face. But what would someone who lived in such a fine house have to worry about?

Two wooden armchairs sat facing the desk. At the gentle pressure on her trembling shoulder, Jenny walked with the housekeeper to one of them and sat down.

Sir Feldon closed the book he had been reading and leaned forward on his elbows, resting his chin on his fist. He was studying Jenny with an intensity that made her wonder, in spite of her fear, if no one in this house had ever seen a dirt-covered child before.

"How old are you?" he suddenly asked, straightening in his chair.

"Ten, sir," she whispered, and when Mrs. Styles touched her arm, she said louder, "Ten, sir."

"You're small for your age, aren't you?"

"Yes, sir."

He was squinting at her now. "What color are your eyes? Gray?"

"My eyes?"

"They are gray, sir," the housekeeper answered for her. "But that's the only resemblance I can see."

Sir Feldon nodded. "Surely Lady Dunley will realize that as well, and all of this silliness will be over."

"You mean you're actually going to send the girl to her?"

"I can't let my wife stay in that room and starve to death. You understand that, don't you?"

"Yes, sir," said Mrs. Styles after a slight hesitation. Jenny could feel the woman's hand tense on her arm when she spoke again. "Sir, may I say something?"

His eyebrows lifted. "Yes, Mrs. Styles?"

"Don't you think it's time you got her some help?"

A shadow crossed the man's face. "You would have me put my wife in an asylum, Mrs. Styles?"

"No, of course not. But surely there's something . . ."

"Lady Dunley just needs time to adjust to her loss. Doctor Clayton says that she'll recover in time."

"But it's been over two years now, Sir Feldon. And in my opinion, she seems to be getting—"

"That will be enough, Mrs. Styles." Sir Feldon stared at the housekeeper with an indignant expression for a second, then sighed and rubbed his temple. "I suppose you'd better clean the girl up," he said. "I want Lenora to get a good look at her, so she'll realize how silly all of this is."

~

Jenny's experience with bathing had always been in the brook that ran behind Uncle Roy's house, except in the winter, when everyone took sponge baths with water heated in a kettle and poured into Aunt Mary's big green-speckled bowl. When she was led up another flight of stairs instead of down to a brook, she imagined that it was to be a sponge bath.

But Mrs. Styles took her into a room larger than Aunt Mary's whole kitchen, which contained a washstand with marble top, several mirrors, and decorated chamber pots. But what caught and held her attention more than any of these was an enormous metal basin that looked like a large feeding trough, only it had one end that rose taller than the other end.

The housekeeper turned and smiled at her. "I'm going to have one of the maids heat up some water. Helene will be in here shortly to comb your hair; otherwise we'll never get the knots out when it's wet." She pursed her lips and studied Jenny's filthy dress. "We'll have to find something else for you to wear. We may have to take a quick stitch here and there, but at least it'll be clean."

In Mrs. Styles's comforting presence, Jenny dared to take a more thorough look around. The room was pleasant, with violets on the wallpaper. There was the familiar pitcher and bowl on the washstand in the corner, but she had a feeling that her bath was going to involve the big metal trough.

"A bathing tub, Jenny," explained the housekeeper. "You

sit inside it." She walked over to the washstand and brought back a cake of soap. "See, you'll smell like flowers." She smiled, holding the soap under Jenny's nose.

Jenny breathed deeply and, for the first time that day, smiled. The soap smelled of lilacs, not like the grainy lye soap that Aunt Mary used. A wave of homesickness came over her at the thought of her aunt, and she looked up at Mrs. Styles with pleading eyes. "I'm . . ."

"Yes, Jenny?"

"I'm supposed to be planting turnip seeds. Aunt Mary doesn't know where I am."

The housekeeper nodded. "When do you usually go home?"

"I don't know," Jenny answered. "When it's almost too dark to see anymore."

It seemed that a muscle moved in the woman's jaw; then she smiled again. "I'm sure we'll be finished with you before then, and you can leave with the other field workers. If not, I'll have someone take you in the gig."

She then started for the door, saying, "Helene will be here in just a minute. Then I'll come see you after your bath."

Alone, Jenny stood in the middle of the room and stared at the doorway. Presently she heard the sound of rapid footsteps, and a tall young woman in a black-and-white uniform bustled through the door with a brush in her hand. She had dark hair pulled back from a heart-shaped face and had a beauty mark under one eye.

The maid's jaw dropped open at the sight of Jenny. Coming closer, the young woman lifted a handful of her tangled hair. "Better sit down, love," she said, taking a stool from the side of the washstand. "And I do hope your head's not tender."

The maid, who told Jenny that her name was Helene,

started brushing the tangles from Jenny's hair. Two other maids came into the room, each carrying a bucket of steaming water. With curious glances at Jenny and then questioning looks at Helene, they left again, coming back a few minutes later with more water.

"All right, it's time to shed that dress," Helene finally told her.

Jenny swallowed and looked up at the three waiting faces. Why were there so many people to tend to her bath when she was perfectly capable of bathing herself . . . and had done so for as long as she could remember? She had even been responsible for the cleanliness of Aunt Mary's children, beginning with Trudy.

"Couldn't I bathe myself?" she asked meekly.

"Only if you want to get us in trouble with Mrs. Styles, love," answered Helene, already going around to Jenny's back to unfasten her buttons. "Just relax and we'll have you clean as a whistle in no time."

~

After her bath, Jenny was perched back on the stool with a linen towel the size of a blanket wrapped around her while Helene combed through her clean hair. One of the maids who had drawn her bath, a tall, freckled girl with coppery red curls, came back into the room carrying a bundle of fabric. "We're to try to make this fit her," she told Helene. "It was sent to the rag bin this morning, but at least it's clean . . . and it's a far sight better than what she had on." She unfolded and held up a faded gingham dress that was obviously too big for Jenny. "Mrs. Styles says we should hurry and that we can cut this down if we have to."

"We'll have to trim off at least three or four inches for sure," Helene mused. "But we won't have time to hem it back up."

The red-haired maid glanced down at the floor, where Jenny's grime-covered dress lay in a heap with her shift and stockings. "No matter," she said, wrinkling her nose.

She breezed out of the room, while Helene continued to comb through Jenny's hair. When the maid came back, she had a pair of scissors in one hand and a sewing basket with a plush red velvet lid in the other. The two maids lifted Jenny up to stand on the stool. Jenny obediently put her arms into the sleeves of the dress, then closed her eyes as it was pulled down over her head.

"Don't they feed you where you come from?" giggled Helene when the dress was fastened in back. She pulled at a sleeve that hung down a good four inches longer than Jenny's fingertips.

The red-haired maid hooted with laughter, which set Jenny's cheeks to burning. Mortified, she wished she had the courage to tell the two of them that she had always been small for her age and that Aunt Mary and Uncle Roy might have been poor, but she had always gotten the same meals at the table that her cousins did.

Helene must have noticed the humiliation on Jenny's face, for she stopped laughing and cuffed the shoulder of the red-haired maid. "Just funning you a bit, love," she said gently. "Don't mean to hurt your feelings."

Jenny swallowed and nodded. For the rest of the time, the maids worked on her dress in silence, only occasionally whispering a suggestion to each other by way of altering the dress. Fifteen minutes later, they were standing back to appraise their work.

"Well, what do you think?" said the red-haired maid, her brows drawing together.

"Pity that Mrs. Pruitt is out orderin' cloth. She could have whipped up a better job than this."

"The dress will do fine," came a voice from the doorway, and Mrs. Styles stepped inside. She smiled at Jenny as the two maids scurried about picking up scraps of cloth. "Ready?"

Jenny didn't know if she was ready—she didn't even know where she was going. But Mrs. Styles had treated her with more kindness than anyone else at the big house, and she knew that somehow she had no choice in the matter, so she answered in a quiet voice, "Yes, ma'am."

The woman helped her climb down from the stool and took her by the hand again. It seemed to Jenny that this time Mrs. Styles held her hand a little more tightly than before. They walked from the bath into the carpeted hallway, past three open doors in which Jenny could see beds and furniture. The fourth door on the right was closed, but this time Mrs. Styles didn't knock. Instead, she bent down to face Jenny, her expression solemn.

"This is Lady Dunley's room," she whispered. "The baronet's wife. She saw you in the fields a couple of days ago and has wanted to meet you ever since."

Jenny was opening her mouth to ask why when the housekeeper said, "Her little daughter, Angelica, died over two years ago, and she misses her. She fancies that you look like her."

Panic set in again. Her heart racing, Jenny asked the housekeeper what she was supposed to say to Lady Dunley.

"I don't expect you'll have a chance to say anything," she whispered back. "Hopefully, the missus will realize her mistake, and you'll be allowed to leave. I'm sorry that I didn't warn you about this, but I had no idea that Sir Feldon would want you to meet her."

Straightening, the housekeeper reached for the knob and opened the door. They walked through two rooms—one just for sitting and the other for dressing. The bedroom was last, papered in gold and dusty rose, with a thick dark green carpet covering most of the wooden floor. Dark furniture filled the spaces, and linen dressed the windows and tables.

Jenny looked around for Lady Dunley, but the woman was nowhere to be seen. Still, Mrs. Styles was leading her to the far wall of the room, where a big bed stood with a graceful fretted top. The bedcovers and pillows were in disarray, and for a second Jenny wondered why, in such a fine house with so many servants, no one had made the bed. Then her eye caught a faint movement, and she realized with a start that someone was under the covers.

"Lady Dunley?" Mrs. Styles said, squeezing Jenny's hand so hard that it hurt. When there was no response from the heaped-up counterpane, the housekeeper added, "The girl that you wanted to see is here."

Slowly the bedcovers began to move, and Jenny pressed close to Mrs. Styles's side. The girl let out a small gasp when a face appeared. The woman's graying brown hair was disheveled, with strands hanging over her eyes. She fixed Jenny with a hard stare that frightened her with its intensity.

But then the hazel eyes softened under the tangles, and the woman's mouth curved into a smile.

"Gray eyes! I just *knew* your eyes were gray."

11

W HEN the train finally came to a stop at Birmingham Station, Corrine tightened the ribbon on her
bonnet, picked up her valise and hamper, and
stepped out onto the platform. She would have to take another train on to Shrewsbury, then try to hire a coach to take
her the twenty miles south to Leawick.

Scanning the people in her near vicinity, she was relieved
to see no sign of Mr. Price, though she knew he was out
there somewhere. He had seemed like such a pleasant man
when he had called upon her at Adam Burke's. A hero, she
thought, who had probably saved Rachel's life. Corrine had
even found him attractive—a memory that now brought back
painful guilt feelings.

Well, she certainly didn't find him attractive anymore! Back
in the compartment, he had reminded her of almost every man
she had been acquainted with in her wicked past. Most had
been married, with leering smiles and pointed comments about
the supposed coldness of their wives, designed to evoke sympathy from her.

Of course, Corrine reminded herself, she had encouraged
and even instigated these flirtations back then, and no matter

how loathsome the memories were to her now, she wasn't going to start casting all of the blame on the men.

The chalkboard outside the booking office in the Birmingham station listed a ninety-minute wait. Corrine felt a tug of disappointment at her heart. After all this time waiting to reunite with her family, she would have to spend the night in Shrewsbury, for she would be arriving there at six-thirty, too late to be starting out on the road.

She had nowhere to go, so she sat on a bench and ate one of the four roast beef sandwiches that Bernice had packed, finishing it off with a pear tart. Then she took out her Bible and read from Saint John until the boarding whistle for the Birmingham Northwestern Railway pierced the air.

~

When she finally disembarked at Shrewsbury, Corrine discovered it was a beauty of a place. It was situated on a bend in the River Severn and had winding streets rich in half-timbered buildings and lovely formal gardens. High above the river, an ancient Norman castle kept watch over the town.

Corrine had been through Shrewsbury once before, eight years ago, when she ran away with Gerald Moore. Back then she had been too enamored of the worldly Moore to be impressed with anything so mundane as beautiful surroundings.

Outside the railway station, she hired a carriage to transport her and her belongings to the Wheat Sheaf Inn, a Georgian-style building just a stone's throw from Saint Mary's Church. The inn's proprietor, a man almost completely bald and wearing spectacles, did not seem to find it odd for a woman to be traveling alone. He carried her valise and hamper to one of the tiny upstairs rooms and told her that, yes, he could arrange for a coach to come by in the morning to take her to Leawick.

He also urged her to go down to the dining room for a good hot meal, but Corrine declined politely, asking that some tea be sent up instead. It was likely that most of the inn's customers were men, and she didn't want to put herself in the uncomfortable position she had experienced on the train.

There was enough food left in Bernice's basket for supper and breakfast, too, which would save her the price of two meals. After years of throwing money around recklessly for whatever happened to amuse her, she was determined to learn not to waste it. After all, the seventy pounds she had received from selling her pearls would seem like a fortune in Leawick, enough to better the conditions of her family.

She still had most of it, too—sixty-five pounds and some change tucked away in the purse inside her valise. Adam Burke had refused to allow her to pay the doctor's fee or any of her upkeep while she was a guest at his house. In fact, the only things she had spent money on—besides her train ticket and now her room—were the small gifts she had bought and wrapped for Adam Burke's servants three days ago.

She closed the door behind the proprietor and smiled, wondering if they had found their gifts yet. Just as they were preparing to leave, Corrine had pretended to go back to her room to make sure she hadn't left her slippers under the bed. While everyone waited outside, she had taken the parcels from the bottom of the wardrobe and left them on the dressing table.

For so many years she had been certain that happiness could be bought. Yet despite her countless acquisitions, Corrine had still needed brandy most nights to dull the emptiness inside and help her fall asleep. Now, for the first time in her life, she had actually *given* something away, not expecting anything in return. And the feeling of satisfaction that came with the act was far better than brandy. In fact, she found herself trying to imagine over and over the surprise and delight on the servants' faces as they opened their gifts.

Turning down the covers of her bed, she decided to have a bath and go right to bed. The sooner she fell asleep, the sooner the morning would come.

~

It had been an easy matter for a skilled detective like Joseph to keep out of Mrs. Hammond's sight when they arrived in Shrewsbury. He had simply waited at the door of his compartment until she was clear of the train.

Then he bought a newspaper from a young boy and watched from the corner of a stack of shipping crates as Mrs. Hammond made arrangements for a carriage. He cautiously skirted his way around her to a chaise at the end of the line, making it clear that the driver would be well rewarded for following a certain other carriage without making it obvious that he was doing so. Shielding his face with the open newspaper, he spent most of the short drive hoping that the man at the reins was competent enough to keep Mrs. Hammond in his sight.

His anxiety ended when the driver pulled the chaise into the shade of an elm tree on the side of the street, then turned to him and pointed up ahead. He peered over the newspaper to see Mrs. Hammond exiting the hired carriage at a building with *Wheat Sheaf Inn* carved on a wooden signpost out front.

Joseph waited outside for half an hour until he was satisfied that she wouldn't be coming out again. The driver informed him that The Dog and Pheasant was the nearest inn to this one, so Joseph asked the man to deliver him there. Then, alighting from the carriage, Joseph gave the man a generous tip in addition to the sixpence fare.

He noticed a family of geese clustered near the entrance to the inn's garden. The sandwiches in his gripsack did not appeal to him now and would be no good by morning, so he took them out and tore them in pieces, then threw them to the birds. They accepted his offering with chattering enthusiasm.

What Joseph wanted—craved, in fact—was something warm and easy on his parched throat. Like soup. Potato soup if possible.

The sound of rattling cups and at least a dozen genial conversations filled The Dog and Pheasant's busy, comfortable old dining room. Joseph gave his order to a woman who brought him tea, and as he waited for his soup, he found himself wishing that he could take a few days to recover from whatever was ailing him.

My fault for not eating proper meals, he thought. *I should have made myself get enough rest.* Right after he had his supper and procured a room here, he would make the necessary arrangements concerning Mrs. Hammond; then he would try to get to bed early. He was certain that he would feel better after a good night's sleep.

The potato soup was hot and well-peppered and felt wonderful going down his throat. Suddenly ravenous, Joseph gulped it down and ordered another bowl. After his meal he went back into the parlor for his gripsack and paid for a room.

But at the top of the stairs, nausea gripped him, and his throat felt as if it were on fire. Fumbling with his key at the door to his room, he made it to the chamber pot just in time.

Spasms gripped his stomach in waves, until he ached all over from dry heaves.

When he could finally stand up straight again, Joseph rinsed his face at the washstand, then walked over to the mirror above the dresser and peered at his face. His eyes were drawn, the skin pale around them, but on his cheeks was a rosy glow. Leaning closer, he touched his skin lightly with a fingertip. A fine rash was the cause of the blush on his cheeks, and he wondered what had caused it. Had it been there all day? And would it be gone by morning?

He turned from the mirror and, without drawing back the bedclothes, lay down on the bed and closed his eyes. He still had work to do, but if he didn't take a few minutes to rest, he wouldn't be able to make it down the stairs.

~

The sun was settling into the treetops when Joseph finally started out for the Wheat Sheaf Inn. He felt somewhat better after an hour's rest, though swallowing was still painful.

Surely after her journey, Corrine Hammond would be resting by now and wouldn't see him. If she did, it would complicate matters, but it shouldn't interfere with the way he planned to capture her. In the tiny front parlor, at a rolltop desk, sat a man he assumed to be the inn's proprietor. The balding man was alone in the room except for a calico cat relaxing in one of the upholstered chairs.

"Will you require a room for the night?" asked the proprietor, looking up through his spectacles.

"No, thank you," Joseph replied. "I have a problem of the most delicate nature and would like to enlist your assistance, if

I may." He pulled his leather pouch from his waistband and held it in his hands.

"I'm not certain that I can help you," the man behind the desk replied, but his eyes, nonetheless, were upon Joseph's purse.

Taking a step closer, Joseph put a hand on the desk and leaned forward on it a bit. "You see, my wife has left me, and I happen to know that she's here."

The proprietor's expression grew wary. "What does your wife look like?"

"Beautiful, with dark hair and gray eyes. She happens to be wearing a gray outfit, too."

"Yes," the man said, nodding. "She's here. But I must warn you, the constable is in our dining room right now. I won't have any commotion in my—"

"I don't intend to make a scene," Joseph cut in, holding up a hand. For a dramatic effect he closed his eyes for a second, took a deep breath as if trying to compose himself, and continued. "But our four children are beside themselves, sir, and I simply would like to get to the scoundrel who's beguiled her into acting this way before she runs away with him."

Lowering his voice, the man said, "You mean a libertine?"

Joseph's nostrils flared as he leaned closer. "The most odious kind, sir! One who uses women until he tires of them, then leaves them bereft of friends and family while he goes on to greener pastures."

"Well, she's met no one here, sir," offered the proprietor, now sympathetic. He squinted at Joseph's flushed cheeks— no doubt he thought his caller had been weeping. "Just went straight up to her room."

"Alone, you say?"

"I took her bags up myself."

After a thoughtful pause, Joseph said, "Then she's meeting him elsewhere. Did she happen to mention her plans for tomorrow?"

The man nodded. "She asked me to arrange for a coach to fetch her as early as possible."

"A coach? Then she intends to leave for good!" Joseph buried his face in his hands.

"Why don't you go up and ask her not to go?" the man suggested. "I can show you her room, if you'll give me your word there won't be a scene."

"No use," Joseph replied quickly. "In fact, if she even suspects I'm here, she'll find some way to meet him tonight. The scoundrel has put a spell on her until she's not the same woman I married, nor the same woman who used to love her children."

"Then what do you intend to do?"

Joseph thought for a minute. "Did she say where she was going?"

The proprietor opened his mouth, then closed it. As sympathetic as he had been, a greedy glint crept into his eyes as he looked at Joseph's money pouch again. "I'm trying to recall," he said, drawing his brows together in thought.

Joseph took two one-pound notes from the pouch. "I must know everything."

First glancing over his shoulder at the open door, the man reached out for the money and drew it back in a flash. "Now, you do give me your word that there won't be a scene?"

"Yes, of course."

"She wants a coach to take her to Leawick. I've already sent a boy to make the arrangements with a driver."

"Leawick? Are you sure?"

The man nodded.

Joseph took another pound note from his pouch and set it on the desk. "Where can I find this driver?"

~

After breakfasting in her room the next morning on some bread and cheese and another pear tart, Corrine chose a simple moss green gown with a single row of black horn buttons up the front. Her bruised ribs had prevented her from wearing a crinoline while recovering, and she had realized how much discomfort she'd suffered in the name of vanity. Now she only wore a shift and a starched petticoat—just enough to give her skirt some flounce while still giving her freedom of movement.

Her hair gave her trouble; she was used to having Rachel, and then Dora, fashion it for her. After several clumsy attempts at a chignon, she simply drew the sides back into a tortoiseshell comb at the crown of her head and allowed the rest to hang loosely. She could learn to style her hair later—reconciliation with her family was more important today.

Corrine thought of Thomas and wondered if he ever imagined that his wife would return to him. It wasn't relevant that she didn't love him, that she hadn't even loved him when she married as a girl of sixteen. If he would have her, her duty was to go back to him. Perhaps love would come in time.

The valise lay open on her bed. She walked over to it to pack her hairbrush inside, and for the first time the notion occurred to her that Thomas might have taken another wife. After all, she had been gone for eight years.

Hope flooded through her, followed immediately by paralyzing shame. She stood there with the brush in her hand, pressing the boar's-hair bristles hard into her palm, and wondered if it was always going to be this hard to do what was right. She shouldn't hope to be released from her commitments; she should be happy to fulfill them, to make amends. Bernice had told her that the Lord gave a new nature to those who trusted him for salvation. Why, then, did her old nature still try to assert itself in her moments of weakness, tempting her to go back to a life of pleasing only herself?

Forgive me, Lord, for not being as good as Bernice, she prayed silently. *I want to be, but my old selfishness gets in the way sometimes.* She stood there, eyes lowered to the floor. Was God disgusted with her? Did he regret allowing her to become his child?

Pain startled her. Loosening her grip on the brush, she stared down at rows of reddened indentations the bristles had made across the inside of her hand. She dropped her brush into the valise and rubbed her hand. Bernice had often told her, *"You're just a baby now. Your faith will grow stronger as you grow closer to the Lord, but you've got to be patient."*

That was it! If she didn't give up, the temptations might not grow weaker, but her faith would grow stronger. Surely God understood that she was still a child in her understanding of the Christian walk. Hadn't he given her his Holy Spirit to nurture and guide her? *O Father,* she prayed, lifting up her eyes, *help me to increase my faith. I want to make you proud of me.*

A voice came to her—inaudible, but so clear in her mind that it startled her. *My child, I'm already proud of you.*

Tears streamed down her cheeks, and Corrine stood still for a long time, feeling a bond with God that she didn't want to end. *I would have become a Christian a long time ago,* she thought, *if I had known about moments like this.*

Wiping her eyes with a handkerchief, she started packing the rest of her belongings. She dabbed a bit of perfume behind her ears and briefly wondered if Jenny would like the light rose scent. *Jenny.* Just the thought of her daughter caused so many feelings of love to well up inside her.

Strange, how she had abandoned the toddler with scarcely an afterthought and, for most of her years with Gerald, hadn't even wondered how Jenny was faring. Now Corrine was certain that she would never feel complete until she held her daughter in her arms.

She was fastening the straps on the valise when a knock came at the door. A lanky man with stubbled cheeks smiled at her, revealing several blackened teeth. "Your coach, ma'am," he announced in a gust of fetid breath.

"My trunk's over there," she said, stepping to the side so that he could see it.

He measured the trunk with his eyes, and Corrine noticed that his shirt and trousers were wrinkled and stained. *As long as he can get me to Leawick,* she thought, *he can wear bearskins.*

"I'll have to get the boy what works here to help me load it," the driver said.

"All right. And I'll be keeping my valise and hamper with me." Nervously, Corrine ran her hands along the side of her skirt as she watched the man disappear down the hall. Her homecoming, her time of reckoning, was getting closer. There was no going back.

~

For all the driver's disheveled appearance, the coach looked fairly new. Its wheels were polished, and four well-groomed horses stood harnessed in front, snorting and flicking their tails occasionally.

"How long will it take to get to Leawick?" she asked as the driver held the coach door open for her.

He scratched his cheek and thought for a second. "Traffic's heavy in town in the mornings. And once we turn off Leominster Road, it'll be slow going. But not more than two hours, I'd say."

Two hours! In just two hours, her life would be drastically changed. Corrine stepped into the coach, set her bag by her feet, and settled back on the thin cushions of the seat to wait.

Twenty minutes later, while she was absorbed in trying to imagine what her daughter looked like, the coach came to an abrupt halt. Her immediate thought was relief that the bumping and jostling had ceased, but when the coach didn't start moving again, she wondered if she should open the door and ask the driver what was wrong.

The corner of her eye caught movement between the gap of the curtains at the opposite window, and before she could move an inch, a man opened the door and quickly stepped into the coach. *Mr. Price!*

He threw a gripsack across the floor, then sat down across from her. Almost immediately the coach started rolling again.

"How dare you?" Corrine sputtered when she was able to speak.

"Don't touch the door," Price growled. His dark eyes were fierce and threatening. Corrine's eyes moved from his face to his hand, and her heart lurched. He held a pistol, pointed straight at her!

"What is the meaning of this?" Her hand trembled at her throat.

"I don't want to hurt you," he said in a cold voice, "but I'll use this if you give me any trouble."

Corrine suddenly recalled how Mr. Price had acted in the train, and indignation rose up within her. "I am a married woman, sir!"

For several seconds he stared at her as if he hadn't the faintest idea what she had just said. Then he let out a scornful laugh. "If you think I mean to seduce you, you are mistaken, Mrs. Hammond."

She prayed that he was telling the truth, but her experience with men caused her to doubt. "Then, why are you here?"

"Perhaps I should ask you the same question. What sheep have you decided to fleece this time?"

Corrine stiffened, feeling the heat rise in her cheeks. This man had no way of knowing about her past. Just what was he insinuating?

"I don't know what you mean, Mr. Price," she answered through trembling lips. "I'm on the way to meet with my husband right now."

To her utter humiliation, he laughed again. "This matrimonial state that you profess—it's convenient at times, isn't it?"

"What are you talking about?"

"Is that how you seduced some of the poor fools you've blackmailed? By letting them believe that you, too, are married and want to keep the affair quiet? With others, of course, you've pretended to be the grieving widow."

Horror rose from deep within her and escaped her lips in a gasp. "Mr. Price!"

"Have I shocked the lady's delicate sensibilities?" he mocked with a cynical voice.

Corrine wanted to crawl under the seat, so great was her shame. But more than that, she wanted to slap the face of the insolent man across from her. Taking several deep breaths, she forced herself to calm down. "I don't know how you found out about me, sir, but I'm not like that anymore. I've changed. Please get out and leave me alone."

He shook his head, though the regret that washed across his face *almost* seemed real. For the first time, Corrine noticed that there was an unnatural redness shading his cheeks. "I would like nothing more than that right now, believe me," he replied. "But I've got a job to do."

Disoriented ever since the man's intrusion into her coach, Corrine finally began to understand. The past she had grieved over had not let her escape so lightly. In the form of the man across from her, it was reaching out to claim her.

She sighed heavily, sagging against the seat. "We're not on the road to Leawick, are we?"

"We should be turning soon." He rested his head against the back of the coach and stared across at her. "We've got a long trip ahead. Our destination is Treybrook."

"Treybrook." It only took her a second to remember York and Squire Nowells. The elderly man had told her that he was from Treybrook. *And then he killed himself because of me!*

Corrine's hand went back up to her throat. "He had grown children . . . a son."

Joseph nodded. "A son who wants to speak with you."

"You mean to kill me, don't you?"

"Whatever he does with you is his business."

No! It can't be. O God, at least let me see my daughter! Her silent prayer bordered on panic. If only her faith had had more time to grow as Bernice had assured her that it would!

The pistol lay on the seat beside him, and he kept one hand on it to keep it from bouncing to the floor below. But even if it were packed in the man's satchel, she had no chance to escape.

Still, she had to try something, *anything*. Leaning forward several inches, she fixed her eyes upon the man. "Mr. Price, I've got a daughter in Leawick. I haven't seen her in eight years."

He sighed, and she couldn't tell if he believed her or not. "You'll have to tell that to the new Squire Nowells."

"And my husband, sir. I told you the truth about my marriage. I just want the chance to let him know how sorry I am." She swallowed and added, "And the chance to hold my daughter in my arms again, sir. Jenny's her name—please let me see her again."

As she wiped away the tears that were burning her eyes, Mr. Price said nothing, just watched her through half-closed lids. Corrine tried to compose herself so that she could plead rationally with him, wondering what kind of man would kidnap a woman and force her to go where she would probably be harmed. *And I thought he was such a wonderful man for saving Rachel's life!*

Then the realization hit her that Joseph Price's presence at her house that day had been no accident. He had been looking for her then and had barely missed her, too!

Corrine regarded him through narrowed eyes. He made money off other people's misery. He was no better than she had been. . . .

Money! If that was what motivated him, she could use it to her benefit. "Mr. Price, I've got sixty-five pounds in my purse right now," she said. "You may have every last penny of it if you'll take me to Leawick."

A slight smile curled the corners of his mouth. "But what about Squire Nowells?"

She realized after a second that he was speaking of the son. "You could tell him that you couldn't find me."

"That would be a lie," he said, an eyebrow raised in amused contempt. "You say you've changed, Mrs. Hammond, and here you are wanting me to tell a lie?"

He was right, of course, though it galled her to admit it. How frightening that desperation could make her revert to her old ways so quickly! With a sinking feeling, she remembered telling Bernice of her desire to repay the people she had hurt. Had she really meant it, or had she thought that just feeling sorry for her misdeeds was enough? God had forgiven her; was there really a need to make reparations on the human side?

She wished she could talk with Bernice! Life seemed so promising and wonderful just days ago, and now her joy had been abruptly yanked away. Was this a test of her faith, to see if she would go through this tribulation like a true believer, even if it meant her death?

Still, with every mile that the coach took her farther from Jenny, the jagged wound in her heart deepened. She didn't see how she could live another day with such sorrow. But maybe her desire to make things right had to begin with Squire Nowells.

"Mr. Price," she began again with a sigh, "I don't want you to lie to Mr. Nowells."

The mocking expression returned. "Well, that's terribly decent of you."

"Just take me to Leawick for a day . . . for an hour, even. Just let me see my daughter and my husband before you take me to Treybrook. I'll still give you all my money."

"I can't do that, Mrs. Hammond."

"I wouldn't leave your sight. *Please,* Mr. Price. You could make sixty-five pounds for just a couple hours' delay."

"And what's to stop me from taking your money now?"

Corrine's pulse lurched in her throat. She hadn't considered that. "Taking my money?"

"I could always use another sixty-five pounds."

She glared at the man. He was certainly scoundrel enough to do it!

Then in a voice that suddenly sounded weary, he said, "I'm not interested in your precious fortune, Mrs. Hammond. But always keep in mind that this weapon is loaded."

"What do you mean by that?"

"Sooner or later the idea is going to come to you that Pete, our fashionable driver, is the one you should be bribing. I will not hesitate to shoot either of you if that becomes a problem."

12

J ENNY'S first thought upon waking to sunlight was that
she had overslept and would be late heading out for the
fields. In a panic she sat up, then breathed a little easier
when she remembered where she was.

She leaned back on her elbows in the soft, high bed and
looked around. Toys—something she had never seen before
except for the girls' straw dolls and Evan's carved wooden
pony—filled the shelves against the wall and overflowed a
mahogany chest at the foot of her bed. She had even been
allowed to sleep with one of the beautiful dolls from the glass
case!

Actually, she'd been *ordered* to sleep with it. That was after
supper at the big table in the dining room. A shiver ran
through her at the memory.

~

It had started out nicely. Jenny had never seen so much food at
one time—roast duckling *and* some type of fish, an assortment
of vegetable dishes, including little onions in cream sauce that
she liked very much, soup, and even something called crepes
for dessert—thin breads rolled around sweetened strawberries,
with cream on top.

At the head of the table, Sir Feldon had been quiet, only making the comment when Lady Dunley brought her into the dining room that it was good to have his wife come down for dinner. Lady Dunley's brother, Mr. Wingate, whom the lady called Neil, had agreed. He was the more jovial of the two men, occasionally making a joke and giving Jenny a smile.

The happiest of all had been Lady Dunley. Her eyes seemed to shine, and there was a constant smile on her face. At her brother's jokes she would throw back her head and laugh. Once when Neil claimed to have found the cook's false teeth in his soup, the lady had laughed so hard and for so long that her husband and brother stopped smiling and looked at each other with worried expressions.

Lady Dunley hadn't seemed to notice. She had leaned over often to fuss over Jenny's plate, cutting her serving of duckling into small pieces and the fish into even smaller pieces as she checked for tiny bones that could catch in the throat.

Mrs. Styles had reminded the woman of Jenny's name, but Lady Dunley called her Angelica once, after the dessert course had been served. Then her husband had abruptly stood, his chair falling to the floor behind him with a loud thud.

"I've had enough of this, Lenora! You promised if I let you see the girl, you wouldn't get carried away."

Lady Dunley fixed glaring eyes upon her husband. "You can't stand to see me having a good time, can you?"

"This child is not our daughter!"

Lady Dunley seemed about to cry, for her mouth curved down and she started shaking. "I . . . know . . . she's not!" she answered, her fists clenched on the table in front of her.

"Then why are you calling her by our daughter's name?

She's got a name—" Abruptly he stopped and looked over at Jenny. "What is your name, girl?"

"J-Jenny," she had answered, trying to slide lower in her chair. Knowing that she was the cause of the whole argument was dreadful, and she wished with all her heart that she were back in the turnip fields.

"See!" Sir Feldon exclaimed. "She said her name is Jenny!"

Mr. Wingate, who had sat motionless through the scene with his eyes downcast, finally looked up and spoke. "Lenora hasn't been this happy in years, Feldon. Why don't you just let her enjoy the girl's visit?"

"Because it's lunacy for an adult woman to be playing pretend games when she knows better!"

Lady Dunley had started crying in earnest then, tears dripping onto her gown.

"Now are you happy, Feldon?" Mr. Wingate asked.

"Do I look happy to you?" Sir Feldon shot back.

"Happier than your wife does!"

With a sharp look at his brother-in-law, Sir Feldon walked quickly around the table to put his hands on his wife's shaking shoulders. "Please don't cry, Lenora. I'm sorry I was angry."

Lady Dunley moaned into her linen napkin.

"Look, you can let the girl stay for a couple of days if it makes you happy," he murmured into her hair. "Just remember that she's . . . she's not Angelica. Promise me that you'll do that."

The woman's moans had quieted, and with her face still buried in the napkin, she moved her head in a slight nod.

"I think it's time for you and me to take a walk." Jenny had been startled to find Mr. Wingate at her right, bending down to whisper to her. He took her by the hand down to the kitchen, where the wide-eyed cook and the kitchen maids hustled to serve them crepes at the worktable, to replace the half-eaten ones upstairs.

Over an hour later, when Helene had found an oversized nightgown for her to wear and tucked her into bed, Lady Dunley had come into the room to sit beside her pillow.

"You may leave now, Helene," she had said. After the door closed behind the maid, the woman just smiled and sat there staring at Jenny until it made her uncomfortable. After a while she wondered if Lady Dunley were waiting for her to speak, so she shyly said, "Good night."

"Good night, you precious baby," Lady Dunley had gushed back, leaning down to place a kiss on her forehead. Then she walked over to the glass case and took out a beautifully dressed doll. "Almost forgot to tuck Frances in, didn't we?"

~

Jenny turned to stare down at the doll. Long golden curls peeked from a bonnet of pink satin, and depthless eyes, painted onto porcelain, stared at nothing. The doll was dressed in a ruffled gown of the same pink sateen as the bonnet.

She had seen girls cuddling dolls before, but she had never felt the desire to do so. Jenny was only four years old when newborn Trudy had been put into her almost constant care so that Aunt Mary could get her work done. The other cousins had followed. They had been her "dolls," their real smiles infinitely preferable to the fake one painted on the face beside her. Carefully she reached out a finger to touch a golden lock and wondered if the hair was real.

Fear of rolling over and damaging such a beautiful creature had caused Jenny a fitful night's sleep, and now she hoped that

someone would put the doll back into the case before something happened to it and she would be blamed.

Also, she needed someone to tell her what to do. Was
she expected to get up and put her clothes on? But her dress
was nowhere in sight, and neither was the one the maids had
cut down for her yesterday evening.

Her dilemma was solved when the door to the hallway
opened and Helene walked in with a pitcher of water. "Oh,
are you awake, love?"

"May I get up now?"

"Of course you can."

Jenny slid to the floor, then turned immediately to make the
bed. The mattress was so high that she had to stand on tiptoe
just to reach for a pillow.

"What are you doing, child?" came the maid's voice from
behind her, after a smothered giggle. A hand touched her
shoulder. "You're not supposed to be doin' that. We'll tend
to it after a bit."

After helping Jenny sponge bathe at the washstand, Helene
said, "Now we've got to get you dressed and down for breakfast. The missus will be up here wondering what's taking so
long. Alice—she's my cousin, and the missus' maid—says Lady
Dunley ain't the most patient woman in the world."

Jenny nodded and looked around the room. "Where is my
dress?"

"That thing? Why it's probably in the rag bin by now. And
the other one we pretty much butchered last night, trying
to make it fit your skinny little bones." She walked over to a
wardrobe and pulled the doors open. "Lady Dunley says you're
to wear the peacock blue poplin. Let's see . . . here it is."

Gaping at the assortment of colors and fabrics, Jenny

wondered how they had gotten so many dresses in her size, especially after having such a time finding something for her to wear last night. "Where did they come from?" she gathered the courage to ask Helene.

"These?" Helene had a child's blue dress by the shoulders, snapping it into the air to shake out some of the creases. "These belonged to the little girl whose bed you slept in last night, love."

"Angel . . ." Jenny's voice trailed off as a shudder caught her shoulders.

"Angelica." The maid finished for her. Lowering her voice, she said, "I can't believe the missus is actually lettin' you wear her clothes. And that doll. Lady Dunley's terrible fussy about her little girl's things, y'know?" She walked over to hold the dress up to Jenny's shoulders. "How old are you?"

"Ten, ma'am."

Helene laughed. "You're a guest here, love. Don't be callin' me ma'am, unless you're out to get me in trouble with the missus." She studied the dress through narrowed eyelids. "Angelica was seven when she passed on. You're a little mite for ten, but I'm havin' doubts about this fitting you."

Jenny glanced down at the dress, then looked over at the wardrobe. "Maybe there's something else in there?"

With a shake of the head, Helene told her that all of the dresses would be the same size. "Every season, the little girl got the latest fashions." She clucked her tongue with disapproval. "Who knows what they did with the old ones? Some of the servants have girls and could ha' used the dresses—I mean they was hardly worn. But I guess the missus didn't want poor little urchins running around Leawick with her daughter's clothes on."

The maid's eyes took on a glint of humor. "No offense to yourself, love," she said with a wink. Helene helped Jenny into the dress anyway, pulling it down over her head. "Now, hold your breath," she said as she fastened the buttons down the back.

The bodice was loose enough to allow Jenny to breathe, but too tight for her to raise her arms up past her shoulders. The waist came two inches higher than her natural waist. Fortunately, the skirt was gathered and full, giving her some measure of comfort, though it met her legs at midcalf. "Angelica loved to wear lots of petticoats, too," Helene declared on her way to a chest of drawers. "Personally, I think it's going to make that dress look funny, flounced out any shorter than it is."

When the ordeal was finished, Jenny was led by the maid over to a glass in the corner. The girl staring back at her had wide, lost-looking eyes. And under the full skirt, her slender legs looked like matchsticks. She smothered a giggle with her hand.

Helene was grinning, too. "Better not laugh too hard, love— you'll pop a button. And hope you don't have to sneeze."

From another dresser drawer Helene brought out a pair of white stockings, and from a cedar chest, two black leather slippers. Jenny was able to make the shoes fit by curling up her toes. Too timid to ask for her old shoes, she hoped that she wouldn't have to wear these for too long.

"Now," Helene said, "let's comb your hair and get you down to breakfast before the missus demotes me to the scullery."

Before they could leave the room, however, the door opened and Mrs. Styles walked in. A flicker of some emotion crossed over her face at the sight of Jenny.

"You couldn't find a bigger dress?" she asked Helene. Before the maid could answer, Mrs. Styles said, "Well, no, I guess you couldn't. Mrs. Pruitt will be back today—perhaps she can let out the hem and seams, if there's any cloth to spare."

Then she walked over to put a hand on Jenny's shoulder. "The Dunleys want me to make arrangements with your family for you to stay here for a while. Is there anything from home that you'd like?"

Jenny's immediate thoughts were of the hillside where she picked blackberries and flowers, the new kittens in the barn, and the children she had tended for so long. Those were the only things she'd had of value at Uncle Roy's cottage, and of course, they didn't belong to her at all. "I don't have anything, ma'am," she answered.

Then the full weight of what the woman was saying sank in. She would be staying here? For how long?

The house was nicer than any place she had ever seen. And people treated her well, even though Lady Dunley was a little scary, hovering over her like she did last night and then having the scene with her husband.

But if she stayed here, she would miss her cousins terribly. These past few days Jenny hadn't been able to be with them much because of her work in the fields, but their times together had been precious moments nonetheless.

Then it came to her. There was no way that Uncle Roy was going to allow the Dunleys to keep her here! Why, the reason he had gotten her the job in the first place was so that she could begin to pay him back for taking her in as an infant. The family needed her wages, he had said most adamantly. Relief washed over Jenny, and she cleared her throat and looked up at the housekeeper. "I don't think Uncle Roy is going to want me to stay here. I've got to work."

The housekeeper's expression grew sad. "Sir Feldon will be offering your uncle higher wages than if you worked in the fields."

Jenny was conscious of a sinking feeling in the pit of her stomach. Even though Mrs. Styles had yet to speak with Uncle Roy, Jenny's fate was sealed.

A few moments later, when Mrs. Styles took Jenny down to breakfast, Sir Feldon and Mr. Wingate were already in their chairs. They stopped talking as soon as she entered the room. Mrs. Styles had just pulled out Jenny's chair when Lady Dunley appeared, splendid in an apricot gown. Her hair cascaded from a gem-studded comb, and her cheeks glowed with excitement.

"Oh, dear, have I kept all of you sweet people waiting?" she cooed as the housekeeper pulled out her chair, then slipped from the room.

Sir Feldon wore an expression of surprise. "You look wonderful, Lenora."

"Oh, I feel wonderful." She was opening Jenny's napkin and tucking it under her collar. "And doesn't our little darling look wonderful, too? That was always my favorite dress!"

Mr. Wingate's smile disappeared. Sir Feldon closed his eyes for a second and took a deep breath. When his eyes were open again, he said in a terse voice, *"Our* little darling?"

"Just a figure of speech, Feldon." She gave him a pleading smile. "Please don't be angry with me again."

He opened his mouth as if to say something, then closed it again and picked up the saltcellar. Mr. Wingate began spreading butter on his toast.

A maid had set a plate in front of Jenny, and Lady Dunley

picked up a knife and fork and began cutting up Jenny's bacon and eggs together. "Nice small bites, the way you like them," she said softly.

Sir Feldon stared for a moment, then set down the saltcellar and frowned. "Don't you think the child's old enough to eat her breakfast without your help?"

A wrinkle appeared at the center of his wife's forehead, but the knife and fork in her hand kept moving. "I always cut up her eggs and bacon."

"You always . . ." Sir Feldon's eyes closed again, this time for several seconds. "Who is she, Lenora?"

"I beg your pardon?"

"The child. What's her name?"

Ignoring her husband, Lady Dunley set down the knife and put the fork into Jenny's hand, closing the girl's slender fingers around the handle in the proper manner. "Now, be sure you chew long enough so that there aren't any large pieces that can choke you," she said.

Sir Feldon observed them through narrowed eyes. *"Lenora."*

Lenora gave her brother an exasperated look, then sighed at her husband. "What, Feldon? Can't you see we're trying to eat?"

"What is the girl's name?"

"I don't want to play these silly games, dear." To Jenny, she said, "Eat your food, dear, before it gets cold."

There was the sound of a boot stomping the floor. Startled, Lady Dunley looked up at her husband. "Tell me her name," the man seethed. "Right now!"

Lenora's face crumpled. "Why are you being so belligerent again?"

"The girl's name is Jenny. Say it, Lenora—say *Jenny.*"

"Jenny!" she cried with a sob as she shot out of her chair. "Jenny-Jenny-Jenny!" She pulled Jenny's chair from the table. "I hope you're happy, Feldon. You've ruined two meals in a row. I can't *wait* for lunch!"

Taking Jenny by the hand, Lady Dunley hustled her out of the room and up the stairs. They went into Angelica's room, and the woman threw herself into the rocking chair in the corner. She drew Jenny onto her lap, pressing Jenny's face into her shoulder.

"Now, now," she soothed, rocking back and forth and stroking Jenny's hair. "Don't let him upset you, darling. He doesn't understand anything, not anything at all."

Jenny fidgeted against the woman's shoulder. She wished she had never come to this house. She had caused another fight between Sir Feldon and Lady Dunley, and this time it looked as if they had been so angry that they weren't going to make up. She wished she had the courage to tell Lady Dunley that if she would only stop fussing over her at meals, her husband wouldn't get so upset.

Besides, it made her uncomfortable, being purred over with such affection by someone who was a virtual stranger to her. The way the woman looked at her was disturbing, too, for she knew that Lady Dunley wasn't really seeing *her*.

"Clouds for baby's pillow, the dew for baby's drink . . . ," the woman began singing softly.

Jenny knew who Lady Dunley was singing to, and it made her shudder to think about it.

13

BEFORE he had abducted Corrine Hammond, Joseph had known that it would be impossible to take the coach all the way to Treybrook without going through towns. Traveling the length of England from one back road to another would take twice as long, and that was assuming all the roads were good ones. But stopping in these towns gave his captive a better chance to escape.

He also had to consider the woman's occasional need for privacy. His low opinion of Mrs. Hammond was irrelevant; he was a decent man and would have to make certain concessions in the name of civility.

But how could he prevent her from taking advantage of these opportunities and trying to escape?

Across from him, her hands folded in her lap, she leaned forward and stared longingly out the window in the direction of Leawick. The futility of her posture would have moved him—*if* he had believed her story about the husband and child.

But he didn't believe it and he never would. What mother could abandon her own child for as long as she claimed to have done? She was a despicable woman, no better than a common prostitute, but he guessed that even female jackals tended lovingly to their cubs.

Joseph's occupation had occasionally taken him to slums in the industrial cities. Even among the lowest dregs of humanity, there was always evidence of the mother-child bond. All over Great Britain, countless women denied themselves, working long hours into the night with needle and thread or with other tools of the cottage laborers so that their children could eat.

He thought of his own mother, Miriam, at the time when his father was trying to start his own bakery. Even though she would be worn out from hours at his side in the shop, she still made time to tend to the needs of her children. He could remember her at his bedside through several nights when he'd had the mumps at the age of five.

A yearning came over him to stick his head out the window and order the driver to take him to Bristol, to his mother. He was feeling worse with each passing hour. His mother, though getting old and not as active now, would know just what to do. She would put him straight to bed and bring him honey with lemon juice to soothe his throat, herbs in strong tea to bring down his fever. And she would tell him not to worry about the patch of white he had found on his tongue in the mirror this morning.

Joseph looked across at Corrine, who was still looking out toward Leawick. *She's probably regretting the loss of the money she could have made there.* That and the loss of her freedom—not to mention apprehension about what lay ahead.

He was not fooled by the offer of her money for a little time in Leawick. Maybe there wasn't a victim there, waiting to be fleeced—he wasn't so sure now. But for whatever reason, she was *too* desperate to get there.

She could be telling the truth about its being her home, he conceded to himself. That would certainly account for the desperation. She could have brothers and kin there who could make things exceedingly more difficult for him.

He cleared his throat, and the pain caused his eyes to water. Again a wave of nausea gripped him. When it passed, leaving him with a clammy coldness throughout his body, he looked with longing at the seat across from him, where his captive sat. Perhaps all the rear-facing traveling he had been doing lately was catching up with him. "Mrs. Hammond?" His voice was beginning to sound hoarse.

Slowly, she turned away from the window and raised her eyebrows at him.

"I must ask you to trade seats with me."

"I beg your pardon?"

"The seats. I can't ride backwards for this long." He held out his hands to take Corrine's so that she could shift in the jostling coach without falling. She shook her head and got up from her seat, bracing her feet on the floor. Quickly he edged around her and crossed over to where she had been seated.

She sat in her new seat watching him, curiosity mingled with the fear in her eyes. Did she suspect that he was sick? He hoped not, for that might embolden her to attempt an escape. He was going to have to bend the truth to keep her from getting away. Unfortunately, lying had often been a necessary tool in his profession. He sometimes wondered if, by the time he retired, he would know what the truth was anymore.

"We've got to discuss something, Mrs. Hammond," he said as his fingers fastened the buttons to his frock coat. He usually found the inside of coaches to be stuffy, but today he couldn't get warm enough. "We should be passing through Harmerhill in less than an hour. We'll stop at an inn for a cup of tea, and I'll give you a few minutes to yourself, to freshen up."

As good an actress as he knew her to be, there was no way that she could disguise the hope that raced across her expression. "I appreciate that," she said quietly, her eyes not quite meeting his.

"There are some things you should know before we get there. You see, I'm not the worst thing that could happen to you."

"What do you mean?"

She still would not look straight at him, but he caught a tremor to her lips that gave him confidence that his deception would work. "In my line of work, I sometimes find myself working hand in hand with Scotland Yard."

The color drained from her face, and this time she met his eyes. "Scotland Yard?"

"I've become acquainted with several of the Yard's detectives over the years."

"But what does that have to do with me?" Her voice trembled anxiously.

"While tracking you and Mr. Moore down for Squire Nowells, I was able to compile quite a record on your activities over the past five or six years." That was true, along with the other things that he had told her. Now it was time to weave in the deception.

Leaning forward slightly for emphasis, he went on, "I just want you to know, just in case you get the idea to ask anyone for help or to try to escape, that it wouldn't be in your best interests. I wish to get this assignment over with as soon as possible, so if I find that you've slipped away, I'll simply give Scotland Yard all the information I've uncovered." What he didn't tell her was that unless one of Corrine's victims made a direct complaint to the authorities, the Yard would have no grounds to arrest her.

After a moment of silence, Joseph was surprised at the bitter laugh that came from her. "Is that supposed to be a threat, Mr. Price? If I do something to rescue myself from your clutches, then I'll likely end up a prisoner of the law. What is the difference?"

"I'll tell you the difference," he replied, settling back in the seat again. "The penalty for extortion is hanging, for women as well as men. With all the evidence that Scotland Yard will have against you, that's what will happen."

"Hanging," Corrine whispered. Her hand went to her neck. "But isn't that what will happen to me in Treybrook?"

"No, I can assure you that it will not." It was a relief to say something truthful for a change, although what lay ahead for her was probably *worse* than a quick, clean death from the rope. He had no intention of letting her know that. In fact, he had to follow up with another half-truth.

"By going with me to Treybrook, you at least have a chance. Squire Nowells—the son, of course—doesn't want the law involved because of the scandal that would follow. You could talk with him—plead your cause, tell him that Moore forced you into it. Whatever suits you."

"You mean lie to him?"

He couldn't stop the cynical grin that came to his face. "Oh, I forgot. You've changed."

"Yes," she replied simply, looking down at her hands. "I have, with the grace of God. But you'll never believe that, will you?"

"It doesn't matter what I believe. What I want to know is

. . . do you understand the consequences of any attempt to escape?"

She nodded gravely. "May I implore you one last time to take me to see my daughter and husband? I'll not give you any trouble."

"No." The disappointment was so great upon her face that he found himself adding, "Sorry."

~

They stopped at Harmerhill at the Swan's Nest Inn. The coachman watered and fed the horses while Joseph escorted Corrine inside the stone and cob building. He paid the proprietress threepence for the use of the water closet, watching Corrine's face for any sign of a plea for help. There was no expression at all from her downcast eyes.

As she started up the stairs with a glance back over her shoulder at him, Joseph pretended to step toward the dining room. Instead, he turned and waited just inside the parlor for her return. *Five minutes,* he told himself, folding his arms and leaning against the wall.

She was back in three. Surprised and pleased that she had caused no trouble, he ordered tea for both of them in the dining room. He could afford to be magnanimous; two and a half more days, and he would be rid of her and on a train to Bristol to be nursed back to health by his family.

They sat at a corner table without speaking. Mrs. Hammond studied the activities of the other patrons scattered about the room with sad eyes. Watching her carefully, Joseph could detect no meaningful glances from her to anyone, no signaling with her expression that she needed help. Instead, she seemed to show a longing to experience the everyday goings-on of people while she still could.

She could be acting for his benefit, of course—putting him at ease so that he would get careless somewhere later on in the journey and let his guard down. He took a sip of lemon-laced tea, and his eyes watered as the hot liquid bathed his raw throat. The only way he was going to let his guard down, he thought wryly, was if he dropped dead in his tracks.

Then he frowned. That was beginning to seem like a distinct possibility.

~

After another three hours of traveling, they stopped for lunch in the town of Wem. This time Joseph bought sandwiches that the driver and Corrine could have on the road. Again she came back after he allowed her the few minutes to herself. He had her wait in the parlor as he bathed the dust of the road from his face. He would not allow Corrine to be alone with the driver at any time, for it had crossed his mind that not only could she offer Pete money to take her to Leawick, but she could hire the driver to kill him on some deserted stretch of the road.

~

"You're not having any lunch, Mr. Price?" Corrine's voice startled him as the coach got on its way again. It was becoming difficult for him to stay awake with the rhythmic sway and his ever-increasing fatigue.

"I'm not hungry." The truth was, he was ravenous, but his burning throat wouldn't allow him to think about swallowing. He looked down at Corrine's hands, which still held the sandwiches wrapped in brown paper. Why was she concerned about his having lunch? Surely she would rather have him starve. "You go ahead and eat, though."

She unwrapped one of the sandwiches and took a couple of bites, then wrapped it again and put it with the others in her basket.

"What's wrong with the food?" Joseph asked.

"Nothing."

He wasn't falling for her play for sympathy. "Don't tell me . . . you're too choked up about your daughter to be hungry."

The look she turned upon him was withering. "Yes, I am, Mr. Price. But what would it matter to you?"

"It doesn't," he said, yawning. "Not one mite."

Her lids narrowed over her gray eyes. "Why do you have to be so cruel?"

"Me? How can *you* sit there and accuse me of cruelty?"

"That was in my past, Mr. Price," she answered in a quiet voice. "I'm not proud of it."

"Tell that to Squire Nowells's widow."

"I will," she answered quietly, her jaw set. "If I'm given the chance. And I will tell her that if I could give my own life so that her husband could live again, I would do it."

He let out a snort of derision, then held up a hand. "Please, stop the high drama. It doesn't become you, Mrs. Hammond."

"It's not drama—it's the truth. I'll regret my part in Squire Nowells's death every day for the rest of my life."

"Because you've changed."

"I have."

"How?"

Taking a deep breath, she replied, "I've become a Christian."

Joseph nodded knowingly. "Oh, so that's what the theatrics with that Bible was all about."

"Theatrics?"

"You looked so devout, there on the train. Charming little act. Be sure and repeat it in front of the squire . . . it just may work on him."

He was prepared for anger, not the sadness that washed over her features. "It wasn't an act, Mr. Price, and I'm not devout. Not like I wish to be."

"Then just what are you?"

For a moment, it seemed that her eyes were locked upon something just above his shoulder, something that only she could see. Then she looked straight into his eyes. "I'm still a child, spiritually, though my sins have been forgiven. I read my Bible and pray because it brings me closer to my God."

"How convenient for you, your sins being forgiven and all of that." He snapped his fingers and added, "You can wipe out the past, just like that."

She shook her head. "God has forgiven my sins, but my past is still with me as far as the people I've hurt are concerned. I can understand their wanting revenge. If the desire wasn't so strong within me to see my husband and daughter, I would willingly go and let them do what they liked with me."

Her words were strangely touching, and Joseph found himself almost believing her. But he reminded himself of the trail of extortion victims this woman had left behind for eight years, then he folded his arms and said, "I understand now."

She tilted her head at him. "I beg your pardon?"

"I can understand how you came to be so successful in your . . . dubious career. You're quite good."

His caustic remark obviously stung her. Her eyes glistened,

and she turned to stare out the window. Or was she still act-ing? Whatever it was, it didn't matter to him.

~

They stopped at Adderly in Cheshire to spend the night.
Joseph was pleased that they were making good time. He
gave the driver some money to purchase supper and to stable
the horses—the man would bed down in the loft of the stable
with other coachmen passing through town.

"I can't have you spending the whole night in a room to
yourself," he informed Corrine as the coach came to a stop in
front of the Coat of Arms. "We'll have to pretend to be husband and wife." At the alarm in her eyes, he growled, "Don't
worry . . . I haven't any desire to go near you. I'll bed down
on a blanket in front of the door."

"I haven't tried to escape yet," she argued. "If I pay for my
own room . . . ?"

"It's not the money. I can't let you have a whole night to
make distance if you decide to slip away."

Turning a deaf ear to her pleas, he took her by the elbow
and led her toward the portico of the inn. His knees felt
wobbly as they walked up the steps.

"I'd like to have some hot soup sent up to our room," he
told the proprietor inside. "My wife has some sandwiches in
her basket, but we want some soup, along with something to
drink." Turning his face toward her, he couldn't resist a
mocking smile. "Would you like to order anything, dear?"

"Just some tea," she answered woodenly.

Their room had sparse furnishings—a bed, a chest of drawers, a chair, and a washstand. Joseph closed the door behind
them and turned to Corrine. "Now, before your sense of pro-

priety is damaged forever, let me assure you that I intend to
pull the carpet over to this door. A blanket and pillow will be
all that I request of you."

They shared another silent meal. Joseph could only finish
half of his bowl of soup, but hoped he had gotten enough
nourishment so that he would feel better in the morning. After
a servant came for the tray, he untied his cravat, draped his
coat across the back of the chair, and pulled the Turkish rug
over to the door. He stretched out on his side with his back
to Corrine, leaving her to extinguish the lamp and change into
a nightdress if she wished.

Joseph regretted what sleeping in his shirt and trousers was
going to do for his appearance, but he had decided to save
the clothes in his gripsack for the last day of the trip, when
he would be meeting again with Squire Nowells. It wasn't a
good idea to look disheveled in front of a client. Until then,
he would just have to wear wrinkled clothing. At least his
coat would be spared somewhat.

Gathering the blanket up to his neck, he wished that he had
left the coat on, too. It was cold here on the wooden floor, in
spite of the huge fire that still burned in the fireplace. When
he had built the fire, piling it up with as many logs as would
be safe, Corrine Hammond had stared at him as if he had lost
his mind.

The room went dark except for the light from the fire.
Huddled against the door, he listened to the sound of a quilt
rustling behind him for a second, and then quiet.

An hour later the fire had died down, and Joseph still lay
there, wide awake and shivering in spite of his blanket. He
considered going downstairs to ask the proprietor for another

one—after all, he was fully dressed—but that would require leaving what little warmth he had.

After two hours, he could still hear Corrine's even breathing over the sound of his teeth chattering. Through the misery of his physical discomfort, the thought struck him that she hadn't tried to seduce him into letting her go. She had offered all of her money, but not herself. For a woman who had used seduction as a means of getting her way for years, why wasn't she attempting it now, when the stakes were so high?

He recalled how she had actually blushed on the train when he had tried to bait her by playing the part of a lecher. His ego had been bruised even though he had such a low opinion of the woman.

What did he think of her now? He was relieved that she hadn't tried to escape yet, though that could still be part of some greater plan on her part. And he was confused by the chaste way she acted around him. It seemed so real. Was she *that* good at acting?

His teeth chattered all the more violently now, and he hugged his arms to his sides. He didn't know what was worse—the chills that gripped his body or the rawness of his throat.

From behind him came the sound of a foot softly hitting the wooden floor. Before he knew it, the weight of a feather quilt settled over him. *What is she up to?* he wondered, lying as still as possible. Had she at last become desperate enough to resort to her old ways? Did he even have the physical strength to push her away if she attempted to get close to him?

He heard another sound—the snapping of dying embers as fresh logs were stacked upon them. Then the footsteps crossed the room, the bed creaked, and all was silent.

14

CORRINE woke up to find Joseph Price seated in the chair beside the window. The blanket and quilt were wrapped around his shoulders, and he was staring down at the courtyard below.

She pulled the bedsheet up over her shoulders to cover her high-necked nightgown and eased up on her pillow. "Mr. Price?"

"What?" He turned his head toward her. "Oh, you're awake." Slowly he eased out of the chair. He folded the covers and set them on the chair, then put on his coat and walked out of the room.

Corrine dressed hurriedly and started downstairs. She assumed that Joseph would be waiting in the dining room—or even at the bottom of the staircase. When he was not in either place, she realized that he must be waiting in the coach for her. She went into the dining room and bought some bread, cheese, and ripe purple plums with her own money.

A door was propped open at the back of the dining room, revealing a glimpse of a kitchen garden and patches of blue sky. It would be so easy for her to slip through it and be gone. Even if Mr. Price alerted Scotland Yard, it would take days to organize a search. The thought of having more detectives on her trail was frightening, but the thought of possibly never seeing Jenny again was worse.

During her years with Gerald Moore, she had socialized almost exclusively with the type of people who used situations to their own advantage. She usually knew how to spot them and had no doubt that she could, in a short amount of time, find someone who could be bribed to whisk her away from this town on a horse or in a carriage. She stared with longing at the back door while waiting for the innkeeper's wife to count out her change. The morning air would feel wonderful on her face, not to mention the sensation of freedom.

But he would know exactly where she would be heading and how desperately she longed to be there. Even if she were able to get away and hide out in another town for months, he would be waiting there in Leawick for her. She might elude Mr. Price, but there could be no freedom for her without the liberty to see her daughter and to ask her husband's forgiveness for her past wrongs.

She prayed silently, her misery like a steel weight in the pit of her stomach. *O God, don't let me die without seeing Jenny again. My heart is sore for the sight of her, and my arms ache to hold her. Please help me!*

On her way to the coach, she reminded herself that there was *some* hope. Mr. Price was gravely ill; she was sure of it after last night. She forced herself not to wish that he would die, though it was a struggle within her.

What if, instead of dying, he got so ill that he couldn't prevent her escape? Surely she could get to Leawick before he had an opportunity to contact Scotland Yard. *If he's as sick as he looked last night, his thoughts would be more on himself than about me.* At least she would have *some* time to spend with her daughter and husband before he recovered and came to capture her again or before the authorities could get to her.

But what would it do to Jenny and Thomas to have her enter their lives only to leave again? Wouldn't it greatly multiply the damage to them that she'd already done?

She felt hope sinking within her. Her only chance was to go with Joseph Price to Treybrook and convince Squire Nowells's son of her deep contrition over what happened to his father. Remorse could not bring back a life, but perhaps the younger squire would listen to her testimony about becoming a Christian and forgive her. She would have to pray that God would soften his heart so that he would receive her words without skepticism.

Doubt immediately assaulted her mind. Could she really hope for forgiveness from the squire's family? Bitterness rose like gall in her throat. If only this hadn't happened now, just as she'd been so close to seeing her daughter!

If only Joseph Price had left her alone! She chided herself for the foolish compassion that had gotten her out of bed last night to give the odious man the quilt and to stoke the fire. Her thoughts must have been muddled with sleep, for she couldn't conceive of helping him today.

He was only doing his job, as he had pointed out yesterday, but his cruelty was unnecessary. She couldn't blame anyone for being disgusted at her past. In truth, it was getting harder and harder to believe it herself—could she truly have been the woman who had performed such heinous acts? Still, Joseph Price's condemnation was almost too much to bear. Jesus had told the men who wanted to stone the adulteress that the person without sin should throw the first stone. Mr. Price was throwing stones at her, but surely he had done things in the past for which he had cause to be ashamed.

Corrine again forced herself not to hope that he would die. It was sinful to wish that upon anyone, and she sent up a reluctant petition for forgiveness.

When she walked out toward the carriage drive and the waiting coach, Pete sent her a leering grin. The driver had not said a word to her since she had hired him—no doubt Mr. Price had arranged that—but his eyes spoke volumes whenever he got the chance to look at her.

Gathering her skirt, she stepped inside. Her captor sat with his arms folded and his head resting against the back of his seat, sound asleep! And the pistol lay beside him!

The coach started moving as soon as Corrine closed the door. As the wheels began to rattle, she stared coldly across at the sleeping man. An image rose unbidden to her mind—a fantasy of Joseph Price jerking his eyes open at the sound of a gunshot, having just enough time before dying to gape down in horror at the growing red stain on his chest. Corrine shook away the thought, wondering how many times on this journey she would be compelled to repent of her thoughts against him.

Across from her, Mr. Price shifted in his sleep. His mouth opened a bit, and Corrine could hear the faint sounds of snoring over the turning of the wheels. Corrine frowned wryly. The man was indeed fortunate that she had become a Christian. Even in her most hedonistic days, she could never think of purposely taking someone's life, but surely she had the right to protect her own.

She stared at the pistol again. Would it be stealing if she took the gun but disposed of it? A smile curved her lips as she imagined Mr. Price's surprise when he realized it was gone.

And how would he feel when he realized his life had been in her hands?

It was too much of a temptation to resist. Slowly, carefully, she leaned forward and took the pistol by the handle. She had never held a gun before and was surprised at how heavy it was—and how nervous it made her. She set it gingerly on her knees and watched through the window as they passed the outskirts of town.

Five minutes later a stand of trees and overgrown weeds became visible from the window. Taking the pistol by the barrel, she extended her arm out the window, then drew back her hand and slung the weapon out as forcefully as possible.

~

She was just finishing breakfast when Joseph finally awoke. He sat up straight and rubbed his eyes, then blinked at her curiously.

"Yes, I'm still here." She regarded him through narrowed eyelids as she brushed the crumbs of her breakfast from her lap.

He looked out the window and back at her, his expression sheepish. "How long have I been asleep?" he whispered.

"About an hour. Why are you whispering?"

His only answer was to put a hand up to his throat and frown.

So, he was getting worse. Besides the strawberry flush to his cheeks, he looked drawn and weak for a man with such a muscular build. "Don't you think it's ridiculous to keep on going when you're obviously very sick? You need to see a doctor, get some rest."

"After," he whispered.

"After you take me to Treybrook, you mean. I don't think you're going to last that long."

He shrugged and turned his head back to the window. In spite of the wool frock coat, he kept his arms huddled to his body.

At last he put his hand down to his side. He had remembered the pistol. He jerked his whole body around and scanned the seat next to him.

"Is something wrong?" she asked innocently, watching him hunch over to search the floor.

"Where is it?" he rasped. He glared at her, then shot an arm out for the valise at her feet. Tearing at the leather straps, he pulled open the bag and looked inside, then started rummaging around with his hand.

Corrine reached for the bag when he was finished. "Perhaps you'd like to search the hamper, too. There's some leftover bread and cheese in there." She smirked, enjoying his panic. "Would you like some breakfast, Mr. Price? The cheese was rather good."

"Where is it?"

"Breakfast? Why, it's right there in your hands. I'm sorry that I couldn't resist finishing off the plums. They were quite delicious, actually."

He threw the basket at her feet, his face a mask of rage. "What did you do with my gun?"

Corrine's gaze drifted toward the window. His eyes widened in response. "You threw it out?"

She nodded.

He made a move toward the door, but her voice stopped him. "It was a long time ago, so you'll be wasting your time by asking the driver to stop."

Defeat and fatigue were etched on the lines of Joseph Price's face as he slumped back in the seat. He stared at her with an expression Corrine was glad she couldn't read.

"I could have used it on you, Mr. Price. Do you realize that?" He didn't answer. "Even if the gun hadn't been here, I could have jumped out the door easily while you were asleep. Your friend Pete wouldn't have even noticed."

His brow furrowed. "Why didn't you?"

"Two reasons," Corrine replied, setting the hamper upright. "I didn't escape because you would only have followed me to Leawick—perhaps even been waiting for me by the time I got there. Or you would have contacted Scotland Yard, if they're indeed after me as you said."

"Why didn't you kill me?"

"Morals, Mr. Price. I realize that you don't think I have any, but you're still alive, aren't you?"

He stared at her for a moment. "You covered me up last night, too. Why?"

She didn't know herself, so she shrugged lightly. "You were obviously cold. I would have done the same thing for an animal."

"You're hoping that I'll change my mind, aren't you?" he whispered. "I can't do that."

"I know," she replied with a heavy voice.

A new thought came to her, and she was relieved that she hadn't taken advantage of her earlier opportunities to escape. After all, it would be better to go back to Leawick without having to look over her shoulder for the rest of her life. The only way she could think of going home would be with the assurance that no one was pursuing her.

I'll offer my money to the Nowells family. Sixty pounds of the

167

money was now hidden away in the pocket of a jacket in the bottom of her trunk—she had put it there this morning for safekeeping. While it couldn't match the amount the elderly squire had given her, it would show that she was sincere in wanting to pay for her misdeeds.

She regretted the thought of going back to Thomas and Jenny with empty hands when the money could alleviate the poverty they no doubt still lived in. But she had no choice. She had told Bernice of her longing to make reparations to her victims, and now that an opportunity to do so seemed to be thrust upon her, she had to take advantage of it.

She knew, however, that she couldn't rely on the money alone. If she did, Squire Nowells would assume that she was simply trying to bribe her way to freedom, just as Mr. Price had thought when she had offered him money. Squire Nowells *had* to see for himself that she wasn't the same woman who had caused his father's death.

Biting her lip, she looked across at Joseph. He could help her if he wanted to. But would he?

"The man who hired you . . . Squire Nowells's son," she began, "he's the one who hired you to look for Gerald Moore, too, isn't he?"

Mr. Price looked back at her through half-closed lids and nodded.

"The reason Gerald beat me was because I was going to try to leave him. You came in after the beating, but you know it happened."

"What does that have to do with anything?" he rasped.

"Surely the fact that Gerald tried to kill me is proof that I've changed . . . don't you think?"

"Of course it is," he answered, but the corners of his mouth twitched, and Corrine realized that he was trying to keep from laughing. She was starting to regret not using the gun on him. Swallowing her anger, she continued to plead her case. "I didn't say that to be funny, Mr. Price. You're the one who said I should try to reason with Squire Nowells. He might forgive me if I can convince him that I'm not the same woman I once was."

When he did not answer but continued to look at her with that maddening expression, she pressed on, "You could help."

His eyebrows lifted as he mouthed, *"Me?"*

"Why not?" Corrine nodded and leaned forward. "You could tell him that I had the chance to escape and didn't. And that I could have killed you with your own gun."

A sardonic look came over his face. "And that you covered me up last night, too, right? Is that why you've become Princess Compassion and Morality, so that I'll put in a good word for you with the squire?"

"I covered you because you were cold," she said through clenched teeth. "I didn't even come up with the idea of your talking to the squire's son about me until just a minute ago."

"Of course you didn't."

"It's true!"

Sighing, Joseph held up a hand to prevent any further words that were on her lips. "I'll be only too glad to tell him about the beating and what a model prisoner you've been—aside from throwing away my pistol, of course."

Corrine let out the breath she had been holding. "Thank you."

~

They stopped for the night in the small market town of Amberton, two hours earlier than the day before. Mr. Price could hardly stay upright in the coach, and he hadn't tried to speak since their conversation about Squire Nowells. Around five o'clock, he reached out the window and pulled on the cord to signal the driver.

As an unsteady Joseph Price accompanied Corrine through the front door to the Briar Rose Inn, he pushed some money at her and told her to deal with the innkeeper.

"Do you want a meal?" she asked.

He shook his head. "I just want to lie down."

Struck by the irony that *she* would be taking control of the arrangements of her own abduction, Corrine walked back outside and handed Pete some coins for the stable and his meal. He had already set her trunk on the ground, and he gave her a suggestive grin when she handed him the money.

Corrine wheeled back around, relieved that she hadn't tried to bribe the driver to help her. *Being alone with him would be worse than with Mr. Price!* She went back to the parlor of the inn and paid the proprietor for two rooms. He wasn't in shape to sleep on the floor tonight, she told herself, and *she* certainly wasn't going to.

Despite herself, Corrine ordered some soup sent up to his room even though it looked like she would have to help him manage a spoon. "You haven't eaten all day," she whispered to his frowning face when the proprietor turned his back for a moment. "You need some nourishment."

~

She was in her room, taking a dress for tomorrow from the open trunk, when she heard a faint succession of knocks in the hall. Someone was waiting at Joseph's door, and she finally stepped out into the hallway. A young woman stood there with a tray.

"I think he's lying down," Corrine told the maid. She walked over to test the doorknob; it was unlocked. "We're coming in, Mr. Price," she called, then opened the door.

Joseph was indeed lying down, under the covers and fully clothed. Only the collars of his shirt and frock coat were visible at his pillow. His face was pale as death, and his teeth chattered violently.

"I'll help him with the soup," Corrine told the maid, taking the tray and setting it on a nearby dresser.

The girl eyed the man in bed suspiciously. "What's wrong with him?"

"I don't know. His throat is sore, and it looks like he's got a fever."

"His cheeks is awful red, too." Fear came over the maid's face, and she backed away with her hand up to her throat. "Scarlet fever!"

Corrine turned her eyes in Joseph's direction again. "I don't think so, but I don't know much about it." She shrugged her shoulders. "My family must have strong constitutions, because I don't remember any of my sisters or myself ever getting sick with anything besides a cold."

Turning her back to lift the cover from the tureen on the tray, she took an appreciative whiff of the soup. "I believe this will make him feel better."

When she turned around again, the maid was gone. Corrine stared at the open door for a second, then took the napkin from the tray and walked over to the bed. "Mr. Price?"

He didn't answer, so she reached out a tentative hand to touch his shoulder. He looked so awful, such a contrast from just a few days ago when he had called upon her in Adam Burke's sitting room. The memory of how attractive she had found him flashed through her mind, and she chided herself for the thought.

"You've got to sit up so that I can help you with your supper," she ordered, a little louder.

Finally a low moan escaped from his mouth. With great effort he pulled himself up on his pillow. Corrine reached over him for the other pillow and pushed it under his shoulders to give him some support.

"Now, I'm going to bring the tray over here—," she began, but a noise from the doorway caught her attention. The proprietor of the inn stepped just inside the room, a handkerchief over his mouth.

"I'm sorry, madam, but you will have to take the gentleman out of here."

Corrine gaped at the man. "But he's sick."

"That is why he must leave. I can't allow others to risk catching his illness."

"I don't think he can move. Isn't there a doctor who can come look at him?"

The man's voice was sympathetic but firm. "Madam, there is no doctor in Amberton. The midwife usually looks after folks, but she's expecting a baby herself. She couldn't possibly risk exposing her unborn child."

"I understand," Corrine told him. "But how can it hurt to let him get a good night's rest? We could keep the door—"

"I'm sorry, but there's too great a risk. We have customers and employees here who have families. The gentleman will have to leave this place immediately, or I will be forced to call the constable. And you must go with him."

She was about to tell him that there was nothing wrong with *her,* when the realization hit her that she had certainly been exposed to whatever illness Mr. Price had. People would likely be just as afraid of being close to her as they obviously were of Mr. Price. A shiver ran through her—not at the idea of becoming ill, for she firmly believed that she was immune to any sickness, but at the thought of the law getting involved.

Corrine looked down at the sick man in the bed, and she briefly entertained the idea of taking the coach and disappearing down the road. Surely *someone* in this village would then see to Mr. Price. Then she remembered the way the driver had looked at her. "All right," she sighed. "Will you send for our coachman? He's at the stables, wherever they are."

"Right away," answered the proprietor, stepping back into the hall. "I'll send for you when he arrives. Please pack up your things and be ready."

Not knowing what else to do, Corrine slipped into her room next door and repacked her trunk, closing the lid and setting her valise on top. Then she came back into Mr. Price's room and looked around. His gripsack lay on the floor, unopened. She set it next to the valise so that it could be sent downstairs, too, and she and the driver could concentrate on loading Mr. Price back into the coach.

When everything was ready, she decided she might as well coax some of the soup into the man until the driver arrived. Likely Pete had already unhitched the horses and would need a little time to get the coach ready again. Where they would go from here, she had no idea. Mr. Price would just have to figure something out, despite his illness.

Corrine brought the tray over to the bed and sat down. "Open your mouth, now," she ordered, testing the soup with

173

the edge of her finger to make sure it wasn't too hot. Listlessly he took the broth, wincing as he swallowed, and Corrine began to wonder at the maid's words about scarlet fever. Fear began creeping in at the thought. Maybe her constitution wasn't so strong after all. But even if it was scarlet fever, there was nothing she could do to keep from catching it. *Oh, please, God, don't let me get sick. I've got to see Jenny.*

When Mr. Price had taken in three or four spoonfuls, he looked up at her and gave a slight shake of the head. "Can't eat any more," he rasped through trembling lips.

"Are you sure?"

He nodded this time, looked up at her again and whispered, "Thank you."

"Oh, think nothing of it," she replied with a hint of sarcasm as she wiped his mouth with a napkin. "After all, I've got to keep up the theatrics of being decent so you'll put in a good word for me to Mr. Nowells."

He winced again, and Corrine wondered if it was his throat or the memory of his cruel words that caused the pain. She rather hoped it was the latter.

The innkeeper appeared in the doorway again, still with the handkerchief over his mouth. "I'm afraid your driver has left, madam."

"What?" Setting the tray on the foot of the bed, Corrine stood, openmouthed. "What did you say?"

"I sent someone to fetch him, but he wasn't at the stables. The coach is gone as well."

"But he has to be there—where else would he be?"

"He's nowhere in town, madam, that's all I know. Was he aware of Mr. Price's illness?"

"I don't know." Corrine turned to seek Joseph's help, but he had sunk back down into the covers and was lying there in a huddle. "What are we going to do?" she turned back to ask the innkeeper. "Are there any other coaches to hire in this town?"

He shook his head. "We're just a small village. What's more, I daresay no driver would want to run the risk of catching the fever."

"Then, we have no choice but to stay here."

The voice coming through the handkerchief was sympathetic, but adamant. "Madam, that will be impossible. I'm sorry, but I have to insist that you leave."

Raising her hands helplessly, she pleaded, "We *tried* to do that, sir, but our coachman left. Would you throw us out into the street?"

He stood there silent for several seconds, glanced over at Joseph then sighed. "Forgive me for asking, but what relation are you to the gentleman?"

"Are you asking if we're married?"

He gave a sheepish nod. "I have a reason for asking."

Corrine frowned. "We shared a coach, sir, and that's all. I already have a husband, but even if I didn't, I would not be romantically inclined toward this man. Never. Does that answer your question?"

"Yes." After another pause, he said, "You see, there's an empty cottage about three miles from here. It's not a palace, but it's clean. The woman who lived there passed away last month."

"Then who does it belong to now?"

"It belongs to me, though I barely have the will to go out there and tend to it since—" His voice softened. "My mother lived there, you see. She had lived in that cottage since she was a young bride and didn't want to leave it."

Corrine nodded, touched by the compassion she now

recognized in the landlord's eyes. "You're offering to let us stay in her house?"

"It's the best I can do. I can't allow my family and patrons to catch the fever. Do you understand?"

"Yes, of course."

"The house is still furnished with Mother's belongings. I can have food sent to the doorstep, as long as you wait until the person delivering it is gone before you go outside to get it."

"How will we get there? I don't think Mr. Price can walk very far."

"I'll drive you there in the wagon," he answered. "I'll put a blanket in the back for him to lie on. I've been exposed more than anyone else, and he'll be downwind as long as I'm driving."

"That is very kind of you. Mr. Price will be able to pay for your services."

The man shook his head. "I've had to burn the money you gave me for these rooms. When he is recovered . . . *if* he recovers . . . you may have the gentleman send me a check."

A new wave of fear caught her, this time stronger. Was scarlet fever so bad that people feared even touching the money that belonged to a stricken person? Her conscience burned her about exposing the innkeeper and his employees. In her past, she had never bothered with learning the little rules in life that most people followed, such as keeping sick people isolated.

"I pray that we haven't given this illness to any of you," she told him with sincerity.

His shoulders came up in a shrug. "You always run that risk when you board strangers every night. And God willing, we haven't been exposed long enough to catch anything. It's all in the Lord's hands."

Something about the tone of his voice when he spoke about God struck a chord in Corrine. *He's a Christian,* she thought with wonder. Of course. There were others out there besides herself and the residents of Adam Burke's house.

"Sir, may I ask . . . do you know the God of whom you speak?"

She could tell by the innkeeper's eyes that he was smiling behind the handkerchief. "I do. And I take it that you know him as well?"

She smiled. "I'm still an infant, but trying to grow."

"Ah, I remember the days," he replied. "How exciting it is to learn more and more about the Savior. I'll keep you and your friend in my prayers. Would you like me to send a Bible out to the cottage?"

"I've already got one, thank you."

"The Gospel of John is inspiring to new Christians. Have you read it?"

Corrine smiled again. "I have."

15

THE tiny stone cottage was just as the innkeeper had described it, nothing close to a palace, but in fine condition. Set between two low hills and shaded by oak and elm trees of the encroaching forest, it looked dark in the dusk of the evening hour. Its yard was choked with weeds, but the innkeeper, Mr. Rhodes, yelled back from the wagon seat that its door and two windows were snug against animals.

He backed the wagon to within inches of the door, apologizing profusely for not getting down to assist Corrine in taking Mr. Price inside. "I'll get your trunk down as soon as you're finished," he told her.

Corrine assured Mr. Rhodes that he had already done more than could be expected, then urged Joseph to a sitting position in back of the wagon. "Come on now, you've got to help me," she commanded.

Letting out an occasional groan from the effort, Joseph leaned on her for support and stumbled into the cottage. Corrine led him past a table and two benches, to a simple low-poster bed. Some bedclothes were folded on the top of a small chest of drawers, but Joseph dropped down onto the bare ticking before she could mention anything about sheets.

A thump came from the doorway. Mr. Rhodes set the

trunk on the floor and in a moment came back with the other bags. "There's some food for today in your basket," he said. Then he tipped his hat and was gone.

"Thank you!" Corrine called out as the door closed. It struck her that the phrase was becoming increasingly natural to her lips. She had said "thank you" more in the past three weeks than she had in her entire life.

The sound of wagon wheels and horses' hooves died away, and suddenly Corrine realized how alone she was. *With only a sick man for company . . . and one whose company I'd just as soon not share.*

She glanced at the bed and noticed for the first time that Joseph Price still had his boots on. Sighing, she walked over and began to pull on them. Why did she bother? He had already ruined the reunion with her daughter and husband, and if he'd had his way, she would still be traveling toward an uncertain future in Treybrook.

She looked over at the door and a wave of longing washed over her. How easy it would be just to escape! With his money and hers combined, she could walk to the next town and hire a coach to take her to Leawick. Mr. Price would die here without anyone to feed and care for him. But no matter how much she might want to leave, she couldn't do it.

She wrestled the pillow from under his head—a little more forcefully than necessary. At least she could put a clean case over the ticking even if the bottom sheet would have to wait for a while. "You'd better be glad that I'm not like I used to be," she muttered to the sleeping man. "The old Corrine Hammond would be heading out of the door with her valise under her arm."

His only response was to moan and thrash about restlessly.

Corrine leaned down and laid a hand on his forehead. "You're burning up, all right. I don't know anything about nursing, but it stands to reason that we should try to cool your fever."

She went across the room to a small cabinet against the wall where a few china dishes and cups were displayed. As she touched one of the delicate cups, her eyes began to burn, and she blinked at the tears. A woman had lived, borne children, and died here. She didn't even know the woman's name, and now she was using her belongings as if they were her own.

Corrine shook her head in frustration and swallowed back her emotions. This was no time to be thinking melancholy thoughts. A sick man, albeit her enemy, was depending upon her.

She opened the top drawer of the chest and found some neatly folded rags. The next drawer held several homemade candles and a tin box of matches. Only then did Corrine realize she had been squinting—the two dusty windows did not let in enough light for the evening hour. She removed the useless stub from the candleholder on the table and pushed a new beeswax candle down into it. Corrine could clean the windows in the morning. For now, one candle was enough for the tiny cottage.

She scanned the room. There was no pump; there had to be a well outside. Setting the candleholder back on the table, she stepped outside and looked around. Sure enough, about eight feet from the corner of the house, she located a round cover of planked wood. Then she realized that she had no bucket. *I've become useless from having Rachel wait on me for so long,* she thought on her way back to the cottage. A bucket sat on a bench against the wall under one of the windows, with a dipper and coiled rope hanging nearby.

When she finally had a bucket of cool water drawn, Corrine struggled to bring it inside to the table, then took a dipper and drank deeply. She poured a dipper of water into a bowl, took a dish towel from the cabinet, and went to Mr. Price's bedside.

To her surprise, the man was awake. He lay trembling on his side in his wrinkled suit of clothes.

"C-cold," he rasped, his eyes pleading to her. "Please g-give me a blanket."

"Of course." She set the bowl of water and dish towel on a little stool, then found the blanket that Mr. Rhodes had put in the back of the wagon. "We might as well let you use this one," she said as she spread it over him. "But I think that's all you should have."

"Still c-cold."

"I don't think it's good for you to lie there and roast under a heap of blankets," she told him. "Your skin's already burning up."

He turned his eyes toward the fireplace. A plank of wood was propped tightly against the opening, no doubt to keep rodents out of the dwelling. "Fire?"

"I'll make a small one later, when it gets cooler." Corrine couldn't help feeling sorry for the man, no matter how much she disliked him, but she couldn't allow any feelings of pity to make his illness worse. Pulling the stool over to the bedside, she picked up the dish towel and dipped a folded corner into the water. As she expected, he flinched and tried to turn his face away.

"Now, Mr. Price," she said, taking his bearded chin in her hand to keep his head from moving. "You're not afraid of a little cold water, are you?"

In no time the rag had lost its coolness, and she had to dip it in the fresh water again. She brought a cup over to the bed and, pulling him up by his shoulders, coaxed him to drink.

"You're going to get well if it kills me, Mr. Price," she declared as she bathed his face again. "And by then perhaps you'll have learned that God can change the heart of a sinful woman." He swallowed and groaned pitifully, and she picked up the cup to coax a little more water through his lips. "And, yes, you're going to tell Squire Nowells everything you've learned. You owe me that much."

~

When he had fallen asleep again, Corrine built a small fire, and with the remaining bed coverings she made a pallet for herself on the hard floor beside the table. She decided to go ahead and sleep in the dress she had worn all day instead of changing into a nightgown. She would probably have to wake up during the night to check on Mr. Price, and propriety demanded that she stay fully clothed, no matter how sick the man was.

As she settled on the pallet, she wondered when modesty had found its way into her character. Had it come immediately with her salvation, or was it the result of her growth process as a new Christian? Wherever it came from, she liked the idea of respecting her own body enough not to put it on display.

But I don't like sleeping on a hard floor, she thought, trying to settle into a comfortable position. She raised her head and looked longingly at the pillow under Joseph's head. The man was unconscious and probably wouldn't even notice if she took it. Besides, he had a soft feather mattress. But could she actually take the pillow from under the head of a sick man? Sometimes compassion was a bother, she thought, resting her head on the crook of her arm.

She was not accustomed to retiring so early, but she was exhausted, and she would no doubt be up checking on her patient several times before the sun came up. As she closed her eyes for her nightly prayer, she realized that the next day was Sunday. Bernice and the other members of Adam Burke's household would be setting out for Pastor Morgan's chapel in the morning, dressed in their best clothes.

For the first time since Corrine had become a Christian, she wouldn't be joining with fellow believers to worship. A sense of loss weighed upon her heart even though she imagined that God understood the circumstances.

She wondered if Jenny or Thomas had ever felt the need to know the Lord. Surely anyone who didn't know God had experienced the kind of emptiness that had consumed her own life, the emptiness that finally made her receptive to the gospel. There on the hard floor, she prayed that her changed life would be a beacon, pointing to Christ.

The light of the fireplace was feeble, but it was enough to illuminate the sleeping, shivering form on the bed a few feet away. Corrine felt compelled to look in Mr. Price's direction, and it seemed as though a voice she had heard before spoke to her heart, inaudible but very clear, *He needs to see that beacon, too.*

Mr. Price? Corrine's thoughts darkened immediately. Surely the sympathy she was feeling for the man's suffering was causing her to imagine things.

~

The next morning Joseph felt the light on his face and opened his eyes. Blinking, he lifted his head and looked around the room, until the effort was too much and he fell back to his pillow. He had caught a glimpse of the woman sleeping on the floor. *She's still here,* he thought. A vague memory came to his mind of Corrine Hammond hovering over him in the light of a candle, her voice coaxing, sometimes scolding, as a cup of water was pressed to his lips. It had happened more than once, he recalled.

He swallowed, searing his throat with fire. The more he tried to keep from swallowing, the more he thought about it, which increased his need to swallow. His stomach was cramped with hunger, but the idea of taking food through his painful throat made him shudder.

He thought about the oranges he had shared with the little boy on the train from Yorkshire and wished now that he could soothe his throat with the juice.

Raising his head again, he glanced at Mrs. Hammond. *Why is she staying?* he wondered. The lie came back to him, the one he had told her about Scotland Yard. That had to be the answer . . . she feared that if she left him, she would only wind up in the hands of the authorities.

But why is she treating me so well? He had accused her of putting on an act so that she could use him to fool Squire Nowells into believing she had changed. He remembered the coolness of the cloth she had used to bathe his face. At first touch it had been a shock to his fevered skin, but after a while it lessened his nausea and made him feel better. *Would someone who didn't have some kindness inside go to that much trouble?*

Just the memory of her fingers upon his brow gave him an almost overwhelming longing to call out to her and ask her to bathe his face again. The irony of such a longing was evident even to his fever-clouded mind. Not too long ago, he would have shrunk from the touch of a woman with her past.

He would not wake her, though, even if he had to lie there

185

and suffer. She was no doubt exhausted from getting up during the night to tend to him. Surely she would be more susceptible to catching his illness if she didn't get enough rest.

Rolling over onto his side, he pulled the blanket back up to his neck and tried not to think about swallowing, or about her soft hands on his face.

~

At the sound of movement from the other side of the room, Corrine groaned inwardly and opened her eyes. It was morning. Asleep in the shadow of the table, she hadn't been aware of the sunlight that now slanted through the windows.

The sound from the bed meant that Joseph Price, if not fully awake, was conscious enough for her to force some more water down him. She wondered if his throat was any better, then made herself swallow. With relief she noted that her own throat was not sore yet. The fear had come to her in the night, during one of her vigils at Mr. Price's bedside, that her strong constitution could fail her. She could very well come down with the scarlet fever, too. How long did it take for the symptoms to show once someone had been exposed?

She remembered the times she had been so tempted to escape, like at the inn back in Adderley. A cold sweat beaded her forehead. What if she had managed to get home, only to bring scarlet fever with her?

And if she came down with the disease here, who would tend to the both of them? Her thoughts drifted, and she started to closed her eyes. But then she remembered that someone was depending on her, and with a low groan, she sat up.

"Mr. Price, are you awake?" She filled a cup with water and walked over to the side of the bed.

"Yes," came the weak voice. She felt his forehead—it was still as hot as it had been yesterday.

"I don't suppose your throat feels better, does it?"

"No."

"I'm sorry to hear that. You need to drink some water, so why don't we try to sit you up a bit?"

With her arm pulling at his shoulder he sat up, but put a hand up to stop her when she brought the cup nearer. "Need to . . ."

She looked puzzled, then comprehended the embarrassment in his eyes. Yesterday evening she had thought about what she should do when this moment came. She took a deep breath and said, "There's a chamber pot under the bed. I'll have to help you with it."

He shook his head, his jaw clenched. "Just . . . help me stand up," he rasped. "Then leave."

"I don't think you can make it," she said. "I know it's going to be uncomfortable for both of us, but as you've been so kind to remind me, I'm not a blushing maiden."

But the jaw clenched tight again, so she put her arm back around him and helped him to his feet. He stood there for a minute, weaving slightly on his feet, then blinked at her and said, "Go outside . . . please. I can manage . . . alone." She understood. He was too modest even to have her empty the chamber pot. A smile touched her lips. In an absurd way, he was finally treating her like a lady.

"Are you sure?"

He grabbed the bedpost to steady himself, then nodded. "Go."

~

Corrine ventured out into the woods on the east side of the cottage, away from the door and windows. She would not walk very far, she decided—she needed to stay within earshot in case Mr. Price called out for her help.

A few more steps, and she heard what sounded like rain, coming from just ahead of her. She followed the sound to a clear brook—narrow, but deep enough to take a decent bath in. She bent down to splash some of the icy water on her face. Perhaps when her patient was well enough to leave alone for some time, she would be able to slip back here and bathe, provided she could stand the temperature.

After several minutes had passed, she returned to the cottage. Mr. Price was back in bed, his breath rapid from the effort.

"Thank you," he whispered. "Hear horses outside."

"You do?" Cocking her head, she listened and heard the rattling of a wagon. She tucked the blankets over her patient's shoulders, then walked over to the window and peered out. "It's Mr. Rhodes with our food for the day," she said. She turned to look at him. "He's the innkeeper, if you don't remember."

The wagon stopped in the yard, and Mr. Rhodes got out and left a large parcel bundled in a hemp sack. He solemnly returned Corrine's wave from the other side of the glass, then got back in the driver's seat and left. Corrine waited until he was long out of sight before opening the door to retrieve the bundle, then she brought it in and set it on the table.

"Looks like we've got quite a feast here," she said over her shoulder, loosening the cord at the top of the sack. She pulled out a cloth pouch of pungent dried herbs and a bag of tea leaves. A piece of paper was curled inside the sack of herbs, and someone, possibly the midwife, had printed neatly, *Brew a pinch of these in the tea, and have him drink it often.*

Soon she had all of the food spread out on the table—a loaf

of bread and some butter, a large wedge of cheese, half of a roasted chicken, two pastries covered with slivered almonds, a cucumber, and two baked yams. A quart-sized jar contained cold beef broth, and at the bottom of the sack were two oranges.

"You know, these might make your throat feel better," she said thoughtfully as she turned and held up an orange for Joseph to see. "Do you think you could eat one?"

Propped up on an elbow, he looked almost ready to smile. "Was wishing for an orange," he whispered.

"Really? God must have been listening. Let me get a fire going for the teakettle, and I'll cut one up for you." When the kettle was hanging on a hook in the fireplace, Corrine brought one of the oranges over to Joseph. "The water should be hot enough for tea by the time you finish this," she said. She sat down on the stool, peeled the orange, and gave him half of a section. "Hurt going down?" she asked when he made a face.

"Hurts." He gave her a grateful look. "But feels good."

She fed him the whole orange, then got up to brew the tea and herb mixture. The note hadn't said for how long, but she waited for a few minutes and brought a cup over to him.

"Now you," he whispered when she took the cup away from his mouth.

"I beg your pardon?"

Joseph inclined his head in the direction of the table. "Need to eat. Don't want you to get sick."

"All right." She was hungry, come to think of it. She'd had no supper last night, and the aroma of the orange had caused her mouth to water. After assuring herself that Mr. Price was settled comfortably, she walked over to the table and took one of the pastries, and then broke off some of the cheese. The remaining orange looked tempting, but it was probably all Mr. Price would have an appetite for today—that and the soup.

Corrine glanced in his direction. He appeared to be asleep again, lying there on his side. Breakfast and tending to his personal needs had probably worn him out. Perhaps she would have time to read from the Bible while she had her own breakfast.

After taking the Bible from her valise, she went back to the table and opened it. It was tempting to go back to the familiar words of Saint John for the third time, but she supposed it was time to see what the other eyewitnesses to Jesus' ministry had to say. Saint Matthew was the logical place to start, being the first book of the New Testament.

As she flipped through the pages to find her place, the movement caused an imperceptible shake of the table. The orange she had decided to save for Mr. Price rolled along the tabletop, coming to a gentle stop at the back of her right hand. She picked it up to set it back with the other foods, then smiled. What would the old Corrine Hammond have thought about her actually putting someone else's needs above her own?

~

Huddled on his side again, Joseph watched the woman at the table. She was looking intently down at her open Bible as she ate. He noticed the little furrow that occasionally came to her brow. She seemed to be not simply skimming as with the pages of a novel, but poring over the words in front of her as if they were of great significance.

He blinked, and her image became fuzzy for a fraction of a second. When his eyes focused again, he realized that for the first time since coming into contact with her, he had forgotten to remind himself automatically of her past. Was it because she looked so strangely at peace, yet somehow vulnerable . . . or because she had taken care of him?

Before she sat down to her breakfast, she had cajoled him into letting her remove his hopelessly wrinkled frock coat in return for an extra blanket on the bed. He was much more comfortable not having his neck and arms constricted. Why had she even bothered?

And just moments ago, she had picked up an orange, run a finger over its skin, and set it back on the table. It was obvious she had given it up for him.

And I've said such hateful things to her, he thought. He had never felt the compulsion to treat anyone so roughly before. In the past, he had hunted people down as a necessary part of his occupation, and he bore no personal grudges. Had he been paying her back for rejecting him on the train in front of others?

In spite of his judgment of the woman, his ego had been bruised. He had assumed she thought herself too good for him. Now he wondered if she truly had changed.

Joseph burrowed deeper into his blankets. *But she's deceived so many people. How can I know when she's telling the truth?* He swallowed and winced. When did he suddenly find truth so important? A major part of the success he'd had in his occupation had been his ability to weave any story that was convenient to the situation at hand.

And who was *he* to be her judge? The men she had conned had not been innocent. Most had been the bored recipients of inherited wealth, all too eager to betray their wives. They probably deserved the loss of money that their philandering had caused, including the elder Squire Nowells. That didn't justify what she had done, by any means, but he didn't have the authority to condemn her.

A picture came into Joseph's thoughts of Corrine Hammond wasting away in a dark cell in Treybrook's rat-infested lockup. As much as he was beginning to question his own judgment where women were concerned, Joseph was dead certain that he had Squire Nowells's character figured out. The man would gladly set out to make every last minute of Mrs. Hammond's life miserable.

Maybe I'd feel the same way if my father killed himself over a woman, he thought, wrestling against the hollow feeling in his chest. *Anyway, whatever happens in the future is between the two of them.*

If he lived through this illness, he would do the job he'd been paid to do. Then he would go to Bristol for an extended visit, until his body—and mind—were ready to take on another job. In the loving company of his family, he would banish from his mind any thoughts about Squire Nowells and Corrine Hammond.

He heard the rustle of pages a few feet away, and the sound caused his sagging spirits to sink even lower.

16

MRS. Styles appeared at Jenny's bedside early Sunday morning, just as the girl was waking. Another woman stood at her side—Jenny couldn't recall seeing her among the army of servants. She was short and wide, and wore her amber hair in a topknot, with dozens of little pinch curls framing her pleasant-looking face.

"This is Mrs. Pruitt," the housekeeper explained moments later as she helped the girl sponge bathe at the washstand. "She is Lady Dunley's seamstress. She's also my friend."

Mrs. Pruitt had already opened the wardrobe and was studying a calico dress she held up by the shoulders. "This room has been like a shrine for so long," she said to Mrs. Styles. "It's been a while since I've seen these frocks. I can't believe the missus is allowing the girl to wear them."

The housekeeper brought Jenny over to the dresser, then picked up a brush and began running it through the girl's hair. "Not *allowing* her, Hannah, but *ordering* Helene to put them on her."

"How peculiar!" Mrs. Pruitt exclaimed, then darted an anxious look at the door.

"Lady Dunley's having her bath now," the housekeeper reassured her friend. Still, she lowered her voice when she said, "It's got the mister and the servants all upset. Sir Feldon had breakfast sent to his room a little while ago. I can just imagine—"

She stopped suddenly and looked down at Jenny. Bending closer, Mrs. Styles cupped her hand under Jenny's chin and raised it to face her. "None of this is your fault, Jenny, so don't let our going-on worry you. We're just trying to figure out what to do about the dresses."

At the sound of her own name, Jenny wanted to throw her arms around the woman and weep. All day yesterday, the other servants had addressed her as Miss Angelica when necessary, especially in Lady Dunley's hearing. Even Helene had taken to calling her by the dead child's name for fear of what the mistress would do if she made a slip.

"The seams aren't wide enough in these frocks," Mrs. Pruitt said from the wardrobe. "I was afraid of that. When I sewed them, I thought I'd never have to be letting them out, as often as the missus had new clothes made for Angelica. Have you talked to her about my sewing up a whole new wardrobe for the girl?"

Mrs. Styles set the brush down on the dresser and opened a drawer to get out fresh stockings for Jenny. "I did yesterday when I saw how tight one of Angelica's dresses was on her. They've got to be terribly uncomfortable."

"What did the missus say?" Mrs. Pruitt had another dress in her arms now, turned inside out, and was squinting down at a seam.

Shaking her head sadly, the housekeeper replied, "At first she seemed agreeable that the girl needed a new wardrobe. But when she woke up this morning, she ordered Alice to tell Helene to dress her daughter in one of her prettiest gowns!"

"Her *daughter?*"

"Now you know why Sir Feldon is having breakfast in his room. Isn't there anything you can do about the dresses?"

The seamstress pursed her lips, running her hand over an emerald green frock. "You know, I still have a bolt of this green cloth in my sewing room. And possibly a good-sized piece of this pink gingham."

"But I just told you that Lady Dunley won't allow any new dresses to be made," said Mrs. Styles. "And she'll recognize it if you patch some extra lengths of fabric to the old ones. You know how fussy she was about Angelica's clothes."

"Yes, I know." After a thoughtful silence, a sly smile came to Mrs. Pruitt's lips. "But what if they looked exactly like the old ones—only a little bigger?"

"You don't mean . . ."

The seamstress chuckled, "By the time I finish sewing up the two pieces of cloth that I've already got, I could have some more cloth sent here to match most of the other dresses. Sally and Gretchen are good with a needle and thread. If you'll give them some time away from their cleaning, we could have the girl some comfortable clothes . . . and nobody'd know the difference."

Mrs. Styles's eyes were sparkling, but there was still a worried frown about her lips. "Nobody except for Sally, Gretchen, you, and me—and Jenny here. Would the two of them keep their mouths closed about the switch?"

"I know they would. They'd do anything to get a little time away from scrubbing floors." Mrs. Pruitt hung the green dress back in the wardrobe and folded her arms. "I can't do it with-out them . . . sew a whole new batch of dresses on the sly and keep up with my other work. Lady Dunley all of a sudden wants a whole new wardrobe for herself."

Taking out a pale pink embroidered frock, Mrs. Pruitt closed the wardrobe door and turned to study Jenny's face. "You know, the missus seems to have come to life again. Maybe it's not such a bad thing having the girl in the house. In fact, it might be good for her."

Mrs. Styles, with a petticoat in her arms, stopped and stared at her friend. "I don't think it's ever good to live a lie," she said. "If she wants to adopt a child to give her someone to love, that's one thing. But to force this one to play the part of Angelica is cruel."

The two women helped Jenny into the dress, leaving the top button at the back of the neck loose so that it wouldn't chafe her neck. "Perhaps some cornstarch would stop the underarms from chafing, too," Mrs. Styles mused. "I'll send for some when Helene gets here."

After helping Jenny squeeze into some white kid slippers, the housekeeper backed away and looked at her. "I'm sorry you had to hear all of this, Jenny. It's unfortunate that Lady Dunley cannot face reality sometimes."

"Why does she think I'm her daughter?" Jenny asked timidly.

Mrs. Styles and Mrs. Pruitt exchanged glances, and then the housekeeper said, "Guilt can do terrible things to a person's mind. But she won't hurt you . . . and there are people here on your side. If you ever need help, you must come to one of us."

Jenny nodded, speechless that two grown women would care so much about a mere child. Why, Mrs. Pruitt had only just met her, and yet she was willing to make her some clothes that didn't chafe and bind—possibly at the risk of losing her job!

"I believe I'll buy the child some bigger shoes, too," said Mrs. Styles, her eyes on the tops of Jenny's bulging feet. "I could give the smaller ones to the servants' children after some time has passed."

New dresses, new shoes—suddenly Jenny understood. She was going to be living in this household for a long time. A cold, hard lump formed in the pit of her stomach, and she found her voice. Turning to Mrs. Styles, she murmured, "Do you know when I can go home?"

The housekeeper laid the petticoat on the foot of the bed. Walking over to where Jenny stood in the center of the room, she put an arm around the girl's shoulders and drew her close. "It might be a while," she answered, her face sad.

"But my aunt and uncle . . ."

"Your uncle gave his permission yesterday for you to stay as long as Lady Dunley wishes." Through the waves of disappointment overpowering Jenny, the housekeeper's voice began to sound like it came through a tunnel. "I'm sorry, Jenny," the woman was saying. "But at least you won't have to work in the fields. And the servants will try to make things here as easy as possible for you. Tell me if any of them don't."

The sound of muffled footsteps on carpeting came from the hallway, and Mrs. Styles took her hand away from Jenny's shoulder. Seconds later, Lenora Dunley came through the door with a silk wrapper tied about her waist. Her hair, washed last night instead of during her usual morning routine, hung down uncombed below her shoulders.

"I just had the most wonderful idea!" she gushed, going over to Jenny immediately to embrace her. "And how is my little darling this morning?" Then she noticed the two women. Without waiting for a reply from Jenny, she asked Mrs. Styles why Helene wasn't in the room.

"I've got her polishing the girl's shoes."

"The balmorals? That's right. I noticed yesterday they had a scuff mark."

"Yes, ma'am."

"Well, good. She can wear them tomorrow. The shoes she's got on will go well with the white lawn dress."

"The white lawn?" Mrs. Styles looked down at Jenny. "But we've already—"

"Yes," Lenora went on, not even seeming to notice that her housekeeper had spoken. "That's the idea I'm so excited about! I thought we would dress alike today. Won't that be fun? My white lawn is only a little different from Angelica's."

Jenny stood on the carpet, feeling the weight of three pairs of eyes on her. Two of the women's faces showed concern; the third showed an emotion Jenny couldn't identify. Even though it was backbreaking, life had been simpler in the turnip fields. At least *there* she had known what to expect every day.

"Begging your pardon, m'lady," began Mrs. Styles, "but it was a struggle to get this dress on . . ." She darted a glance at the seamstress. "The child. For her sake, can't she wear the white dress tomorrow?"

"Today," Lenora ordered, already wheeling around to head for the door. "Now I've got to get dressed myself, or we'll be late for church. Be sure she puts on the white silk bonnet after breakfast."

She was out the door, and Mrs. Pruitt raised her eyebrows at Mrs. Styles. *"Church?"*

"Master Neil must be taking her."

"But why now? She hasn't gone since the funeral."

The housekeeper wore a puzzled expression. "I don't know." Turning to Jenny, she said, "Mrs. Pruitt and I will be in the balcony, so don't worry. Everything will be fine."

~

"I'll be wearing the white lawn today," Lenora announced to Alice as the girl combed the tangles from her hair. "And put enough pins in my chignon to keep it from bouncing loose in the carriage."

"It's a pretty day to go riding, missus," Alice said meekly.

"Isn't it!" Lenora smiled at herself in the mirror at her dressing table. "The most lovely day I've ever seen. In fact, I feel like really dressing up today. Isn't my rouge pot still in this drawer?"

The maid leaned over for a second to pull out a wide, shallow drawer. "It's still there, ma'am, and your powder, too. Would you like me to help you with it?"

"I'll wait till you finish my hair and do it myself." Hugging herself, she let out a little laugh. "I feel like I could do just about anything today!"

"It's good to hear you so happy, missus," the girl mumbled.

Lenora shot the girl's reflection a smile. She could afford to be magnanimous today. After all, life was so good! And it was going to get even better!

Within the hour, she would be on her way to church with Angelica at her side. They would look radiant in their white lawn gowns—like angels, she thought. All the townspeople would stand and gape at the beauty of her darling daughter. The embarrassment on their faces, when they remembered their silly letters of condolence, would be almost comical to watch.

But she wouldn't laugh at them. No, it wasn't ladylike to harbor bitterness. She would accept their acknowledgments of how wrong they had been with a gracious nod of the head.

If only Feldon would come with us. Things would be just

perfect then. His eyes would be opened, and he would finally understand what she had been trying to tell him. Why did he have to be so stubborn, refusing even to see her this morning? *Maybe Neil will help him understand.* That was one hope. Her brother could explain to her husband how everyone in Leawick knew that Angelica had come back to them.

A little nerve began to throb in Lenora's temple, and she rubbed at it with her fingers.

"Did I pull your hair too tight, ma'am?"

Blinking, Lenora looked up at the girl's reflection. "What?"

Alice's face became wary. "I thought I pulled your hair."

"Oh. No, you didn't." But seconds later, Lenora was rubbing her temple harder, humming a low tune to drown out the voice that was trying to tell her something she didn't want to hear.

~

"Now, darling," Lenora crooned, her fingers straightening the ribbon of Jenny's silk bonnet as they sat next to each other in the rolling carriage, "be sure to remember to curtsy to Reverend Coleridge. But take a step back if his wife tries to kiss your cheek—she reeks of camphor and will make your dress smell."

From the facing seat, Neil Wingate had been watching the two with an expressionless face. At this last instruction, though, he leaned forward and said, "You can't have her insulting the vicar's wife like that."

"Well, then perhaps you should tell her that she stinks. You'd likely be doing her a favor—I can't be the only one who's noticed."

Wide eyed, Jenny tried to picture in her mind an evil-smelling woman trying to kiss her. How could she possibly refuse to allow an adult to touch her? All this affection lavished upon her lately was so disconcerting. Physical affection from Aunt Mary had been rare, and nonexistent from Uncle Roy.

From the corner of her eye, she observed the woman who now clung to her hand so possessively. The baronet's wife had applied makeup with a liberal hand. Fawn-colored powder was already caking in the lines around her eyes. Even more noticeable was the rouge, almost two perfect circles on her cheeks, each the size of a small apple.

"Be sure to sing loudly," Lenora continued to Jenny. "I want everyone to be green with envy that their little brats don't have the voice that you do."

"You haven't been to church for two years, and that's the only concern you have?" Mr. Wingate asked in a flat voice. "Showing off? Insulting people?"

"Of course not." Rolling her eyes at her brother, Lenora squeezed Jenny's hand. "Don't listen to him, Angelica. He wouldn't even be going today if he wasn't afraid of my misbehaving."

"I didn't say that, Lenora," her brother snapped.

"You didn't? What about the lecture you gave me this morning about not parading Angelica in front of everybody? And we look so nice, too." She flounced the hem of her white lawn dress with her other hand and giggled. "Why, we could pass for sisters!"

But the smile left her face seconds later, replaced by a pout. "I only wish your father cared enough to join us," she murmured, bringing Jenny's hand up to her cheek. "After all, he's the head of the household and is supposed to be in charge of our religious instruction."

Jenny saw a look of pain wash across Mr. Wingate's face.

He opened his mouth to say something, but then closed it again and began watching the passing hedgerows.

"I believe all the men in my house are afflicted with terminal stuffiness," Lenora whispered in Jenny's ear with a giggle. "Just wait. I doubt if anyone pays attention to the vicar's dull words. All eyes will be on my beautiful Angelica."

In the distance ahead came the resonant sound of the bell from the tower of Church of the Cross. From the other side of the village, Jenny had heard the same bell, but she had never even imagined that one day she would be inside that magnificent church. No matter that some in the village declared the church to be too small and ugly. Besides the wonderful iron bell, the flint building had a steeple as high as the clouds and windows of colored glass formed in the shapes of people and angels.

But as much as she had longed to peek inside the church building, she felt nothing but dread right now. Her feet were beginning to ache, and her neckline still pulled at her throat. Her underarms felt chafed in spite of the cornstarch Mrs. Styles had sprinkled there. And worse than that, Lady Dunley would probably cling to her the whole time, like she was doing now.

In front of the church, Mr. Wingate helped Lady Dunley and Jenny out of the carriage, then signaled to the driver that he could take it farther down the road to find some shade. "They've likely rented out the Dunley box after two years," he whispered to Lenora as they walked toward the door.

"The things you say!" Lenora returned forcefully, glancing ahead at the group of people standing at the door. "And you were worried about how *I* would act!" She lifted her chin and walked toward Reverend Coleridge, her white-gloved hand extended. "How pleasant to see you this morning, Vicar," she purred, ignoring the stunned look on the man's face.

The vicar, a white-haired man in his sixties whom Jenny recognized from the village, recovered in time to take Lenora's hand. "Why, Lady Dunley! What a wonderful surprise!"

Still holding Jenny's hand with her left hand, Lenora giggled softly and inclined her head toward her brother, standing rigid at her side. "I don't remember if you've ever met my brother, Mr. Wingate."

While the men shook hands, a woman came from the inside of the church to stand next to the vicar. Her gray curls peeked out from a flowered hat. "Did I hear Lenora Dunley's name?" she exclaimed.

The smile froze on Lady Dunley's face, but her pressure on Jenny's hand increased. "Yes, good morning, Mrs. Coleridge." She tugged at Jenny's arm and said, "Well, we mustn't be late." With that, she disappeared through the open church door with Jenny in her wake. Jenny looked back in time to see Mr. Wingate whisper to the vicar and his wife.

Trying to keep up with Lady Dunley, Jenny didn't have an opportunity to look around the inside of the church building until she was seated on a polished wooden bench in a small compartment with low walls. Mr. Wingate plopped down on her left side a moment later, his cheeks almost as red as his sister's.

"Why did you do that to me?" he seethed quietly over Jenny's head.

The two adults argued in whispers while Jenny looked around. She wondered why there were only three other compartments like the one they were sitting in. Filling the rest of the sanctuary were long wooden pews. She looked up to see more pews on the second level, behind them. Hushed voices drifted down from up there, and Jenny searched the faces for any sign of Mrs. Styles and her friend Mrs. Pruitt. Sure enough, they were there in the first row. Both waved down at her.

"Turn around, dear," came the voice from beside her. "The service is about to start."

The vicar was indeed up at the pulpit. A note sounded from an instrument that resembled the pianoforte at the Dunley manor, only sounding softer and trembling somewhat. The entire congregation rose to its feet. Feeling the now familiar tug at her hand, Jenny got up and stood between Lady Dunley and her brother. All heads lowered, and Jenny lowered hers while the vicar prayed out loud. After a few minutes, voices joined him with "Amen," but the people did not sit down yet.

Instead, there was a rustling of pages. Jenny noticed that everyone seemed to have the same dark blue book, and the instrument began playing again. Jenny looked around as much as she dared. The members of the congregation stared at their open books for a few seconds, then all began singing as one: *"Come, thou Almighty King, Help us thy name to sing. . . ."*

"Angelica," whispered the woman beside her, leaning closer, "you know this one by heart. Sing loudly so they'll hear you."

Mouth agape, Jenny looked up at her. "Ma'am?"

"The song, child. Show them what you can do." There was a strange gleam in the woman's eyes, and Jenny found herself pressing closer to Mr. Wingate's side.

"What's going on, Lenora?" came Mr. Wingate's voice.

Ignoring her brother, Lady Dunley peered about the sanctuary with narrowed eyes. Then she turned back to Jenny. "Sing!" she pleaded in a loud whisper. She made a sweeping motion with her arm. "Let these peasants hear your beautiful voice."

"She can't do it, Lenora," said her brother. "Leave the girl alone." Voices were beginning to taper off in the near vicinity, while everyone watched the goings-on in the box.

"Of course she can!" An open hymnal was thrust in front of Jenny's face. Feeling all eyes upon her, she tried to make sense of the unfamiliar markings on the page. Before she could stammer that she couldn't read, the book was snapped shut.

"Why won't you sing, child?"

"I-I don't know how."

The woman next to her burst into tears, just as the singing stopped completely. After the organ had played several unaccompanied notes, it stopped, too.

"You're still angry with your mother?" Lady Dunley sobbed. "I tell you, it wasn't my fault!"

Mr. Wingate reached over Jenny to take his sister's arm. "That's enough, Lenora," he said carefully. "We're leaving."

"Leaving?" Lady Dunley wiped her eyes with the back of her gloved hand, smearing streaks of rouge all over her cheeks. She seemed oblivious to the shocked stares coming from the faces around her. "But she—"

"The child can't do what she can't. Now let's go."

"Let us take her back to her family," a soft voice said from behind Neil. Uttering a small cry of recognition, Jenny wheeled around to find Mrs. Styles there.

Mr. Wingate shot the housekeeper a grateful look. "That would be good of you." Still holding his sister's arm, he directed an apologetic look at the vicar and began to lead Lady Dunley down the side aisle toward the door. Placid and dull eyed now, the woman leaned on her brother's shoulder, and he matched his steps with her own.

17

LACING her fingers together so tightly that they hurt, Lenora Dunley looked up at the granitelike face of her brother as they rode back in the carriage. "You're angry at me?"

Neil shook his head and sighed, "I'm not angry, Lenora. It just makes me so sad seeing you carry on this way."

She blinked, vaguely recalling that someone had caused some commotion in church. It was on her lips to ask her brother who had been responsible. But something in his face told her that it had been herself. "I embarrassed you?"

"That's the least of my worries. It's you I'm concerned about."

More memory found its way into her thoughts. "What did you do with the girl?"

"The child?" Neil was now giving her a stare of intense disbelief. "You mean *Jenny?*"

"Jenny."

"You've been calling her something else for two days now."

"I have?" Lenora rubbed her temple and tried to think. She could remember asking Feldon to allow a child she had seen in the fields to visit, but only bits and pieces of anything else. She couldn't even recall arriving at the church, though the scene inside was becoming more and more clear. "What did I call her?"

A look of pure agony crossed his face, and he spoke the name.

"I did not!"

"You did, Lenora."

"Well, perhaps I did," she conceded after chewing her lip and staring at him for a while. "But it must have been a slip of the tongue." Her own voice began to sound tinny, as if from far off. The disorientation was so frightening that she began firing out her words in a rapid pace, hoping her voice would sound familiar if she talked long enough.

"Angelica is in my thoughts all the time, so that's a natural slip of the tongue. Any mother would make that mistake—once you have a child, her name is engraved on your heart forever."

Lenora fixed unblinking eyes upon her brother's face and spoke even faster. "I don't think the child should come back to visit, because I would have to let her play with Angelica's dolls. I don't think anyone should be allowed to play with Angelica's dolls. Not anyone."

"All right," Neil mumbled with a shrug of the shoulders.

"You can't go telling children that they can't play with toys that are right in front of them, so be sure to ask her not to come back."

"I said I would!" Neil snapped. After a wary silence, his voice softened. "You don't have to keep saying it, Lenora."

"Don't have to keep . . . ," Lenora echoed, her eyes now vacant. "Need to put the dolls away."

~

Roy Satters usually spent Sundays sharpening and oiling his tools and seeing to minor repairs in the harness and wagon.

He would have gladly used that day to thatch roofs. Sunday was the same as any other day to him, but the people of Shropshire were either too religious to hire anyone on the Lord's Day or too superstitious to ignore the customs of the religious folk among them.

Still, his ears perked up at the sound off in the distance— filtered through the noises of his children playing in the yard—of a horse and carriage wheels on the dirt road. Usually the only visits his family had were of a business nature. Perhaps he would have another thatching job next week. *No, that would have to be the week after.* Finally, there seemed to be a demand for his work. He hoped it would continue.

Hanging his shears on the hook in the barn, he walked out into the yard just in time to catch sight of a gig as it crested the low hill in front of his home. Two women sat in the seat, one of them holding the reins. Roy brought up a hand to shield his eyes from the sun overhead. He thought he had caught sight of a third person between the two women.

Seconds later, he realized that this third person was his wife's niece. The children had noticed, too, and Rebecca and Diana were hugging each other with glee. "All of you go in the house!" he barked in Trudy's direction. "Get on, now!"

The children obeyed immediately, darting furtive looks back over their shoulders on their way to the door. Seconds later, Mary's face appeared at the window, but the look he sent her kept her inside.

"Good day, Mr. Satters," the woman who held the reins called out as they got closer. Roy recognized her as Sir Feldon's housekeeper, who had come to speak to him just yesterday about Jenny. She expertly brought the horse and gig to a halt just a few feet from where he stood. Jenny sat mute beside her, eyes huge with fright in a face as colorless as whey.

Ignoring the greeting, Roy walked up to the carriage and directed a withering stare at the girl. "What did she do?"

The housekeeper glanced over at the other woman, who appeared to be near the same age, then gave Roy a hesitant smile. "She didn't do anything, Mr. Satters. Not anything wrong, that is."

"Then why are you bringin' her back here?"

Mrs. Styles drew a deep breath. "Let me explain." Motioning toward the other woman, she said, "This is—"

"You don't need to go into all that, missus," Roy cut in impatiently. "Just tell me why you brought the girl here."

"Because Lady Dunley is . . . not feeling well. It would be better if Jenny stayed here, at home."

"This ain't her home. It's my home, and I'm hard pressed to feed the ones what rightly belong here." His eye detected a slight movement, and he noticed that the housekeeper had slipped a hand down to hold the girl's hand. This simple gesture angered Roy. *He* was the one more deserving of sympathy, working his calloused fingers to the bone to take care of his family.

"There's nowhere else the child can go," Mrs. Styles was saying. "Mrs. Pruitt and I live in the manor house, too, so we can't take her with us. It wouldn't be good for her to go back to the Dunley house now."

Roy thought about the shilling he had been paid in advance for his permission to have the girl stay at the manor house for a week—twice as much as she would earn in the turnip fields. He had snatched up the offer with private amusement, for he would have gladly settled for the same salary—and would have had one less mouth to feed. His hand automatically formed a fist at the thought of the coin in the canvas pouch under his mattress. Jenny had stayed with the Dunleys for only two days. Would Sir Feldon be sending someone around to demand the balance of his overpayment?

Roy glared up at the housekeeper. He couldn't carry his anger against Sir Feldon *too* far. After all, the man was his landlord. But he would good and well speak his mind to these two servants. "He should ha' thought about that before he sent you over here to ask if she could stay."

"Are you saying that we can't leave her here?"

"What I'm saying is she was supposed to stay there for a week. Now she's got to be fed for five more days."

"You would have to be responsible for her meals if she were still working in the fields, so you're not losing any money. And if I'm not mistaken, Sir Feldon paid you a substantial amount over her salary."

The money he had been paid was a dangerous subject— Roy knew that if he didn't back down, it might be mentioned that he owed Sir Feldon a refund for the five days. He shifted tactics to whining. "Well, what about her old job? We were countin' on that to make ends meet."

Mrs. Styles's jaw tightened. "I'm not in charge of the fields, but I don't see why Mr. Blake wouldn't take her on again." Looking down at the man with clear disapproval in her eyes, she added, "If that's what you *want* to do. Field work is hard for one so young."

So the snooty woman's going to sit up there and look down her nose at me! Roy fumed. *A man's got the right to say what goes on under his own roof and with his own kin.* He turned glaring eyes to Jenny, whose face whitened even more. "Well, get down from there and help your aunt fetch some dinner." Turning on his heel, he stalked back to the barn.

~

"Well, I suppose I should help you climb down, child," Mrs. Styles said after letting out a low whistle between her teeth. She handed the reins to Mrs. Pruitt and let herself out of the driver's seat, then reached for Jenny.

When her feet were on the ground, Jenny found herself being drawn into Mrs. Styles's embrace. "Maybe it's for the best after all," the woman said in a wavering voice.

"Thank . . . thank you for being so kind to me," Jenny whispered. Now that Uncle Roy was no longer nearby, she began to feel a measure of optimism. She was back at what she had considered home for most of her life. There was no doubt in her mind that she would be back in the fields come morning, but at least she would be able to spend some time with her cousins today.

Mrs. Styles had climbed back into the carriage and was taking the reins when Jenny remembered that the dress she wore was not her own. "Ma'am?" she called up. "I don't have another dress to put on. But won't she want this back?"

"That's more than likely," Mrs. Pruitt said to the house-keeper. "She's got Angelica's things memorized down to the last detail."

"Isn't there *anything* at the house we can give her?"

After chewing her lip for a second, the seamstress smiled down at the girl. "I'll get Sally and Gretchen together as soon as we get back, and the three of us can likely have you another dress made before the sun goes down. Won't have any frills in that short bit of time, but it'll be a lot more comfortable than what you've got on."

Mrs. Styles looked from Jenny to Mrs. Pruitt, her face distressed. "But, Amelia . . . sewing on a Sunday? Maybe you should wait until morning."

The stocky woman crossed her arms and answered, "And what did our Lord Jesus say about pullin' an ox out of a ditch if it needed doing on the Lord's Day? Do you want that girl havin' to spend one day planting crops in that tight frock? Not to mention what the missus would do if it came back stained."

"Ah, the voice of reason," replied the housekeeper. "Well, we'd best be on our way so that you can get to work. You know I'll have to give Sally and Gretchen a half day off tomorrow to make up for their Sunday afternoon."

"Why don't you give 'em the whole day?" Mrs. Pruitt countered. She winked at Jenny. "Maybe if they work fast enough, we can add a frill here or there."

With a final wave the women left, turning the carriage around in the yard. Jenny had taken two steps toward the house when the door opened and her aunt came running out to grasp her by the shoulders. "The children are so excited!" she whispered after a furtive glance toward the barn. "Come inside and let them see you."

Jenny found herself surrounded by her young cousins the moment she stepped into the cottage. "I've missed you all so!" she exclaimed, bending down to lift little Evan into her arms. Even Rebecca, the most serious of the children, was grinning while Trudy touched the ribbons in Jenny's dress with reverence.

"I have to give it back," Jenny told her cousin. "I wish I could give it to you—it would fit you a whole lot better."

Suddenly she remembered how sore her feet were, and she put Evan back on the floor and walked over to a rush-bottomed chair. "I'll be glad to give these shoes and stockings back!" she exclaimed, wriggling out of them.

Her feet loosened from their bonds, Jenny set to work helping her aunt. Lunch was a simple meal of warmed-over porridge and cooked pears, eaten in silence as usual because of Uncle Roy's sullen presence. Jenny's bowl held the least amount of food, even less than the baby's. Darting a sidelong glance at the head of the table, she hoped that Aunt Mary's husband had noticed that she was trying not to be too much of a burden.

Before Jenny had been summoned to the great manor house, she had wondered why meals at Uncle Roy's table couldn't be shared in a setting of harmony, as she imagined they were in other people's homes. But having sat down at the Dunley table, too, she now began to wonder if mealtime was naturally a time of tension, no matter what family.

When I'm grown, she thought as she tried to keep her spoon from making a noise on the stoneware bowl, *I won't even think about marrying anybody unless he'll promise to be kind to the children . . . most especially when they're trying to eat.* It was unlikely that anyone would ask for her hand, now that she was destined for the turnip fields for the rest of her life, but she would keep that resolution stored away in her mind just in case.

~

True to Mrs. Pruitt's word, one of the baronet's servants showed up at the door right before bedtime with a package for Jenny. The girl was already in the loft, tucking the children in for the night, when she heard Uncle Roy speaking with the man at the door. She had begun to worry that she might have to wear the white dress to the fields in the morning.

After changing into her worn nightgown earlier, Jenny had folded the dress as neatly as possible and had put it with the shoes, stockings, and petticoat on the table so that Aunt Mary could give them back in case someone actually did come around from the manor house. She peeked down from the side of the loft and discovered that the bundle was gone now—her aunt must have given it to the man at the door.

"Jenny?" Aunt Mary's voice startled her. She hadn't noticed anyone standing at the bottom of the ladder.

"Yes, ma'am?"

Her aunt held out a square of fabric, her tired face as near to a smile as Jenny had ever seen. "Your dress is here. They sent back your shoes, too, only somebody polished them up."

Assuring baby Evan that she would return, Jenny gathered the hem of her nightgown in one hand and scurried down the ladder. The dress was of sea green calico, with a collar and elbow-length sleeves of white dimity. Lengths of emerald braid were sewn around the collar and at the edge of the sleeves, drawing attention away from the simpler lines of the rest of the garment.

"It's too pretty to wear in the fields!" Aunt Mary exclaimed before clapping a hand over her mouth and turning to see if her husband had heard. In his chair by the fireplace just a few feet away, Uncle Roy did not look up from the scythe handle he had been carving. He hadn't heard—or more likely, he had heard and didn't care.

"Thank you, Aunt Mary," Jenny whispered before darting back up the ladder. After allowing her cousins to caress the fine fabric, she hung the garment on the nail where her old dress had hung for so long. Then she blew out the candle on the lone shelf and nudged Becca over so she could slide onto the mattress with the others.

As happy as she was to be back with her cousins, it was a while before Jenny's thoughts calmed down enough for her to drift off to sleep. So many unsettling things had happened today.

She couldn't help but feel bad that she had made Lady Dunley cry in church. If only she had been able to sing. Better yet, if only she could really *be* Angelica so that the woman wouldn't be so sad. It had to have been terrible, losing her daughter like that.

But she couldn't be anyone but herself. Mrs. Styles said something about it not being right to live a lie, and instinctively Jenny knew she was right. Still, she couldn't help but hope that Lady Dunley's feelings hadn't been hurt too badly.

~

"Feldon?"

When he received no answer, Neil Wingate held the candle closer to his brother-in-law's bed and repeated the name.

Sir Feldon shot up in bed this time. "Who's there? What—Neil?"

"Your wife, Feldon. She has the servants in a tumult."

"What's she doing this time?" the man sighed, lifting the quilt so that he could swing his legs over the side of the bed.

"It's the child. Mrs. Styles tells me that Lenora has been crying for the girl for two hours now."

"Two hours?" In the circle of light from Neil's candle, Sir Dunley took a pair of trousers from his wardrobe and pulled them up over his nightshirt. "Why did Mrs. Styles let it go on for so long?"

"I don't know, but she's out in the hall wringing her hands now."

Sir Feldon fastened his suspenders and took the candle from his brother-in-law. In his bare feet he walked out into the hallway. Mrs. Styles had a lantern, so the baronet handed the candle back to Neil. "What's going on here?"

Mrs. Styles's face was drawn with worry, and before she could answer, a low, wretched moan drifted from several doors down the hall. "The missus," the housekeeper answered with a glance over her shoulder. "I'm afraid she's going to hurt herself, sir."

"She's crying for the child?" He rubbed his brow for a second and asked, "Which child? Angelica? Or the girl from the fields?"

"I believe both, sir. She's calling out for your daughter, but it's the other child she's got her mind fixed on, I think."

"How do you know this?"

"Because it all started when she came upon Mrs. Pruitt downstairs, giving one of Angelica's dresses to the laundress. It's the one Jenny wore today. The child, you know."

"Yes, I know." Turning to Neil, he said, "Didn't you tell me that Lenora doesn't want that girl here anymore?"

"That's what she said, and I took it to mean she didn't ever want to see the child again."

Another moan, broken by sobs, chilled the atmosphere in the hall. "Shouldn't we send for Doctor Clayton?" Mrs. Styles asked.

"Why? So the man can take money to tell me that Lenora should be sent to an asylum? He doesn't even examine her anymore when I send for him."

"The missus won't let him, sir," the housekeeper said in a

217

quiet voice. "Do you remember she threatened to slap him last time if he touched her?"

"She was joking," said the baronet. "You know how she used to joke."

"Doctor Clayton didn't seem to think so," whispered Neil.

Sir Feldon turned upon him with fury in his eyes. "So what would you have me do? Send your sister away?"

"No! But perhaps if you sent for the child again. She was much calmer when the girl was here."

"Calmer, Mr. Wingate?" Mrs. Styles challenged. "You can't mean you approved of the way she acted!"

"Well, at least she slept nights!" came Neil's retort.

"And what about what happened at church?"

"What happened at church was the result of Lenora's trying to do too much at once. It was her first outing in two—"

"That's enough!" Feldon ordered. His voice was sharp, and his expression wore the strain of constantly trying to draw his wife back into the bounds of sanity. Rubbing his forehead again, he lowered his voice and asked Mrs. Styles if the girl's family would allow her to return. "Tonight, I'm talking about."

The housekeeper's face fell. "Oh, please, sir," she pleaded. "Don't bring Jenny back into this. It's not right to keep sending her back and forth."

"That's not what I asked you, Mrs. Styles."

After a sigh, she replied, "Her uncle would gladly give her over to you tonight. As long as you pay him, the man doesn't care a whit about what happens to the girl."

Another wail, this time louder, floated down the hall. Feldon realized that the sound was coming from Angelica's room. Turning a haggard face back to his brother-in-law, he asked, "Do you know where the girl lives?"

"I could have Harold drive me. He delivered some of her things to her earlier."

"All right." Sir Feldon turned back to Mrs. Styles. "I can't bear to be around her when she's like this. I'm going to try to go back to sleep. Wake me if she doesn't calm down when the girl gets here."

"You mean, when *Angelica* gets here, sir," the housekeeper murmured as her employer started to turn away.

"What?" He pivoted back around, his expression mirroring disbelief that a servant would talk with him in such a manner.

"Begging your pardon, sir," Mrs. Styles said with gentle boldness. "That'll be what Lady Dunley will insist that we call the girl. Can you live with hearing your child's name over and over in such a disturbing way?"

"I can live with anything that I have to, if—" His voice broke, then he took a deep breath and went on. "If it'll keep Lenora from just giving up and dying. It's bad enough to have my daughter's death on my conscience . . . I can't have my wife's on it, too."

~

"You, girl!"

Jenny could hear the voice and feel the touch of the rough hand on her shoulder. For several seconds she thought she was still at the Dunley house. Then, blinking her eyes open, she recognized Uncle Roy's face in the semidarkness.

"Get up and get dressed," he ordered before turning to climb back down the ladder. Jenny could see the amber light from a candle creeping up over the edge of the loft, and she could hear the sound of Aunt Mary weeping. *What have I done?* she wondered, quickly jumping from the mattress and getting her dress from the nail.

"Don't make her leave again!" came her aunt's voice from below.

"Go back to bed, Mary!" Her uncle's voice sounded irritated, unrelenting. "This ain't for you to decide."

After reaching behind herself to fasten as many buttons as her shaking fingers would allow, Jenny knelt down by the mattress again.

"Hurry, girl! You got people waiting."

She quickly kissed each sleeping cheek, pausing only long enough to brush a lock of hair from little Diana's closed eyes. As soon as her feet touched the floor below, her uncle was at her side. "Now this time, you'd better behave, you hear?"

Numbly, she nodded. With Uncle Roy hurrying her to the door, she darted a look at Aunt Mary, who was sitting on the side of the big bed with her hands covering her face.

"Good-bye, Aunt Mary," Jenny ventured when they reached the door. There was no answer from the bed, only a muffled sob.

Outside, Mr. Wingate and another man sat in the Dunleys' gig. Uncle Roy boosted her up between them. "Don't be bringin' her back here again!" he growled, then turned to go back in the cottage. As the driver turned the horse around, Jenny stared longingly at the door that had just slammed shut.

She sat, stiff and wooden, between the two men as the gig rattled up the dirt road under the light of the stars. When the outline of the manor house was finally visible ahead, she began to feel an overwhelming sense of resignation. Somehow she sensed that she might never see her cousins and aunt again.

The gig finally came to a halt in front of the house, and

Mr. Wingate turned to Jenny with an apologetic look before helping her to the ground. "I must take you up to see my sister right away, but don't worry—you shan't be mistreated."

Jenny could only stare at the man, and from somewhere in her mind came the thought that she was already being mistreated. The door to the only home she had ever known was shut to her forever it seemed, yet this place could never be her home. Was there any place in the world that she belonged?

"Mind you don't trip over the stones," Mr. Wingate warned gently as he led her up a dark footpath to the portico.

Mrs. Styles met them at the front door, a lantern in her hand. "I'm so sorry, Jenny. I tried to keep it from coming to this." The two adults and the girl started for the staircase. A low wailing drifted down from the darkness above. Strangely, the sound evoked more pity than fear from Jenny.

"It sounds worse than it really is," Mr. Wingate assured Jenny when she hesitated at the foot of the stairs. "I'm sure she'll settle down when she sees you."

Mrs. Styles touched Jenny lightly on the back. "We had better go on up there, child," she said with a heavy voice.

~

A sliver of light shone under the door of the room where Jenny had stayed just the night before. Jenny could hear a muffled rhythmic sound going on and on, and for the first time felt a tinge of fear. After pausing for a moment, Mr. Wingate opened the door and motioned for Jenny to follow him inside.

The back of the rocking chair was the first thing the girl saw, and then she realized that Lady Dunley was seated there, facing the window and rocking frantically.

"Lenora," her brother said. The woman ignored him, so he

nudged Jenny to walk over to the chair with him. "She's back, Lenora."

Slowly, the woman turned her face toward them. Her eyes were swollen, reddened slits over splotched cheeks, and her graying brown hair disheveled about her shoulders. The white lawn dress she had worn to church, wrinkled now, bore stains on the bodice, as if she'd spilled food or drink there earlier.

At first Lady Dunley fixed a blank stare on Jenny, which made her wonder if the poor woman had lost her mind completely. Then, slowly, recognition began to show in her eyes.

"Angelica?" came a weak whisper from Lady Dunley's lips. "My baby?" She held out her arms, and Jenny felt Mr. Wingate's hand on her back, nudging her closer.

"Oh, my baby!" With a strength that belied her fragile appearance, the woman pulled Jenny onto her lap. "You came back to me!" she exclaimed, stroking Jenny's hair. "You came back!"

18

"I THINK you should have some more of the herbs and tea,"
Corrine told Joseph Price Monday morning as she poured
water from the bucket into the teapot. She tried to keep
any worry from her voice, but Mr. Price's appearance had
shocked her when she had bathed his face a moment ago. He
had opened his mouth to try to talk to her, and she had caught
a glimpse of fiery red patches on his tongue.

Is that supposed to happen? she wondered, hanging the teapot
on the hook over the fire. *And does it mean he's getting better
. . . or worse?* Corrine wished she had someone to ask. Again
she chided herself for acquiring so little rudimentary knowledge during her lifetime. *Now, if someone asks me which shoes
would go with a peach breakfast gown, I could answer right away.*

After the tea was brewed, she brought the cup over. "It
seems a little too hot," she declared, testing it with the tip of
a finger. "I'll just set it here on the table until it's cooled down
some. No sense in scalding your throat."

"Talk?" Joseph rasped.

"I know, it hurts."

"I mean . . ." He glanced at the stool at his bedside. "You?"

Tilting her head at him, she wondered if she had heard him
right. "You want *me* to sit and talk with you?"

"Please?" He gave her a weak smile and touched his throat. "Takes mind off."

"All right," she replied, wondering what she could possibly say that would interest this man. In his eyes, she wore a cloak woven from the strands of her shameful past—a covering that prevented him from seeing the woman she had become. Still, she sat down on the stool. "What do you want to talk about?"

"Hope you . . . don't get sick."

Corrine shrugged her shoulders. "I hope so, too, but that's out of our hands."

"My fault if it happens," he whispered.

"No." As much as she still disliked him and blamed him for ruining the reconciliation with her family, she could not hold him liable for the disease, even if she ended up catching it herself. *The old Corrine would have—in a heartbeat,* she thought. "I've asked God not to allow me to get sick," she told him quietly. "Perhaps he'll grant me that favor. Either way, he's blessed me more than I deserve."

Joseph stared at her, clearly baffled. "Even?"

She knew what he meant. "Even with the way things turned out? Yes, even so. He made me his child—and I've got a bright future promised to me, in spite of my dark past."

He looked as if he were considering her words, and Corrine wondered if he thought she had only spoken them in the hopes of his good testimony about her to Squire Nowells. Did all new believers have to battle their past reputations? What about the woman at the well? Had everyone believed her story about being cleansed by the Living Water? For the rest of her life? Or had there been some doubters who refused even to listen?

"Can't let your tea get cold," she said, reaching over to test the dark brew with a finger again. It seemed to be just the right temperature, so she helped Joseph ease up onto his elbows. "Just sip it. It's probably best that the herbs stay in your throat for as long as possible."

With a grateful nod he obeyed, taking short swallows and wincing every time. "Thank you," he whispered when the cup was lowered from his lips. He lay back on his pillow to catch his breath, his eyes watching her.

"Are you ready to try to have some breakfast?" Corrine asked after a length of silence. The man's unreadable expression was beginning to make her uncomfortable. What was he thinking about as he watched her?

He shook his head slightly. "Talk more? Please?"

"All right," she shrugged.

"Your family?"

"Are you asking about my husband and daughter?"

He only nodded.

Corrine frowned. Why ask her about the people he had refused to believe existed? Was he just humoring her because she was taking care of him? "So you believe me about that?"

He gave another weak nod.

Sick or not, Corrine couldn't let him forget the accusation he had made about her reason for wanting to go home. "And how do you know I don't have a potential 'sheep' waiting in Leawick to be fleeced, Mr. Price?"

He watched her with a pained expression for a moment, then whispered, "Sorry."

"So you really do believe that I've got a family? How did this come to pass?" Corrine asked, folding her arms.

"Been thinking about it. On the train you didn't . . ."

Corrine shook her head in amusement. It obviously

bothered the man that she hadn't responded to his flirtations even though they had only been an act. If there was one thing she had learned about men, it was that they took rejection deeply to heart. "I didn't flirt back with you . . . is that what you mean?"

"Yes."

"And so now you conclude that my lack of interest was because I was telling the truth about my husband and child?"

He nodded again, and Corrine had to struggle to keep the smirk from her lips. It was probably wrong, baiting a sick man like this, but she was enjoying herself for the first time since she had been abducted. "Maybe the reason I didn't fall into your arms was because I didn't find you particularly appealing," she said innocently. "Did you ever consider that?"

This time Joseph looked startled, and Corrine got up from the stool before he could utter a response. "Now, Mr. Price, I've got things to do," she said, favoring him with the sweetest smile she could muster. She had spent enough time on this foolishness. If not for him, she would be with Thomas and Jenny now. She certainly wasn't going to go into details about her family just to help this man pass the time.

~

All morning she moved about the cottage, performing chores that were unnecessary and avoiding looking at Joseph. He was probably hungry, but she had already done her duty by asking earlier if he wanted breakfast.

By noon Corrine was miserable. Here she was, claiming to be a Christian, but acting like a spoiled child. Would Jesus allow a sick man, even one who had been cruel to him, to suffer? Hadn't he even forgiven his tormentors from the cross?

She walked over to the bed. Joseph was lying there on his side, awake. "Mr. Price," she said, touching his shoulder when he didn't look up at her. "Would you like me to heat up some soup?"

~

The rest of the afternoon Corrine devoted herself to tending to her patient, but she was still not in the mood for conversation. Bernice had once explained to her that Christians should always try to go the extra mile, yet Corrine figured she could go the extra distance without being required to chat the whole way.

Joseph didn't try to talk, either. Occasionally she caught him studying her with a puzzled expression before he would avert his eyes.

She heated a pitcher of water and set it on the stool by the bed so that he could bathe himself. Before taking a walk to give him privacy, she took his clean set of clothes from his gripsack and laid them out on the table.

"Your clothes are beginning to smell, Mr. Price," she told him bluntly as she helped him to his feet. "I'll wash the ones you have on in the morning."

When she came back after a long walk, Joseph was in much better spirits. He was sitting up in bed this time and had even put on some water for tea.

"Feels good to be clean," he whispered. "Thank you, Mrs. Hammond."

"I'm sure it does," Corrine replied. He seemed so anxious not to offend her that her reserve thawed just a little. "And you're welcome."

After brewing a cup of herb tea, she sat down on the stool beside him.

"You have some, too?" he asked, his face still anxious. He looked like a little boy who didn't want to get in trouble, and she had to smile.

"I'll make myself some when you're finished," she told him. She helped him manage the cup, occasionally wiping his beard with a dry dish towel.

"Thank you again, Mrs. Hammond," he whispered when he finished.

Corrine set the cup aside and frowned. "Look, Mr. Price. It's painful enough for you to say anything at all. Just call me Corrine until you get better. Or don't call me anything. After all, there's nobody else here that you'd be talking to."

He nodded and smiled up at her. "Call me Joseph?"

"I don't think I'd care to do that," she replied, rising abruptly to set the cup and napkin on the bedside table.

"You angry?" he whispered, clearly taken aback by her response.

"Angry? Not one bit, *Mister* Price." Without another word she snatched up her valise and pushed through the front door of the cottage. She marched through the woods until she came to the brook, then dropped her valise on the ground and dug inside for her cake of soap and towel.

Corrine's jaw tightened as she fumbled with the buttons at the back of her dress. Mr. Price had to be the most infuriating man she'd ever met! What did he think—that they were chums now, just because she had been forced to take care of him? Did he actually think she wanted to be his *friend? And when he's recovered, he can haul his new "friend" up to Treybrook,* she fumed silently. *"It's been jolly good knowing you, Mrs. Hammond—sorry you won't be able to see your husband and daughter. Be sure and write from whatever dungeon they boot you in."*

The suggestion that Mr. Price should use her given name had been a simple act of trying to make it easier for him to speak—nothing more. Yes, she felt compassion for him, but she would have the same compassion for an animal that was suffering. *Maybe even more!* she told herself, stepping into the chilly water.

Despite the temperature, she took her time bathing, enjoying the mental picture of Joseph Price holding his throat and groaning for a cup of water. Or better yet, she thought with a smirk, urgently needing her to help him get out of bed again!

Corrine was soaping her hair when she thought she heard a sound. Her pulse jumped. Had Mr. Price called out for her? Almost immediately she realized that it had been the crinkling of lather at her ear. *Anyway, how could he call when he can barely whisper?*

Her "revenge" began to feel hollow. What if he was in there suffering? She had told him that she had changed, had become a child of God, yet within a span of hours she had lost her temper twice. What if he needed her while she was down here sulking?

Quickly Corrine rinsed the soap from her hair and got out of the water. She dried off and put on the clean clothes, then made her way toward the cottage with her valise in one hand and her wet shift wrapped in a towel in the other. She was halfway there when a powerful urge came over her—the urge to get back as fast as she could. Setting her valise and wet clothes at the base of an oak tree, she gathered her skirts in her hands and started running. "Mr. Price!" she called out before she was even halfway through the door.

She hurried over to the bed, panting to catch her breath. The man was still lying there on his back as she had left him, his eyes closed. Peaceful. Yet Corrine was becoming increasingly aware that *something* was odd. Touching his shoulder, she whispered, "Mr. Price?"

Joseph opened his eyes, looked at her, then turned his face away. For a second Corrine thought that his condition had worsened. His eyes were red rimmed . . . and watery.

When he sniffed, Corrine's mouth gaped. Had Joseph Price—the muscular and menacing detective, the man who had kidnapped her at gunpoint—been lying there weeping? She frowned, folding her arms. *Of course.* The way she had grabbed her valise and stormed out of the cottage, he must have thought she was leaving. Then he would have to capture her all over again—if he didn't die from having no one to tend to him.

He sniffed again. Corrine rolled her eyes and thought, *For all of your tough talk, you're just a frightened little boy. And a selfish one at that.*

"Haven't cried in years," Joseph's raspy voice mumbled, though his eyes were still turned away from her.

"Well, you needn't have," she snapped as she fetched a handkerchief from one of the drawers. Coming back to the bed, she dropped it on his chest. "I didn't run off to Leawick."

Joseph lay still for a few seconds longer, then picked up the handkerchief and wiped his eyes and nose. "Didn't think you had."

Corrine's brows shot up. "What?"

"Knew you'd come back," he said, returning her gaze.

That settles it! she thought. *The fever has baked his brain.*

"Well, that's good to know." She picked up the handkerchief, dropped it in the basket in the corner, then started toward the table to warm up some more broth for his supper.

But her steps halted. Crossing her arms, Corrine turned to stare at Joseph. "Just so I'll know," she said, "in case I *do* have the chance to live to be an old woman and find myself wondering one day, why were you crying if you were so sure I'd be coming back?"

Joseph swallowed and winced. "Because I knew you'd come back."

She cocked her head. "I beg your pardon?"

"Told the truth," he whispered. "You did. About changing."

His answer stunned her. After she had tried and tried to convince Mr. Price that she was no longer the Corrine Hammond who destroyed people, what opened his eyes was the fact that she had stormed out of the cottage in a fit of anger?

Brushing a strand of damp hair from her eyes, she said, "I *could* be putting on an act so that you'd have more nice things to tell Squire Nowells about me. Remember your point about theatrics?"

"Not acting," he rasped, giving a slow shake of his head.

"And how can you be sure?"

Joseph swallowed again, his face showing the pain that speaking caused. Corrine noticed and held up a hand. "We can talk about this later, Mr. Price." Hesitating for several seconds, she then added, "But thank you for saying that."

~

Joseph tried to drink down some of the broth, but the swallowing gave him such agony that he had to give up, despite Corrine's coaxing. He couldn't even eat the other orange, but was able to take little sips of the juice that she squeezed into a cup for him.

After Corrine had helped him drink another cup of tea brewed with herbs, Joseph closed his eyes and pretended to sleep so that she would sit down and have some supper herself. He listened to the faint noise of her spoon against a tin soup bowl and tried to recall the moment it had struck him that Mrs. Hammond had been telling him the truth.

The sound of the door slamming behind her when she had left with her valise had caused him to panic. How would he manage without her? Was he going to die, all alone in this cottage?

Then as quickly as the panic had set in, it went away. A feeling of relief had washed over him, although where it came from, he had no idea. She would not leave him to perish. He hadn't known where she had gone or when she would return, but when she finally burst back through the door, he hadn't been surprised.

That was when the tears had come, and they had startled him as much as they'd startled Mrs. Hammond. But he knew why he had wept. He had never broken his word to a client in his life. And he would still have to take her to Treybrook.

19

JOSEPH Price was barely able to whisper for the next three days. He lay huddled in such lethargy that it took nearly all of Corrine's strength to persuade him to drink the tea and the broth that Mr. Rhodes delivered every day.

On the fourth morning, Friday, she went to his bedside with a cup of herb tea. The rash had disappeared from his face, and he was covered with sweat.

Panic gripped her and she shook his shoulder. "Wake up, Mr. Price!"

His eyelids fluttered open. "Huh?"

"You're sweating. Is that good or bad?"

"Must be good," he whispered, giving her a weak smile. "These blankets are too hot."

She set the tea aside and took both blankets away, leaving him between sheets that were drenched with sweat. "I'm going to have to change these after you have your tea," she told him, reaching over to put a hand on his forehead. The coolness of the skin under her palm came as a shock. "You'll have to change your clothes, too. I'll set them out for you and then go for a walk."

"Thank you." He swallowed hard. "Throat feels better, too. My tongue hurts, though."

"Open your mouth and let me see."

Joseph looked up at her with alarm in his eyes, then shook his head. "Will get better," he said through closed teeth.

"Well, just let me look at it."

"Embarrassed," he whispered, then pressed his lips tight.

"To have me look inside your mouth?"

He nodded.

"Why? Are there warts on your teeth?"

A laugh came from Joseph's throat—he winced from the pain of it, but the smile stayed on his lips.

Corrine marveled at the change in his expression, realizing that this was the first time since he had captured her that she had seen him laugh without a superior smirk on his face. *He's really quite handsome.* The thought passed through her mind before she could stop it.

Chagrined, she took a step back. *Not again!* She had allowed herself to think of him as a man instead of someone she happened to be taking care of, and now guilt raged through her again. *Forgive me, Lord . . . I should be thinking about Thomas.*

That was the solution. If she kept her mind on her husband, there would be no room to have disturbing thoughts about other men.

"All right," Joseph whispered. He had been watching her with some confusion in his eyes. "Don't be angry."

"What?"

"I'll show you my tongue."

Corrine sighed and stepped close again, bending to peer inside his open mouth. His tongue was no longer the color of strawberries, but now was covered with darker crimson patches where the skin looked raw.

Concern for her patient overshadowed her feelings of guilt. "You say your tongue hurts?"

He nodded. "Burns."

"Do you think you could still drink some tea? I don't think you should stop."

"Try. Not warm, though."

"All right. We'll let it cool a little while longer."

Thirty minutes later, she helped him to the bench at the table so that she could change his sheets. "I'm going to wash today," she told him, setting the sweat-soaked sheets on top of the basket of towels and clothing.

"Wish I could help."

She turned to him with a small laugh. "Oh, you do? Are you a laundress as well as a detective?"

Joseph shrugged his shoulders and smiled back at her. "Do you know how?" he whispered.

Already on her way to the chest to get fresh sheets, she nodded. "I didn't always have a maid, Mr. Price. When I was growing up, my sisters and I had chores. And before I left Leawick, I had to care for my husband and . . ." Her voice caught, and she began pulling at the corners of the bottom sheet.

"Your daughter," he finished for her. "You miss her."

She could feel her pulse, sluggish in her throat. Longing to see and hold her daughter brought an ache to her heart. "Does that mean anything to you?" she asked slowly.

"Yes." His sorrowful, mulberry eyes were fixed upon her face. "But I gave my word to Squire Nowells."

~

Joseph's throat was remarkably better the next day, though the patches on his tongue were still quite painful. He spent most of the afternoon listening to the thunderclaps outside and watching Corrine as she went about the cottage doing chores.

She had barely spoken to him all day, but he sensed that it was sadness, not anger, that kept her quiet. When she supposed him to be napping, he had watched through half-closed eyes as she folded the wash she'd brought inside just before the thunderstorm set in. She had paused several times to wipe her eyes.

After she helped him spoon down some broth for his supper, Joseph could stand it no longer. "Please, talk with me," he said, grateful that the pain in his throat was easing.

"Sorry, but I don't feel like talking."

"Please?"

For several seconds she didn't move. He saw her shoulders heave, then with a sigh she turned around, came back to his bedside, and sat on the stool beside him.

"You've taken good care of me," he began. "I'm very grateful."

"You're welcome." She took his empty bowl and started to rise from the stool.

"Please don't go."

She settled back on the stool and folded her hands in her lap. The apricot gown she wore set off her flawless complexion—flawless but for the shadows of fatigue under her eyes. "Mr. Price, I don't want to hear any more explanations of why you have to take me to Treybrook," she said. "You were hired to bring me in, so there's nothing more to say."

"You're not making this any easier on me."

"I don't see that I'm required to." Giving a heavy sigh, she bit her lip. "My money's gone. Most of it, that is."

"What?"

"I noticed it this morning while you were still asleep, when

I took this dress from my trunk. I had put the money in the pocket of my jacket when we stopped at Adderly."

"Are you sure you didn't put it in some other pocket?"

She shook her head. "I've gone through every dress in my trunk. Twice."

"What do you think happened to it?"

"I believe Pete took it. He was alone with my trunk for a while at Amberton. And he acted funny when I came out to speak with him."

"I'm so sorry. I never should have trusted him alone with the trunk."

She accepted his apology with a somber nod. "I was going to give it all to Squire Nowells to pay back the money I took from his father."

"Again, I'm sorry. Would you allow me to pay you back what you've lost?"

"I don't want your money, Mr. Price. I appreciate the offer, but my days of taking money from men are over."

"I only meant . . ."

"I know." She was quiet for a spell, her gaze fixed upon the rain swirling against the window glass while Joseph tried to keep from staring at her. He was disconcerted to find that he liked looking at her face, especially when she was deep in thought. Sometimes she seemed to possess such enviable peace, and at other times there seemed to be a struggle going on within. He decided that this time she was struggling, and his impression was confirmed when she finally spoke.

"I was wrong to put such stock in offering Squire Nowells the money," she said, her gray eyes serious upon his face. "I've been praying for God to touch Squire Nowells's heart when he sees that I've changed. It was wrong of me to keep trying to figure out another way. I've just got to trust God."

There was so much hope in her voice that Joseph felt a pang of regret at the deception he had fostered upon her. He had told Corrine that if she went with him to Treybrook, she would at least have a chance. But it had been a lie. There could be no possibility of mercy from a man so obsessed with revenge.

It would have made his job much easier if she had lived up—or rather, down—to her reputation. Why did she have to turn out to be so decent? The Corrine Hammond he had been hired to take to Treybrook had a wicked past and had hurt people, but sometimes it seemed that he had captured the wrong woman. At times she seemed so vulnerable that he found himself wanting to protect her.

She had nursed him back from the brink of death, and now, as soon as he was able to travel, he was going to have to take her somewhere where she would probably not last a year. The irony of the situation struck him like a blow. She, the deceiver, had been honest with him. He had lied to her.

Well, maybe it was time for a little truth of his own.

"Mrs. Hammond, I don't think he would have been interested in the money anyway."

"Well, perhaps not. I suppose I thought offering it would prove to him that I want to make amends."

"I don't think he's interested in 'amends' either."

"Meaning what?"

He blew out a sharp breath. "He's bent on revenge, ma'am. Likely you'll be put in jail."

"Jail?" Tears welled up in her gray eyes, and she wiped them with the back of her hand. "For how long, do you think?"

"Please don't ask me that," he answered in a grim voice.

A tense silence surrounded the two of them. Joseph watched Corrine stare out the window, and he thought that it might have been better for her if she had shot him that day in the coach.

Corrine turned grave eyes upon Joseph. "I'm not going to let my faith weaken. I'm still praying that God will soften the man's heart." Hesitating, she added, "And I'm hoping that you will speak for me."

"Of course I will," he said quickly, but he was certain it would do no good.

"You know," she began, her expression thoughtful, "I'm still glad I didn't try to escape." With a wry smile, she went on. "I'm sure you know that I was tempted a couple of times. But if you had contacted Scotland Yard, I don't think they would have allowed me the opportunity to ask Squire Nowells's forgiveness. At least this way I have a *chance* to start all over again."

Her honesty, her vulnerability, stabbed at his conscience like a knife. Joseph closed his eyes, unable to stop a groan from coming to his lips.

"Mr. Price?"

Opening his eyes again, he saw the worry in hers. "Mrs. Hammond . . ." He gave a deep and troubled sigh. "I never intended to tell Scotland Yard about you."

"But you said . . ."

"I said that so you wouldn't try to escape. Scotland Yard can't arrest you unless someone brings in a complaint . . . someone who has been hurt by you. I'm sure you realize there's no chance of that happening."

She glanced up at the door and then back at him. "You mean I could have . . ."

"You could have left me here to die and gone on to Leawick—that's what I would have done in your place. I have no right to expect you to accept my apology for the lie, but I do regret it."

After another length of silence, Corrine said in a quiet voice, "I can't fault anyone for lying. Not when I've told so many myself."

"You're not angry?"

"Well, to be honest," she sighed, "I wish that our paths had never crossed. But I'm glad I didn't know the truth about Scotland Yard. The temptation to leave was hard enough as it was."

"You wouldn't have let me die."

"I hope that I wouldn't," said Corrine. "But the main reason I didn't escape was that I knew you'd eventually come for me if you lived." Her voice filled with irony. "You or Scotland Yard."

"But you would have at least had a little time with your family."

Corrine shook her head. "If I'm ever back with my husband and daughter, I don't want to be taken out of their lives again. I can't do that to them—once was bad enough. And I don't want to have to listen for footsteps outside my door either. Squire Nowells just *has* to forgive me."

~

"You never did tell me about your family," Joseph said cautiously to Corrine the next morning after breakfast. His voice was only slightly hoarse, and for the first time in days, he had been able to eat some bread and cheese, washed down with the ever-present herb tea. "Does it make you angry when I ask about them?"

"No, I suppose not." Just a few feet away, Corrine sat on the bench, her back resting against the table. She had found some sewing supplies and was patching one of the blankets she had washed two days ago. "There's not much to tell," she said, drawing the thread through the wool draped over her knees. "My parents died in a fire shortly after I married. My sisters are all married and scattered, except for Mary. She lives in Leawick, too."

"And your husband?"

"Thomas?" Her fingertip felt a stab of the needle, and she had to put it to her mouth for a second. "He's a charcoal maker," she said when the finger had stopped bleeding.

"Did you hurt yourself?" Joseph had pulled up on one elbow and was watching her.

"The needle bit my finger," she answered, scowling down at the row of slightly uneven stitches in the wool. "It's been a long time since I've sewn anything. I suppose you think I'm totally helpless."

"Helpless? I'd match your nursing skills against Florence Nightingale's anytime."

She was about to ask him who Florence Nightingale was, then decided that just because she was ignorant, she didn't have to advertise the fact. Surely that wasn't being dishonest.

"Your husband," Joseph went on, relaxing against the pillow a bit. "Are you eager to see him?"

"Of course," she answered right away.

"And your daughter?"

"I think of almost nothing else. My whole being aches for her." Fighting back tears, Corrine stopped sewing and clutched the blanket to her chest. "Have you any children, Mr. Price?"

she asked, changing the subject for the sake of her own composure.

"I've never married. Would you please call me Joseph?"

She shook her head.

"You're still that angry at me?"

Again Corrine shook her head. There was no point in being
angry anymore. However, she couldn't let their relationship
get any more familiar than it had already become. The attrac-
tion she felt for him was becoming more and more intrusive
in her thoughts, but she intended to do her best to fight it.

She went back to her sewing, glad to have something for her
hands to do. She had already done the scant chores necessary
to keep the cottage tidy, and she couldn't concentrate on her
Bible when he was awake and pretending not to look at her.

~

As evening drew on, a chill permeated the inside of the cottage. Corrine built a little fire in the fireplace, then began
straightening out her pallet on the floor. But before she could
put out the lantern, Joseph asked her to sit with him again for
just a little while.

"Are you having trouble sleeping?" He had been silent for
so long after supper that she assumed he had fallen asleep a
long time ago.

"Yes," he answered as she took her place on the stool.
"My thoughts are quite troubling for some reason."

"My friend Bernice used to pray for me when my thoughts
kept me awake. Would you like me to pray for you?"

She really means that, Joseph thought, touched that she
would suggest it. "All right . . . please." He closed his eyes and
waited, but no words came from her mouth. After a while he

opened one eye to look at her—Corrine's head was bowed and her lips were moving slightly. A little while later, when he thought it was safe, he opened both eyes and looked at her. She was watching his face, but averted her eyes quickly.

"I didn't hear you praying," he said with a smile.

"I've never prayed out loud before. God heard me though, Mr. Price."

Joseph felt his eyes smarting as he gazed up at her. *She almost looks like an angel sitting there.* "You really believe that God is listening, don't you?"

"Yes, I do. And sometimes I can hear him talking to me."

He raised an eyebrow. He'd never heard of such a thing mentioned in the church services he had attended with his family while growing up in Bristol. "Are you sure?"

Corrine smiled. "Very sure."

"What does he say?"

"It's hard to explain, Mr. Price. I don't know that I could make you understand." She was quiet for a long moment, then said, "Have you ever seen a couple who looked to be truly in love? The way they seem to speak to each other without words?"

Joseph thought about the man and woman on the train from York. "I saw what you're speaking of just recently, in an older married couple."

"Good," she said with a pleased nod. "Sometimes when I'm praying, I can 'feel' God's love being directed at me."

"You can?" He tried to keep the skepticism out of his voice.

She didn't answer right away, but took a second to wipe her eyes with the back of her hand. "You have to understand what that means to someone like me, Mr. Price," she said at length.

"To know that I'm *clean* in the sight of my Father is the most incredible thing that's ever happened to me."

She really means what she's saying, Joseph thought. An ache came to his chest. Would she still have that faith after months in Treybrook's dark lockup?

If only he hadn't gotten sick! He would have had her delivered to Squire Nowells and been on his way to Bristol by now, filled with satisfaction that he had stopped an extortionist from hurting anyone else. There wouldn't have been time for him to get to know the Corrine Hammond sitting there beside him.

"Thank you for praying," he managed to say around the lump in his throat.

~

Extinguishing the lantern, Corrine crawled onto her pallet. She had fashioned a makeshift pillow by folding a blanket and wrapping a sheet over it, but it still took her a while to relax on the hard floor.

An hour or so later as she was just beginning to dream—she was a little girl again, playing with her sisters—Joseph's voice brought her back to reality.

"Did you say something, Mr. Price?" she called out, rising on one elbow.

His tone was apologetic. "Were you asleep?"

"I was, Mr. Price." Corrine couldn't keep the irritation out of her voice. "If you'll lie still for a while, I'm sure you'll be able to sleep."

"I'm not going to take you to Treybrook."

This time Corrine sat up straight, bumping her head on the table's bench. "What did you say?"

"I'm going to send Squire Nowells back the money he paid me to find you."

Tears began to flow down Corrine's cheeks. "But you were hired . . ."

"That's why I had trouble sleeping. But I've worked out a way to tell the squire that I can't find you—a way that will also keep him from hiring someone else to look for you."

Corrine's shoulders fell. It was too good to be true. How could he possibly do that without lying . . . and how could she allow a lie to be perpetrated on her behalf? *O God, is this a test?* she prayed under her breath. *I want this so much, but what would you have me do?*

"Mrs. Hammond?"

"I'm here," she said, biting her knuckle to stifle a sob.

"When you became a Christian . . . isn't that called being 'born again'?"

"It is, Mr. Price. The words came from Jesus."

"And so you became a new person?"

"Not *physically*, but yes, that's so."

"Well, what happened to the former Corrine Hammond?" Joseph's voice said from across the tiny room.

Corrine bit her lip. How could she make the gospel clear to him when it had sounded so mysterious the first time she had heard it. "Well, my old nature . . . died. God's Holy Spirit came into my soul and made me into a child of God."

"And that's the message I intend to send to the good squire."

Corrine could not see Joseph, but she could tell by his voice that he was smiling. How could he be so flippant about something that had brought meaning to her life?

"Mr. Price . . . I don't know what to make of what you're saying."

A chuckle came through the darkness. "Don't you see? It'll be the truth if I tell him that the Corrine Hammond he hired me to capture is *no longer alive*. Because according to your faith, she isn't! I can see that with my own eyes!"

Corrine sat there speechless. The man she had once despised was offering her freedom! But was it right for her to take it? "Mr. Price," she said, her voice shaking, "I can't allow myself to be involved with anything illegal anymore. If the law says I should—"

"The law has *nothing* to do with this. You're not wanted by the authorities—just by a vengeful man who wants to bend the law to his own purpose so that he can watch you die a slow death."

She was quiet for a long time, digesting this information. "You mean, if I go to my family, no one will come looking for me later?"

"Squire Nowells was the only person wanting to find you. The others would just as soon forget about that part of their lives. I don't think you'd have to worry about being taken again."

It was almost too good to be true! Wrapping her arms around her knees, Corrine breathed a quick prayer of thanks. "Mr. Price, I don't quite know what to say!"

"Just say 'good night,'" he answered, "because I think I'm going to be able to sleep now."

She laughed, almost giddy from the joy. "Good night, then." She started to lie back down on her pallet when a disturbing thought occurred to her. "But what about your reputation? This won't hurt your career as a detective, will it?"

"I hadn't thought of that," he answered with a degree of uncertainty.

Why did I bring that up? she thought. Would he change his mind now?

"I don't think it will affect my career, because no one will know the difference. Besides," he continued, his voice filled with humor, "if it does, I know of a bakery in Bristol that would probably give me a job."

20

M RS. Pruitt appeared in Jenny's room just as Helene was helping the girl with her bath. "Oh, good, you're not dressed yet," she said, breathing heavily from a sprint up the staircase. She held out two orchid dresses, complete with lace and carved-ivory buttons—identical except for the fact that one was a good two sizes larger than the other. "I had the girls up late finishing this last night. Too bad you had to wait so long, but none of Angelica's dresses were simple."

Jenny still couldn't quite understand why anyone would go to so much trouble for her. Two days ago, Mrs. Styles had shown up with three pairs of shoes that actually fit her, hiding away Angelica's smaller matching ones. It had been such a relief to not walk around with cramped toes yesterday, and now it looked as if she was about to get some more comfortable dresses.

Jenny reached out a finger to touch one of the rosebud-shaped buttons. "Thank you," she whispered, her voice thick with emotion.

Mrs. Styles and the seamstress had decided that Helene would have to be let in on the dress-switching secret, since she was the one who saw to Jenny's wardrobe. "Oh, lookit!" she exclaimed, taking the larger dress from Mrs. Pruitt and examining the lace. "It's just like the other one!"

Mrs. Pruitt beamed. "We'll just hide the smaller frock in my room and get started on another one," she told Jenny with a wink. "I've ordered pieces of cloth that match most of Angelica's dresses, so we'll swap out as we get them made. Then if you get to go back home, you can keep the dresses that fit you, and we'll put the old ones back in here."

The seamstress's words brought a lump to Jenny's throat. *"If you get to go home," she had said. Not "when." So, she had been right—when she left Uncle Roy's house in the middle of the night, she left it for good.*

Not wanting to hurt Mrs. Pruitt's feelings, she managed a smile. "Do you think I could wear it today?" she asked Helene.

Helene looked at Mrs. Pruitt, who raised a hopeful eyebrow, and then back to Jenny. "Well, missy, we could hurry and get the dress on you before the missus comes in to pick out your clothes." She raised her chin, threw her hands in the air, and said in a mocking tone, "Maybe the missus will be in an *orchid* mood today."

The seamstress left with the smaller dress folded under her arm, lest Lady Dunley walk in and surprise her. Helene helped Jenny into her petticoat, stockings, and shoes, then slipped the new dress over the girl's shoulders.

Lady Dunley walked in just as the maid was fastening the last button. She wore a mauve gown with lace panels trailing down the bodice, and a matching ribbon threaded through the curls in her chignon. Just recently she had started washing her hair in the evening so she would have more time to spend with her "daughter" in the morning. She stopped just inside the door and regarded Jenny with a huge smile. "My, don't you look like the perfect lady!"

Feeling Helene's gentle pressure on her shoulder, Jenny made an attempt at a curtsy.

"Oh, you little clown!" Lenora giggled, rushing forward to embrace the girl. "Right foot forward, and you know it!" Immediately, she straightened and frowned at Helene. "The dress won't do."

"But you said she looks—"

"I'd like her to wear the pink gown," she declared, bending again to cup Jenny's chin with her hand. "The one with the little embroidered pansies. We're going to walk in the garden after breakfast, and my little angel will be the most beautiful blossom in sight."

"Yes, ma'am," Helene replied, a tiny note of resignation in her voice. With a glance at Jenny, she added, "Perhaps she could wear this one tomorrow?"

"I don't know . . . we'll have to see." Lenora gave the girl another quick embrace and said, "You know, a ribbon would look nice in your hair, too. I'll see if Alice can find another to match mine and be back to fetch you for breakfast."

~

His plate cleared, Feldon Dunley glanced up at the mantel clock, then quickly dabbed his fingers in the finger bowl and wiped them with a napkin. *I shouldn't have come down so late,* he thought, listening for the sound of footsteps in the hallway as he got up from his chair.

He didn't hear anything, but to play it safe, the baronet left the room through the door leading to the kitchen staircase.

Better to go through the kitchen and take the servants' stairs back up to his study than run into his wife in the hall.

Breakfast was the only meal he took in the dining room since Jenny's return, and always early enough not to be forced to witness Lenora's constant attention to their young visitor. He was resigned to the fact that Jenny had to stay in order to keep his wife happy, but the happiness was colored with a disturbing hue.

Of course, this whole arrangement was quite a boon for the girl. She had been rescued from long days in the fields and from nights in what he supposed to be a miserable hovel. She was given the best meals, a comfortable room, pretty dolls and clothes, and servants to attend to her every need. In his eyes, if anyone benefited from this situation—other than Lenora— it was the child.

Like the children at work in his fields, she had been given the privilege of helping her family earn a living—and while living in the lap of luxury, no less. He hoped she had the sense to appreciate her situation. If not, well, people suffered every day. The ones with character were strengthened by affliction, ultimately becoming strong enough to change their circum- stances. And those without character deserved to have their circumstances determined by other more powerful people. Like himself.

But even if he hadn't been born into a family of wealth and power, Sir Feldon would have triumphed. He would have pulled himself out of the gutter by sheer determination and strength of will. Until the death of his child, however, he had never been called to prove these claims. Now his wife's declining mental state and her incessant mad whims sapped his energy, demanding more than he could give. Acquiescence was his only option.

~

". . . And so your Uncle Neil and I slipped out of the bedroom window while our governess was asleep," Lady Dunley went on. Her eyes were lit with excitement, and she used her hands, when she was not holding Jenny's, in spirited animation. "Oh, don't look so shocked, dear! I was quite the little tomboy in those days, and it was nothing to scamper down a nearby birch tree."

Jenny nodded, trying in vain to picture Lady Dunley playing childish pranks and acting normally. It was so tempting to allow her thoughts to drift from the woman's long disjointed narrative, but then she would have to remind herself that her lot was far better than those out in the fields today. No doubt Mrs. Farrel would love to be allowed to sit in the garden and just listen.

That was basically all that was expected of her, Jenny now realized. Make Lady Dunley happy. And that was best done by paying attention, even when she had no idea what the lady was talking about.

". . . And the look on Metta Hansworth's face when you came out to recite!" Lady Dunley continued, jumping to another subject. "Her oldest daughter, Eloise, has always been such a toad. Oh, they boast that their seamstress is from France, but I say you can't make a silk purse from a sow's ear."

Lady Dunley grinned and squeezed Jenny's hand, the incident of some three years past still bringing triumph to her face. "Do you remember the horrible song Metta had that little pygmy of hers sing?"

"Yes . . . Mama," Jenny answered dutifully.

"I told your father that Metta shouldn't have worn green that afternoon. After she heard *you* sing, there was enough green in her *face* to dye a dozen dresses!"

A breeze fresh with violets wafted across Jenny's brow, stirring wisps of hair around her face and filling her with a longing to run about the garden, burying her face in patches of flowers. She remembered the joy that had come to Evan's face the first time he had tasted honeysuckle nectar. Before the memory had a chance to make her sad, Jenny realized the woman beside her had stopped talking.

"Yes, Mama," she said, hoping Lady Dunley hadn't noticed that her attention had drifted.

"Angelica," Lady Dunley whispered.

Jenny swallowed. The way Lady Dunley was looking at her was even more unsettling than her strange narrative had been. "Yes, Mama?" she said again.

But the lady shook her head. "You're not Angelica, are you?"

Glancing back at the house, Jenny wished Mrs. Styles were here so that she would know what was expected of her. "No, ma'am," she finally answered.

"Angelica is gone." A tear was making its way down Lady Dunley's cheek. "And it's my fault."

"No, it wasn't," Jenny answered timidly. She had no idea what Lady Dunley meant by blaming herself. Angelica had drowned—how could it be anyone's fault?

There was a long silence while Lady Dunley stared at a bee hovering over some roses on the trellis. Then she turned to Jenny again, her bottom lip trembling. "You're wearing her clothes."

Jenny nodded, a little fearful that her admission would bring about anger. Instead, the woman's voice went flat.

"I ordered you to, didn't I?"

"Yes . . . ma'am."

A sob came from the woman's lips, and she rubbed her temple. "I was so scared! I thought I was going to die!"

"Yes, ma'am."

"I didn't realize Angelica needed her father. The water was so cold . . . do you understand? And so deep. It pulled at me and I couldn't move my legs. Do you think she would understand?"

Jenny could only gape at her. After a moment the question was repeated. "Do you think she would?"

"Yes, ma'am."

"I didn't even *want* to go to the lake that day. Angelica knew that, too. She would remember my saying that. She would forgive me, don't you think?"

The misery in those hazel eyes stirred in Jenny more compassion than she had ever felt for Lady Dunley. Lifting a tentative hand to pat the woman's back, she replied, "Angelica would forgive you."

"Are you sure?"

"I'm sure, ma'am." Jenny then mustered up the boldness to take Lady Dunley's hand and get to her feet. "We should go inside now."

For a few seconds Lady Dunley didn't move, but only looked in the direction of the house as if trying to make up her mind. Finally she stood, still allowing Jenny to hold her hand. "I think I should lie down and take a nap. I'm so tired, all of a sudden."

"A nap will make you feel better, ma'am." Jenny led her out of the garden and around to the front of the house.

"You won't play with Angelica's dolls, will you?"

"No, ma'am."

"I just can't stand the thought of anyone playing with her dolls."

"I won't even touch them."

Mrs. Styles took over when they got inside. Not knowing what else to do, Jenny went up to Angelica's room and sat in a wing-back chair to wait. Surely any minute, someone would come through the door and tell her it was time to go back to Uncle Roy's. The thought should have made her happy, but instead it filled her with concern. Would he even allow her inside the door, or would he send her to an orphanage somewhere?

Think about nice things, she ordered herself. Anything to keep Uncle Roy's scowling face from her mind. *The violets smelled so nice outside. And the roses.* She willed herself to think even harder. What would it be like to be a bee out there in the garden? No worries, just moving from one lovely flower to another.

She found her eyelids growing heavy, and she rested her head against the cushioned chair arm.

~

"Jenny?"

She jolted her head up at the sound. Helene stood bending over her, her eyes concerned.

"I fell asleep?"

The maid laughed. "For two whole hours, love. You must have been awful tired, sleeping the mornin' away like that."

"Is it time to go?"

256

"Time for lunch is what it is. Let's get you freshened up and downstairs."

The answer confused Jenny. "You mean I'm not being sent away?"

"Sent away?" Helene shook her head and gave a sad smile. "Lady Dunley's down there wondering why Angelica's not at the table yet."

21

M R. Rhodes!" Corrine called out as the innkeeper dropped off the day's parcel of food.

The man paused, one foot up on the wagon frame. "Oh, good day, Mrs. Hammond!" he said, removing his straw hat. "How is your patient?"

"That's what I want to ask you. Mr. Price's fever's been gone for four days now. How can we tell when he's completely well?"

Mr. Rhodes smiled. "That's a good sign—the fever leaving. How is his throat?"

"Better every day, he says. He's getting his strength back, too."

"And what about his tongue?"

Glancing over her shoulder at Joseph, who sat peeling potatoes at the table, she turned back and nodded to the innkeeper. "Better, too. The raw patches are healing."

"Then it looks like just a few more days, and your friend will be completely well."

My friend. For the first time, Corrine connected those words with Joseph Price. She supposed he was indeed turning out to be a friend, though she must not allow herself to think of him that way.

"What about the people at your inn . . . and your family?" she called back to Mr. Rhodes.

"Nothing yet," he answered with enthusiasm. "I believe the danger's past, thanks to your being agreeable about getting Mr. Price away from the town."

The danger was past? She had been exposed to Mr. Price's illness for a longer time than Mr. Rhodes and his employees had been. Did that mean for certain she wasn't going to come down with scarlet fever after all?

The innkeeper seemed to read her thoughts. "So I take it that you didn't get sick, either."

"God took care of me," she answered.

"Took care of all of us, didn't he?"

From the table, Joseph said with only a shade of hoarseness in his voice, "Please thank him for the food again, and tell him I'll send a check as soon as I reach Bristol."

She relayed the message, and when the innkeeper had left with a wave of his hand, Corrine walked outside to pick up the food parcel. Coming back inside, she set the sack on the table and began rifling through the contents. "More oranges," she declared with a smile.

Joseph smiled back. "From now on we share them."

"So, you're going to visit your family?" she asked as she sat down at the other end of the bench.

"I haven't been there for a while," he answered. "As soon as I'm well enough to get my hands on some transportation out of Amberton for the both of us, I'll head over to Nantwich. There's a train to Bristol that stops there."

"Both of us? But I'm going . . ."

"To Leawick—I know. But you'll need a coach to get you there."

She was opening her mouth to protest that she couldn't take money from him, when he held up a hand. "Mrs. Hammond, you would still have your sixty pounds if I hadn't stepped into your life."

"I told you that I will not accept any money from you, Mr. Price. Please don't embarrass both of us by offering again."

"If you insist," he told her. "But you can't stop me from hiring a driver for you, whether you decide to set foot inside his coach or not. *At least* let me do that, in return for your nursing me back to health."

"All right," Corrine answered with a sigh. She didn't see where she had a choice, if she wanted to see her family. "If we can consider it payment for nursing services rendered, I suppose it wouldn't be improper for me to take you up on your offer. I certainly can't get home by walking."

Joseph picked up another potato and began peeling away the skin in long strips. "I don't suppose you know how to make potato soup, do you?"

"We've got a quart of chicken broth and an onion in the sack. I believe I could have a pot ready by lunch." She motioned toward the two potatoes he had already peeled and quartered. "You'll need to cut those up in smaller pieces."

"I'll do it. I'm glad I can help you a little with the chores now."

Leaning forward on her elbow, Corrine said, "You'll be well enough to travel before you know it."

He nodded. "Thanks to you."

"God deserves some credit, too."

"Yes, of course. Please thank him for me."

"Why don't you thank him yourself?"

Joseph actually blushed. "I've never been much of a praying

man, Mrs. Hammond. I'm sure that it does some good . . . after all, I do believe in God. But the idea of approaching him with my petty concerns is rather intimidating."

"I felt the same way not too long ago," Corrine said gently, "but a good friend taught me that God is eager to hear from his children."

"I guess I've never thought of myself as his child . . . or even wanted to think of myself that way."

"Why not?"

He shrugged. "Pride, I suppose. That would be admitting that I can't take care of myself." Setting down the knife and potato, he looked across at her. "But I do envy the faith you have. If I had that much faith, I would probably believe, too."

Corrine's heartbeat quickened. She remembered the message that God had seemed to put in her heart that first night at the cottage, about Joseph Price needing to see Christ through her. It was clear that he was searching for *something*.

"I don't think I have a lot of faith," she answered truthfully. "I still worry about things that I should be trusting God for. But I have much more than I had when I first became a Christian."

"Then how did you become one?"

Smiling at the memory of her conversion, Corrine explained, "Back then, all I needed was enough faith to trust him to save me. That's all you need right now, Joseph."

His face lit up. "You called me Joseph."

"I'm . . . I'm sorry," Corrine stammered, chiding herself for the slip. He had looked so anxious to hear what she had to say about faith, and now she had broken the mood.

"No, don't be sorry," he was saying. "I like hearing you say my name."

"That's not a good idea," Corrine replied. She occupied herself with taking food from the sack and setting it on the table.

"But why not?"

"Because I'm a married woman."

"I know that. But I like to believe that we've become friends."

She shook her head, clenching her jaw. "We're living here in the same house, Mr. Price. We had no other choice but to do so, and we've done nothing to be ashamed of. But it would be highly inappropriate for us to display any sort of affection for each other."

"But friendship?"

"What kind of true friendship wouldn't be based on affection?" she answered with a sad smile. "I'm grateful to you for letting me go, and I'll pray every day that God blesses you for it."

"But you don't want to be my friend."

I want to be more than your friend. Corrine shook the thought away. "I cannot," she replied over the pounding of her heart. Turning her back to him, she took the fruits and vegetables over to the bin in the kitchen. When she turned around again, she was startled to find Joseph standing right there.

Perplexity filled his eyes . . . mixed with something akin to longing. "You haven't seen your husband in eight years, you told me."

"Yes," she whispered. She tried to walk around him, but he stepped to the side to block her path.

"You wouldn't have left a man you loved, would you?"

For several seconds, she could not answer. She dared not look up at him, either. For the first time since she had met

Joseph Price, she feared she would totally lose control of her emotions.

"Do you love him, Corrine?"

"Mr. Price, I do not want to discuss my husband with you." The truth was, she needed to talk to someone, *anyone,* about the apprehension that continually tormented her, more and more now that the date of her reunion with Thomas neared. But the man in front of her was the last person she could confide in about that subject. *If only I could speak with Bernice again.*

"You've told me you're not the same person you were," Joseph said in a thick voice. "And you've proved it, over and over. I don't know how you felt about your husband when you first married him, but I can tell you have no feelings for him now. It's your daughter who lights up your face when you speak, not him."

Corrine shook her head, stifling the sob that threatened to rise in her throat. "It is *because* I've changed that I must go back to my husband."

She could feel the heat of his gaze upon her face. "But what about love?"

Again she was silent, but her heart hammered wildly against her chest. *Give me strength, Father.*

When she could finally raise her head to look at him, she said in a much calmer voice, "I'll tell you about love. It was love that sent my Savior to a cross . . . love for a woman who was no better than a streetwalker."

"But what does that have to do with—"

"Everything. If Jesus was willing to die for me, then I should be willing to live for him. He would have me return to my husband, so there is no question of what I should do."

~

Joseph left the cottage and walked through the woods to the brook Corrine had shown him. Why had he made such a fool of himself? He knelt on the bank of the stream to bathe his face with the cold water.

Suddenly he knew why, though the revelation brought him nothing but pain. *I don't want to leave this place. And I don't want her to leave.*

Except for his illness and the guilt that had torn at him for deceiving her, Joseph realized, the days spent in the cottage in these woods had been almost idyllic. Her occasional smile brought a lightness to his soul he had never before experienced.

The happiest moment of his life had come when he told her that he wasn't going to take her to Treybrook.

Why did she have to insist on going back to her husband when it was plain to see that she didn't love him? He would have laughed at the irony of it if he didn't feel so dead inside. The goodness of her soul had drawn him to her, and now it was causing a barrier between them that could never be removed.

Joseph picked up a stone and chucked it into the water. *I hope he realizes what a lucky bloke he is.*

~

"It's good to finally speak to you in person, Mr. Price," the innkeeper said Thursday morning as he pumped Joseph's hand. "You certainly look better than you did two weeks ago!"

"I'll never be able to thank you enough for giving us a place to stay . . . and sending food," Joseph told the man. "Just name your price, and I'll gladly send payment."

"Whatever you think is fair," Mr. Rhodes answered. "No one has ever taken advantage of me yet."

Together they hoisted Corrine's trunk up onto their shoulders and brought it out to the wagon. "There are two coachmen at my inn, eager to take on passengers," the innkeeper told him, leaning back against the wagon to catch his breath. "The railways have cut into the coaching business quite painfully."

Joseph nodded. "I appreciate your handling that for us."

They could see Corrine though the window, taking care of some last-minute tidying up of the cottage. She wore an aqua gown, high necked, with lace trim around the collar. She had managed to sweep her hair up in a chignon, though some tendrils were escaping from the pins at the nape of her neck. "You know," Mr. Rhodes commented, "Mrs. Hammond is a lovely woman. Mother would have been happy to have her tending to her house."

"Yes, I suppose she is," Joseph answered, brushing a bit of grass from his sleeve.

~

For the ride back to Amberton, Joseph insisted that Corrine take the seat up front next to Mr. Rhodes while he sat on a crate in the back. They reached the inn just after eleven. "Just in time for an early lunch before you get on the road," the innkeeper declared. "My treat."

While Mr. Rhodes got back to his duties, the two sat across from each other at a table against the wall in the almost empty dining room. Both ordered roast duckling, the house specialty, but Joseph felt he could generate the same enthusiasm for a roasted brick.

Joseph watched Corrine in silence, but she would not meet his eyes. In just a little while, she would be gone, and he would never see her again. He had grown weary of the uneasiness that had settled over the two of them since he had started recovering. He liked it better when she hated him—at least then he got a response.

"Why won't you look at me?" he asked suddenly. "Just because you're married doesn't mean you have to treat me like a stranger."

Corrine raised her eyes from her plate. "I'm sorry. I was just admiring the china."

"Then perhaps I should wear a cup on my head. Would that get your attention?"

His quip brought a smile to her face, and for a moment she almost looked like the Corrine he had first met. "Mine and everyone else's in the room."

"I just want to know that you'll be all right."

"Of course I will."

"If you're worried about anyone causing you any trouble, I can postpone my trip to Bristol for another day or two. I've always wanted to see Leawick anyway." He was grasping at straws, and he knew it, but he had to do *something*.

Corrine smiled again and shook her head. "I appreciate your kind offer, but I'm sure my reputation there is damaged enough because I left with a man who was not my husband. I wouldn't want to show up with another man . . . do you understand?"

"Of course." He leaned forward, and before Corrine could move her left hand, he covered it with his own. "Don't look so scared," he said gently when he saw the panic in her eyes. With his other hand, he reached into his waistcoat pocket and produced a piece of paper. "I just wanted to give you the address of my father's bakery, in case you ever need my help."

He reached over and slipped the piece of paper into her hand. She looked back at him with eyes the color of smoke and eased her hand into her lap. Clearing her throat, she murmured, "Thank you, Mr. Price. I hope that your visit with your family is filled with joy."

I can't say the same about yours, Joseph thought. Yet seconds later he found himself saying, "And I hope the same for you."

~

Thirty minutes later, Corrine was alone in a rattling coach headed for Leawick. Now that her route had been detoured, it would take two days to get there. She wasn't concerned about being the lone passenger, for she had met the driver, and he turned out to be a newly married young man—quiet, bashful, and earnest about his job.

The old fear and excitement about going back to Leawick returned. To think that she would be embracing Jenny again very soon! That was, if the girl would allow it. *And Thomas, of course.*

She wished fervently that she still had the money that had been stolen, to give to her family. Thomas could have used it to buy new equipment, maybe a bit of land, and they would have been assured of food on the table for a long time.

Something else besides the missing money weighed her spirits down, causing a great sense of loss within her. Corrine knew what it was, but whenever she caught herself tempted to think about it, she would pray.

She found herself having to pray several times on the road to Leawick.

22

IN bed for her afternoon nap, Jenny was dreaming of
blackberries and honeysuckle vines and purple-stained
smiles when she felt a touch on her arm.

"Darling, wake up!" For a second Jenny imagined that little
Evan was waking her. When the words were repeated, the fog
cleared from her mind and she opened her eyes. Lady Dunley
was leaning over the bed, her eyes sparkling.

"Yes, Mama?" Jenny responded automatically. Even in her
sluggish state, she could tell that it was time to be Angelica.
Since that time in the garden, Mrs. Dunley had only come to
herself once, and only for part of an afternoon.

"I want to take you somewhere—a surprise!" Covering a
giggle with her hand, she said, "Your father and Uncle Neil
are in town doing something or other, and so there won't be
anybody grumpy around to spoil our fun."

Helene appeared in the doorway, and Lady Dunley ordered
her to help the girl into another change of clothes.

"What should she wear now?" Helene asked. This morning
Lady Dunley had insisted on Jenny wearing the rose gingham,
one of the frocks that had yet to be switched by Mrs. Pruitt.
There were four new larger dresses in the wardrobe now,
with the seamstress and her assistants still working on other
replacements.

Lady Dunley walked over to the wardrobe and, after a moment's thought, pulled out a jonquil-and-white striped gown with a starched white collar. "Put this on her, and hurry about it." After draping the frock over a chair, she started for the door. "And I'll send Alice up with some daisies for you to pin in her hair. I want her to look beautiful."

When she was gone, Helene sighed and rolled her eyes. "Well, at least she's picked out a dress that will let you draw a decent breath. Good thing Mrs. Pruitt sent this up last night."

Helene's cousin Alice came in to help, and the two were just starting to pin the flowers in Jenny's hair when Lady Dunley returned with a pot of rouge. "Put some color in her cheeks, too," she ordered, walking up to the dressing table. A trail of overwhelming perfume followed her and surrounded all of them.

"Yes, missus," Helene replied after exchanging quick glances with her cousin. Lady Dunley's cheeks were two bright spots of red, and there were smears of rouge on the front of her pale yellow gown, where the woman had apparently wiped her hands after decorating her face.

Helene dabbed a bit of the rouge on her fingers and smeared it on the little girl's cheeks, spreading it out so that only a hint of a blush could be noticed.

"Not enough, you silly girl!" The woman shooed the two maids out of her way, picked up the pot of rouge, and dug two fingers into it. Barely daring to breathe, Jenny held her breath and watched in the mirror as the red paste was caked onto her cheeks.

"Now!" exclaimed Lady Dunley, wiping her hands on the skirt of her dress. She reached down to take Jenny's hand. "I've got Harold waiting with the carriage."

In the carriage, Lady Dunley wrapped her arm around Jenny's shoulders and drew her close. "We're going to have such fun!" she giggled when the wheels started moving.

Jenny could barely breathe, her head beginning to ache from the heady scent of perfume. She worried that some of the rouge on her cheeks would rub off on Lady Dunley's dress, but she didn't want to hurt her feelings by pulling away.

At least she was thankful that today wasn't Sunday. She never wanted to live through a repeat of the scene at church. But where were they heading?

At the end of the carriage drive, the horses did not turn in the direction of Leawick, but instead turned onto the road leading to the west. They passed hedged fields, landscaped lawns, and four or five homes along the way. None of the homes were as fine as the Dunley estate, nor as humble as most of the cottages in Leawick.

Lady Dunley sat with glazed eyes and a frozen smile as they bounced along, occasionally humming some disjointed tune. She came alive when the chaise pulled into the carriage drive of a two-story home of umber brick.

"Remember this place?" she whispered, brushing back a stray wisp of hair from Jenny's face. "Mrs. Hansworth. I thought it would be fun to pop in for a visit."

"Yes, Mama," Jenny answered dutifully. The driver came around to help them from the carriage, but Lady Dunley seemed not to realize he was there.

"The woman had the gall to ask for one of your dolls," Lenora said. She was quiet for a moment, working her lips and searching for her next thought.

"A long time ago," she continued shortly. *"Something for Eloise to remember Angelica by,"* she said in a mocking voice.

271

"After all, they were best friends!" She frowned, her eyes becoming glaring slits while her voice increased in volume. "She'd like to think so! As if any of the spawn of Metta and that mule-faced husband of hers could come even close to being your best friend!"

An elderly footman had come out of the house and was walking down the portico steps, raising questioning eyebrows at Harold, the driver. Lady Dunley glanced down at both of them but went on, uncaring who should hear. "Your dolls are special, not to be handed out like party favors!"

"Lady Dunley?" came the driver's meek voice beside the chaise.

"What?" She fixed an irritated stare on the man.

"Shouldn't we go on back home now? The horses could use a feeding." Harold had the look of someone caught between two catastrophes. Jenny had seen that look before—the expression of a servant trapped in an impossible situation. What would the baronet do when he found out that he'd taken the mistress for a drive? But how could he have refused Lady Dunley?

"Go back?" She blinked and looked over at the footman, now standing next to Harold. "Why, no," she replied, her voice turning as calm as the eye of a storm. "We came to visit Mrs. Hansworth and the children. Are they at home?"

"I don't think . . . ," the footman began, but just then the front door opened, and a woman stuck her head out.

"Brewster, I'll need you to . . ." The woman's voice trailed off as she stepped out onto the porch. She was tall and plump, with an attractive round face. Her hair, wheat-colored like Jenny's, was drawn up into a topknot. "Lenora?"

Quick as thought, Lady Dunley flashed a smile. "My dear

Metta! Forgive me for not sending a note ahead of time, but it's such a pretty day, and Angelica and I suddenly felt like company!"

"Well, that's, uh . . . so nice," the woman replied, walking closer, to the edge of the portico. Her head tilted, she eyed them both with a mixture of curiosity and pity. "Truth is, Lenora, little Ansen has a bad cold. I would hate for either of you to catch it."

"The poor, dear child! Have you tried a mustard poultice?"

"Olivia is up there now, changing it. I'm sorry I can't invite you in. . . ."

"Think nothing of it," Lady Dunley replied in a compassionate tone. "We'll come back another time. Just take care of that sweet little boy. Tell him I'll have Cook send some of her special sweetmeats for him."

She leaned over to tell the driver to take them home, but he was already hustling toward the front of the carriage. For the first mile or two she was silent, her lips pursed in thought. Then she turned to Jenny and said, "The poor woman. Her children are so sickly, it seems. I can tell that she worries about them."

Lady Dunley looked at Jenny as if she expected an answer. "I hope the little boy gets well," Jenny said at last.

"That's so like you!" Lenora gushed, reaching an arm over to give the girl's shoulders a squeeze. "Here you are . . . your outing is ruined, and your only concern is for someone else!"

"Th-thank you."

"Well, I'm not going to have you go back home disappointed." Leaning forward in her seat, she called out for the driver to take the turnoff leading to Lake Chestnut. "I know it's not a happy place, Angelica. But we'll have so much fun this time that you'll forget to be afraid."

When they arrived at the lake, however, Lady Dunley was too frightened to get out of the carriage. "It looks so . . . deep," she breathed, sitting tall and rigid and clutching Jenny to her side. Jenny could feel the woman's heartbeat, pounding so rapidly that she wondered if she were about to faint.

"I . . . can't," Lady Dunley said with a sob in her throat. "We have to go home." She looked down at Jenny, tears welling up in her eyes. "I'm tired and I need a nap."

~

Early in the evening, Jenny sat in the rocking chair by her window in still another change of clothing and waited to be called down to supper. She could see nothing but trees and fields and streaks of orange sunset, but by squinting her eyes tightly, she imagined she could see the hill in front of Uncle Roy and Aunt Mary's cottage. It *could* be their hill, she told herself.

She heard the door behind her open, and she looked over her shoulder to see Mrs. Styles coming into the room.

"Is it time for me to go downstairs?" Jenny asked.

"Not for a while, dear," the housekeeper said, walking over to stand beside the chair. "Lady Dunley's just waking from her nap. Please keep your seat," she said when Jenny started to get out of her chair. "I just wanted to see about you."

"See about me?"

Mrs. Styles took the girl's hand and stood there, facing the window. "I heard you had an unsettling day."

Jenny nodded slowly. "She was so angry at Mrs. Hansworth until she came out onto the porch. Then she changed and was sweet to her."

"There is nothing I can do to keep Lady Dunley from acting like that," the housekeeper said, her voice shaded with sadness. "Just remember that she doesn't realize what she's doing most times. It's as if she were sick."

"Yes, ma'am."

"You aren't frightened of her, are you?"

After a moment's thought, Jenny shook her head. "I don't think so."

"Good! If you ever *are* afraid, keep in mind that you've got people surrounding you who care about you, like Helene, Mrs. Pruitt, and myself. Come to one of us if you ever need a sympathetic ear."

Jenny had never heard of anything called a sympathetic ear, but she understood Mrs. Styles's offer. "Thank you," she said in a small voice.

The housekeeper smiled back. "I did bring some good news, however. Sir Feldon has sent orders to the stables that no one is to take Lady Dunley out riding unless he or Mr. Wingate comes along. You won't have to worry about a repeat of what happened today."

"Yes, ma'am."

Jenny felt her hand being squeezed, and then Mrs. Styles said, still looking out through the window glass, "You know, I'm called 'Mrs.' because it's customary to address the housekeeper as such, but I've never been married. My dream was to have a house full of children, but it never happened."

Turning her face toward the woman beside her, Jenny said, "Oh, I'm sorry."

Mrs. Styles gave her shoulders a shrug. "I haven't had a bad life. I started out as a parlor maid, and now I've got a big household to tend. I like making everything run smoothly."

"But you never had children."

"In a way, I did for a while. Ever since the accident, Lady Dunley won't allow any of the servants to keep their children in the servants' quarters, but for years we had five or six at a time living here, and I was an unofficial aunt to most of them."

"Where did they go?"

"Some, like Sally, became servants themselves as they grew older. But the children who were around here at the time of Angelica's death . . . well, some of the servants had to leave and find other positions, because they had no place to keep their children. Especially husbands and wives who worked here together. Some had relatives who could take them in, so they can only go and visit their children on their half days off."

"The poor children!" Jenny cried.

Mrs. Styles nodded. "It was difficult for the parents, too. Sad, when families can't stay together." Quickly a look of concern washed over her face. "I'm sorry, child," she said gently. "I wasn't even thinking about your situation."

"I miss Aunt Mary and my cousins," the girl said, fighting back tears.

"I know you do, Jenny." She squeezed the girl's hand again. "Would it make you feel better to talk about them?"

"I want to talk about them." The truth was, she *needed* to, for ever since she had come to live here, her whole personality was being forced into a mold that did not fit—just as her feet had been forced into Angelica's too-tight shoes. She had a life that was separate from Angelica Dunley's, and as bad as it had been at times, it was the part of her that couldn't be taken away unless she allowed herself to forget it. And she never would. She was *Jenny,* not Angelica, and she would always be Jenny. Even if only in her own mind.

The housekeeper let go of Jenny's hand, took the dressing-table bench and set it next to Jenny's chair. "How long have you lived with your aunt and uncle?"

"Since I was little," Jenny answered. "But my father died not too long ago."

"I'm so sorry," Mrs. Styles said, her face grim. "And your mother?"

"You don't know?" More than once, she had heard Uncle Roy tell Aunt Mary that her sister, Jenny's mother, had scandalized the town and brought shame upon the whole family by leaving with another man. Visitors who came to arrange thatching jobs with Uncle Roy had sometimes stared at her, their thoughts obvious on their faces.

"No, Jenny, I don't," Mrs. Styles was saying. "Did your mother pass away also?"

"No." She frowned. "She was Aunt Mary's sister, and she went away. I don't know where she lives now."

The housekeeper shook her head, but then arranged an encouraging smile on her face. "So your Aunt Mary took care of you. How fortunate that you had other family. You could have wound up in an orphanage if you hadn't."

"Yes, ma'am." A wistful look came across the girl's face. "I wish she had told my father and me that she was going to leave. Maybe we could have been nicer to her and she would have stayed with us."

"Dear, you can't blame yourself . . . you were just a baby."

Jenny didn't look convinced. "But Aunt Mary said that I cried a lot when I was little." After a moment's hesitation, she confessed, "I remember that Rebecca was the same way, and sometimes after I tried to rock her and walk her, I just wanted to run outside and get away from the noise."

She turned to the older woman and put a timid hand on her arm. "Becca wasn't a bad girl . . . it's just that some babies are more fussy than others."

"And you think your mother left because you were a fussy baby?" Mrs. Styles asked with a sad smile.

"I wish I hadn't cried so much. I don't even remember why I did it."

A strange look crossed the housekeeper's face. "You did it because that's what most babies do. I don't know why your mother left, Jenny, but you mustn't blame yourself."

When Jenny didn't answer, Mrs. Styles changed the subject. She motioned toward the dolls on display in the cabinet. "You know you're allowed to play with any of the dolls you'd like. The cabinet is unlocked now, so you just have to unfasten the latch on the side."

Jenny looked across at the collection of frozen porcelain smiles and unblinking eyes. "I don't want to," she answered flatly, then, worrying that she had been rude, said, "Did Angelica love her dolls?"

"She did at that," the woman replied with a smile. "She was a lonely child, and they were her only friends. Also, I think they reminded the girl of herself."

Glancing at the dolls again, Jenny said, "Of herself?"

"Angelica wasn't allowed to play with the servants' children or, really, with any other children. It would have been hard for the child to play anyway, because Lady Dunley didn't want her to get her clothes mussed."

"What did she do?"

"To pass the time? Played with her toys—the dolls mostly, as I said."

"But why did they remind her of herself?"

Mrs. Styles drew a deep breath. "Because they were pretty things meant for display. That's what Angelica was—or that's how her mother treated her. The girl's duty was to dress up, sing and recite nicely, and impress people. Lady Dunley was proud of her daughter's looks and abilities, but unless there were people around, the girl was basically ignored."

"That's so sad!" Jenny exclaimed.

"Oh, the missus loved her daughter—don't think that she didn't. But she just didn't know how much the girl craved some of her time. The baronet did more things with Angelica than Lady Dunley did. Lady Dunley always seemed to be wrapped up in planning for houseguests or organizing some social function. I think that's another reason she's never gotten over the poor child's death. Regret over the past can be a damaging thing."

For the first time, Jenny felt a kinship with the girl whose room she occupied. She understood the pain of longing for a mother. "But her mother didn't leave," she said solemnly. "At least Lady Dunley was here where Angelica could see her and talk to her."

"Yes, she was," Mrs. Styles agreed. "But sometimes being near someone who is too busy to spend time with you is worse than being alone." Glancing at the mantel clock, she patted the girl's arm and stood. "We'd better get you down to supper, or the missus and her brother will wonder what's happened to you."

23

CORRINE chewed nervously on her lip as the passing landmarks grew increasingly familiar. The rain that had accompanied the coach for the past five miles or so had settled down to a light drizzle, sending a fine mist through the window to bathe Corrine's face as she held the canvas curtain to the side.

Give me strength, Lord, she prayed. Her whole body felt weak, and it seemed that she could not draw enough air into her lungs. In just a little while, she would be looking at the faces she had dreamed of almost every night lately.

She had given the driver, Amos, directions to the hut she had shared with her husband and daughter, but at the crossroads just before Leawick, the coach came to a halt. The young man came to the window to make certain that he was at the correct crossroads and would still be taking a turn to the right.

Corrine stifled a laugh at Amos's comical face. He kept his eyes focused on her chin so that he would not appear to be too forward. The slightly built, clean-shaven man was a refreshing change from Pete. *He probably doesn't steal money from trunks, either.*

After they made the turn, the road eventually tapered off into little more than a cow path, lined with trees from the forest on both sides and rutted with holes. Corrine was glad that Bernice could not see her, holding on with both hands to try to keep from being thrown against the sides of the coach. *She would lecture me about knocking about and hurting my ribs again.*

Corrine wondered if Bernice and the other servants at Adam Burke's house were worried about her. She had promised to write as soon as she was settled in Leawick; she just hadn't known that she would be delayed for two weeks because of Joseph Price.

With that thought came a mental picture of Mr. Price, looking up at her with gratitude in his eyes as he sipped tea from the cup she held at his mouth. "No," she murmured, banishing the image from her mind.

They passed a number of half-timbered cottages, most with tidy gardens and pigpens or chicken yards. "It's this one!" she finally called out to the driver. He pulled the horses to a stop, and Corrine had the door open before he could come around to offer his assistance.

When her feet were on the ground, she froze. Her home with Thomas had always been barely more than a hovel, not even as nice as the cottage she had shared temporarily with Mr. Price. But the dwelling standing before her looked uninhabitable. The door stood open, and both front windows were broken. Weeds choked the yard, which was littered with broken bottles and rusting food tins.

"Ma'am . . . are you sure this is the place?" Amos asked, coming up to stand a respectable four feet from her side.

"Yes," she mumbled. Holding the hem of her dress above the mud, she walked up the remnants of a path to the door, with the driver following. She eased the front door open another inch. The loud groaning of rusty hinges startled her, but not as much as the sounds of scampering feet inside.

"I wouldn't go in there if I were you," the young man advised from behind her. "Sounds like rats."

"Yes, it does." Still, she took a step closer and leaned forward to peer inside. In the darkened interior she could see broken dishes and bits of furniture. The smell hit her then, a mixture of rodent droppings and rotting food. She quickly drew her head back, holding her hand to her mouth to keep from gagging.

"They must have moved," she said to Amos. "Why don't we go ask someone?"

He nodded and started back for the coach. Three minutes later, she was knocking on the door of the last cottage they had passed. *Fuller,* she remembered, was the name of the family that lived here.

The door was immediately opened by a middle-aged woman wearing an apron. "Yes, what do you . . ." She stopped abruptly. Cocking her head, the woman studied Corrine's face, then let her eyes travel enviously down the length of Corrine's attractive burgundy calico. "You're Corrine Hammond, ain't you?" She frowned.

"Yes, Mrs. Fuller. I was wondering where—" Before she could finish her question, the woman slammed the door in her face.

Amos, who had hung back near the horses, came running over. "Are you all right, ma'am?"

"I didn't really expect people to welcome me back with open arms," Corrine said through her tears. Amos looked puzzled, but she was too upset to explain. "Perhaps we should go to my sister's. She would know where my husband and daughter are."

~

"Curse this rain!" Roy Satters muttered from the box of his empty wagon, though the sky had finally cleared a few moments before. Looping the reins around the back of the seat, he jumped down and slogged to the wobbly rear wheel. The weather had cost him most of a day's work, and now, just as he had been about to turn down the road leading back to his cottage, the wheel had splashed through a puddle concealing a rock. He gave a futile effort to push the hub more securely on its axle. The wheel would not budge. Well, there was no use trying to fix it until he got home. He would just have to inch along for the half-mile left and hope that his wagon did not come apart under him.

He was just about to climb back into the box when he heard a sound—a wagon or carriage, coming his way. He squinted off in the distance. *No, a coach.* Curious, he stepped closer to the front of his wagon and watched the vehicle being drawn by two horses down the muddy road. The driver nodded down at him and then slowed as he drove past, probably so as not to splatter him with mud. Roy glanced at the body of the coach and was startled to see a woman's face at the window, looking right at him.

"Amos, stop!" he heard her call out. When the coach came to a halt, a few feet ahead of his horse, the woman eased the carriage door open and peered out. "Roy?"

Roy's jaw dropped open. Of all people to come breezing back to Leawick, just when he'd made such a cozy arrangement with Sir Feldon! Every week Jenny stayed at the manor house was a week that brought money to his pocket—his just reward for caring for the girl for so long. *And now she shows up!*

he thought bitterly as he walked over to the coach. "Corrine," he said, his face as cold as granite. "What are you doing here?"

"Hello, Roy." Corrine wore a fragile smile, but there was some apprehension in her eyes. "I was just on the way to your house. I can't find my husband or Jenny."

"Thomas is dead," he told her bluntly, taking a perverse satisfaction in the stricken look that came across the woman's face.

"Dead? Thomas?" She shook her head, her eyes wide. "But how?"

"Consumption. Brought on by drinkin' himself to death. Guess I don't have to tell you why."

She let out a sob, covering her face with her hands, but Roy could hardly keep from smiling. It was true, he thought, the old saying that every dog has its day. "What happened to that rake you ran away with?"

She ignored the question and wiped at the tears on her face. "Is Jenny at your house?"

"Why do you want to know?"

"Because I want to be with her if she'll let me."

"She ain't at my house," Roy answered, his mind working at some way he could keep her from taking the child.

"Where is she?"

"She's in a nicer place than most folks ever live in." Roy looked the coach over, with its black luster paint and gold trim. Was it hers? Perhaps he could come out ahead financially after all. One nice lump sum would be better than a shilling dribbled out every week.

He inched forward a bit. "What's it worth to you to get her back?"

~

Corrine couldn't believe what was happening. She had finally made it to Leawick—to Jenny—and now her own brother-in-law stood between her and the fulfillment of her dream.

"What are you saying?" she asked.

"I'm saying, I know where the girl is, and I'm the only one who can get her back. How much are you willin' to pay me to do that?"

"You would charge me money to get my own child back?"

He frowned. "Don't go preachin' morals to me, Corrine. What's it worth?"

With shaking hands she brought out a beaded purse, grateful that she still had a little money inside. When her hired coach was miles from Amberton, she discovered that Joseph had paid Amos a generous amount in advance for hers and the driver's meals and lodging. "I've got over three pounds here," she mumbled, digging through the bag. "The rest of my money was stolen." She held the money out to him. "You can have it all . . . just take me to my daughter."

He spat on the ground. "I don't think so, Corrine. I think it's time for you to leave, just like you did last time. And don't get any ideas about visitin' your sister—you've caused Mary enough trouble."

"What do you mean?" Corrine said, her face ashen.

"When you sailed out of town with your fancy-man, it was Mary and me what took Jenny in to raise. Your Thomas weren't in the state to take care of himself, much less a baby."

"I'm grateful to you, Roy. If you only knew how sorry I am for leaving like that . . . please understand that I want to make it up to her."

"Make up for eight years gone? And how would you take care of her? How will you buy food when your money's gone?"

Corrine's shoulders fell. She had made no plans to fall back on in the eventuality that Thomas wouldn't take her back. The thought of her husband's death brought another sob to her throat. *Poor Thomas . . . he didn't deserve any of this.*

But she couldn't break down. She had to be strong. She had to think about Jenny now. The cottage was still standing, such as it was. She had enough money to make repairs—that is, if Roy didn't end up insisting on taking her three pounds—and she could try to get her old job back at the dairy. She said as much to Roy, but he just laughed.

"Corrine, there ain't a soul in Leawick who would hire you. Do you understand? You can't even stay at the *inn* for one night, because of the scandal you caused there."

Biting her lip, Corrine tried not to cry. She had met Gerald Moore at Leawick's Gaston House Inn, spending a night there with him and leaving the next morning. Did everyone still have bad feelings toward her after eight years?

"Mrs. Hammond . . . is everything all right?" Amos called down from the driver's seat.

Corrine opened the door a little wider and stuck her head out. "Y-yes," she answered in a shaky voice. She looked at the hostile face of her brother-in-law and knew that he was speaking the truth about the way people felt about her. Why, growing up, she could remember her mother and aunts talking about people who had disgraced the community decades ago . . . and those were minor scandals compared to what she had done.

"We can try to start over somewhere else, Jenny and me," Corrine told him. "Another town . . ."

"And what are you gonna do there? Find another man to take care of you?"

~

As soon as Roy had said the words, he regretted them. His mind had suddenly lighted on a plan to protect his income by keeping Jenny at the Dunleys. But he couldn't carry it out by angering his sister-in-law. "You've got to understand our bein' bitter," he said in a more conciliatory tone. "We've watched the girl suffer, bein' raised without a true mother and father."

He waited while she covered her face and sobbed, then, when she quieted down, said as gently as possible, "I'm just helping you plan ahead, Corrine. If you go ahead to another town and get a job like you did at the dairy, you'll be gone ten to twelve hours a day while the girl pines for you at home. Or maybe you'd have to hire her out as a servant to make ends meet."

Corrine put a hand up to her throat and gave a choked gasp. "Why are you saying this?"

"I'm wantin' you to think about Jenny, for the first time in your life. She's got a real mama and papa now."

"A real mama and papa . . . ?" she echoed. "Where is she?"

"Fancy dresses and toys," Roy continued, "and always enough food on the table. A big house, too, with servants and horses. And they bring her to church. A family that any child would consider itself lucky to have."

"I want my daughter," Corrine insisted.

"Now, ain't that a change." Pushing back his straw hat,

Roy scratched his forehead easily. *"You* want, Corrine? Look what your *wants* have already done to Thomas and Jenny. And now you want the girl back. Don't you even care about what's good for her?"

"She would want her mother!"

"She doesn't even know you! You think she'd want to leave two people who love her, who *dote* on her, to go with a stranger?"

"My baby . . . ," Corrine mumbled, her face showing the strain of the battle raging within her. Roy took this as a sign that his words were taking effect, and he pressed on.

"You know, Jenny took her papa's death hard," he said, making sure a touch of sadness colored his expression. "The people who took her in—they lost their little girl two years ago. She were about the same size as Jenny, I hear." Stepping even closer, he said softly, "Seems like they was meant to be a family, Jenny and the Dunleys."

"Sir Feldon?" Corrine said in a weak voice. "Is that where she's staying?"

Roy cursed under his breath for the slip, then nodded. "They love her, Corrine, and she loves them. You take the girl away from the place she's come to know as home, and she'll hate you."

"She won't hate—"

"Yes, she will! You almost ruined her life once. Do you really want to do it again?"

"No," she moaned, her hand pressed against her forehead. "I don't know. Please let me talk with Mary."

"No, I won't have it. The best thing you can do is have that boy turn this coach around and be on your way."

~

"I can't believe I let you talk me into this," Neil Wingate told his sister from the opposite seat of the carriage. They were just on the outskirts of Leawick, heading toward the main street of town.

Lady Dunley laughed and winked at Jenny. "It's stopped raining. Tell Harold to stop so you can put the hood down."

"Stopped raining?" Holding his hand out from under the fringed top, Neil noted that the drizzling mist had indeed ceased. "It could always start again. I don't think we need to put the top back."

"Weren't you the one lecturing me on getting out in the sunshine and fresh air not too long ago?"

Neil gave a sigh and called out to the driver to stop, then did what Lenora wanted, grumbling under his breath that the air was still so damp that they'd all likely have colds in the morning. "Why in the world do you want to go to town now, anyway?"

"Angelica and I were bored," Lenora replied, trying to keep her voice patient. Neil could be such a grouch. After grudgingly agreeing to escort the two of them on a ride, her brother had raised a fuss about the rouge on their cheeks, refusing even to go down to the carriage until she and Angelica had washed their faces!

She looked down at the girl beside her, dressed in a splendid ivory silk-and-lace gown with a matching bonnet, her hair trailing in ringlets over one shoulder. A secret smile touched Lenora's face. She hadn't washed *all* of Angelica's rouge away . . . and Neil hadn't even noticed. Her brother just didn't understand the necessity of keeping up appearances. Angelica ok—

was the most beautiful child in town, wore the most fashionable clothes, and was most beloved by her mother. People needed to remember that, and a ride through town every so often was a proper way to make sure that they did.

Actually, it was Lenora's *only* avenue of showing the girl off. Feldon had forbidden her to set foot inside the church again, especially if she intended on bringing the girl with her. Just yesterday she had come up with the idea of having a dinner party, perhaps even a ball. But her husband had refused even to consider it, instead stomping down the hall to his study and slamming the door behind him.

As the first dwellings of Leawick appeared, she sighed and straightened the bonnet of the girl beside her. "Smile, dear," she whispered, then lifted a regal hand to wave to the vicar's wife and sister, both watching openmouthed from the carriage drive of the rectory. *They can't keep their eyes off my daughter,* she thought, her eyes shining with pride.

~

"Turn around when you can," Corrine called to Amos with a shaky voice. "We're going on to town."

Roy gave her a withering look as the coach began to move. "So, you ain't gonna listen to me."

"I'll die if I don't see her," Corrine answered.

Minutes later she felt the coach slowing again and watched from the window as the shops and cottages of Leawick came in sight. Only a few people were about in the streets. She cared nothing for the sights of the village where she had been raised—her thoughts were occupied with the manor house at the opposite end of Leawick. Would the Dunleys allow her to see Jenny? Did she have the right to demand that they do so after abandoning the child for eight years?

Fresh tears came to Corrine's eyes, and she wiped at them with her sodden handkerchief. What about what Roy said, about ruining Jenny's life? Was she really being selfish? But how could she come this close and not be with her daughter?

The coach slowed to a snail's pace, then pulled up to one of the iron posts in front of Gaston House Inn. Though no people were out on the lawn, Corrine felt like slouching down in her seat. *Why are we stopping here?* she thought. Amos appeared at the window a moment later, his hat in his hand. "Mrs. Hammond, do you mind if we get something to eat?" he asked. "I've got to water the horses, too."

"Of course not," she replied. Consumed with thoughts about her family, she hadn't realized that the man had not eaten since breakfast. She glanced at the stone building with its grasshopper-shaped weather vane and timber porch. "I'm not hungry, and I don't want to go in there. You go ahead."

"I'll just buy some sandwiches for both of us then," Amos told her. "You might get hungry later, and I can eat mine while I drive."

He was gone before she could thank him for his thoughtfulness. It was good to have one person treat her kindly in a town that apparently would never forgive her.

Her thoughts turned back to Jenny, bringing a new ache to the pit of her stomach. She steeled herself not to cry this time—she would need to keep her composure when asking the Dunleys to give her back. *They can't love her more than I do,* she told herself. *She's just got to want to be with me.*

She noticed a carriage coming down the road from the opposite direction. The driver had pulled its two horses to a walk, a courtesy to keep mud from splattering any pedestrians. Corrine shot to the edge of her seat when the vehicle drew closer. Lady Dunley was inside, older now but still easily recognizable, seated across from a man Corrine assumed was her husband.

The baronet's wife smiled and lifted a hand to wave at Corrine as they passed. Her other arm was draped lovingly around the shoulders of a little girl . . . a beautifully dressed little girl with dark eyes, glowing cheeks, and a smile showing from beneath a silk bonnet.

"Jenny!" Corrine whispered, opening the door so that she could follow the carriage with her eyes. She stepped out of the coach, dragging her skirt in the muddy street. "Oh, Jenny!" she cried into her fist. She was certain that it was her daughter, and the fact that she looked so happy in the arms of her adoptive mother stabbed into her heart.

When Amos came back to the window a moment later, Corrine was huddled in the far corner of the coach.

"Mrs. Hammond?"

Corrine blinked and looked up at him. "It's two hours to Shrewsbury," she said in a tired voice. "Can we make it there before dark?"

"Shrewsbury?"

She nodded. "I've got to catch a train in the morning."

"It'll take longer than two hours, what with the muddy roads," he answered, his young face a picture of concern. Reaching through the window, he set the wrapped sandwiches on the seat. "But we'll get there before dark."

As the coach started moving again, Corrine returned to her huddle. Every lurch of the wheels compounded her sense of loneliness and loss. Roy had been right . . . Jenny obviously fit right in with her new family. It was selfish of her to be distressed at her daughter's happiness. Had she wanted to find the girl miserable?

She tried to pray but couldn't, and she began to wonder if even God had abandoned her.

There was only one place she could think of going now, and she wasn't even sure if she would be welcome there so soon after leaving. London . . . and Bernice.

~

Saturday evening, Corrine stood under the portico roof of Adam Burke's house and chided herself for the impulsiveness that had brought her here. Why hadn't she tried to locate one of her other sisters? What did she expect Bernice and the others to do for her? True, Adam Burke had invited her to stay for as long as she liked, but it was generally understood that once a houseguest left a place for good, she had no right to pop in and out.

Still, she had no choice but to impose herself upon their charity once more until she could find a job and a place to live. Even though she had traveled third class from Shrewsbury to save money, she was down to two pounds sterling and some change, all the money that she owned in the world. Swallowing her pride, she reached for the brass knocker.

But the door swung open before she could knock. "Mrs. Hammond!" Bernice exclaimed, her ruddy face glowing. "And I thought Lucy was imagining things when she said you were gettin' out of a carriage out front." Upon closer inspection of Corrine's face, the cook's joyful countenance fell. "What's happened, dear?"

Corrine fell into her arms and began to weep. "Oh, Bernice!" she sobbed. "They're both gone!"

24

IN Bristol, Joseph set out for his usual two-hour morning walk—from his parents' house above their bakery on Market Street, along the banks of the River Avon, to the Prince Street Bridge, and back. Shopkeepers, sweeping their front walks, nodded greetings as he passed, and the streets became busier with people and vehicles by the minute.

Under the care of his family for the past two weeks, his health had been fully restored—in fact, he was convinced that he felt better than he had in years. The bells from the church of Saint John the Baptist began pealing out the first measures of "Come Thou Fount of Every Blessing," a pleasant backdrop to the noises of the wakening city. It was good to be in the only place he could really call home, but he knew that it would be time to be moving on soon. Already, two requests for his services from potential clients had arrived with his father's mail.

As usual, his thoughts turned to Corrine as he walked along, and he wondered how she was faring in Leawick, back in the arms of her husband. Of course the lucky bloke would take her back—he'd be a fool not to. The thought brought such a feeling of emptiness to his chest that he kicked a loose stone in his path, chiding himself for harboring the selfish wish that something had gone wrong with the reunion.

I've got to stop this or I'll go crazy! he thought. Yet at the same time, he found himself remembering the worried expression in her gray eyes as she had bathed his face or helped him manage his soup spoon.

~

That afternoon, over his mother's protests, he went down to the basement to help out in the bakery. His brother George had mentioned during lunch that the mixer's gears had jammed four or five times that morning. Joseph liked to tinker with machines, and having something to keep his mind occupied would be good for him. Besides, he welcomed the opportunity to repay his family in some way for their care while he regained his strength.

The mixer, a large metal contraption operated with foot pedals, had to be completely taken apart. While his brothers George and Collins and several other employees scurried about in flour-dusted aprons, loading lumps of dough into great brick ovens, Joseph worked quickly. The machine could take the place of half a dozen pairs of hands and was needed as soon as possible.

His mother had worried that the heat of the bakery would cause a recurrence of Joseph's fever, but he did not find the atmosphere too stifling. Besides, he had spent many hours of his childhood down here helping out. Wide, short windows at street level surrounded the room on all four sides, allowing enough ventilation to give the workers some fresh air.

His task was completed in less than two hours. He wiped his grease-covered hands with a towel and called out to his brothers, "Ready to see how she works?"

Collins set down a canister of flour and came to inspect the repairs. "Well, I believe you've got it," he declared, testing the pedal with his foot. "So you're good for something besides running about the country after all."

Grinning, Joseph went upstairs to the shop, where Benton and his wife, Mavis, were working. The bell at the door jingled as two customers, both older women, were just leaving with their purchases. "Would you like to try some of this chocolate torte?" his sister-in-law asked, pointing to the display case.

"I'd love some." Joseph reached for a saucer from the shelf behind him. "You don't have to wait on me, though—I'll get it myself." As he bent down to cut a slice of the dark, rich cake, the bell jingled again, and a man and woman entered. Quickly Joseph stood and moved aside so that Benton and Mavis could wait on the new customers. He leaned on the side of the counter, speared a piece of cake with his fork and, as discreetly as possible, resumed his old habit of people watching.

The man was smartly dressed, in a suit that looked brand-new. Joseph couldn't see all his face, for it was shaded by a hat, but he was obviously much older than his companion.

In fact, she's little more than a girl, he thought, switching his attention to her. She wore an excessive amount of makeup for the daytime and for her age and carried herself with a swagger that sadly reminded Joseph of the women loitering on the street corners near the docks.

"May I help you?" Benton asked the young woman. The man hung back, watching the girl with his arms folded across his chest.

"We'll take some of those cinnamon rolls—a half dozen," the girl answered with a haughty tilt to her chin. She squinted at the other items on display. "And that lemon cake—give us half of that . . . and a dozen of those almond buns." Turning to the man waiting behind her, she said, "Did you want anything, sugar?"

"Not right now, I don't," he snickered loudly. Joseph's dish crashed to the floor at the sound of the man's voice.

"Pete!" Joseph snarled, sprinting from behind the counter as swiftly as a cat. The man turned to run for the door, but before he had taken two steps, Joseph was upon him, locking his arm behind his back.

"Let me go!" the coachman yelled, struggling to get away.

The young woman at the counter turned around, her eyes two glints of fire. "Hey! You leave my fiancé alone!" Drawing back her arm, she swung her beaded handbag toward Joseph's face. But he was too quick for her, and it only grazed his cheek.

The girl cursed and was raising her arm to swing again when Benton grabbed her from behind.

"Mavis!" Joseph said to his sister-in-law, who stood there white faced and frozen. "Send someone to get the police!"

"No!" the man yelled, struggling harder. "I don't want to go back to prison!"

"You stole the money from Mrs. Hammond's trunk!"

"I didn't do it!"

"Mavis! The police!" Benton called, involved with his own struggles with the girl. This time Mavis moved around the counter and started for the door, intent upon fetching the police herself.

"Wait!" Pete called out as her hand touched the doorknob. "I'll give you back the money!"

Mavis stopped, obviously unsure of what to do, and Joseph swung the man around and grabbed him by the stiff new collar. "It looks like you've spent it all!"

"I still got most of it! Please, don't get the police!"

"Why? So you can steal from someone else?" Even as he spoke, Joseph realized that he had no proof to offer the authorities, not without Corrine's word as well. And he knew that as much as she feared winding up in the hands of the law, Corrine wouldn't want to come from Leawick to testify. He tightened his grip on the man's collar. "How much do you have left?" he sneered.

"Pete!" the girl screamed, her eyes wild. "You said you'd buy me that bracelet!"

"Shut up, Nadine!" Pete yelled back. He turned pleading eyes on Joseph, his breath coming out in short gasps as he spoke. "Forty-eight pounds I got in my pocket right now, mister. That's all what's left, but you can have it all. *Please* don't turn me in to the police!"

Joseph loosened his grip just a little. "Hand it over."

~

Two days later, Joseph was on a northbound train, rationalizing to himself that he couldn't trust sending that much money by post. Besides, if he sent a check, how could he be certain that it would wind up in Corrine's hands?

She didn't have to know that he had added twelve pounds to the envelope containing the money he had recovered from Pete. She would have every bit of her sixty pounds back. Joseph smiled wryly. No doubt she would give God the credit for this latest blessing when *he* was the one who had wrestled Pete and had made up the difference from his own pocket.

Then it occurred to him that perhaps God had chosen to bless Corrine through him, but he dismissed the thought from his mind. Joseph didn't know a lot about God, but he was pretty certain that the good Lord didn't work in that manner.

~

Instead of hiring a coach upon his arrival at Shrewsbury Wednesday afternoon, he paid the owner of a stable for the use of a sorrel gelding. The weather was good and the roads dry—on a horse he could make the trip to Leawick in only an hour and be back at Shrewsbury before nightfall. Just enough time to hand Corrine Hammond the money without intruding into her life. Even if she asked him into her home to meet her family, he would politely respond that he had to get back to taking care of his own business.

As the thatched and timbered cottages of Leawick began to appear along the road, at first a scattering here and there, and then closer together, Joseph wondered if Corrine had lived in one of these meager homes. In the town itself he was relieved to find an inn on the main road, an old stone building with a grasshopper-shaped weather vane. He tied his horse to a hitching post out front and went inside to have a cup of tea and ask directions.

He found himself in a smoke-filled, noisy dining room, its walls decorated with cheap prints of the crowning of Charlemagne and of the princes in the Tower waiting to be murdered.

"Corrine Hammond ain't lived here in years," the innkeeper's sister, a buxom woman with a missing front tooth said in a whisper after bringing his tea to the table. She glanced around the room before adding, "Her man, Thomas Hammond, died back in January. Some folks wondered if she might come to town for the burial, but she didn't show."

Joseph sat there, stunned. Corrine's husband, dead? After the shock wore off, he raised his eyebrows to the woman. "Wasn't Mrs. Hammond here just recently?"

"Here in Leawick?" The woman snorted and shook her head. "Folks would have noticed the likes of her."

That didn't mean that she hadn't come, Joseph thought. *Maybe she left town with her daughter right away, after she heard about her husband.*

"What about her daughter?" he asked. "Jenny's her name, I think."

The woman's lips tightened with disapproval. "Her sister's been raisin' the child."

"And her sister's name?"

"Mary Satters," she replied. "Her husband, Roy, thatches roofs. Don't say much to nobody." She glanced around again. "Kind of a mean-looking sort, if you ask me."

~

With the directions to Roy Satters's cottage in his mind, Joseph thanked the woman with a generous tip and went back outside. *Surely Corrine couldn't come to such a small town without people knowing about it,* he mused as he headed the horse back in the direction he'd just come from. After all, inns were the hubs of gossip in towns of any size.

Just past a dairy, he reached a crossroads and turned to the right, as the woman from the inn had instructed. The road led over a hill and, a quarter of a mile later, ended at a small half-timbered cottage. A group of children playing in the yard ran inside at Joseph's approach. He wondered if one of them might be Jenny—from a distance, none had looked big enough to be ten years old.

A tired-looking woman came to the door that the children had left open. She wore her light brown hair pulled up into a tight chignon, and her only resemblance to Corrine was a delicately cleft chin.

"Mrs. Satters?" Joseph asked.

"My husband's not here," she answered curtly. A small lad clung to her skirts. She did not invite the stranger at her doorstep inside, but stood there waiting for him to leave so that she could close the door.

Joseph shook his head. "I'd rather speak to you, Mrs. Satters. I'm looking for your sister Corrine. I thought she would be here."

At the sound of her sister's name, the woman's face clouded with uneasiness. "How . . . how do you know Corrine?"

"I shared a coach with her and found some money that she lost. I'd like to make sure that she gets it."

"I don't know where she is." She stood on tiptoe and glanced over Joseph's shoulder. "You'd better leave before my husband gets home."

Joseph wasn't about to give up so easily after coming so far. He was becoming increasingly worried about Corrine. She had been so intent on coming to Leawick. What had happened to her? "Her daughter, Jenny. Is she still staying with you?"

Mary absently gathered the collar of her faded dress with thin, trembling fingers. "Watch Evan," she said to the three girls who had been standing a few feet behind her.

Joseph stepped back out of the woman's way as she came through the doorway. She closed the door behind her, then turned to face him again.

"Are you a friend of my sister's?" she asked, searching his face with her dull gray eyes.

"Yes, a friend."

She looked over his shoulder again. "Corrine came here to get Jenny, but my husband talked her out of taking the girl."

"How could he do that?" Joseph asked, shaking his head. Hadn't Corrine told him that her soul ached for the child?

She hesitated, the fear evident on her face.

"I won't tell anyone that you told me," Joseph assured her in a gentle voice.

"He told my sister that Jenny is at Sir Feldon's and that she's bein' treated good. But I worry."

"Sir Feldon?"

Darting anxious looks up the road, Mary explained to him how her niece had gone to live in the manor house. "Jenny's had a longing to see her mother since she was left here as a baby. The Dunleys ain't family, and besides, people around here say that Lady Dunley is . . . not right in the head."

"Are you afraid the girl's being mistreated?"

"I don't think so." Her eyes became moist, and she looked up at Joseph with a pleading expression. "But she'll always wonder about Corrine if she don't get a chance to see her. Jenny's a loving child. It weren't right for my husband to send Corrine away."

Joseph nodded his understanding. Corrine had shown up in Leawick with almost no money only to find out that her husband was dead. She had been a target for her brother-in-law's lies that the girl would be better off with a wealthy family.

"You don't have any idea where Corrine would go?" he asked Mary.

She shook her head. "I didn't even get to see her. But my other sisters don't live close, and they've got bigger families and smaller houses than mine. They never got along with Corrine anyway." Giving Joseph a wan smile, she added, "Corrine was the only pretty one of the lot. They were jealous."

Joseph gave a weak smile. From the way things looked right now, they had little to envy.

25

N o job yet," Corrine told Bernice and Lucy Wednesday evening. She came through the kitchen door and sat down at the worktable, taking off her shoes to rub her stockinged feet.

Bernice raised her eyebrows and set a cup of hot tea in front of her. "You were gone an awful long time. We were startin' to worry."

"After I tried the Lambeth Pottery Factory, I stood in line at Bryant & Mays—the match makers—for five hours. When there were only about a dozen people in front of me, the manager came out and said that there weren't any more positions." Corrine shuddered at the memory. "Most of the women in line looked even more desperate than me—several were younger than Lucy here. There was almost a riot when the announcement came."

Bernice's daughter, Lucy, stood at the other end of the table, blinking her eyes as she minced onions on a cutting board. "I don't see why they wouldn't hire you right away," she said with a sniff. "You bein' so pretty and all."

Corrine gave the girl a strained smile. "Thank you, Lucy. But I wouldn't want to work for anyone who hired me just because of my looks." A meaningful look passed between Corrine and Bernice. "Those days are over."

"You've chopped enough onions," Bernice said to her daughter while wiping her eyes on her apron. "Go add them to the soup pot. You've got us all sniffing."

"Thank goodness!" the girl exclaimed, immediately raking the onions from the cutting board into a bowl.

"Actually, they smell rather good to me," Corrine remarked with a wink at Lucy. "I've been sniffing sulphur for five hours. I can still smell it in my hair and on my clothes."

"Well, it's a good thing you didn't get a job there!" Bernice pulled up a chair beside Corrine. "There's no telling what breathin' those chemicals does to a person's lungs."

"It would have been a job, though," Corrine replied sadly. "I could have looked for something else later."

"There's no rush for you to go out and do that," said the cook. "I know that Mr. Adam and Miss Rachel would say that to you."

"But I don't want to impose upon their hospitality one day more than necessary. It puts an extra burden on all of you when you've already been more than good to me."

Out of consideration for Bernice, Corrine didn't add that having a job to perform for eleven to twelve hours a day would keep her mind occupied so that she couldn't dwell so much on her daughter. She had cried enough on the good woman's shoulder. The cook could hardly look at her without sadness taking over her expression.

"Six guest bedrooms there are in this house, that aren't bein' used," Bernice countered. "You've been cleaning your own room and helping out with the kitchen work. How are you putting an extra burden on us?"

"I've got an idea, Miss Corrine," offered Lucy, coming over from the stove. "You could look for a position as a governess or a nanny."

Corrine smiled again at the girl. "I don't think I could do that yet . . . be around children."

She thought about Jenny, wondering for the hundredth time that day what the girl was doing at this very moment. Roy had been right, though it was painful to admit it. How could she possibly support a child when the only employment she'd been offered so far was from the owner of a millinery shop, to assemble ladies' hats and bonnets at home? It wasn't that she was too proud to do piecework, but like most cottage industries, the salary was adequate only to cover food and other necessities. Rent was out of the question.

She would eventually find a job that paid enough to rent herself a jerry-built tenement somewhere, but she would have no money left for her daughter's schooling. How could a ten-year-old girl be happy, locked indoors and alone every day while her mother worked?

Sometimes the emptiness threatened to consume her, and she would have to go to her room and pray. It was good to be able to talk with God again, though for a while the temptation to turn away from him had been strong. Then she had finally realized that God knew just how she felt. He had given up his only Son once. How vacant heaven must have felt without Jesus!

And while she had the comfort of knowing that the people Jenny lived with were kind and loving to her, God had known that his Son would endure the hatred of most of the people he lived among.

Still, she thought of Jenny almost constantly and found

comfort in praying for her daughter. Corrine didn't forget her promise to pray for Joseph Price, either. She faithfully uttered short prayers for his continued health and that he would see his need for God in his life. Then, after praying for the man, she would try to banish from her mind all recollections of the time she had spent with him. Somehow, it seemed disloyal to Thomas's memory to be thinking about someone else.

~

After speaking to Mary Satters, Joseph headed back toward Gaston House Inn. He had to have time to think. Clearly there was a need for some sort of action on his part, but he wasn't sure exactly what it was. Should he try to locate Corrine first and let her know how much Jenny missed her so that she could come back to claim her? With her money returned, Corrine would be able to hire a solicitor to aid her, in the event that the Dunleys refused to let the girl go.

He had a strong hunch that Corrine was in London, back at Adam Burke's house, where he had first met her. She had obviously been close to the people who lived there—in fact, she had told him that one of the servants, a cook, had shown her how to become a Christian. Where else would she be?

And if Corrine wasn't in London, surely the cook would at least have some idea of where to reach her.

Joseph had a nagging feeling that he should at least see about the girl before leaving town. After all, he was only a few miles away from the house where she was staying. He didn't know if it would be possible to actually *see* her, but he had to make an attempt.

After stabling his horse behind the inn, he went inside and

procured a room. Once upstairs, he sank into a comfortable upholstered chair and set himself to working out a plan for the morning.

The first thing he had to do, he decided, was find out all he could about the Dunley manor. That could probably be taken care of at supper, especially if the innkeeper's sister was still in the dining room.

Then he needed to have a reason to actually *go* to Sir Feldon's home. *Easy,* he thought, *I'll go looking for work.* In the probable event that he didn't get a glimpse of the girl, at least he would look for an opportunity to talk with some of the servants—as many as possible.

At any rate, he wouldn't leave Leawick until he knew for certain how Jenny Hammond was being treated. Then he would find Corrine and advise her to come back here and fetch her daughter. If she asked for his assistance, well, of course he would accompany her. He would accept her gratitude with aplomb, letting her know by his words and actions that he was only doing what any decent man would do, and not because he longed to be near her again.

Joseph went to the washstand to rinse the dust of the road from his hands and face. As he dried his face with a towel and caught a glimpse of himself in the mirror over the pitcher and bowl, he studied his face. Had Corrine found him at least a little handsome? *You sorry rake!* He scowled at his reflection in the glass. *She's just found out that her husband is dead!*

With a flash of pain and shame, Joseph recalled the harsh things he had said and thought about the man. *He never did anything to me, and here I was almost hating him because . . .*

Because why? he asked the solemn-looking image in the

mirror. The answer came to his mind immediately. *Because I wanted to be him.*

~

Near midnight, Lenora Dunley propped herself up on her elbows. "Can't sleep," she murmured, rubbing her temples viciously. "So tired."

Moving her covers aside, she turned over and sat up in bed. She reached over for the brass candleholder on the night table, but her hands grasped empty darkness instead.

"Alice!" she called, waiting for an answer. When there was none, she felt for the candle again, this time frowning. For two years now, the maid had slept on a cot in Lenora's dressing room with the door propped open in case her mistress should need something during the night. The girl was a light sleeper and usually only had to be called once.

"Alice!" Lenora called, louder. "I want some hot chocolate!"

There was still no answer.

This time Lenora lunged for the candlestick, almost knocking it over. Slipping her legs over the side of the bed, she felt for the tin box of matches. With the candle burning, she got out of bed and walked barefoot over to her dressing room. She stepped through the open door. "Alice?"

The maid's cot was rumpled, but empty.

"Where are you!" Lenora demanded, holding the candle higher to check out the dark corners of the room. Her temples throbbed, bringing stabs of pain with each beat of her pulse. Angered by the silence of the room, Lenora walked over to one of the windows and glared out toward the carriage house. "Stupid girl is probably out there entertaining the gardeners," she muttered.

~

Sir Feldon Dunley sat on a leather chair in his library and stared at the open book in his lap. *Frederick the Great.* He had just read two pages describing the attack on Saxony and realized he couldn't recall one sentence. Setting the book on a nearby table, he picked up the pamphlet he had already read twice today. As with the pages of the book, his mind still refused to absorb the printed words in front of him.

"Pinel Sanitarium for the Mentally Disturbed," he read again, thankful that neither *lunatic* nor *asylum* was on the page. He continued on. "Located in Combe Down, just south of Bath . . . founded on principles of Parisian physician Philippe Pinel . . . compassionate treatment . . . no physical restraints."

Sir Dunley lowered the pamphlet and let out a sigh. How could he send Lenora away? What if, instead of getting well, she became worse?

"Sir Feldon?" Alice, Lenora's maid, stood in the doorway. "May I speak with you?"

He sighed again and wished he had gone on to bed, like everyone else in the household. *Most everyone,* he thought, for there was no telling the scenario his wife was acting out upstairs at the moment. "Is it Lady Dunley?"

"She's in her bed, sir," was the girl's timid answer. "I didn't want to leave her till she fell asleep."

"I appreciate your loyalty," he said, though he was not used to giving compliments to servants. He nodded toward a chair three feet away. "Sit down, then, if you have something to say to me."

Quickly, Alice slipped into the chair and cleared her throat. "It's me cousin, sir . . . Helene."

"Surely Mrs. Styles can handle any problems you're having with your cousin."

"Oh no, sir—we get along just fine. And I would go to Mrs. Styles, but she's asleep."

She's got two minutes to get it all out, Sir Dunley thought, *then I'm going up to bed myself.*

"You see, I don't want Helene to lose her job." Her brown eyes welled up, and she wiped at them with the back of her hand.

"What do you mean?"

The girl swallowed. "The last thing Lady Dunley said to me when I helped her to bed was that Helene weren't fancy enough to be Angelica's maid. She—"

"Jenny."

"Beggin' your pardon, sir. Jenny."

"You're saying that Lady Dunley wants to dismiss your cousin?"

"In the mornin', she says. She says she's going to replace her with one o' those French maids who can fix hair in the latest styles."

If the situation weren't so tragic, Sir Feldon would have smiled at the worry on the girl's face. Instead, he yawned, then said, "Unfortunately, Lady Dunley will most likely forget anything she told you tonight."

Glancing down at the pamphlet on his lap, he added, "Even if she does remember, I can assure you that you have nothing to worry about."

~

Still wearing her nightgown and holding the candle, Lenora padded through the dressing room to the hallway. She would wake Feldon and demand that he send the girl packing in the morning! And if he became angry because of the late hour, she would tell him to stop avoiding her in the daytime, and she wouldn't have to disturb his precious sleep!

Feldon's door stood open, and his bed was undisturbed. Where could he be?

Lenora walked back out into the hall, not quite sure what to do next. No light showing under Angelica's or Neil's doors. Maybe Feldon was in his study. That had to be the answer. He had been acting so strange lately; she wouldn't put it past him to be at work while the whole world was sleeping.

"Well, all the better," she mumbled. "He can go out there and find that girl and send her away right now." Holding the candle aloft, she descended the stairs to the ground floor and walked down the hallway to his study. The room was empty as well, she discovered, but when she walked out into the hallway, she heard what sounded like a female voice from the direction of the library.

Alice? she wondered. What would Alice, who probably couldn't even read, be doing in there? And where was Feldon?

Lenora opened the door and stepped inside. There sat her husband and that servant!

"What is this?" she shrieked.

Feldon was on his feet in an instant. "Lenora, what are you doing out of bed?"

"What am *I* doing? How dare you ask me that question!" She turned glaring eyes upon Alice. Face white with terror, the girl was trying to press herself back into her chair as much as possible. The vulnerability of the maid's posture enraged Lenora even more. "I suppose you come here every night when I'm asleep, you little—"

313

Her husband clamped a hand on her arm. "It's not at all what you think, Lenora. The girl needed to talk to me."

"Trying to steal my husband, are you?" she screamed. She pulled away from Feldon and lunged for Alice, dropping the candleholder on the carpet. "I'll tear you apart!"

"Stop it, Lenora!" Feldon pulled her away from the maid. As he pinned Lenora's arms to her sides, he stomped at the charring place where the candle had landed. To Alice, he said, "Go on, get out."

"Yes! You get out!" Lenora screamed at the girl's retreating back, struggling to get free of her husband's arms.

When the door had slammed shut, Feldon loosened his hold just a little and whirled her around to face him. "The girl and I were just talking."

Tears of rage and humiliation coursed down Lenora's cheeks. "How could you!"

"How could I what?" he answered, meeting her accusing gaze without flinching. "She was worried about her cousin losing her job, that's all."

"How can you act like you didn't even do anything wrong?" she sobbed.

His hands tightened on her arms. "Because I didn't!"

"Yes, you did! How many other times have you been with that doxy?"

"I won't honor that question with a reply. Besides, if I *had* been unfaithful, it would have been your fault."

"My fault!"

"You spend all your time with that child, pretending she's our daughter! Well, she's not—and I'm sick of seeing you act that way!"

The throbbing in Lenora's head returned, so intense that

she thought she might faint. Lenora pulled one arm free to rub at her temple. "Sick of seeing me . . . ," she repeated. "My fault . . ."

Feldon sighed and loosened his grip. "Go back to bed, Lenora. You need to get some rest . . . we both do."

~

Mrs. Styles was out in the hallway with a lantern when Lenora walked out the library door. "I'll show you to your room, Lady Dunley," she said quietly.

They walked up the stairs to Lenora's room together, then the housekeeper straightened the covers on the bed and fluffed the pillows. "I'll sleep in the cot in your dressing room," she said.

Lenora climbed into bed, allowing Mrs. Styles to pull the covers over her shoulders. "He said it was my fault," she murmured, looking up at the housekeeper with red-rimmed eyes.

"Now, m'lady," Mrs. Styles said in a soothing voice, "just close your eyes and try to get some sleep. Things will look better in the morning."

"It was so cold, the water. My legs wouldn't move."

"Of course they wouldn't," Mrs. Styles whispered.

"So cold," Lenora whispered, turning to lie on her side. "Not my fault."

26

THE next morning, Joseph went down to the dining room and ate a big breakfast of sausage and eggs. It was good to have an appetite again. He winked and smiled at the innkeeper's sister, who had graciously told him during supper last night how to get to the Dunleys'.

After he paid for the room he took his satchel with him out to the stables. There was no telling where he'd end up sleeping tonight, so he would need the extra clothing with him. The possibility of actually being hired on at the Dunley estate was remote, but there was always a chance.

As he saddled the horse, he wondered what Corrine Hammond would think if she knew how close he was to her daughter's new home. She probably thought he was still convalescing in Bristol . . . if she ever thought of him at all.

~

Sir Feldon Dunley, dressed in riding breeches and coat, went downstairs before his solitary breakfast was to be served. "I've got to post a letter," he informed Mrs. Styles on his way to the door.

The housekeeper looked surprised. "Wouldn't you rather Harold do that?"

Shaking his head, the baronet touched the corner of the envelope in his coat pocket. "I need to post this one myself," he answered sadly.

~

Jenny knew as soon as she got out of bed that something was wrong. Helene had helped her sponge bathe in silence, and the somber-looking maid took a dress from the wardrobe without waiting to see which one Lady Dunley would choose.

A periwinkle-and-white striped muslin, one that Mrs. Pruitt had substituted, slid over Jenny's arms comfortably. Helene sat the girl at the dressing table, tied her hair behind her ears with a wide blue ribbon, then finally spoke in a flat voice. "Mrs. Styles is coming up to take you to breakfast."

Jenny nodded timidly, wishing she had the courage to ask what was wrong. She liked Helene. Whatever it was she had done to make the maid angry, she wouldn't do it again if she knew what it was.

"Oh, don't look so pitiful," Helene scolded gently, reaching around Jenny's shoulder to touch her cheek. "You didn't do anything. I'm just upset 'cause my cousin is talking about looking for a position somewhere in one of the big towns."

"I'm sorry," Jenny said. She had seen Alice often, tending to Lady Dunley's many demands. Like Helene, she was friendly and laughed a lot.

Helene shrugged. "Well, maybe I can talk her out of it. She's just a bit miffed because of what happened last night."

Jenny nodded as if she understood. What had happened? And where was Lady Dunley, she wondered. Was she sick? Was that why Mrs. Styles would be taking her to breakfast?

Minutes later, the housekeeper came into the room, her

face as somber as Helene's. Still, she managed a smile. "How nice you look!" she said, taking Jenny's hand.

They reached the dining room at the same time as Lady Dunley's brother. "She's still asleep," Mrs. Styles said in a near whisper to Mr. Wingate as she led Jenny into the room.

He shook his head, his brow furrowed.

"Why don't you stay and sit with me and the girl," he said when the housekeeper was about to leave. "I know she'd feel more comfortable with you here."

Mrs. Styles pulled out the chair next to Jenny, on the opposite side of where Lady Dunley usually sat. She declined Mr. Wingate's offer of food, saying that she had already eaten in the servants' hall.

Jenny served her own plate from the sideboard, taking an extra strip of bacon. Lady Dunley always hovered over her, reminding her again and again to chew her food, like she was a baby instead of a grown girl of ten. This morning she would take advantage of Lady Dunley's absence. She would chew the meat just enough so it could be swallowed, but not a bit more.

While she and Mr. Wingate ate their breakfasts, Mr. Wingate and Mrs. Styles talked quietly about the humidity, the health of one of the older gardeners who had gout, and the likelihood of the civil war in the United States dragging on forever. It seemed to Jenny that their conversation was stilted, as if they were both working hard at talking *around* something. She wondered if that something was connected to Lady Dunley's absence. They obviously weren't going to say anything in front of her, so she went back to concentrating on not chewing her bacon.

Mrs. Styles turned to her and smiled, seeing that the girl's plate was clean. "Would you like to go play in the garden?"

"Yes, ma'am," she answered at once.

"Pick yourself a bouquet for your room if you like," Mr. Wingate said from across the table. He looked at the house-keeper for confirmation. "Couldn't she do that?"

"Of course," said Mrs. Styles. "Go through the kitchen and ask for a jar. Later we'll find a nice vase for you."

"Thank you." Jenny got up from the table and left the dining room, wishing that all the mealtimes at the manor house could be as undemanding as this one had been. Feeling guilty for the thought, she reminded herself that Mrs. Dunley couldn't help being the way she was.

She walked downstairs to the kitchen and timidly asked a scullery maid for a jar, as the housekeeper had suggested. Then she went through the back door and, with the jar under her arm, skipped all the way to the garden. In spite of her pity for Mrs. Dunley, she relished the freedom of being able to move about outdoors without a hand clinging tightly to hers.

The garden bore a heady scent of flowers, green leaves, and soil. A house martin, collecting mud for its nest from a large earthen pot of ferns, cocked its head and stared at Jenny for a second before taking flight. His short, feathered legs made him look as if he wore little white stockings.

Jenny stretched up to smell a particularly inviting crimson rose on one of the trellises and wished she had thought to ask for a knife so that she could put some roses in her bouquet. But violets were almost as nice, and she walked deeper into the garden to collect some.

"Angelica!"

Jenny froze. Lady Dunley was seated on the garden bench, wearing a rumpled white cotton nightgown with her hair wild about her shoulders. Her hazel eyes were shadowed under-

neath, and she was rubbing her upper arms with her hands as
if she were cold.

"You came to see your mother!" the woman said in a voice
that sounded strangely hoarse.

When Jenny still hadn't moved, Lady Dunley smiled and
beckoned for her to come over. A little fearful at the woman's
disheveled appearance, Jenny set the jar down on the grass,
then walked over to the bench and sat next to her. Lady
Dunley immediately took her hand in her own.

"You were going to pick flowers?"

"Yes . . . Mama."

"I always liked daisies the best, even if they don't smell."
She let go of Jenny's hand and began rubbing her arms again.
"Happy flowers, that's what I call daisies," she said in a child-
ish voice.

Calmly, so as not to upset her, Jenny said, "Would you like
me to ask Mrs. Styles to come here?"

"Mrs. Styles?" Lady Dunley echoed. "Perhaps I should go
fetch her." But there was no movement on her part to rise.
"I'll never figure how Simone manages to keep those children
in such fine clothes," she murmured, staring at something on
the other side of the garden. "Kendall boasts every time he
opens his mouth, but his debts are no secret from anyone
in the family. I'm sure he's asked your father to lend him
money."

"Yes, Mama."

Lady Dunley nodded and gave a sigh. "I figured as much.
I'm going to have to talk to your father." Turning to give
Jenny a knowing smile, she said, "Your father's very clever
with numbers and financial things, so don't think I'm saying
that he's not. But you'll learn that men have weak spots for

their relatives. Particularly male relatives that they're bound to by their boyhood memories."

"Yes, ma'am."

"There's just no way to understand it." She leaned down to scratch the top of one of her bare feet, then was still and quiet for a long time, again staring out at something in the distance. "People just say any old . . . ," she mumbled, and as her voice trailed off, a thread of saliva made its way from her bottom lip down to the bodice of her nightgown.

Jenny sat in silence with her hands clenched in her lap. After a while, the baronet's wife cleared her throat and turned again to look at the girl beside her. "You know that it wasn't my fault, don't you?"

"Yes, Mama," Jenny answered dutifully.

"Why did he have to say that? He knew I couldn't move my legs."

"It wasn't your fault."

"You know that?"

"Yes, ma'am."

The woman stood abruptly, then held out a hand for Jenny. "I've got to make you understand. I can't have you turning against me like *he* did."

With no other choice, Jenny stood and slipped her hand into Lady Dunley's. They walked together through the garden and across the lawn. A gardener, digging a hole several feet away, straightened and called out, "M'lady . . . can I help you?"

Ignoring the man, Lady Dunley squeezed Jenny's hand tighter. "I think he just doesn't want to remember. It's not fair . . . his not remembering how it happened. I tried my best. . . ."

"Yes, Mama."

They reached the stables. A young man wearing work clothes and carrying a bridle came out of one of the stalls, took in the sight of Lady Dunley's nightgown, and asked the same question the gardener had asked.

"Yes," she answered. "I need you to get the gig ready."

His eyes widened. "Ma'am?"

"The gig, Dustin—I need it now. And don't hitch Bluebell up to it. She's too lazy to run."

"Bluebell, ma'am?"

Her voice took on a sharper edge, to where the hoarseness almost disappeared. "My mare, you idiot!"

The man blinked in bafflement and looked in the direction of the house. "Perhaps Mr. Wingate—"

"Now! Or pack your things and leave!"

The gig was ready in five minutes. Lady Dunley, now all smiles, allowed the groomsman to help Jenny and her up into the seat. Just as she picked up the reins, they both caught sight of a red-faced Mrs. Styles coming halfway across the lawn.

"Lady Dunley!" the housekeeper called out, waving a hand.

"We'll be back later!" she called, then gave the reins a snap.

~

The horse's hooves sent up great clouds of dust as the gig passed the gatehouse and tore down the road. Jenny kept a white-knuckled grip on the seat. At first she thought Lady Dunley was taking them out to the fields, but just as the two barns were in sight in the distance, the woman steered the horse to make a sharp turn to the right, down the path leading to Lake Chestnut.

They passed the boathouse and pulled to an abrupt stop in

front of the pier. "Now, wasn't that fun?" Lenora exclaimed, pushing the hair away from her face.

"Yes, Mama," Jenny replied. She didn't like being here alone with Lady Dunley in such a state. What if she tried to hurt herself? She was about to ask if they could go back now, but remembering the hair-raising ride she had just survived, Jenny kept quiet and hoped instead that her wildly beating heart would have time to calm down before Lady Dunley wanted to leave again.

"I wish your father had come with us."

Jenny wondered if anyone from the house would be coming for them. "I wish so, too, Mama," she said soothingly. "Maybe he will next time."

"He blames it all on me, you know." Lady Dunley stared out at the water. "That's not fair."

"It wasn't your fault."

The woman turned to direct a blank stare at Jenny. "It couldn't have been," she whispered as if talking to herself more than to the girl. "I could have saved you if he hadn't made my legs go numb. I could have."

Not bothering to tie off the reins, she began climbing out of the gig. "Let's get out."

~

Just settling down in his favorite chair in the morning room with a two-day-old *London Times,* Neil started at the sound of rapid footsteps in the hallway. Mrs. Styles came through the door before he could stand, holding her side as she caught her breath.

"Lady Dunley—," the woman said between gasps. "She took off in the gig—she's got Jenny with her."

He put down his newspaper. "Where did she go?"

"I don't know. None of the maids even saw her slip out of the house this morning. She's still in her nightgown."

"Didn't anyone follow her?"

Mrs. Styles shook her head. "She's got the whole staff afraid of her . . . especially after what happened to Alice."

Sighing, Neil got to his feet and said, "She probably went back over to the Hansworths' place, showing off her 'daughter' again. I'll saddle up and try to catch up to her before she causes any more trouble."

~

At the first crossroads on the outskirts of town, Joseph reined his horse to the left as he had been instructed. He passed hedged fields on both sides and wondered if all of this land belonged to the Dunleys.

Returning his attention to the road ahead of him, he noticed a cloud of dust in the distance and then made out the form of a horse and rider. He kept his horse at the same pace and watched the man and animal draw near.

When he was several feet away, the man raised a hand. Even from that distance, Joseph could spot the hatless man's pale complexion and anxious expression. He didn't look like someone who ordinarily went out riding.

"Are you coming from Leawick?" the man asked when he had reined to a stop. He drew in deep breaths as he spoke.

"Yes, I am." Joseph reined in his own horse. "Is something wrong?"

"Did you pass a woman driving a carriage?"

"I didn't pass anybody, man or woman."

The man's face fell. "Are you certain? She would have had a little girl with her."

"A little girl?"

"Surely they didn't go to the lake," the man said, mostly to himself as he looked back over his shoulder. "Lenora said she never wanted to go back there."

An uneasy feeling settled in Joseph's chest. He detected a tone of fear in the man's voice, enough to convince him that he had to get to that lake, wherever it was—and fast.

"Where's this lake?" he asked.

"Oh no. She couldn't—"

"Show me the way!" Joseph ordered.

~

"See?" Lenora held Jenny's hand and guided her slowly down the pier. Jenny's shoes were the only sound against the oak boards—Lady Dunley was easing one bare foot down in front of the other, as if afraid to make a noise.

"Let's sit," she said when they reached the end. She looked down at Jenny's dress and smiled vacantly. "That looks nice on you. Mind you don't snag it on the boards. I ruined one of my favorite gowns that way . . . only it wasn't on the pier." Pursing her lips in concentration for a few seconds, she finally gave up and shook her head. "I forget just how I did it . . . but my mother was so angry!"

They both sat down, their legs dangling down over the end. "You make me so happy," Lady Dunley said, looking away. Jenny couldn't see her face, but could tell by her voice that she was crying. "Don't ever believe what *he* says about it."

"No, ma'am," Jenny answered. It would have been pleasant, sitting out here like this if Lady Dunley wasn't acting so strangely. The lake was pretty, with water sparkling in the places where sunlight filtered through the trees. Once in a while a fish jumped, sending out rings that grew wider and wider until they were captured by the calmer water. She could be having a lovely time if her cousins were here, too, and she didn't have to worry about the woman beside her.

Suddenly Lady Dunley started rubbing her own arms again. She stared out at the lake with unblinking eyes and mumbled something that the girl couldn't understand. As the woman's voice grew louder and more agitated, Jenny realized that she was arguing with someone who wasn't there. She wondered if Sir Feldon was the object of Lady Dunley's anger.

"You know that's what you're thinking—I've known it for too long! You blame me for everything!" She rubbed her arms more furiously, then whispered, "I've known it."

Jenny's neck prickled, sending a shudder down her spine. What should she do? "Mama," she ventured carefully, "don't you think we should go back home now?"

"I don't *want* to go boating!" the woman beside her yelled hoarsely into the air. "Let Simone learn not to make promises!"

When the voice died down, Jenny straightened and tilted her head to listen. She was hearing a sound in the distance . . . thunder?

~

Why is the water always so cold? Lenora thought, rubbing her arms even harder. It was impossible to get warm with its wetness plastering her clothing against her body, saturating even the pores of her skin. Yet she couldn't allow the chill and darkness of the water to distract her from doing what she had to do. Angelica was depending upon her, and this time she wouldn't fail her daughter.

"I'm going to save her!" she raged at Feldon, whom she could see standing on the opposite bank, pointing his finger and mocking her. "You'll see! I'll get her to the boat!"

But where was it? The boat was their only chance, and now she couldn't find it. She could see her husband shaking his head at her helplessness. She kicked her legs to stay afloat and scanned the surface of the lake with her eyes.

Then she saw it—the hull of the overturned boat floating just ahead of her. Renewed hope set her heart to racing. She hadn't expected the boat to be so close. No wonder she had missed seeing it!

There was no time to waste! Ignoring the skirts that clung to her legs, she turned to her daughter.

~

Jenny watched with horror as Lady Dunley, still seated beside her, kicked her legs back and forth over the edge of the pier, as if she were running. Suddenly Jenny felt a strong hand at her back. Her arms shot down to grab the edge of the pier . . . but too late. She hit the water with arms flailing out and eyes wide open.

A cold blackness cut off her screams and burned its way up her nose and mouth. Terrified, she kicked her legs against the icy water and flailed her arms in search of something solid.

Finally her face broke the surface. She sputtered and coughed, then heard a splash close by. Water slapped her in the face again.

Jenny cried out for help as the water started closing in around her again. She gulped in a deep breath just before going under and kicked her feet furiously. When she came up again, Lady Dunley was moving in the water next to her, her mouth and eyes wide open and her hair plastered down against her head.

"Keep paddling your feet!" the woman ordered, inching toward her in the water.

Jenny remembered the pier and turned her face to look. A ladder reached down from the side. It must be close, but it seemed so far away. Her feet went numb, and she started to go under. *No!* her thoughts screamed.

She felt an arm grab the shoulder of her dress, pulling her back to the surface. "The boat!" Lady Dunley shouted. "We've got to make it to the boat!"

The woman was dragging her through the water, but—to Jenny's horror—they were moving *away* from the pier.

"Not that way!" she managed to gasp, her chin barely above water.

"Take hold of the boat!" Lady Dunley sputtered.

Jenny grabbed hold of the woman's arm—whether to wrench free or to keep from sinking, she didn't know.

But it no longer mattered. They both began to sink.

~

Once Joseph could see the lake, he urged his horse even faster, leaving a gap between himself and the other rider. At the sight of an empty gig several yards from the water's edge, he slowed his mount. The other horse looked up at Joseph, then went back to pulling grass from a nearby patch.

He thought he heard a voice and jerked around to look at the water. Nothing was moving as far as he could see. He rode quickly over to a long covered pier, and when the animal balked at the entrance, Joseph jumped from the saddle and ran out to the end.

On the surface of the water, about six feet from the pier, floated a blue hair ribbon. *O God, help her!* he prayed, as he yanked off his boots and lunged into the water.

Seconds later, his hands brushed against something—a dress, perhaps. He grabbed it and swam for the surface with his heavy burden. When he broke into the air, Joseph immediately hooked his arms around the waist of a girl and brought her head out of the water. The man who had met him on horseback stood a few feet away, holding on to a ladder at the edge of the pier. "Bring her here!" the man called.

Joseph dragged the child to the ladder, and when the man had her firmly in his grasp, Joseph dived back into the water. This time he had to go under several times. Fatigue was starting to set in when he finally located a second body and brought it up to the surface.

The girl lay on the deck, and the man left her to help Joseph get the limp woman up the ladder. They turned her onto her stomach, and the man started pounding on her back. "Come on, Lenora!" he cried. "Breathe!"

Joseph crossed over to see about the girl. She lay on her stomach, too, as still as death, her face turned to the side and her mouth partly open. "I heard her cough a minute ago!" the man called.

Joseph lifted the girl by the shoulders. Her eyelashes fluttered and she coughed again, then began heaving water from her throat.

~

Joseph had been waiting in the sitting room for nearly an hour. At last the door opened and a woman entered. Her lined face was drawn and tired looking, but there was a strength about the way she carried herself that impressed him. Joseph started to rise.

"Please keep your seat," she told him, walking toward the high-backed chair adjacent to his. "I'm the housekeeper here—my name is Mrs. Styles."

Joseph waited until the woman had seated herself before taking his own chair again. "How is Jenny?"

"Resting, but fine, thank God." She glanced at the dishes and tray on the tea table in front of him. "I hope you had enough refreshment."

"More than enough," he replied. "I appreciate your hospitality."

"It was fortunate that you had some dry clothes with you."

"Yes."

"And it was a blessing from God that you came around when you did."

"How is Mrs. Dunley?"

"Lady Dunley is resting as well. Her husband is with her now, but he would like to thank you himself if you don't mind waiting."

Joseph nodded. "I would like to speak with him, too."

The housekeeper's eyes lifted. "Are you looking for a position, Mr. Price?"

He decided to tell the truth. When he and Mr. Wingate had brought Jenny and the baronet's wife to this house, he had heard the pale and shaking girl tell Mrs. Styles that she had been pushed into the water. There was absolutely no way he could allow Corrine's daughter to stay in this place one more night. If he had to take her at gunpoint, he would do so.

Perhaps Sir Feldon would listen to reason and it wouldn't

come to that. "I'm working for Jenny's mother, Mrs. Hammond. She desperately wants her daughter back. Her trip to Leawick was . . . delayed . . . or she would have been here weeks ago."

He thought he detected a tightening of a muscle in the woman's jaw, and he leaned forward in his chair. "Mrs. Hammond is a good woman, Mrs. Styles. A Christian."

"Then why did she abandon the girl?"

Groping for an answer, he said, "Because Mrs. Hammond wasn't always the woman she is now. I can tell you for a fact she is not the same woman who walked out on her daughter and husband eight years ago. But she *is* Jenny's mother, and she loves her dearly. She has changed—can you understand that?"

"Yes, I can," she answered with a slight smile. "Then you think Mrs. Hammond will give Jenny a good life?"

"I *know* she will."

"Then I shall go upstairs and ask Sir Feldon to speak with you at once."

Joseph smiled back at her. Corrine would be comforted to know that this good woman had been here to look after Jenny. "I wouldn't want you to get in trouble with your employer. I can wait a bit."

But Mrs. Styles was already standing, her shoulders straight with determination. "After forty years of loyal service, it's about time I put my foot down. Jenny doesn't need to stay here, and she certainly doesn't need to end up back with her uncle."

~

"Does my mother really want me?" Jenny gazed into Mrs. Styles's eyes.

"Very much so, according to the gentleman downstairs."

Jenny thought about the possibility of never seeing her cousins or Aunt Mary again, and a lump came to her throat. "I don't know if I could leave my cousins," she said in a somber voice.

"That would be hard," the housekeeper agreed. "It's always hard to leave loved ones. But how much time would you be able to spend with them if you went back?"

A frown came to Jenny's face as she remembered her uncle's words. *Don't be bringin' her back here again!* he had said. If he did take her back, he would put her back out in the fields, and she would have scant time to be with her loved ones. And every time she ate a meal, she would see the reproach in Uncle Roy's eyes for taking food from his family. *His* family, where she didn't belong. And if he didn't take her back . . . well, she didn't even want to think about what would happen then.

But what was her mother like? The girl shuddered at the memory of what happened at the lake. She looked up from her pillow. Mrs. Styles would tell her the truth.

"Is my mother like . . ." Her voice trailed off. Lady Dunley was sick. It would be disrespectful to speak badly of her.

Mrs. Styles reached over to brush a strand of hair from Jenny's forehead. "Is your mother like Lady Dunley? Is that what you're afraid of?"

Jenny flushed. "Yes, ma'am."

"No, dear. Your mother will be different."

"Do you know what she looks like?"

"Your mother?" The housekeeper smiled, her eyes glistening. "I expect that she looks like you, Jenny."

Jenny nodded, hardly able to take in the wonder of it. "I'll be leaving today, then?"

"I think it's best . . . if you're up to it."

"I'm up to it." Excitement flooded through her, and then she suddenly realized that she would most likely never see the kind face above her again. "But I'll miss you . . . and Helene and Mrs. Pruitt."

The housekeeper took a handkerchief from her apron pocket and wiped the corners of her eyes. "We'll miss you, too, lass," she whispered. Clearing her throat, she added, "But when you get settled, we can post letters back and forth. That'll be nice, won't it?"

"But I can't read," she choked out.

Mrs. Styles laughed and patted her hand. "I'm sure your mother will be taking care of that. Until then, why don't you ask her to write them for you?"

Jenny considered that for a moment. "Do you think she would mind?"

"I have a feeling she would do anything for you."

~

An hour later, after Mrs. Styles had decided Jenny had rested enough, Jenny said farewell to Helene and Mrs. Pruitt.

Mrs. Pruitt, her eyes rimmed with red, handed over a small carpetbag. "I packed up your new dresses and shoes while you were asleep."

Struck speechless with emotion, Jenny embraced the portly seamstress, and then Helene.

"You'll be the most fashionable girl in London," Helene quipped, though wiping at her eyes, too.

"Thank you for everything," Jenny finally managed.

Mrs. Styles held out a hand to her. "We'd best get you downstairs now. Mr. Price is waiting."

In the hallway they passed the door to Lady Dunley's room. Inexplicably, Jenny found herself stopping.

"Jenny?"

She peered up at the housekeeper. "Lady Dunley will miss me, won't she?"

"She will, dear," Mrs. Styles said softly. "But Sir Feldon says she'll be going somewhere to get help soon."

"Do you think I should say good-bye to her?"

The housekeeper thought for a moment and shook her head. "No, child. Let's leave things as they are."

~

After Mr. Price and the girl were gone, Sir Feldon Dunley went back upstairs to see about his wife. "Is she still asleep?" he asked Alice, seated beside Lenora's bed.

"She's stirring a bit again, sir."

"I'll take over for a while," he said, motioning for the girl to leave. When she was gone, he pushed the chair even closer to the bed, sat down, and took his wife's hand. Lenora lay there, more peaceful than he had seen her in weeks.

Bringing the fingers, still so soft and feminine, up to his lips, he thought about how she had looked as a bride. "You were the most beautiful thing I had ever seen," he whispered.

Her eyelids opened slowly, and she turned on her pillow to look at him. "Feldon?"

"I'm here, Lenora."

She blinked, and a radiant smile came to her face. "I saved her this time, didn't I?"

Sir Feldon swallowed hard and gave her hand a gentle squeeze. "Yes, Lenora. You saved her."

27

"MISS Corrine made this bread herself," Bernice announced to the others around the table.

"You don't say!" Jack exclaimed from beside her, in the process of spreading butter on a second slice. "This is right fine bread, it is. And I thought it came from my dear wife's hands."

"Thank you, Jack," Corrine smiled at the gardener. She had finally persuaded Adam Burke's servants to stop addressing her as Mrs. Hammond. It had taken some doing, but they were finally getting into the habit—even shy Irene—of at least calling her Miss Corrine. Titles and surnames caused distance between people, no matter how warm the relationship. Still hurting from the loss of any possible relationship with Jenny, Corrine found that she needed intimacy with friends right now, not deference from servants.

"You know," Hershall said, "I'd like to know what fellow it was who first discovered you could use bugs to make bread."

Lucy stopped chewing and wrinkled her nose. "Bugs?"

"You know, in yeast, to make the dough rise. He was a brave man, don't you think?"

"Or maybe he were just weak sighted," Jack quipped.

"They're too little for you to see 'em," Dora said to Lucy, who didn't look reassured. "You've got to use one of those looking glasses."

Corrine cleared her throat and sent Hershall a tactful smile. "Actually, yeast is made from plants."

The manservant's eyebrows went up. "Not bugs?"

"I'm afraid not," she answered gently.

"That means it's safe for Lucy to eat her bread again," teased Marie, for Lucy had consigned her slice to the edge of her plate. The girl blushed but joined in the laughter.

Corrine laughed, too, for the first time in days. Then it came to her that she actually possessed a bit of information that other people hadn't known. It was a comfort to know that her mind did contain some practical knowledge after all. *I wouldn't have known about the yeast if Mr. Price hadn't told me,* she reminded herself. On one of their last days in the cottage, he had told her all about the bakery his father owned in Bristol, even explaining how bread was made to rise.

She remembered the light in the man's eyes when he spoke of his family. How sad it seemed to her that he was employed in such a solitary occupation. Perhaps as long as she was praying for Joseph Price, it would be good to add that he find a wife and have a family of his own one day. But the thought made her uneasy, so she pushed it aside and turned her attention back to her friends at the table.

Dora was in the process of telling everyone about a production she wanted to see at the theater on her day off, when her sister raised a hand to quiet her.

"I thought I heard a knock," Marie said, tilting her head.

The sound came again, and Hershall rose from his chair. "I'm finished with my plate. I'll see about it."

~

"Are you sure she wants to see me?" Jenny asked Mr. Price as they stood under the portico and waited. She hoped the man didn't mind that she had already asked that same question twice on the train. But she was filled with doubts about whether she had made the right choice. She wished she'd had more time to think over what she should do, but Mrs. Styles had told her that she must hurry and decide before Sir Feldon got back.

The man who had saved her from drowning now looked down at her and smiled. "Does she want to see you? More than anything in the world, I'd say."

His assurance made Jenny feel a little better, though she couldn't stop trembling. Her mother might change her mind. After all, Aunt Mary had said that her mother was beautiful. What if she took one look at Jenny and decided that she was too ugly to have as a daughter?

"Are you still worried?"

Biting her lip, Jenny nodded up at Mr. Price. He reached for her hand and held it in his. "You're going to love each other. Trust me."

They heard the click of a latch, and the door swung open. A graying man wearing a black suit bowed and said, "May I help you, sir?"

"My name is Joseph Price. I'm looking for Mrs. Corrine Hammond. Is she staying here again?"

When the servant hesitated, Mr. Price squeezed Jenny's hand and added, "Her daughter has come to see her."

~

The conversation around the table ceased as Hershall came back into the room. He walked purposefully over to where

Corrine was seated and put a hand on the back of her chair. "Miss Corrine," he began, smiling down at her in a curious manner, "you have guests in the drawing room."

"Perhaps someone from one of the shops in Mayfair, where I applied this morning," she said to the others, getting to her feet as Hershall pulled out her chair. She hadn't even dared to hope for an answer so soon, but who else would be coming to see her?

"Perhaps so," Hershall answered, yet the mysterious smile remained on his face.

Pausing just inside the door, Corrine turned and looked back at her friends. "I'm a little nervous. Please pray for me." She hurried down the hall to the drawing room, went through the open door, and stopped in her tracks.

Joseph Price was standing by the fireplace, a huge smile on his face.

"Mr. Price?"

"You didn't expect to see me so soon, did you?"

At the sound of his voice, Corrine's heart began pounding in her chest, and she felt an almost overwhelming urge to run over and lose herself in his arms. Instead, she took a couple of steps forward and said in the most cordial tone she could manage, "Why, this is a surprise."

"Yes, isn't it? But an even bigger surprise is the friend I brought with me." He nodded toward the sofa, where a wide-eyed little girl sat perched on the edge of the seat.

Corrine's hand went up to her heart. It couldn't be!

"Don't you have anything to say to your daughter?" asked Joseph.

"Jenny?"

The girl gave a shy nod, and Corrine was at her side in an

instant. "Oh, my Jenny!" she cried through tears. "I can't believe you're here!"

She was startled and hurt when the girl stiffened in her embrace. At the touch of a hand on her shoulder she looked up—Joseph stood there, his expression now turned somber.

"Jenny's had a bad experience," he said, his eyes gentle. "Let her get to know you better first."

"All right." Though she didn't understand, Corrine backed away a little, wiped her eyes with her sleeve, and smiled at her daughter. It seemed as if her own gray eyes stared back at her. "You're beautiful," she whispered, wondering if she had ever felt as much love for a person as she was feeling right now.

The girl's eyes opened wider. "You still want me?" she whispered back.

"Want you?" Saddened that the child even had to ask, Corrine had to restrain herself from taking Jenny into her arms again. "I want you more than anything in the world."

Corrine didn't know how she was going to care for the two of them without a job and place of her own to live, but she had learned that some steps had to be taken in faith. Besides, now that she had seen her daughter with her own eyes, she couldn't even think of giving her up again.

"Do you think I could hold your hand?" she said carefully to the girl. When Jenny gave a hesitant nod, Corrine took the little hand gently in hers. And she knew she had never felt anything more precious.

~

Later that night, Jenny lay tucked into a soft bed in one of the guest bedrooms—utterly exhausted, but too overwhelmed by everything that had happened to fall asleep. A low light from a lamp left burning on a nearby stand took the edge off the darkness. Her mother—her *mother*—had promised to come and see about her all during the night, in case she became frightened. They had been together for almost an hour, her mother seated at the side of the bed, until Jenny couldn't stop yawning every few seconds. "I'll go so you can sleep," her mother had finally whispered, pressing a kiss to her hand before leaving the room.

Jenny tucked the hand that her mother had kissed between her pillow and her cheek. Once again, her life had changed drastically in a matter of hours. This time, though, the change felt right and good. Her mother did love her, after all. She was *wanted*. Not because she was a substitute for someone else and not because she could earn money . . . but just because she was alive. Just because she was *Jenny*.

She let out a contented sigh, her mind beginning to relax into sleep. Mother had told her, as she sat at the side of the bed, that God had brought them back together. Jenny's knowledge of such things was limited at best, but she knew in her heart that her mother was right. God had done something very special for her.

~

"I promised to check on her every hour or so," Corrine told Joseph. They sat on a cast-iron bench in the conservatory in a circle of amber light from a single candle. The room was redolent with the scent of earth and petals and greenery, and stars peeked down at them through the glass overhead. "I can't believe she's here!"

"I don't think she can believe it either," Joseph said, smiling.

"And I believe Mr. Burke's servants were almost as happy to see her as you were."

Corrine returned his smile. "Bless them for their kindness—and you for yours. It's almost as if this whole evening has been a dream." Her daughter was back, and Joseph had informed her that all of her money had been recovered!

Corrine turned the conversation to more practical matters. "There are some small terrace houses in Hackney renting for fourteen pounds yearly—I read about them in Marie's newspaper just yesterday, never thinking I would be able to afford one. If I take in piecework for millinery shops, it will give me the chance to stay home with Jenny, at least for a couple of years."

"What about her schooling?"

"Schooling?" she echoed, chiding herself inwardly for not thinking about that right away. Tears welled up in her eyes. She lifted a helpless hand, then let it fall to her lap. "All of this . . . being a *real* mother . . . is so new to me. I want so desperately to do what's best for her."

"You're going to do just fine," Joseph assured her. "I have no doubts about that." With a careful smile he added, "I would be happy to sponsor Jenny's—"

Corrine shook her head, and the rest of his words hung there, unspoken. "You know I can't accept your money," she said with quiet firmness. "You paid for my carriage out of Amberton, and for that I am grateful. But please don't offer again."

"All right," he sighed. "Then may I make a suggestion?"

"Please."

"When you find a place to live, go ahead and pay the first

six months' rent with part of your sixty pounds. Then invest the rest."

"Invest? But where?"

"I'm sure Mr. Burke could give you some guidance, when he gets back, as to opportunities here in London. You should receive more than enough in interest to pay for Jenny's tuition at a church school. Their fees are quite reasonable."

Corrine felt almost light-headed from relief. "That's what I'll do, then."

"Only . . ."

Her spirits began to sink at the uncertainty that had crept into Joseph's voice. Had he discovered a problem with his plan? "Only what?"

"Piecework?" he answered, looking at her with a tender expression. "Do you remember what happened back at the cottage when you tried to sew? Your poor fingers."

"That was a good lesson," Corrine answered with a smile. "It reminded me to respect the point of a needle." She could feel her cheeks burning from the intensity of his gaze, and she looked away.

"Would you at least allow me to buy you a thimble?"

A protest rose to her lips, but she let it die. "A very *inexpensive* thimble," she whispered, wishing that her heart would stop beating so loudly. "No more than a farthing."

"A *farthing?*"

"Not a bit more than that." As she looked into his mulberry eyes, she thought of all the wonderful things he had done for her—and the wonderful things God had done through him. "God alone knew what a blessing you would be when he allowed you to come into my life."

"You mean *barge* into your life, don't you?"

She laughed. "Yes, that would be more like it. But even then, God was looking ahead to the future."

A silence stretched between them for several minutes—not an awkward silence, but a comfortable one. Finally Joseph spoke. "Your faith is quite beautiful to see. Perhaps one day mine will grow as strong."

Corrine tilted her head and looked into his eyes. Was he saying . . . ?

"Why are you looking at me like that?" Joseph asked, a slight smile on his lips. "Did you think I was too hardheaded to ever see my need for God?"

In her joy, she put her hand on his shoulder. "You've become a Christian?"

"Just last night."

"How did it come about?"

The smile vanished from his face, and he reached up to cover Corrine's hand with his own. "Yesterday. I looked into the face of death again, Corrine."

"Jenny," she whispered.

"And Lady Dunley. *Especially* Lady Dunley, for it took so long to revive her." Joseph shook his head. "I've watched people actually die before, but it has never unnerved me as much as what happened yesterday. That woman was just a breath away from eternity. A second longer in the water, and her family would be preparing her body for burial now."

The thought sent a shudder down Corrine's spine.

"In my room last night," he continued, his eyes sober, "I couldn't get the thought out of my head that I'm just a breath away as well. Three times in my life I almost died . . . once by sickness when I was a boy, another time when I was jumped by some thieves, and then the scarlet fever. Who knows how many times a person can get away with cheating death?"

Corrine nodded understanding. "When Gerald almost killed me, it made me realize how close I had come to meeting God. I didn't want to face him with such wickedness in my soul."

"That's how it was with me. But more than that, I realized there was something in your life that was obviously missing from mine."

There was another long silence, and then Corrine said, "I'm happy for you, Joseph."

His somber expression melted into a smile. "Happy enough to call me *Joseph* now, are you?"

Suddenly Corrine realized that her hand was still on his shoulder, captured by his hand. She made no attempt to move it. "Happy enough to call you *Joseph,*" she echoed, meeting his smile with one of her own.

"That in itself was worth the trip to London," he quipped. Then, with obvious reluctance, he said, "I should go and let you get some sleep. You and Jenny will have a lot of catching up to do tomorrow."

Together they got to their feet and started slowly for the French doors. "I can never repay you for everything you've done for me," Corrine said.

Joseph still had her hand in his. "You've already repaid me. You led me to God." He cleared his throat, his steps slowing. "I'm leaving for Chesterfield in the morning—a new client wants to hire me. I don't know how long it'll take, but when the job is finished . . ."

Corrine felt her pulse begin to race. "Yes?"

"May I come back to see you . . . and Jenny?"

"I would like that," she answered. After a thoughtful pause, she added, "Do you know how long this job will take?"

"I'm afraid I don't." Joseph smiled tenderly at Corrine, drawing her hand up to his cheek. "But I intend to work faster than I've ever worked before."

A Note from the Author

Dear Reader,

Thank you for reading *Measures of Grace*, the story of Corrine Hammond's learning the infinite length and breadth of God's grace as she searches for the daughter she abandoned.

Isn't *grace* a lovely word? Even the sound of it, the way it floats past our lips. No wonder many girls are named Grace. Its definition is even more special than the way it sounds: "unmerited favor." Aren't you glad for the times you've chosen to extend grace to someone else?

One such occasion comes immediately to my mind. Our eldest son, Joe, telephoned from school in a panic to say he had forgotten an important assignment at home. I immediately went into the busy-stressed-out-mom routine, scolding him for his carelessness.

"Would you please just not be angry?" he finally pleaded.

The way he said it stopped my tirade. I had a choice, I realized. I could extend grace to the son I loved. And I did. My attitude changed from irritation to calmness. That feeling of serenity accompanied me all the way across town to deliver the assignment.

I have had grace extended to me many times too, as I hope you have. May we strive to live our lives as vessels, overflowing with so much grace that it spills out onto everyone around us. And may God send a special blessing your way, dear reader!

Warmly,

Lawana Blackwell

About the Author

Lawana Blackwell is an accomplished novelist whose books have found a strong following. Her books include *The Widow of Larkspur Inn*, *The Courtship of the Vicar's Daughter*, *The Dowry of Miss Lydia Clark*, and *The Maiden of Mayfair*. She and her husband live in Baton Rouge, Louisiana, and are empty nesters who love every opportunity to get together with their three recently married sons and their wives. Besides writing, Lawana enjoys Home and Garden television, vegetarian cooking, and garage sales.

Lawana welcomes letters written to her in care of Tyndale House Author Relations, P.O. Box 80, Wheaton, IL 60187-0080 or by e-mail at lawanablack@yahoo.com.

Turn the page

for an exciting preview

from Lawana Blackwell's

next HeartQuest book,

Jewels for a Crown

J enny looked up at the sound of someone clearing her throat. Mrs. Ganaway stood in the doorway, hands clasped in front of her ample body. "I thought you were going to try to be more patient with the girl," she said with an injured air.

Jenny sighed. "I suppose patience is not my strong suit, Mrs. Ganaway. But I really did make an attempt to get along with her."

"Well, it's no matter now. Mr. Harrington would like to see you in his office."

"Couldn't I just leave?"

The housekeeper shook her head, and this time she looked truly sad. "You'd best come along, Miss Price. If it's any consolation, you're not the first to have this happen. I'm sure you did the best you were able."

In silence they walked downstairs, through the great hall, to a door opposite the front parlor. Mrs. Ganaway gave a soft knock.

"Come in," came a masculine voice from the other side.

Jenny stood back while the housekeeper opened the door. "Miss Price is here, Mr. Harrington."

"Please ask her to come in."

"Yes, sir. Will you be needing me as well?"

"No, Mrs. Ganaway."

The woman turned and put a hand on Jenny's shoulder. Immense regret showed on her careworn face. "I'll have someone finish your packing for you, dear."

"Thank you," Jenny whispered, her eyes growing moist. When the woman was gone, she walked with stiff dignity into Graham Harrington's office. He looked up at her from behind a massive oak desk, then got to his feet.

"Please close the door," he said, then motioned toward a chair in front of the desk. Jenny took the chair, surprised that Celeste wasn't in the room.

"I had Miss Barton take my daughter out into the garden," Mr. Harrington explained, as if he knew what she was thinking.

Hands folded in her lap, Jenny nodded.

"I'll get right to the point," the man said when he had sat down again. His brown eyes were serious. "This is only your first week here, yet my daughter has told me some things that are quite disturbing."

Jenny fought the urge to lower her eyes. She had decided on her way downstairs that she would readily admit to being wrong, but that her only crime had been a lack of patience, not larceny or murder. Raising her chin with a cool stare in his direction, she replied, "I'm sure she has, Mr. Harrington."

"I must admit to being surprised. You were so highly recommended."

"And because Celeste is your daughter, you believe her." Jenny stated this as a fact, not a question.

"She's never been one to lie to me."

"Well, sir, I suppose there is nothing more to say." Jenny rose to her feet. "If I could trouble you for a carriage . . ."

Obviously startled, he lifted a hand. "Please wait, Miss Price. I would like to hear your side, too."

"You would?"

"Of course. Only a fool makes a decision before he has heard all of the facts."

"I appreciate that," she said, lowering herself back into the chair.

Mr. Harrington was watching her thoughtfully, and Jenny realized that he was waiting for her explanation. "I suppose it was a mistake for me to be assigned here," she began. Her own voice sounded weary in her ears, and she wished she could just leave. "But I would like you to know that I did make several attempts to befriend your daughter."

"It doesn't sound that way to me."

Jenny uttered a deep sigh. "I can't defend myself until I know what I've been accused of, Mr. Harrington."

He nodded, as if that were a reasonable request. "Did you tell Celeste a frightening story one night about a cat, after she had warned you that she was prone to nightmares?"

Jenny's mouth fell open. "She told you *that?*"

"Yes. Do you deny it?"

"Of course I do! Please send for Alma, the maid who watched that night, and she'll verify it."

Mr. Harrington's expression turned a shade unsure. "Actually, Miss Barton also said it was untrue."

"She did?"

"Yes. But Celeste believes that you two are conspiring against her."

Jenny couldn't believe her ears. "Miss Barton and I have

only known each other for six days. Why would we conspire against a twelve-year-old girl?"

The line between his eyebrows grew deeper. "Celeste must have imagined it all, then. But what about the incident at the zoo?"

"There was, indeed, an incident at the zoo. And I seem to remember your daughter telling you shortly afterward that I was a wonderful nurse."

He absently ran a hand through his shock of light brown hair. "Yes, that's true."

"Let me ask you . . . why would Celeste refer to me as 'wonderful' if I had mistreated her during our outing or had terrorized her with stories of cats?"

"I thought we already settled that, Miss Price. Celeste was mistaken about the story. She has a very active imagination."

"Mistaken?" Leaning forward, Jenny gathered the courage to press her point. "Within the space of three hours your daughter has referred to me as an ogre and an angel. Both can't be true, Mr. Harrington. And you don't think she would tell a lie?"

"She told me that you struck her at the zoo, Miss Price!"

"I have never struck any child in my life," Jenny said with quiet forcefulness. "I simply refused to hand over the sixpence that she demanded of me."

His face reddened. "Surely she was asking to borrow—"

"Demanded, Mr. Harrington!"

"All right then, that was wrong of her. But I don't see why you couldn't have appeased her, out in public like that. You would have been repaid, and I would have spoken with her about it as soon as it was brought to my attention."

"And what if she had demanded that I buy her a pony? You would have wished me to appease her then as well?"

"Of course not!" Graham Harrington got to his feet, the veins standing out on his temples. "If you knew anything about children, *Miss Price,* you would know that most of them don't understand the concept of money!"

"And if *you* stayed here long enough to get to know your daughter, *Mister Harrington,* you would realize that a twelve-year-old who threatens to have someone dismissed if she doesn't pay up understands the concept of money all too well!"

His jaw dropped and he gaped at her silently. After several seconds he asked in a quiet voice, "Is it possible that you misunderstood her?"

The tinge of hope in the man's question was obvious, but Jenny had to be truthful. "Absolutely not."

~

Graham Harrington sank wearily back to his chair. *I've been a blind man,* he thought, rubbing his forehead.

For the past five years or so, Graham had noticed there were new faces among the servants almost every time he came home, particularly those servants who had to deal directly with his daughter. He pushed aside, however, any possible connection between this and Celeste's behavior. Mrs. Ganaway had never complained about the girl, he rationalized. But he had ignored the fact that the housekeeper needed her position and would likely never complain.

Graham looked at the young nurse. Miss Price seemed ill at ease, but she sat there regarding him with intelligent gray eyes.

At the risk of her job, she had found the nerve to speak some harsh words to him. *Harsh but true. I've ruined my daughter.*

"Mr. Harrington?" Miss Price finally ventured.

Still mute with self-recrimination, he merely stared back.

"I shouldn't have said the part about your not being here," she continued, her gray eyes suspiciously moist. "You have a business to oversee."

"No, I appreciate your honesty," Graham replied with a bleak voice.

The young woman shifted in her chair. "But it wasn't my place to lecture you."

"I wish someone would have had the courage to do so a long time ago." Graham paused to collect his thoughts for several seconds. "When Celeste's mother passed away, I should have stepped in to fill the void. I assumed nannies and nurses could better teach the child how to become a woman."

"We can't take your place, Mr. Harrington," Miss Price said gently. "And we can't teach her anything at all if we live in constant fear of being dismissed."

Her words were painful to hear, but he needed to hear them. He frowned and said, "And I've blamed the high turnover of servants here on their lack of understanding for a sick child."

"It's not my place to say so, but perhaps that's the problem."

"What do you mean?"

"The 'sick child,'" she answered. "Celeste isn't *sick*. She's a perfectly normal girl who sometimes has seizures."

"But we cannot just ignore the reality of her condition." A picture flashed across his mind, of his child thrashing about on the floor . . . and of himself helplessly wringing his hands while calling out for assistance. He shook the thought away. "She has limitations that other children don't have."

"Of course she has. But they aren't so drastic that she can't overcome them."

How does a little girl overcome a monster? he wondered, but he kept silent.

"Ever since I was told of this assignment, I've been reading about epilepsy," Miss Price continued, her gray eyes eager now. "Are you aware that George Frederick Handel had epilepsy? He lived for seventy-four years, Mr. Harrington, and I would say that he overcame his limitations."

Graham raised an eyebrow. "Seventy-four years?" Somewhere in the far recesses of his mind, he caught sight of a glimmer of hope. "Please . . . continue."

HEARTQUEST

HEART
QUEST®

Visit

www.heartquest.com

and get the inside scoop.

You'll find first chapters,

newsletters, contests,

author interviews, and more!

Must-Reads!

HEART QUEST.

OVER A MILLION BOOKS SOLD!